# Dark Rising

Book Two *of the*

ARCHANGEL PROPHECIES

MONICA McGURK

This book is a work of fiction. Names, characters, businesses, organizations, places, events, and incidents are either a product of the author's imagination or are used fictitiously. Any resemblance to actual persons, living or dead, events, or locales is entirely coincidental.

Published by River Grove Books
Austin, TX
www.rivergrovebooks.com



Distributed by River Grove Books

For ordering information or special discounts for bulk purchases, please contact River Grove Books at PO Box 91869, Austin, TX 78709, 512.891.6100.

Design and composition by Greenleaf Book Group and Kim Lance
Cover design by Greenleaf Book Group and Kim Lance
Cover images: [girl] ©Thinkstock/janniswerner; [stairs] ©Thinkstock/mkirstein; [birds] ©Thinkstock/gepard001; [tower] ©iStockphoto/digitalimagination

Publisher's Cataloging Publication Data is available.

ISBN: 978-1-63299-033-4

First Edition

Other Edition(s):
eBook ISBN: 978-1-63299-034-1

*To victims and survivors of modern-day slavery everywhere.*

*You are so much more than your circumstances.*

*May you know the joy of freedom and the knowledge*

*that your worth is boundless.*

*A portion of the proceeds from the sale of this book and its predecessor,* Dark Hope, *will be donated to organizations that fight human trafficking, especially the sexual trafficking of minors.*

# one

## TURKEY

It was cold.

Not the kind of cold that nips your nose and makes you laugh as you stomp your feet to warm up, the briskness bringing a rosy glow to your cheeks and a sparkle to your eyes.

No, this cold was damp and insistent, working its way into my bones, dull and persistent, slowly eating away at me like nagging doubt.

Or loneliness.

I coughed, a harsh barking sound that echoed off the cobblestones of the empty courtyard, and three heads swiveled in unison to stare at me.

The looks on the angels' faces couldn't have been more different. Raph held nothing but disdain for me—the whole reason we were in this mess and a visible reminder of all he hated about humanity. Enoch, on the other hand, knowingly searched my face, deftly cataloging each and every sign of frailty or pain as if he could single-handedly take them away and make me whole again.

And Michael? Michael just frowned, his eyes remote, before turning away to stare once again up the crumbling, steep steps that led to the church's gate.

We'd set off for Istanbul only a day ago but now that we were here, everything that had happened in Las Vegas already seemed a distant memory.

*More like a nightmare*, Henri whispered in my mind.

I sighed, willing Henri, my guardian angel, away and walling off my thoughts from him. I knew he was right. Nothing had gone right since Michael came into my life back in Atlanta. I thought I'd made a new friend, getting off to a clean start after I filed for change of custody and moved in with my mom after years of living with my dad. I was in a new school, where nobody knew about how I'd been abducted as a child. Nobody knew about the Mark and how it had materialized, unbidden, upon my neck during my disappearance.

I traced its strange outline with my fingertip, lost deep in thought.

Nothing was as it seemed. I thought nobody knew about the Mark. But Michael may have, and it may have been the real reason he was interested in me to begin with. It designated me as part of an ancient Prophecy, the Bearer of the Key to Heaven's Gate. And because Michael wasn't just a teenage boy, but the Archangel charged with guarding Heaven's Gate, that meant . . .

Even now, I could barely bring myself to think it.

It meant he couldn't have possibly ever loved me. For I was the Bearer of the Key. The one, according to the Prophecy, from whose hands the Fallen would receive the Key that unlocked Heaven's Gate to them, allowing them to overturn Heaven. How could

Michael love me when he knew he might have to kill me to prevent that from ever happening?

*Unless we found the Key and destroyed it before the Fallen Angels got to it,* I reminded myself. If they got it, they'd use it to storm Heaven and fulfill the Prophecy. But we could find it first if we could only figure out where to look.

That's what took us to Las Vegas. We'd gone to see Enoch, Heaven's Librarian and an angel who had once been human himself. Enoch gave us the entire Prophecy but left it to us to decipher. We made no headway until after The Incident.

That's what I call it. The Incident. It sounds so innocuous, so clinical. It helps me skip over all the confusion of Before and After, the jumble of emotions that welled up in me when I remember what happened.

We were playing a dangerous game, talking our way into gambling with the Chinese syndicate that was responsible for the human trafficking ring that whisked my friend Ana from her hometown in Mexico to Atlanta and, eventually, to Vegas. I made Michael promise to help me find her, my own condition for going willingly with him to Las Vegas to search for the Key—the ancient artifact that would somehow open Heaven's Gate. The Prophecy mentioned it but didn't tell us what it was. The Fallen Angels—Michael's rival, Lucas, chief among them—mistakenly believed I was the Key. Our only chance of beating the Fallen, then, was to find the real Key before they caught up with us. If we found it, we could destroy it and prevent them from using it to gain entry into Heaven, overthrowing it, and casting the entire world into chaos. Michael grudgingly went along with my condition, impersonating my father in order to skirt airline procedures and accompany me, a minor, to Las Vegas. Once there, he pretended to be one of the traffickers, weaseling his way into their good graces in hopes of finding Maria. While doing so, he went hot and cold on me and treated me so callously it was easy to believe he wanted me dead.

I still felt a twinge of guilt, thinking of how my mother would blame my father for my disappearance, knowing that he would fall under suspicion and that it might make things even worse between my estranged parents. Michael assured me that the best way to protect my father was to create a trail of evidence that meant it was impossible for him to be with me. But still, as crazy as he might seem sometimes, he is my father, and I wish we'd been able to avoid dragging him into this. I couldn't help but wonder if our attempts to protect him made it worse for him instead.

In our search for the Key and Maria, we shut everything out. I was isolated and alone, unsure of whether I could trust Michael. As the Head of God's army, Michael had a special responsibility to defend and protect the innocent on Earth—refugees persecuted for their religious beliefs, peoples ravaged by war or brutalized by their own governments. Throughout history, he guarded them and saved them in the most improbable of ways. Yet, because of me, he has now abandoned his charges, blocking out their insistent cries for help in order to focus on me and our search. Whether it was as a reminder of his neglected duties, or a punishment for failing to take my life, God hounded Michael with unrelenting, crippling pain. He was warping under the weight of it, so that I couldn't tell if he really did hate me, or if it was part of his act.

When he surprised me with dinner on the night of my birthday, I let down my guard, believing him when he told me that he loved me. *So naïve*, I thought bitterly. But how could I have known that an Angel's love was not meant for humankind? What started out as a gentle kiss grew into much more, until the intensity of our need, the depth of Michael's emotion, literally turned him to flame.

*My love is meant only for God*, he'd explained, too late, when I'd woken up in a hospital bed to find that the flames had engulfed me, too.

I looked at my shiny skin, scarred everywhere he'd touched me. I bent my fingers, forming a fist and winced at the tightness, the pain.

Was it love or hate that caused him to throw me into that inferno? Did he mean to hurt me that night? I could never know for sure, but my marred skin would serve as a painful reminder of what happened.

That, plus the new powers of intuition that transferred from Michael to me. "God's cosmic joke," Henri called it. Just in case a human survived an encounter with an angel, He'd rigged it so the human would absorb the angel's powers. Just as our search was getting more dangerous, Michael was drained, unable to rely on the unerring instinct that guided him in the past. My own hunches often felt like stabs in the dark, but they helped us find and free Maria from the traffickers. And my newfound instincts revealed to me that the Key we were looking for wasn't a literal key; it was the rock that Cain used to slay his brother, Abel, millennia ago, a symbol of the divide over mankind's fate that rent the angelic host in two. How fitting that if it were recovered, the Fallen would use the very thing that had turned them against humanity—and God's authority—to overtake Heaven's Gate?

Henri would have called it another of God's jokes. It was because of Cain's crime that so many angels turned against humanity. And it was because Michael had protected Cain that so many angels hated Michael. Michael hated that rock, which humans came to treat as a sacred relic, twisting it into something to be venerated. He'd wished it away, resenting that it came to be associated with him. And now we must find it before it is too late.

That's what brought us here. My gut told me we would find the rock somewhere sacred to Michael, perhaps lost along the pilgrimage routes of the Crusades or buried under rubble along the way. When Michael told me about the Michaelion, the ancient church that the Emperor Constantine had dedicated to him, it sounded right. So we came to Turkey to look for it.

That was my first mistake.

The ancient sanctuary was gone, of course. What was once wild, isolated countryside had now been swallowed up by the waves of growth that turned Constantinople into modern-day Istanbul. The distant shores of Istinye were now just another city neighborhood. Where the shrine had stood, a modern shopping mall, all polished steel and glass, now reigned exultant.

We stood in the center of the mall, surrounded by shops that could have been in New York or Paris or Tokyo, and waited for some inspiration to guide me.

But nothing came.

Nothing but bitter accusations from Raph, the other Archangel whom Michael had roped into joining us, ostensibly as protection. Whether he was to protect me from Michael, or Michael from me, I wasn't sure.

Enoch—the other part of the security detail, and the one who'd revealed the full Prophecy to Michael and me—had told me to ignore him, but it was hard when I knew Raph blamed me for leading Michael astray and putting him at risk of Falling.

"So much for her vaunted skills," Raph spat out in anger, oblivious to the happy din of shopping that swirled about us. "We're lucky she didn't lead us straight to Lucas and the Fallen Ones."

"She's young," Enoch interjected, "and new at this. She is just learning her own powers. We shouldn't expect her to do it all alone. Plus, she's tired. She has barely slept since Las Vegas."

"Ah, yes, human weakness. How quaint. Just what we need at

a time like this," Raph retorted. "What are we supposed to do now? Shop?"

The bickering escalated until Michael made what he called "an executive decision," forcing us out of the mall to wander the rain-swept streets of Istinye, dragging our duffels and backpacks behind us. It was an assault on my senses—the incessant honking of traffic; the booming horns, blasted by ships as they passed; the way modern streets would give way to narrow alleys, punctuated by coffee shops and fruit stalls and bakeries that seemed to have grown in that very spot hundreds of years ago; the juxtaposition of mosque with high rise; the strangeness punctuated by the sight of a woman wrapped in her headscarf climbing one foot out of her apartment window, high above the street, vigorously washing the glass in the sputtering rain; and, every now and then, the haunting song of the call to prayer, wafting over the chill air. After hours of searching, slowly winding our way down the hill and closer to the water, we found ourselves in the most run-down of alleys. I would have said we were lost, but Michael—far ahead of me now—had somehow found these crumbling steps and was climbing them with purposeful, renewed energy.

The two other angels moved about him, subtly shifting with his and my every move, shielding him from my view, and building a buffer of wind-driven space between us. They served as a wall—a wall of flesh and bone, meant to keep me away.

I trailed behind them as they climbed, watching for worn spots and crumbling rock, wary of falling. Their heated whispers bounced off the old brick and stone.

"You're lucky to have found it," Raph muttered. "There's not even a *here*, here. And after she said she knew where it was . . ."

"She never said that," Enoch grunted with the effort of the climb. "She simply said she felt we were supposed to come to Turkey."

"Enoch's right," Michael added quietly, sighing. "I was the one who said we should come to Istanbul. The Michaelion was my idea. It seemed as good a place to start as any. And to be fair, I should have realized it wouldn't be here any longer. It's as much my fault that I didn't know where to find the church that had been rebuilt from its ruins. At least, not without some searching."

"It's a wild goose chase," Raph protested. "She has no idea what she's doing. How can you entrust this to her?"

"It's her Prophecy, Raph," Enoch chastised gently. "We have no choice but to trust it to her. Without her, we are all lost."

A metal gate, as gray as the weary sky, arched gracefully over the steep steps, and I stopped beneath it to rest. The delicate ironwork didn't seem of this age. I reached out my hand to touch the filigree, tracing the symbols, wondering what they meant. Droplets of water clung to the metal until my finger interrupted their tenuous hold, and they fell, one by one, like tears, my finger leaving a track against the cold metal.

"Better keep up now, Hope."

I looked up, startled, to find a red-faced Enoch had descended and was waiting a few steps above me. He reached out and proffered a bottle of water.

"Important to keep hydrated."

I took the bottle and skeptically eyed him as he wheezed with obvious strain.

"You're a funny one to be handing out health advice."

He snorted with a smile, waving me up the stairs. "Such impudence. Come on."

We began to climb slowly, side by side, Enoch leaning heavily on his cane. The frigid wind carried a faint whiff of his cologne past my nose.

"Enoch," I began, my curiosity piqued. "If you can choose how you materialize when you appear here on Earth, why do you choose . . ." I paused, trying to find the right way to phrase my question. "Why don't you pick a human body more like Raph's, or Michael's?"

He fixed me with a stare from behind his aviator glasses. "You mean all 'hot'?"

He saw my embarrassment and laughed, a hearty sound that bounced off the ancient bricks and stones, filling up the emptiness around us.

"That is the word you teenagers use, isn't it? Why?" he demanded, sweeping an arm over his overweight, lumpy body like a showgirl. "Is the view not to your liking? Or are you worried I won't be able to protect you, if it comes to that?"

I blushed, hurrying to correct myself. "It's not for me. It just seems so hard for you. And unnecessary. Why not at least have a younger and healthier body?"

He leaned into the cane and hoisted himself up the final step, then stopped to catch his breath.

"I loved being human, Hope. Perhaps I didn't realize how much until my human life was gone. When I have the chance to be human again, I like to take the form I had back then, to remind me of what it was like."

He peered ahead into the dark shadows of the church's portal. "Some look at human frailty and see only weakness and heap their scorn upon it. Others see it as an invitation to put themselves in the hands of God and accept his grace. How one views it is a choice."

He reached a hand down the steps and pulled me up, gently. "This is what is left of Michael's famous shrine, the Michaelion: a chapel built from its rubble. They are waiting for you inside." With a tiny push, he sent me ahead of him.

I quickly took in the church, moss growing in the cracks between the stones, modest on a patch of dirt and worn grass. It seemed built into the surrounding buildings and hillside, engulfed—or perhaps protected—by the shelter they provided. A cement sidewalk ran the width of it, leading to some distant apartment buildings. The yawning distance to the stoop of the church seemed impossible to cross, but I forced my feet to shuffle across the stones and ducked slightly to enter. As I did, a fat cat perched in one of the windowsills looked at me imperiously and, with a whisk of its tail, disappeared from the ledge.

It took a moment for my eyes to adjust to the darkness. The few high windows cast little light in the fading shadows of late afternoon, leaving it to the stands of flickering candles to show the way. A gallery graced by pillars marked off the entry, which gave way to a small, open space, cut in half by an aisle that led in a straight line through a jumble of folding chairs. Stained glass windows, a simple pattern of circles, ran the length of the chapel, casting a dull glow of scarlet, peacock, and emerald, even in the day's gloom. A simple altar stood at the end of the aisle. Above it hung a stylized crucifix, flanked on either side by portraits of a winged, armored angel wielding a flaming sword, striking down a serpent whose long tail was entwined about the soldier's feet.

*Michael.*

I walked wordlessly down the aisle, drawn to the strangely flat portraits. I searched the painted plane of his face, looking for anything familiar, waiting for a flicker of recognition or a surge of insight to overtake me, but nothing came.

"Just paint and gold leaf, I'm afraid," Enoch said quietly from over my shoulder. "But beautiful in their own right."

I nodded, trying to swallow my disappointment.

The echoes of feet on the stone floor drew my attention. I turned around to find that Raph and Michael had joined Enoch.

Raph crossed his arms with obvious impatience. "Anything?"

I shook my head, casting my eyes down to stare at the worn stones, which priests and pilgrims had tread for untold years.

"No, of course not," Raph mocked. "Michael, your prophetess is failing you. What say you now?"

Michael's face was blank, as flat as that on the painting that hung on the wall. He looked at me coolly, appraising me with a distanced eye. Only the vein throbbing in his forehead gave away that he had any feelings at all.

I tried to drag my eyes away from his penetrating look but found I couldn't.

"I think we need to give thanks," he said, his eyes never leaving my face. "And pray for a successful start to our journey, for this is only the start, I am sure. Raph, give me your change."

Raph started to protest, but a sharp look from Michael cut him off. Indignant, he dug into his pocket and drew out a handful of coins, thrusting them into Michael's upturned hand.

"Go ahead." Michael's eyes directed me to the low rail at the side of the altar. Behind it stood a bank of pillared candles and votives, some already dancing with little flames. A utilitarian metal box stood in front on a low table. I saw something move in the shadows and noticed a small woman, folded into a shawl, tending the candles.

I walked over to the table, unsure of what to do.

"Give me your hand," Michael instructed as he edged in next to me. I hadn't been this close to him since Las Vegas, and the sudden burst of his scent, the feel of the heat radiating from his skin, was a shock. Swallowing hard, I turned my palm up. He cupped the underside of my hand and my entire body quivered as a jolt of heat raced up my arm. He didn't move, steadying my shaking hand as he dropped the coins in one at a time.

"Place your offering in the box and light the candles."

Behind us I heard Raph shuffling his feet. "It's a silly human superstition, Michael. Why are you even bothering?"

Michael shrugged, looking up at me as he spoke. "It may be silly, but it can't hurt anything. Go on, Hope. Maybe you can bring us some luck."

I swallowed, not wanting to pull my hand away from Michael's. But I did, closing my fingers so tightly around the coins that their worn edges seemed to cut into my skin. I turned to the table and noticed a cushioned place to kneel. I lowered myself onto it and then dropped the coins, one by one, into the box, each one clanking against the emptiness inside.

I looked up and saw the old woman watching me intently. She gave a subtle nod, encouraging me on.

A cluster of long matches stuck out of what, long ago, must have been a pitcher. I drew one out. The woman bustled forward and drew out a matchbox, pointing to the strip of sandy paper on its side. I dragged the match against it and watched the flame burst to life. The woman beamed, her mouth a gaping hole with only a few yellow teeth. She muttered something to me, drawing me closer to the candles, nodding at me to continue.

I looked at the candles. What, exactly, should I pray for? I could imagine what the few lonely souls who lit candles before me had asked for. Recovery from an illness, or perhaps just cessation of pain. Entry into Heaven for a loved one who had passed away. Peace from whatever troubles kept them awake at night.

But how could I ask for what I needed? Please, God, let this journey end? Please, God, let me wake up and find it has all been a dream? Help me find The Key before it is too late?

Please keep Michael from killing me?

Or what I really wanted to pray: Bring an end to his pain, God, for I can see his agony. And please, God, let everything he said to me not be a lie.

*You're so melodramatic*, Henri, my guardian angel, whispered in the back of my mind. *Let's get this over with.*

I sighed, defeated and betrayed by my own thoughts and leaned over to light a candle. I watched the flame flicker and dance, growing stronger and leaping up high until it drew back into a steady burn.

"Time to go," Enoch intoned. "I think we've done enough for the day."

I pushed myself up and turned to go, leaning instinctively toward Michael. The urgent, hurried voice of the woman tending the candles chased after me. She hurtled herself around the tiny shrine and thrust herself upon us, her voice insistent as she took my hands in hers and repeated herself over and over in a language I didn't recognize.

"What is she saying?" I asked, looking around at the men. Enoch looked amused, Raph indignant, his hard face turning several angry shades of purple.

Before they had the chance to answer, the woman reached out and took Michael's hand, placing it firmly in mine, squeezing our fingers closed so they clasped. She gave a satisfied pat to our entwined hands, squeezing them once again, firmly, before letting us go.

Reaching into her dress, she pulled out a folded pamphlet and shoved it against Michael's chest, her speech now coming with staccato insistence. She poked a finger at his chest until his other hand snuck up to take the flimsy piece of paper in hand.

She beamed at us both. Then, satisfied her work was done, she bustled back into the shadows, leaving us standing in the twilight of the church, holding hands.

"What is it?" I asked. Reluctantly, I let go of Michael's hand to take the pamphlet. I opened it up, smoothing out the wrinkles from where Michael had clutched it. I held it up to the meager light from the windows, trying to make out what it was. All the writing seemed to be in Turkish, but the text was peppered with pictures of churches, mosques, and ruins.

Michael drew the paper away from me. "Let me see that." He flipped the paper over. Perplexed, he shot a glance over his shoulder at the woman, now nearly invisible in the darkness. "How did she know?" He handed the paper off to Enoch, who glanced at it quickly before passing it to Raph.

"Know what?" I pressed.

Raph cleared his throat. "It's a map."

"A map of what?"

"It's a tour of all the shrines and churches dedicated to our friend here. Every one of them, in the entire city of Istanbul."

"What?" I snatched the map out of Raph's hands. "Let me see."

In the dim light I could make out the crosshatch of city streets, the winding Bosphorus and Sea of Marmara that made up the city map. Little red crosses studded the sprawl of the city. I scanned it quickly. Nearly twenty, I estimated, my heart sinking.

"We'll never be able to search them all."

Michael reached down to take the map, his hand closing over mine. I looked up, startled by the deliberate contact. His steely eyes glinted, his jaw set hard. Whatever we'd shared just a moment ago was gone. He was angry, and determined, once again.

"You'll just have to try harder, then, won't you?" His words hit me like a slap in the face. I felt tears gathering in the corners of my eyes, threatening to take away my last shred of dignity.

"It's not for want of trying, Michael," Enoch intervened, reaching between us to take the map and stepping in to separate us. He folded the map carefully as he spoke, regarding Michael with caution. I took advantage of the distraction he was causing to wipe away the errant tears with the back of my hand.

"Look, night descends. You have need of sleep and food. We all do, in this human guise. As you said, we are just at the start of this quest; you cannot wear yourselves, or each other, out so soon."

Michael's lips pressed together in a hard line as he looked down on the shorter Enoch. "Fine," he capitulated. "Have it your way, old man." He brushed through us, stalking down the aisle and out of the church, Raph trailing after him. My eyes followed him despite myself.

"I'm doing the best I can," I whispered weakly as the door slammed behind them.

"I know, Hope," Enoch said, patting my head awkwardly. "He's not himself. Not now. He probably won't be as long as we are searching for that blasted rock. Best for you to get used to it now."

"Why can't I tell where we are supposed to go?" I asked, desperate for a solution. "I thought with Michael's powers . . ." I let my voice trail off, unsure how much I should say.

Enoch's voice became eager. "So it's true. It really happened."

"Yes," I admitted, my misery only deepening. "But I didn't mean for it to happen. I didn't know."

"Of course not, my dear. I can't really say why it isn't working for you; perhaps it will only come in flashes. But we must be very careful. Michael is quite vulnerable in this state. His normal instincts cannot be relied upon. And he is equally unpredictable. His emotions are getting the best of him. As is the pain."

I thought of how easily Michael seemed to swing from gentleness to disdain for me and nodded.

"You must be careful around him, Hope. You should spend the time you need with him to figure out this mystery, for I'm guessing it will take both of your skills to do so. But I would keep it at that.

You don't fully understand your own feelings for him; and his for you . . ? Ah, those only God knows. Best not to stir the pot. The most important thing is that we find the Key."

I nodded dumbly, knowing what he was saying was true.

The door to the church swung open, banging hard against the massive stone walls. Raph's voice rang out.

"We're waiting."

Enoch leaned into his cane to create the momentum for the walk down the aisle. "Help me, my dear, would you?"

I scurried to his side and took an arm.

"Thank you," he said, pulling me along as he began his shuffling walk down the aisle.

I stole a quick glance at his face as we moved. I could barely make it out in the waning light. I still found it unsettling that I couldn't see his eyes behind the pair of sunglasses he always wore, but then again, there wouldn't be anything to see in those blind eyes. Was it that which made his expression so hard to read?

We swung the door open and stepped out into the night. I shivered, the chill reminding me I had only a hoodie to protect me against the sharp air.

"We must get Hope indoors," Enoch pronounced, watchful of my every move.

"Sultanahmet," Michael said, taking the map back from Enoch and shoving it into the back pocket of his jeans. "The Old City. We can be there in an hour, maybe a little longer."

Enoch raised an eyebrow. "You are thinking of a hotel there?"

Michael shook his head curtly. "No. We have arranged for a house in the back of the quarter."

Enoch wrinkled his nose. "Why, for heaven's sake? Are you deliberately trying to increase your misery?"

Michael turned, dismissing Enoch's complaints. "It will be safe."

"From what?" Enoch shuffled after him, awkwardly negotiating the steps. "There is nowhere you can seek shelter that you cannot be found by the Fallen."

"The Fallen are not all we have to worry about," Michael said gruffly, not slowing his pace. He was headed back toward the traffic of the financial district, drawing us out of this ancient place back toward the bustle of the modern day. In the distance I could hear honking horns and the occasional blast of a ship heading in or out of the harbor.

Enoch looked over his shoulder to where I stood at the top of the steps.

"What is he talking about, Hope?"

I shrugged. "I'm not sure."

Michael laughed out loud, more of a bark than a laugh, as he turned to face us both, throwing his duffle bags down on the glistening pavement in frustration.

"Not sure? Let me clarify. We are in Istanbul, long-time bridge between East and West, nexus for trade and transport. The modern age has not changed the unique aspect of geography that is and always will be its entire reason for being; it has just made it more sordid. You are standing in one of the human trafficking and slavery capitals of the world. Every day war-ravaged and desperate people hand over their life's savings, hoping for an escape to the promise of a new future that so easily slips from the lips of the men who guarantee them safe passage, if just for a little more money. Every day, they are packed inside of trucks and ships, packed so tight, and so full of expectation, that they cannot breathe, dreaming and wishing against reason that, finally, they will be safe. They believe, because they have no choice, that there really is a way out, that there really is a job waiting for them at the end of their hellish journey, that this is their new beginning. And every day, they are lucky if they find themselves in servitude at the end of their trip, instead of sinking to the bottom of the stormy ocean or being abandoned in the cold and wild halfway through, their money disappeared, cast off in a strange no man's land.

"You, Hope, who outwitted one of the most violent trafficking rings in the world with the stunt you pulled back in Las Vegas, you are in their territory now. Do you think they will just let you go? Who knows what sort of tentacles they have, reaching all the way even to this place? This place you have chosen to begin our search may be the exact place we need to be, but it is one of the worst places in the world for you to be right now. So we need to lay low." He cut off his speech, glowering at us both.

"Does that explain it to your satisfaction, Enoch?"

Enoch nodded grimly. I swallowed hard.

"I didn't realize," I said simply.

"No, of course you didn't," Michael said stiffly, turning on his heel. "You never do. And really, how could you? Let's go."

Raph fell in silently next to Michael as they strode away, Enoch and I struggling to keep up.

We reached Sultanahmet—the district that was the oldest and at the very heart of the city—after night had fully shrouded Istanbul. The bright lights of the old mosque quickly gave way to dark alleys. Michael and Raph negotiated them with ease, sure of their direction as we went deeper and deeper into the maze of old buildings, ignoring the watchful eyes that stared out from noisy cafés and tiny shops. Here and there, fat stray cats, content with the kibble that was strewn across the cobblestones for them, lounged, never bothering to move, but tracking us with heavy lidded, vigilant eyes as we invaded their neighborhood. Block by block, we seemed to go back in time, until we found ourselves facing rows of ramshackle wooden houses, upper stories jutting out to claim the street. The wood was black with age and rot. The scent of mildew and decay floated in the air, mingling with the ever-present salt of the sea. For once, I was glad that Enoch had gone a little heavy on his cologne; it made the smells from the street a little bit easier to bear.

"Here we are," Michael said without ceremony as we approached a lonely house on a corner. The homes surrounding it seemed abandoned, no welcoming lights shining in the windows.

Raph sniffed. "Not much to look at."

"Which is exactly how I want it," Michael said emphatically. "There is no one of consequence on this block or the next. Any uninvited visitors will be easy to spot."

He swung one duffle bag behind him, his shirt stretching across his strained shoulders, and walked up to the door to rattle the knob. He drew out a key and worked the stiff lock until the door swung open. "You and me first," he said to Raph. "You two stay here until we are sure it is safe."

I looked over my shoulder. I wasn't sure waiting in the deserted street was the safer option, but I didn't want to annoy Michael, so I kept my mouth shut as they disappeared inside the house.

"It's a shame," Enoch murmured, staring at the decrepit buildings that occupied the length of the street. "This used to be so beautiful. People used to fight for these homes, especially the ones with the views of the sea or the strait. And now look at them. Passed over."

"You've been here before? I thought you'd been trapped in the desert, waiting out your punishment all this time."

Enoch waved his cane in the air as if dismissing my question. "It was a long time ago."

I looked around, trying to imagine what it had been like. I struggled to see any sign of beauty amidst the ruin and waste, my eyes drawn to the persistent weeds and debris.

Raph poked his head out of the door. "You can enter."

Lonely, tuneless howls split the night, one after another, and Raph smirked.

"Some things never change," he said, his ear tilted to the night sky. "You'd best come in before the wild dogs get here." He disappeared into the dark maw of the house, not waiting for us to follow.

I went through the door first and began climbing the stairs, listening for Enoch's thumping cane behind me. I couldn't see anything, but felt my way with my hands, the wood of the narrow walls rough beneath my fingertips where strips of wallpaper hung like ribbons.

I emerged into a small vestibule. Across the room, a wide arch beckoned me into the large, open space ahead. The dim light of a fire glowed, filling the room with a soft haze and the gentle crackle of shifting logs. I moved instinctively toward the promised warmth, crossing the hall in a few easy steps.

A gasp of delight escaped my lips as the firelight shifted and I looked around me. "Oh."

The room was much larger than I had even guessed—perhaps a ballroom in a previous life. And somebody had taken obvious care with it. The wooden floors were polished to a golden sheen, reflecting back the dancing flames. White walls looked freshly painted—only a few cracks and holes in the plaster gave away the wear of time. Intricate moldings wrapped around the length and breadth of the walls, and graceful swags and garlands decorated the mantels above the fireplaces that stood at either end of the room. Enormous windows, stripped of what surely had been grand curtains, looked out upon the very tip of Istanbul, the few lights of homes on the hill below us twinkling like stars and the waves beckoning where the strait met the ocean.

I turned around, only then noticing the exquisite tiles that surrounded the fireplace where Michael crouched, shifting the burning logs with a poker. The light from the fire reflected off the vibrant blues of the tiles, making the scattering of delicate flowers painted across their surface seem to sway, as if the wind had caught them in an open field.

Michael stood, examining my face and obviously enjoying my reaction. "Iznik tiles," he said quietly. "Famed for their beauty. Very rare."

"I would have never guessed," I breathed, stepping closer to absorb the warmth of the fire and give myself a better view of the delicate hand-worked tiles. "From the outside, it looked like it was about to fall down around us."

I scanned the walls of the room, noting the sheets that covered mirrors or paintings. It was as if someone had moved away and time stood still, eating away at the outside of the house, but leaving the inside pristine.

Michael smiled. "Some things are not as they seem. You'd be wise to remember that. Come, take a seat." From a dark corner, he pulled up a plush, comfortable-looking chair. "You, too, Enoch."

Enoch emerged from the dark and approached the fire. "Not bad, Michael. Not bad at all. Now all we need is to get some food in this girl, and she'll be better in no time."

I collapsed into the deep seat of the chair and Enoch followed, throwing his cane down and easing himself onto the floor beside me.

"I'm too tired to eat," I said, letting my body sink into the cushions and relax. I hadn't realized how tired I was, but now that we'd stopped moving and the heat of the fire was draining the chill from my bones, I could feel the insistent exhaustion coming back to the surface, along with the surging pain from my healing burns.

"Besides, don't you guys have a supply of manna that just shows up? You can eat that while I get some sleep."

Michael eyed me sharply. "You're feeling okay?"

I let my eyes drift closed for just a second before replying. "I just need some ibuprofen and some rest. Then I'll be good as new." No sense in worrying him by mentioning my nerve endings, screaming for relief.

Just then, Raph emerged. "The bedrooms are made up, as the owner promised. We'll keep the central one for Hope and take turns guarding the door."

I struggled to pull myself up by the arm of the chair. "I don't need guarding. Besides, as long as you are in human form, you'll need sleep as much as I do."

"It's not up for debate," Raph said sharply. "I'll take first shift. Michael, you take your rest, too."

Michael looked at me again, something like doubt clouding his blue eyes. "You're sure, Hope? We can call a doctor. It's not that long since . . ."

He couldn't bring himself to finish his sentence.

"I don't need a doctor. Just show me this bedroom, Raph." I pushed up from the chair and grabbed my bag, trudging after him. As we were about to leave the room, one of the draped shapes on the wall caught my eye. I reached out to tug the trailing sheet to find that it was hiding a big-screen television.

Before I could say anything, Raph frowned. "Leave it," he said in a low voice, turning abruptly and proceeding down a dark hallway.

Confused, I dropped the sheet to the floor and followed after him. He was waiting for me outside a lone door. "It locks from the inside. I suggest you keep it locked at all times. Keep away from the window if you can. If you need anything, I'll be outside." He was nothing but polite. Although I couldn't see his face in the dark, I could tell it pained him to be so civil toward me and that his curt instructions amounted to nothing but a dismissal.

"Raph, back there, with the television . . . ?"

Even in the dark I could feel his black eyes boring into me. "The last thing you, or any of us, need is for Michael to accidentally see a news program and be reminded of all the havoc taking place out there."

"Out there?"

"In the real world."

His unspoken accusation hung before us. The world Michael left behind, abandoned to its fate, while he watches over me.

Raph did not move. His body was like a massive rock wall, looming in front of me, daring me to defy him.

"Is it getting worse? Out there?" My voice was timid and small. I didn't want to hear Raph's answer, but I needed to know.

Raph grunted, crossing his arms as he answered me in a sullen voice. "We have to be sure Michael doesn't find out."

A surge of guilt swept through me. I knew Michael was neglecting his charge to protect the faithful on Earth in order to stay with me and search for the Key, but I hadn't realized the consequences would escalate so quickly. How many thousands of people were suffering because of me? And how long before Michael's pain—the punishment God inflicts on angels who disobey him—got even worse as he ignored his duties as the defender of the innocent?

"Thank you," I said, looking down at my feet, unable to meet Raph's incriminating stare. "Thank you for letting me know." The massive shape of Raph's body barely moved in the dark shadows, just enough to open the door to my bedroom. I slipped by him, his presence overpowering the narrow hallway, wondering how much he blamed me for Michael's obvious suffering.

I shut the door and turned the key where it waited in the lock, then leaned against the door, exhaling heavily. Almost there.

I crossed into the main part of the room, fumbling toward a curtain, careful to avoid the hulking, sheet-covered armoire that nearly reached the ceiling. I flicked the drape aside to let in a little light from the window. The moonlight illuminated the large iron bed, making the white sheets glow in the dark. I slipped out of my shoes, dropped my backpack and slid under the crisp, cotton sheets, not bothering to change out of my clothes.

As I sank into the pillowy mattress I could feel the tension seeping out of my aching muscles. *I really should take some ibuprofen*, I thought to myself, trying to remember where in my backpack I'd last seen the bottle. But before my mind could envision it, I was drifting away into a dreamless sleep where neither worry nor pain could reach me.

The sliver of daylight that jutted across my wall told me I'd only slept until early morning. The room was still very dark and cool, the heavy draperies muffling out the sounds of the waking city below. I stretched out, testing the dull ache in my muscles, and wondered if anyone else was awake yet. A sense of dread stole over me. If yesterday had been tense, today, I knew, would be even worse: with everyone in our search party following me, hanging on my every word, waiting for my newfound instincts to kick in, waiting for me to cough up some coherent idea of where to search next for the missing Key.

It was laughable, really. And the pressure of knowing they were counting on me would just make it harder.

Steeling myself for whatever the day held in store, I rolled out of bed.

I turned the key and cracked open the door. Nobody standing watch. I slipped out into the dark hallway and worked my way back to the great room, hoping, as I shivered in the cold, that someone had started the fire again. I padded with bare feet across the smooth wooden floor to find fading embers in the hearth. I poked at them, hoping to find a stray spark, but the fire was truly dead.

I stared into the dark, gaping fireplace and realized I was alone.

A thrill shot through me.

Quietly, I dashed into the open rooms and peered out onto the balcony. Yes, it was true—the house was empty. It didn't matter to me whether the others were still in bed or had gone out. I crept back into my bedroom and began rifling through my backpack to fish out my forgotten running clothes.

*You aren't really going to do that, are you?* Henri butted in, voicing his skepticism directly into my mind. *Michael will be furious. Besides, those clothes aren't nearly warm enough for this weather.*

"Leave me alone," I muttered under my breath as I pulled out a tissue-thin T-shirt. I hated how my guardian angel could simply butt into my thoughts at will. As far as I could tell, I could block him out—but only if I realized he was there, watching me. Where he went when he left me to my own devices, I wasn't sure. "If I could just have a few moments alone, out in the city, I know something will come to me. And I'll be back before anybody realizes I'm gone. Now go away. I need to change."

I barely paused to acknowledge his harrumph of displeasure.

Exhilarated by the promise of freedom, I threw on the T-shirt and tights. I pulled on the same stinky pair of socks I'd worn yesterday and thrust my feet into my shoes, fumbling with the laces.

Of all the things that changed when I moved from my Dad's house in Alabama to live with my Mom in Georgia, the freedom of being able to run outside was one of the best. I'd forgotten how it felt, how much it meant to me, until just now.

I slipped out of my room and down the gloomy stairway to emerge, shivering, into the sunny street.

I was so happy, it felt like my very cells were singing.

I tried to recall the tiny crosses marked out on the map that Michael had tucked away; they seemed to have been scattered across the whole city, so it probably didn't matter where I headed. *Remember*, I warned myself as I started up the alley, back toward the direction we'd come from last night, *just a short run. Just long enough to loosen the hinges of your rusty brain*. But my mind was working as fast as my feet as I raced up the cobbled way. Over the rooftops, the spires and domes of various buildings poked their heads. I set my sights on one and ran even faster, barely pausing to note the landmarks, so I could eventually make my way home.

I ignored the chill that threatened to sink into my very bones, pretending not to see the clouds of steam that I puffed into the cold air with every breath. I stretched out, willing my muscles to work even harder, as I wound through the twists and turns of the old city, eventually picking up the tracks of a trolley or train to follow. I was alone in the dawn, only more stray cats, nestled into shuttered shop-door stoops, to keep me company.

Every now and then I would lose my landmark to the looming rooftops, but I would turn a corner to see its dirty marble rising, catching the sunlight, ever closer, back into my line of sight. At first, the sounds of the city waking up—the vendors pulling up the doors that protected their shop windows overnight, the mothers calling out to their children as they left for school—barely registered as I focused on my breath, in and out. But as I came closer, another sound, a sound I couldn't place, broke into my consciousness.

I came to a major boulevard at the end of the warren of streets; crossing it, I stepped into an alley teeming with activity. Merchants called from tiny stalls whose wares—carpets and silks, books, and pots—threatened to spill across the paths through which shoppers wandered. Hunched men, wizened by years of heavy labor, skillfully negotiated heaping carts through the lane, ducking into passageways emerged from the long, low building that stretched alongside the outdoor market. They shouted cheerfully at one another in their rapid guttural language, chastising young helpers who were not fast enough on their feet. But that was not the sole source of noise. I froze: Underneath the noise of the market a rhythmic chanting emanated from somewhere deeper inside the city, beyond the stalls.

I pushed my way through, ignoring the curious looks and the repeated calls that followed me:

"Would you like to buy some jeans?"

"A leather jacket? Please, let me show you what I have for sale."

"Hello? Hola? Salut?"

"Hey! Where are you going, lady?"

Cheeks hot, I stared determinedly at my feet and kept moving.

The alley opened up to a large square. A throng was gathering in front of an impressive gate, the only gap in a high stone wall. Behind the wall, set back behind leafy trees, stood the tower I'd used as my landmark. Young people, dressed in mostly Western attire, shouted and waved signs in front of the gate, which was swathed in an immense Turkish flag. More and more people were joining the crowd, jostling me as they rushed past, towing banners and makeshift cardboard signs behind them. I moved deeper into the crowd, trying to make out what they were protesting. I peered up at the sign above the gate—*Istanbul Universitesi,* it read. I looked around nervously and realized that they all seemed to be students, some of them were wearing gas masks.

I was pressed against the backs of the people in front of me as the students pushed forward. From the street, sirens wailed. I tried to fight my way through, but I was trapped, forced to march along with them as they thrust themselves forward. I could no longer see anything ahead or around me, my view blocked by the unfurled banners and swaying Turkish flags. Helplessly, I was swept in the tow of the mob as they took to the street. Through the chanting, a stern voice blasted over a bullhorn, warning the students.

*Just a short run, eh?* Henri's voice, sarcastic as ever, snaked into my panicked brain.

*Why don't you do something useful and get me out of this mess?* I shot back, looking about wildly for a way out.

Just then, a scream rose over the din. Then another. Sirens, whining insistently, drowned out the shouting. The bullhorn reprimands grew more insistent, the voice rising shrilly.

A loud shriek went out, and then a blast of water pushed us all back in a wave.

It hit me like icy needles, sending me gasping for breath as I fell, my body glancing off of others as I tumbled to the hard pavement.

I was shoved against the ground, pinned down by the people falling on top of me. I pushed up onto my hands and knees and began crawling, trying to avoid being trampled by the running students who were now retreating from the challenge of the police.

Then, in the chaos of the crowd, I spotted him. He was bigger, and dressed differently, but the sneer on his face was unmistakable.

It was one of Lucas's Fallen Ones—the one who picked on me at school.

I gasped.

A wicked grin stole across his face as he relished my shock. He looked past me, though, and I followed his eyes to see others, inexorably working their way toward me.

*Over here,* Henri whispered. *To your left.*

I dragged my body toward his voice, trying to block out the keening sounds of the police sirens, the sickening thuds of people being beaten, and the cries of resistance being cut short. Several times I was buffeted in the head, but I kept making my way through the chaos, only daring to look over my shoulder for a moment to be sure the Fallen weren't gaining on me.

Suddenly, I could see a gap in the thicket of feet and legs. I crawled faster, ignoring the gravel that pressed into the heels of my hands.

I blinked at the light. I was in an alley. Alone. Sighing with relief, I crawled over the curb and pulled myself up against the side of a building, leaning back to scan the crowd.

The angels had disappeared, melting back into the crowd. I shrunk farther into the shadows of the alley, hoping I was right and they really were gone.

When I'd retreated a bit farther, I stopped to assess the damage. My tights were ripped, the skin on my left knee grazed just enough to be bloody. My T-shirt was ripped as well, but more than that, I was soaked through, having been caught in the direct blast from the hose. I brushed off my hands, picking the bits of gravel out of my palms and noting with amazement that I had no further injuries. Hopefully, no tell-tale bruises would emerge later to give me away.

From the safety and distance of the alley, I watched the crowd disperse, a handful of students getting marched and shoved unceremoniously into waiting police vehicles.

"What was that?" I wondered aloud.

*That,* Henri answered, *is just one of the things that has gone awry since your beloved Michael decided his time was better spent babysitting you. The people are rising up to protect their rights, because no one else is doing it for them. And they are paying with imprisonment and sometimes their lives. The fact that the Fallen were among them should not surprise you. Wherever there is chaos, you will find them. This was their warning to you. Why they did not take you when they had the chance, I do not know.*

I gulped hard, trying to swallow back my guilt.

*You don't have time to feel sorry. You need to get back to the house before the Fallen change their mind, and before your absence is noticed.*

I nodded, knowing he was right. I looked around, trying to reorient myself. I didn't dare find the train tracks; I would be too exposed. I needed to wind my way back through the side streets and alleys. As I peered back into the emptying square, a flock of birds rose up, startling me.

Were those pigeons, or something more sinister?

The fact that the Fallen might still be all around me, that they might have been trailing me this whole time, spurred me to my feet.

I didn't try to run. I was too winded. The adrenaline that had coursed through me now waned, leaving me spent. Instead, I clung to the sides of the buildings as I limped my way back. Every now and then, I darted a glance at the rooftops, hoping I wouldn't spot a stray raven trailing me back to our hiding place.

I managed to creep up the stairs of the house—attracting only a baleful stare from the cat that had apparently taken up residence at our doorstep—and snuck into my room. Slowly, teeth chattering, I peeled off my clothes, shoving them under the bed where I hoped they would not be found. I longed to climb back into bed, piling the covers on top of me to ward away the cold, but I knew I couldn't linger here, avoiding the angels forever. Instead, I forced myself back into yesterday's clothes and headed out into the living area.

Michael crouched down before the hearth, coaxing the glowing embers back to a roaring fire. I breathed a sigh of relief, knowing I'd barely made it back in time to escape his notice.

The room was flooded with light from the bank of windows and seemed to catch his blond hair so that it shone in the morning sun. He leaned into the fire with a poker, his tight T-shirt clinging to his broad shoulders and back as he poked and prodded the reluctant flames. The fire shifted and sprang to life, a real fire now, and Michael stood up, throwing the poker down to look at the fire with satisfaction. My eyes were drawn down the length of his body, admiring how his muscular back gave way to his narrow waist.

Suddenly, he turned to find me staring at him. There was a light in his eyes, the tiredness and frustration of the previous day seemingly forgotten. He bent his head quizzically as he waited for me to speak, a slight smile on his lips.

"Good morning," he said, almost asking it as a question.

I cleared my throat, finding myself unable to respond as I drank in the sight of him. "Morning," I mumbled, awkwardly hiding my hands behind me and hoping he couldn't tell the effect he was having on me. "I need coffee."

He nodded. "Nothing here, I'm afraid. The water is turned off, so I sent Raph out to look for coffee or tea."

I groaned. "No water? But I'm desperate for a shower," I added, hoping that the cold blast of water I'd endured had managed to rinse away most of the sweaty smell of my run.

He nodded, ruefully. "We'll have to use the public baths."

"Public baths?"

"Just like the days of old. Some are still operational, though often just for tourists. We'll take you to one of those, where they are more likely to speak English."

"What do you mean, public baths? How public?"

He shrugged, watching me squirm under his gaze, my panic at the thought of bathing in public obvious. Slowly, he let a wicked grin spread across his face, letting me know how much he was enjoying my embarrassment.

"It's no big deal, Carmichael. Hundreds of thousands of women and men have done it over the centuries. In fact, people pay big money these days to have this kind of authentic *Istanbullu* experience. Consider yourself lucky."

I was so stunned that he'd lapsed into his old nickname for me that I almost didn't catch what he'd said. "Women and men?" I asked quickly.

He didn't even bother to hide his amusement. "Separate baths, separate entrances. Totally above board." A light chuckle escaped his lips. "You know, for a modern woman, you really are a prude, Hope."

He stood there, relishing my discomfort, when a shadow crossed his face and the set of his jaw turned hard. "Of course, you are probably worried about more than your modesty."

I frowned at the sudden change in his mood, until I realized he was talking about my scarred skin.

"Michael," I said quietly, knowing it was dangerous to even approach the topic. But it was sitting there, the obvious issue between us. If we didn't confront it, we would never be able to trust one another.

I took a deep breath and pushed on, looking up at him tentatively. "It will heal in time. You said so yourself."

He scowled, his fist curling on the top of the mantel as if he would hit something. "And yet you won't let me help you. You refuse the very help that Raph could give you. You do it deliberately, to spite me," he growled savagely, the words nearly torn from his mouth, as he moved threateningly close.

I backed away, his show of frustration frightening me. But, of course, he was right. I had refused Raph's healing powers, all because I wanted Michael to be reminded of what he'd done to me. And I didn't mean just the physical damage covering the length of my body with sores and scars. I wanted him to feel the distrust, the regret, and the anger. I wanted him to feel all of that. And yes, at the core of it all, I wanted him to feel the longing that could never, ever be filled.

I raised my chin, refusing to be cowed.

"I'm not afraid of you," I breathed, knowing the words were lies.

"You should be," he glowered, closing the distance between us in a few strides.

I looked down at his clenched fists, wondering just how far things would go before he would snap. We stood there, our breaths coming heavily, staring each other down. I longed to reach out and smooth away the furrow of pain, anger, and worry that was etched into his brow, but I didn't dare move.

The door slammed below us, and we heard the heavy tread of footsteps on the stairs. Still, we did not move.

"What's going on?" Raph exclaimed from behind me. I heard him drop something to the floor and, in the instant it took for him to understand the situation, he leapt into the little space between Michael and me. "Get away from him, Hope. Just back away."

"I didn't do anything," I protested, refusing to move.

"I didn't say you did," Raph said tersely, spreading his arms out to force some distance between us. "But you need to back away. *Now*."

The urgency in his voice spurred me to back up.

"Now, your turn." Raph directed Michael, his hand remaining on Michael's chest. Michael's nostrils flared at the disrespect of being ordered about, but he obeyed, turning and striding to stand in an empty corner. He stretched his arms out to lean against the barren wall, his back rigid from the strain of holding his temper.

"Where is Enoch?" Raph demanded sharply, addressing Michael's back. "The only thing he had to do is babysit the two of you and what does he do? Leave you unattended until you're about to tear her apart. Enoch!" He shouted, his voice echoing through the empty room. He turned toward the gaping archway and shouted again. "Enoch, where in God's name are you?"

A door creaked somewhere down the hall, and we heard the telltale thump and shuffle of Enoch and his cane.

"I wasn't going to hurt her," Michael said, barely making himself heard over the sound of Enoch walking.

He turned from the wall, his eyes shining and full of tears, and walked straight to Raph. "I wasn't going to hurt her," he repeated, now looking over Raph's broad shoulder to me, then Enoch as he entered at the far end of the room. "I would never hurt her."

"Then why the hell are we even here?" Raph threw his hands up in frustration. "Isn't that the whole reason you asked us here? Because you weren't sure if you could trust yourself? My God, man. Love the girl if you must, but keep your wits about you. Keep away from her, so she has a chance to find this Godforsaken rock. If you don't, we'll all be dead."

He stormed away, kicking over the bag of morning takeout he'd fetched for us as he left the room. I stared after him. The black stain of spilled coffee spread slowly over the polished wood, an accusation. I rushed over, kneeling next to the mess, and reached into the bag to find napkins. Deliberately, I began dabbing at the spill, mindful not to lift my eyes.

"Hope."

I kept mopping at the mess until there was nothing left to clean. I could hear Enoch slowly crossing the room. I bent my head closer to the floor, rubbing away at an imaginary stain. Over the lingering smell of coffee, I caught a whiff of sulfur and choked back a sob. I dashed a tear away and kept wiping.

"Hope." Michael's voice was close now, practically in my ear. His hand closed on mine, stopping me mid-swipe.

I looked up from the floor to find Michael crouched beside me, desperation in his eyes. Carefully, as if afraid of my reaction, he dropped my hands and then held his own out, palms raised—a gesture of futility and confusion.

"I promise you, Hope, I won't hurt you."

"I know," I whispered, wanting to believe it. But I had to look away.

I focused, instead, on Enoch's last few steps toward us, until he was close enough to lean over and place a heavy hand on Michael's shoulder.

"Raph is right. You shouldn't be alone together. It will be better this way," he said, his face grave. "Easier for both of you."

I continued to watch them out of the corner of my eye. Michael swallowed hard, his Adam's apple bobbing in his throat, and shook his head silently. His head fell down, his pose one of defeat. Enoch waited until Michael took a deep breath and rose to his feet, stretching out of his crouch to full height.

He stood tall over Enoch, but his eyes were as lost as a little boy's.

Enoch patted him on the back and led him away, leaving me to sit in the crumpled mess of damp napkins and soggy food.

*You're running out of time,* Henri whispered.

# two

## GEORGIA

The fluorescent light was giving Mona a headache. Or maybe it was the slightly burnt coffee from the FBI's kitchen. Or the uncomfortable chairs. She'd been here too long to know what exactly was causing her headache, and she didn't really care.

She knew she could go home. That she probably *should* go home. But it made her feel more in control, to be here in the center of the investigation, even if she really wasn't doing anything. At least she could walk down the hall and ask questions and get answers, instead of waiting by the phone for them to call.

If she ignored the fact that the answers never changed—*no new leads*—she could feel some semblance of control and hope. So, every day she bundled herself into Arthur's hulking SUV for the ride to and from the FBI offices, pretending to herself that the trip was as routine as the countless airport runs on which Arthur had chauffeured her over the years, so she could keep her vigil. She could have driven herself, but Arthur had insisted and, frankly, she appreciated his comforting, calming presence by her side as she went back and forth, the days stretching on with no resolution.

But there was a reason for optimism, she reminded herself. Her daughter's friend, Tabitha, had called after receiving a message from Hope. Mona didn't yet know what Hope had said, or how long the message had been, but surely something would come of that phone call.

So Mona waited, resolute in her conviction that something would happen to give them new leads about her daughter's disappearance.

A brief knock at the conference room door interrupted her thoughts. An agent she didn't recognize was leaning through the opening of the door, careful not to violate her space.

"Do you want to talk to your daughter's friend with us? She and her parents just completed their formal statements."

Mona pushed away from the table. "Of course," she nodded, her throat suddenly dry.

She followed the agent through the corridor to another dimly lit conference room. The room was smaller—closer to an interrogation room like the one that had held her estranged husband, Don, who'd been a suspect just a few days ago.

*Don. Would he be there, too?* She squared her shoulders and let the agent open the door for her, trying to ignore the riot of emotions surging through her at the thought of him.

An empty chair was waiting at the narrow Formica-topped table, beckoning Mona to join Agent Hale and Don, who'd already taken their seats. Don smiled at her and, despite herself, happiness surged through her; but it was a joy quickly chased by irritation at her own weakness.

*It's just because you're tired. You're worn down*, she reasoned with herself, ignoring the memory of the awkward conversation she'd had just the other day with her boss, Clayton—while having him arrange for help from the FBI—a conversation during which she realized she still had feelings for Don. Really, what right did he have to be here, she reminded herself, trying to stir up some indignation, some old hostility built up over the decade; anything, really, to push away the giddiness that threatened to overtake her. But even that didn't work, because, she grudgingly admitted, he had every legal right to be there. And in the back of her mind, she knew he had even more than that, for it had been on Mona's watch that Hope had disappeared—this time. Swallowing her chagrin, she squeezed in between the FBI agent and Don, doing her best to avoid brushing up against either one of them.

Across the table, sandwiched between her parents, sat Hope's friend Tabitha. She perched on the edge of her chair, ramrod straight, her hands clasped in front of her on the table. Mona had to look twice to be sure it was her. Tabitha had been stripped and scrubbed of all signs of rebelliousness—the funky hair, the fake tattoos and piercings, the ripped clothing—all of it was gone. Her hair was straightened and smoothed into a conservative flip. Pearls—just like her mother's—graced her delicate collarbone and splayed against the subtle herringbone weave of her navy wool dress. She seemed smaller to Mona, the bravado of her larger-than-life alter ego gone, swallowed up inside her grown-up clothes. Mona could hear her nervously tapping her foot under the table and watched as she lifted her shaking hand to tug at the collar of her dress.

Tabitha's mother reached up to smooth Tabitha's collar and took Tabitha's hand in hers, giving it a little squeeze. Ever so subtly, Dr. Franklin shifted closer to his daughter, as if he could prop her up in the chair through force of will and proximity. He was wearing his ministerial collar, giving him an air of quiet authority and calm that seemed to suffuse the room.

As she watched, Mona felt a little pang of regret that her daughter's friend had been drawn into something so sordid. But just as quickly, she pushed it aside, knowing she couldn't afford to feel sorry for Tabitha nor her parents. Not when her own daughter's life was at stake.

"Tabitha. Dr. and Mrs. Franklin. Thank you for coming," Mona said quietly as she took her place between Agent Hale and Don. "I know this must have been terribly inconvenient for you."

Tabitha smiled nervously back at Mona, then darted a glance at Hale before answering. "No ma'am. I mean, I want to help."

Mona smiled, a sad turning of her lips that did not reach her eyes. "Of course you would. You are a good girl. A good friend to Hope."

Hale cleared his throat. "Normally we wouldn't involve either one of you so directly in the investigation, Mrs. Carmichael," he began. He had slipped into the formality of his official role, warning her that as far as he was concerned she and Don were still persons of interest and potential suspects. "But Tabitha wanted to speak with you personally to tell you what she knows. We thought it might be helpful to see if you can piece some of it together."

Mona nodded, on her guard.

Mrs. Franklin patted Tabitha's hand. "Go on, Tabby. Tell Mr. and Mrs. Carmichael what you know."

Mona startled at the use of her married title. Mrs. Carmichael. Cheeks flushing, she stole a glance at Don. The slightest hint of a smile had crept across his face. He reached down the table, proffering his upturned hand. Slowly, as if not sure what she was doing, Mona took it, bracing herself for whatever Tabitha had to share.

Hale prompted, "Start from the very beginning, Tabitha. From the last time you saw Hope."

Tabby shifted in her seat. "The last time I saw Hope was after school. We'd been working on our Contemporary Issues project. You know, the one with the shelter."

Mona leaned her head in recognition. "Yes. Street Grace." Don shifted in his seat, transferring his attention from Tabitha to her. She could see Agent Hale watching them both out of the corner of his eye, most likely watching their every move, every facial expression, for any signs. She felt herself flushing, cursing herself for not being able to stop it.

Instead, she ignored Don, willing herself to bring her attention back to Tabitha, stating simply, "The girls were doing a research project about human trafficking and had interviewed a young woman at the shelter about a month ago."

"What's that?" Don demanded. "You didn't mention that to me." Mona pulled away her hand and shot him a cold look, refusing to answer. She wasn't in the mood to hear his criticisms of her parenting and knew that if it had been up to him, Hope would never have been allowed anywhere, least of all a home for girls like her—girls who had once been abducted.

"Human trafficking. That's interesting," Hale said, leaning forward onto the table.

"Exactly," Tabitha said. "We'd been arguing because we were having trouble getting all the information we needed for our paper, and we knew we'd get a bad grade if we didn't get it all done."

Mona's forehead crumpled. "Arguing? You and Hope?"

Tabitha leaned forward, eager to have the adults' attention. "No," she said, her face becoming more animated as she recounted her story. "Hope and I wanted to go back to Street Grace and interview that girl we'd talked to before. Maria. But Michael didn't want

Hope to go back there. He didn't think it was safe. They had a big argument about it. I sided with Hope, of course."

"Hope never mentioned that."

Tabitha shrugged slightly. "Michael is always really protective when it comes to Hope, but this time he was a little overbearing, in my opinion. It turned out it didn't matter, though, because when Hope called down to see about setting up a visit, we found out that Maria had disappeared."

"Disappeared?" Don asked. "Just like that?"

"We just agreed we'd have to finish the paper the best we could. We had divided it all up, so we just had to work on our own pieces and then I was going to put it all back together."

"When exactly was this?" Don countered, deeply interested.

Tabitha looked at her mother. "We think it was a Wednesday or Tuesday. Because the paper was due that Friday."

"Right before her birthday," Mona mumbled to herself.

Hale interrupted. "It sounds like the right window for the night of her disappearance, as best as we can tell."

"That was the last you saw her?" Mona was impatient to hear the rest of Tabitha's story.

Tabitha nodded and licked her lips. "And Michael. He's been gone since that day, too."

Mona could hear the clicking of the industrial clock mounted on the wall. Michael? Missing, too?

"Michael. And Hope. Tabitha, do you think they are together?"

Tabitha bit her lip. "I don't know, ma'am. Michael used to miss a lot of school, anyway, with his emancipated teen status. It's just that . . . "

"What?" Mona demanded, a bit too sharply.

"Well, usually he comes back after a few days. But he hasn't come back this time. I mean, at least not yet."

Mona's mind raced. "Does he tell you where he goes when he misses school?"

Tabitha's face fell. "No, ma'am. And I don't ask him, because I really don't care. We don't get along all that well."

Mona found this last statement curious. Michael was extremely likeable and had been nothing but a positive influence on Hope, as far as she could tell.

"Why not?"

Tabitha squirmed in her seat once again and stared down at the tabletop. "I guess I didn't like how he was with Hope. It was like . . ."

"Like what?" Mona prompted, finding herself unable to breath.

"He just didn't want anybody else around her. He was kind of bossy." She looked up, somewhat sheepishly. "I mean, I know I am bossy, too, but he was a different kind of bossy. Like he wanted to control her or something."

This was new, an angle she had not considered. Had Mona missed the signs of something more insidious in Hope's relationship with Michael? Had she been encouraging Hope in her blossoming friendship, when all along he was a threat? What if Don was right, and she'd been too lax, too absent, to be a good mother to Hope?

She shot him a glance, wondering if this newest revelation would cause him to blame her, but his face was calm. Only the slight wrinkle in his brow gave away the fact that he was troubled by what he was hearing.

"I don't think Michael would hurt her, Mrs. Carmichael," Tabitha whispered. "I don't think he would force her to go with him, either. But I can't figure out why they would both be gone like that."

She nodded, trying to gulp down her fears. "And then you got the phone call from Hope?"

"First, she sent me her and Michael's part of the paper. That was a few days before the phone call. She left a short message, just saying to tell you she was okay."

"We listened to the message and took the SIM card, so we can analyze it further," Hale interrupted.

"She didn't tell you anything more? Like where she was or what she was doing?" Mona prompted, frustrated to have such a tenuous tie to her daughter's whereabouts.

"No, ma'am."

Mona swiveled in her chair, turning to Hale. "What about this other missing girl, this Maria? Is that a possible connection?"

Hale nodded. "We're running that one down. Given what we know about Las Vegas, it is a possibility."

"What about Las Vegas?" Tabitha pressed. "Is Hope in Las Vegas?"

Hale shook his head curtly. "We can't comment on that at this time."

Tabitha, undeterred, thrust her chin out. She was a dog with a bone, again, the spirited young woman that Mona recognized from those afternoons in her kitchen, and Mona smiled despite herself.

"Maria probably left to go find her little sister. She didn't trust the people at the shelter, or the police," Tabitha said pointedly, shooting a poisonous glance at Hale. "Maybe Hope was going to help her with that."

Hale perked up, but tried to appear casual as he probed Tabitha's statement. "Why would you think that, Tabitha?"

Tabitha began slowly. "Hope really identified strongly with Maria. She was very worried about her, and they seemed to . . . connect. She even gave Maria her phone number, in case Maria ever needed any help. The more we researched, the more obsessed Hope seemed to be with trafficking and about Maria. "

The words were spilling out of her, the relief on her face palpable.

"She wasn't sleeping well. She was working at all hours, doing research online. And she was frantic when Maria went missing."

Hale scribbled a few notes down on his yellow legal pad while he peppered Tabitha with questions. "What do you know about this sister?"

"Not much. Her name is Jimena. She was younger than Maria, and they got separated before the raid that brought Maria into Street Grace."

"Any idea where they were from?"

"A border town in Mexico. It's all in our paper," she said, drawing out a plastic binder. "I brought a copy, just in case." She slid the paper across the shiny table toward Hale. The plastic was black and pink, the colorful font of the title page and curlicue decorations belying the horror of their subject matter. Mona's heart broke, thinking of Hope staying up at night, worrying herself sick about this other girl—and likely her own past. How could she not have seen it? She understood now why Michael was arguing with Hope—he was trying to protect her from herself, something she, Hope's own mother, had failed to do.

Hale flipped through the paper, skimming the pages for anything that jumped out at him. "Traffickers," he muttered, slamming the cover shut. "There's our Vegas connection."

Tabitha's eyes widened, but she didn't say anything.

Hale picked up the paper and ripped the top sheet off of his notepad, handing both wordlessly to one of the anonymous agents in the back of the room. "Find out what you can."

"You've been very helpful, Miss Franklin," Hale said, standing up to conclude the interview. "Dr. and Mrs. Franklin, they can validate your parking at the front desk. We'll be in touch if we need anything more from you or your daughter." He looked down at

Mona, still seated in the hard plastic chair. "Mona and Don, we'd like you to stay a few minutes, if you don't mind."

"Of course," Mona said. Her brain was feverishly trying to piece together the implications of what she'd just learned, but nothing seemed to fit. Nothing.

From across the table, Mrs. Franklin reached over and touched Mona's hand. Mona looked down, startled, to see she'd been gripping the edge of the table so tightly that her hand was turning white and bloodless.

"I'm sorry," Mrs. Franklin said. "So very sorry."

"We'll pray for you. And for Hope," Dr. Franklin added.

Mona was surprised by how good it felt to have that little touch, the words of comfort. But she could feel the walls of her defenses shifting, knowing if she indulged in that moment of sympathy and self-pity, the entire thing would come crashing down around her.

Instead, she smiled politely and drew her hand away. "She's fine. I know she is."

A knowing look crossed both of the elder Franklins' faces. "Of course she is," Mrs. Franklin added. They rose to their feet, bundling Tabitha before them, looking anywhere but at Mona as they made their way to the door. As they shuffled out of the too-small room, Tabitha shot one last glance behind her.

"You did well, Tabitha," Mona said to her as she paused at the door. "Thank you."

Tabitha's eyes welled with tears. "I feel like it's my fault, ma'am."

"Why ever would you say that, Tabitha?" Mona answered, surprised. "Of course you're not to blame."

"If I hadn't pushed her so hard . . . "

"About the paper?" Don asked, finally breaking his silence.

"About the paper, and about Stone Mountain, and her tattoo . . . "

Tabitha choked back a sob as both Mona and Don froze in their chairs.

"Her tattoo." Don's voice was flat, dead, as he repeated Tabitha's words.

Tabitha nodded. "I didn't mean to make her feel bad. I thought it was so cool, and to be able to read it . . . I guess I was showing off. I didn't know it would make her upset. Please, you've got to believe me, I'd do anything to have her back. She was my only real friend." Mrs. Franklin held her daughter's heaving shoulders, trying to comfort her.

Mona's mind was racing now. Tabitha said she could read Hope's Mark. Clearly, Tabitha didn't know Hope's history or some of this would make more sense to her. Would Agent Hale be piecing this together? She knew Don already had. He was pressing her knee under the table, silently urging her to be careful, to not let this opportunity slip away.

She had to figure out a way to get more out of Tabitha before she and her parents left the room—and do it in a way that Hale wouldn't pick up on. Before she knew what she was doing, she was pushing away from the table and moving to Tabitha's side.

"Tabitha," she soothed, bending at the knees to get closer to Tabitha's height, "of course you did only what you thought was best for Hope. We know that, and we know how good of a friend you were to her. Don't worry about it, sweetie." She beamed at Tabitha, her best "trust me" smile, able to dazzle CEOs and Chairmen of the Board around the world, and leaned in to give Tabitha a big hug. She lingered there, murmuring her hasty instructions to Tabitha, then kissed her above the ear.

"Thank you for being such a good friend to Hope, Tabby," Mona said, holding Tabitha's shaking hands in hers and stepping back to look at her appraisingly. "Thank you."

Tabitha looked up at Mona, blinking away her tears before nodding quickly. Then, she slipped out of Mona's grip and slid silently out of the room, her parents closing flanks behind her. Hale closed the door behind them.

"That ended up being more promising than I'd anticipated," Hale intoned, yanking the knot of his tie loose and plopping himself down in a chair. "Sometimes, with a little extra time, witnesses come up with a few things they forgot the first time they give their statements. Like this girl, Maria."

Mona wasn't going to tolerate chitchat. "What do you have, Agent Hale?"

He ran his fingers through his hair so it stood on end, another visible sign of the long days and nights he'd been keeping.

"We had the time to check into this Michael character, in between her first statement and when we pulled you in to talk to her. You know this kid?"

Mona nodded, knowing that Don would be listening keenly for details. "He spent a lot of time with Hope. He was one of the first kids she met when she started at her new school. Very mature for his age, it seemed. But I guess you'd expect that from an emancipated teen."

"Emancipated? So you never met his parents? No guardians?"

"No."

"How close were they, Mona? Were they dating?" Don's voice had an edge to it, accusing.

Mona closed her eyes, picturing the way Hope's face lit up when Michael walked in the room; the way her body subtly turned to address his whenever he moved; the way Hope spilled out her secrets, counting them out and sharing their burdens, which Michael gladly took up for her. How could you know that if you hadn't been there to see it for yourself? She settled back down into her chair, trying to determine how, exactly, to describe their relationship.

"No, they weren't dating, but I think they were very close."

Hale sighed, rubbing his face. "So, here's the thing. You remember him. Tabitha Franklin remembers him. The people at the front office of the school remember him. But there is no actual record of him being enrolled in Dunwoody High School. No registration forms. No parking passes. Nothing about his emancipated teen status. No grades reported in the system. We tried to go to his home and confirm his whereabouts that way, but we can't even find an address for him in the school IT system. It's as if the kid never existed."

Mona's mind went to the obvious explanation. "It's the IT system. It's horribly antiquated. They probably have paper copies of all of those things sitting in some dusty pile somewhere."

"We thought so, too. But then we used our own systems to try to track him down, looking for the court records from his emancipation hearing, social security information, any public record of him. Nothing."

He let his words sink in.

"Like I said, it's as if the kid never existed."

He leaned in close to Mona. "Mona, are you sure you knew this kid? I mean, really knew him? Did you trust him with your daughter?"

She was gripping the table again. What was he saying?

"I did." She whispered. "I trusted him. He was so good to Hope."

Hale did not back away but raised a skeptical eyebrow. "Really? Sounds like a jealous bastard to me." The way in which he dismissed her was unmistakable. She felt her cheeks burn red with anger, the implied inattention and naïveté on her part an insult. Hale rose back up to his full height. "But that's not all."

"What more could you have found?" Mona whispered, afraid to ask.

"We were able to track the call Tabitha received back to Nevada. It was made from a hotel well outside of Las Vegas. Our agent on the ground questioned the staff. They reported seeing three girls together in the time frame we are talking about. Two Hispanic, one Caucasian. One was limping. One, the Caucasian, was badly scarred on her face and arms. Looked like burns, according to the night clerk. The clerk said it was hard to gauge the recency of the injuries, because the scarred one was pretty mobile for being that messed up. But it fits our time frame. And it could place your daughter with this Maria."

"Was Michael with them?" She whispered, not sure if it would be a good or bad thing if he were.

Hale shook his head. "The clerk only saw the girls. But we're running through all the security cameras to make sure there was nobody else with them who came in separately."

Mona sat in silence, her logical mind shifting the pieces of the puzzle around. She could make no sense of it. She was acutely aware of Don, glued to his seat next to her. She sensed the quiet anger mounting in him, anger she remembered from the early years of their marriage, when she'd discovered the intensity of it—his absolute cold control—which made her yearn for the messiness of a real argument.

Hale looked at her, furrowing his brow. "You know I am only telling you these things as a favor to our friend Clay. But maybe I should stop. Sometimes it's actually harder for family members to have the details as they unfold, when there are no answers."

He paused to assess her reaction. Mona felt keenly that this was a test of some sort.

"No," she sighed. "I appreciate being kept in the loop. Especially when I know I am still not officially in the clear." She smiled grimly. "I want you to keep telling me as much as you can."

"As you prefer. But if that is the case, you may want to see one other thing. Come with me." He looked perfunctorily at Don. "Both of you."

Hale steered her out the door, not bothering to wait for Don, and led her back down the hallway to what had become the central command post for the investigation. The bank of screens, blinking with data and video feeds, was overwhelming, but, at the same time, reassuring. Even as they puzzled things out for themselves, the FBI's algorithms and search functions were systematically looking for Hope, leaving nothing unexamined.

"We got a data feed from the interrogation of the Chinese traffickers we picked up after that fire in Las Vegas. Only one of them talked, but what he had to say was, well, interesting, to say the least."

He guided her to a desk and held the chair for her as she sat down. The video was poised to run from the desktop monitor, the little triangle for "Play" blinking patiently.

Hale tapped the "Play" button and sat down on the edge of the desk, next to Mona.

The camera angled in closely on the face of the man being questioned. The bags under his eyes and faint stubble suggested he'd had a rough night. Despite that, Mona could tell he commanded the room. Fatigue did nothing to undercut the presence of a man who was accustomed to ruling with impunity, a man who was routinely obeyed. His expression was unruffled by the circumstances in which he found himself. Only a faint hint of irritation, found in the disdainful curl of his upper lip, suggested anything even unpleasant about his interrogation.

Hale narrated over the close-up. "This is Chen. One of the leaders of the Triad trafficking group, as far as we can tell. This is about halfway through the session we had with him."

Off camera, Mona heard the agent questioning Chen.

"You are sure? You are sure that is the man you gambled with? The man who came to your compound last night?"

Chen looked straight at the camera. "You must find more interesting interrogators. I find this one to be repetitive and slow-witted." He shifted his gaze, presumably to address his questioner. "Yes. As I told you before, I am sure this is the man. I will never forget his face."

"Can you pick up the book and point to the man in question? Hold it up to the camera. Let's get a close-up," the voice said, giving instruction to the cameraman.

The camera zoomed out and Chen wearily lifted a heavy book, flipping it so the open pages were visible. He pointed at the third picture in the middle row.

"This is him. Mr. Carmichael." The camera zoomed back in for the tight shot. Chen's finger rested on a snapshot of Mona's estranged husband, Don.

Mona's head began to swim.

"Careful, Mona," Hale soothed, watching her reactions as closely as he watched the evidence before him. "Remember, we already knew there was someone out there who looked like Don."

She nodded, unable to speak, unable to look at the *real* Don, standing right behind her, her eyes riveted to the video.

"You're sure?" the off-screen agent asked again.

"Yes," Chen sighed, snapping the book shut and dropping it on the table in front of him. "For the last time, I am sure this is the person. What I want to know is why you are so interested in him."

The cameraman reset the angle, giving Mona a fuller picture

of Chen. Even the poor quality of the recording couldn't hide the glint of interest in his keen eyes.

"You don't need to know that. Why were you working with this man? What were your business dealings with him?"

Chen's face broke into an open sneer. "You think I would work with such a man? I would kill him if I had the chance. But perhaps you will find him and deal with him before I can."

There was a long pause. Mona knew the technique. The interrogator was drawing out the uncomfortable silence, laying the trap, hoping the awkwardness of the silence would draw out the nervous chatter that often spelled the downfall of people with something to hide.

Chen just sat. He was too good to fall for such a ploy, Mona could tell.

The interrogator tried again. "Does this man traffic, like you? Is he Triad?"

Chen smiled, thinking he had won. "I don't know what you mean."

"Did he run your operations in Atlanta?"

"What operations? I am a simple Chinese businessman. I don't have any dealings in the United States."

Mona heard a shuffle of papers off-camera. A few brisk footsteps, and the agent filled the screen, dropping some papers in front of Chen before disappearing once again.

"Do you recognize this girl?"

Chen picked up what looked like an 8x10 photo and glanced it over. He shrugged noncommittally, tossing it onto the table in front of him. "What if I did? There are lots of girls in Las Vegas. They all run together in my mind."

"Look again."

Chen raised an eyebrow and picked up the photo. He then picked up a few other snapshots. The corners of his mouth turned up, just slightly. "Yes, this girl I do remember." He cocked an eyebrow, enjoying the cat and mouse with his questioner. "What do you want to know about her?"

"How do you know her?"

"Can one ever really say one knows another human being?" Chen philosophized, taking his time answering the agent. "I mean, really knows someone? Take Mr. Carmichael. I put my faith in him. And then he turned against me. If I could make such a mistake with him, I doubt whether I can trust my own judgment and say I really know anybody."

Mona was losing patience. She heard the agent scrape his chair. "Do I need to turn off the camera, so we can have a private talk, Mr. Chen?"

Chen laughed derisively. "Your American laws will keep you from doing that." He leaned back in his chair and gestured magnanimously. "I had hoped you might indulge me in conversation, but I see I overestimated you. So, you want to know about the girl. She was with Carmichael. He said she was his niece. I have no reason to think otherwise."

"Keep talking."

Chen had baited his hook and was enjoying stringing along the agent.

"It was a funny thing. She was clearly very special to him. He would not let her out of his sight, but for a minute. And for good reason. Every time she was alone, she caused great trouble. She was a very disobedient young lady."

"What kind of trouble?"

Chen's eyes twinkled as he recounted his story. "It is of no matter. What matters is how Mr. Carmichael dealt with it. At first I thought him weak. But then he did something I am not sure I could even do, not to one who is a particular favorite."

He leaned into the table, and the camera zoomed in once again. He had delicate, manicured hands, Mona saw. They gestured with precision as he continued.

"He wanted to prove he could control her, I think. To establish goodwill. Seal our bond." He clasped his hands together, a physical demonstration of the kind of bond about which he was talking. "He brought me the girl, to show me for myself, and I was astonished."

Mona was holding her breath.

"What did he do?" the agent prompted, his voice sounding strangely hollow from off-camera.

"He burned her!" Chen announced, his eyes wide with crazy admiration.

Behind her, Mona heard the sharp intake of Don's breath, but it seemed a million miles away. She couldn't drag her eyes from the screen. Chen expressed crazy glee as he told his story, relishing the details.

"I didn't have time to ask him how—battery acid, I would presume. Her face, her arms, her hands, her body. Everywhere, burned. And then he made her stand there, so I could inspect her. If I hadn't seen it with my own eyes, I would not have believed it. Great, oozing sores. She could barely stand."

Mona's stomach was beginning to roil, but she couldn't look away, couldn't form the words to ask Hale to stop the tape.

"Such a pity," Chen continued, shaking his head, a tiny smile still evident on his lips. "She was so beautiful; but then, what did it matter? He still thought she was beautiful. Even though he had to destroy her, he still loved her. He even worried about her pain. He is quite a sensitive man, I think, our Mr. Carmichael." He paused, tutting softly. "And the poor thing, I think she loved him, too, despite it all. Maybe even because of it."

Mona felt the bile surging up her throat and reached about her, blindly, for the trash can. She found it just in time.

Over her retching, she was vaguely aware of Agent Hale turning off the video, of Don awkwardly patting her back and holding her hair.

She hovered over the trashcan. When she was sure nothing else was coming up, she dragged her sleeve across her mouth and straightened up in her chair, shrugging off Don's touch.

"Okay?" Hale asked gently.

She nodded, her back still to him.

His voice was soothing now, trying to paper over the horrible hole that had been ripped in her heart. "What Chen said seems to corroborate what the hotel clerks said, though the disparity in the extent of the injuries is puzzling. We've updated the missing persons alert to reflect her reported injuries."

Mona didn't say anything. Her mind was blank, refusing to accept what she'd just heard.

"Mona." He said her name, quietly. She braced herself for whatever he said next. "The thing is, when we went back to the casinos to look for room records or gambling records for our perp, nothing shows up. The forms this man had to file to get his markers to gamble are gone. Even the security videotape from Wynn—the tape *we all saw*—is gone. It's nothing but static now. Car rental, same thing."

He paused, waiting for her to comment, but she was uncharacteristically quiet.

"The only organization that has the reach to do that is Triad. Or maybe one of the Russian trafficking operations. And the evidence . . . "

Don finished Agent Hale's sentence, his hard words full of judgment. "The evidence looks as if somehow her friend Michael was involved, too."

Hale nodded. "Whether as a victim or not, we don't know. But I feel like I need to tell you, trafficking cases often start with a so-called boyfriend luring a young girl into trusting him. Trusting him so much that by the time she realizes his intentions, she's cut off from her family. Trapped."

Mona swiveled on her chair to face Hale, unwilling to believe it. Her eyes were wet with tears. "Why? How?"

"We don't know yet, but we'll find out. I promise you. With a proven Triad link, this is moving out of our normal jurisdiction. I need to take our search international, start cooperating with some other agencies. With Triad or other trafficking connections there's no telling where they could have taken her."

Her shoulders sank, a quick nod giving her assent.

He cleared his throat to broach a more delicate subject. "With the evidence we have in hand, there is really no reason for us to keep Don in custody or file any charges. Nor to have you here, for that matter. I think it would be better for you both to go home. I promise we'll keep you up to date."

"Okay," she numbly agreed, recognizing his not-so-subtle attempt to move them both out of the picture. "I'll get out of your way."

"It might be better for the time being," Hale continued. "Don, do you think you will stay in town, or go back to Alabama?"

The subject of her estranged husband was hard for her to take right now, when the images of his face from the video were still fresh and her own confused feelings for him still unresolved. Before he had a chance to speak for himself, she announced, "He'll be going back to Alabama."

Her words hung in the air awkwardly, but Don did nothing to dispute her decision. Finally, Hale cleared his throat.

"Fair enough. I'll clear it with your employer, Don, if that's what you really want to do. You'll just have to stay where we can find you. Just in case. Neither one of you should talk to the press or attempt to interfere in the investigation. And then there's the matter of security . . ."

She looked up, confused.

"Given what you just saw, we thought you might be more comfortable with a security detail. In case the traffickers trace Hope back to you, or try to make good on that threat to kill Hope's kidnapper. Remember, Triad won't know that Don is not their man. They could come after you with everything they've got."

"That's not necessary," she said, her voice firm.

"I know it seems like an imposition, but you should think it over, Mona. For your own peace of mind. And what about you, Don?" He peered over Mona's head, to where Don still stood behind her. "With the physical resemblance, and the perp using your name as an alias . . . " he left his thought unfinished, knowing they would fill in the blanks themselves.

"I don't need security," Don answered simply. "I'll be fine on my own in Alabama. After all, it's a flyover state, right? Nobody would think to look for the kidnapper there," he joked lamely, trying to make light of the situation. "I'll just need to get my truck, Mona. It's parked at your house."

Hale began to argue, but Mona cut him off.

"Don is Hope's father and an adult. If he doesn't want a security attachment, you can't force it on him." Her words came out more sharply than she meant, but she was tired and losing patience.

Hale sighed and then threw up his hands. "You're right. I can't force you. But if you change your mind, we can have a detail there in minutes. Don't forget."

He pulled the bits and pieces of his files back together and, before leaving, reached out to squeeze Mona's shoulder.

"She's alive, Mona. If Chen is telling the truth, we have that going for us." He gave her shoulder another quick squeeze and began winding his way through the cubicles back to his own office, leaving her alone with Don.

All she could think was, *She's alive—but for how long?*

# three

## TURKEY

The disastrous morning with Michael boded ill for my next adventure—the trip to the public baths. And, indeed, the outing began on a sour note. I emerged from my room having changed into a pair of jeans and a T-shirt, the only clean clothes I had left.

"You can't go out in that," Michael said, abruptly. He looked me up and down with a critical eye. "That won't do at all."

"Why not?" I demanded.

"First of all, it's too cold out. You're not used to the wind off the water—it can be biting and will cut you to the bone in no time at all."

"So I'll put on a sweatshirt when we go out."

"Second, there is the matter of your skin."

He stopped talking and all the air seemed to get sucked out of the room. I was vaguely aware of Enoch and Raph watching us.

"What about my skin?" I said, trying to keep my tone even, challenging him to even speak of it.

Michael, sensing he was in dangerous territory, adopted a reasonable tone. "I think you'll be more comfortable covering yourself. Especially in a Muslim city."

Enoch spoke up. "This is a secular country, Michael. They do not practice sharia law here. She has no need for covering."

"It's changed," Michael asserted, looking at me as if he dared me to contradict him. "It is not as safe for an uncovered woman to walk through the city. You can feel it everywhere. And the government. . . . Even this morning, there were more protests."

I felt myself flushing. Had he been near the university that morning, just as I had been? Did he already know I'd been there? And did he know I had encountered the Fallen? I stared at him, hard, refusing to be drawn out. Besides, I knew what was really motivating his insistence. My chin lifted in defiance as if daring him to say what he really thought about my uncovered skin—that he couldn't stand to be reminded of the damage he had done.

"You said we were going to a tourist district for this bath, correct?" I very consciously kept my tone steady, my voice calmer than I was feeling on the inside.

"Yes," he acknowledged, his eyes wary.

"They are not going to expect tourists to obey Muslim law. I'm going uncovered. I'll wear the sweatshirt and that's it. Deal?"

"She's being very reasonable, Michael," Enoch added, trying to smooth things over.

Michael shot an annoyed look over my head at Enoch. "Fine," he said, turning on his heel and walking away. "We leave in five minutes."

Raph brushed past me, clearly annoyed. "Why must you provoke him? You're only making things worse."

"That's not fair," I called after him as he pounded down the stairs. I moved to follow him, but Enoch grabbed my arm and held me back.

"Hope, there is only so much he can take. You must choose your battles."

"I'm not going to veil myself, Enoch. That's completely ridiculous."

"I don't suggest that you do. But think about what you say to him. Please. For me."

I looked up into the lenses of the shiny aviator sunglasses that were perched on Enoch's nose. I wished I could see into his eyes instead of seeing my own, powerless figure reflected back at me.

I sighed, knowing Enoch was right. "I'll try, Enoch. I promise."

*The old man is the last person from whom you should be seeking advice*, Henri whispered to me. *After all, look at what happened to him. But*, he continued begrudgingly, *this time I happen to agree with him. Don't provoke Michael if you can avoid it.*

I thought about what Henri was implying. He was right, in one sense. Enoch had followed his own way and ended up banished to the outskirts of Heaven, sentenced to live an eternity in solitude as punishment for giving voice to the Prophecy—the Prophecy that foretold the rise of the Fallen Angels and spelled almost certain death for me.

I went cold at the thought of it and shivered.

"See?" Enoch tutted at me, patting my hand. "Michael was right. You'll be much too cold in such light clothing."

I forced a smile, never completely sure if he could really see me through his seemingly blind eyes. "I'll go get my sweatshirt."

"Good girl," he said.

We walked in silence from the house, working our way back through the labyrinth of streets toward the heart of the old district. Michael and Raph kept tightly together, leaving Enoch and me to straggle behind.

"Enoch, have you ever been in the public baths?"

"No, my dear. When I was human, we did not have such niceties. I was more likely to clean myself off with sand."

I tucked my hands deeper into my pockets, head down against the wind, and kept walking, wondering what was in store for me.

We had apparently reached the more touristy part of Sultanahmet. Crowds milled about, holding up their cell phones to get the perfect photo and straining to listen to the tour guides shouting out their litanies of dates and facts. A swarm of young men, watchful, circled around the tourists, looking for the lone, hapless ones, offering their helpful guidance and asking if maybe, just maybe, they would be interested in a carpet. They gave us a wide berth, apprehensive of the warning silently flashing from Raph's black eyes. We cut through them all and headed for the other side of the square.

I tilted my head back, agape at the minarets soaring above me, left and right. The white marble seemed to draw the smallest bits of sun from behind the clouds, which floated, a radiant mix of orange and gray and purple, against the muddy sky. Everything was reflected in the wet puddles of the square, still slick with rain. On the opposite side, brick, stone, and marble rioted on the façade of another massive complex, glowing pink with morning radiance as the sun managed to peek out from behind the clouds.

Suddenly, a grand flock of birds wheeled overhead, silhouetted against the sky. I gave a start.

"It's just seagulls," Raph volunteered, understanding my fear that the Fallen had found us. I took a shaky breath, grateful for his reassurance, and looked back up to the sky. Entranced, I watched the birds whirl and streak across the sky before the gigantic domes ahead of us, majestic and grand, commanded my attention.

"What are those buildings?"

"Ayasofya and the Blue Mosque," Michael answered over his shoulder. "But we'll be going to the building between them."

I reluctantly dragged my eyes away from the spires to where Michael was pointing. Across the square, past a dancing fountain, sat a slightly smaller, more austere complex. Only between such magnificent structures could this third site have been deemed humble. It stretched the length of the square, row after row of domes that spoke of untold wealth.

"That's a bath house?" I gaped, incredulous.

"A *hammam*," Michael corrected me, pausing for me to catch up. "Most Ottoman homes didn't have private baths, so hammams like this were vital to the public. And this one was special. It was designed by one of the most famous architects of the Ottomans, built for a slave who became the powerful wife of the sultan."

"This was built for a slave?"

"She didn't remain a slave. Roxelana grew powerful in her own right. These were just recently restored after having fallen into great disrepair. Imagine, hawkers were using the navel stones to display carpets to tourists."

"Navel stones?"

"You'll see," he said, a slight smile on his face as he began walking swiftly across the square, following the cobblestone path toward the fountain.

I didn't have time to wonder what had improved his mood. Raph had already moved ahead and was consulting with a street vendor next to the fountain. When we caught up with him, he turned from the vendor, who resumed the business of peddling his wares from under his red and white striped awning, his voice cutting through the low murmur of the crowds and the gurgling fountain.

A deep frown marred Raph's dark face. "I'm not sure this is such a good idea," he began, looking at me doubtfully. "We will have to part here. Even the entrances are separate. I think we should skip the baths."

My heart sank. I could practically feel the dirt between my toes. Any inhibitions I had felt earlier were quickly slipping away. I wanted—no, needed—that bath.

"I promise, I'll be watchful. Besides," I added, pointing at the crowds milling about near the building, "nothing could happen to me in there, not with all these people around to witness it."

Michael seemed to be weighing the risk, looking about the square for any sign of danger. His eyes narrowed as a particularly loud group of young men cut across the lawn, which, despite the grayness of the day, glistened a dewy green.

"Maybe one of us should go in with you. As a woman, of course," he declared hastily, lest any of us mistake his meaning.

I felt my face turning a deep red. Of course, any one of them could shape-shift at will and take the form of anybody they pleased. I became indignant at the thought of it.

"No way," I said in a clipped voice. "That is not going to happen. You can forget about it right now. I'd rather stay filthy than have one of you watching me taking a bath."

Raph shrugged, his black eyes glittering with amusement. "It is a logical solution," he said, struggling to keep a sardonic smile from stealing across his hardened face. "But I would never impose against your wishes." He gave a short, mocking bow and backed away, leaving me to square off with Michael.

Behind me, Enoch gave a snort. "She's surrounded by people in there, Michael. Let her go. Set a time and place to meet and be done with it."

Michael rolled his eyes. "Fine. We'll split up here. You're going to go around the other end to the women's entrance. Pay with this," he said, thrusting a credit card into my hand. "They'll issue you a cloth and slippers and take you into the *camekan*. It's like a locker room. You'll change there and then make your way into the main baths. You'll see what to do once you are there."

He put his hands on my shoulders and squeezed gently. A shimmer of heat ran through my body. He looked at me intently, as if he were trying to memorize my face in case we never saw each other again.

"Don't let yourself get trapped alone."

"It's just a bath," I whispered, my voice catching in my throat. My skin was singing at his touch, the heaviness of his hands upon my shoulders the only thing keeping me grounded.

*You have more to fear from him than from anything that could happen to you in those baths*, Henri whispered.

Michael's voice cut off Henri's taunt. "Promise me."

I nodded and looked down at the ground, my morning encounter with the Fallen an all-too-real reminder of the danger I faced. "I promise."

"We'll give you an hour. Come to the fountain when you're done."

He released me and waited for me to go.

"Enoch?" I said, turning behind me to find the old angel leaning into his cane.

"Don't worry," he said, grinning. "I'll make sure neither follows you in."

"Thank you," I said, grateful he was on my side.

I turned and started walking toward the side of the hammam. Now that I was close to the complex, I could see how the two ends were composed of alternating white and red bricks, towering above the deep pink walls of the two inner domes. The entire building was topped with a slate gray that matched the cloudy sky.

The feeling of eyes boring into my back made me pick up my pace as I made my way toward the women's entrance.

I turned the corner, out of sight, following the discreet signs. There was no line. I climbed down a staircase, taking a deep breath before slipping through the massive wooden door.

I found myself in a high-ceilinged hall, steps leading down into a square, sunken room lined with low cushions. The interior was bright and clean, calming cool white walls reaching up two stories to a tidy dome bathed in blue. Polished wood, gold as it caught the light of scattered lamps, glowed from the upper floors. Brass plaques and stained glass warmed the walls, giving the place a cozy feel. Across the room, up the stairs and behind a polished wooden desk, stood a lone attendant. She was wrapped in a turquoise skirt and top, her glossy black hair falling in waves beneath her shoulders. She smiled expectantly.

"English?" she asked, scanning me up and down as I crossed the room and climbed the stairs to her.

"No, American," I answered, my gesturing hands broadcasting my nervousness. She caught a glimpse of my reddened skin, and her eyes flamed with curiosity. But just as quickly, she looked away, burrowing in her desk in pretended distraction. My cheeks flushed with embarrassment, and I pulled the sleeves of my sweatshirt over my fingertips.

The woman pretended not to notice, keeping up a cheerful chatter. "For you the distinction is so important. American, British—you have fought wars to be what you are. But for me, it means nothing. You read your services in English, no?" She looked up from her desk, her eyes twinkling, and handed me a laminated menu. I scanned it quickly, looking for the simplest thing I could find.

"This," I said, pointing and showing her the card. "The basic service, please."

She nodded, taking the card from me, her eager eyes taking in the shiny skin on my fingertip. "No special needs, then?" She waited politely for me to respond. When I said nothing, she nodded her head and continued on. "Your attendant's tip is included in the price, Miss. If you would like to pay now?"

I dug into my pocket and handed her the credit card. She took it from my hand, and I noticed how elegant her slender, manicured fingers looked next to my dirty, scarred skin. Ashamed, I snatched my hand away.

She turned behind the desk and smoothly executed the payment, and then offered me a pile of fluffy linens.

"This is your first time in a hammam, *yes*?" She didn't even wait for me to answer before continuing. "Come with me." She whisked me up a flight of wooden stairs, a study in grace, guiding me to one of the airy, rattan-like cubicles against the corridor.

"This is your changing room. You can leave your clothes inside. Put these on," she said, handing me a neat pile of slippers and fabric. "You may come back down when you are ready to meet your attendant."

I peered around the inside of my personal locker. Empty hooks awaited towels and discarded clothing. I laid out the things she handed to me. The linen unfolded into a towel-sized wrap of thin, purple cotton, white fringe decorating each end.

Swiftly, I pulled my clothes off, stacking each piece into a neat pile on the bench. I didn't look at myself in the mirror; I didn't want to see the welts of angry flesh, the hardening scar tissue that I knew marked my body. Instead, I wrapped myself snugly into the towel, fastening and refastening it about my chest, and slid my feet into the too-tight slippers, clearly not made for large, corn-fed American girls. I tugged at the wrap, which barely covered my thighs. Resigned, clutching the thin fabric about me, I headed down the stairs to meet my waiting attendant. Michael's words of caution hurried me along.

She was dressed in a smart, dusty-rose uniform. Stretching out her hand, she beamed at me. "Come. I will show you." She grasped my hand firmly and led me through a narrow arched door.

I felt an immediate change in temperature as I slipped into the next corridor. The air behind me swirled, chilly and dry, as I moved deeper into the moist heat that was beckoning from the other side of the narrow space. I looked up and saw that the ceiling here was considerably lower than that of the changing room—no dome here, just a hallway. Beads of perspiration began to form above my lip. I dragged an arm across my face and kept walking, careful not to slip on the increasingly slick floor. My attendant gripped my hand more tightly, checking that I was safe. To my side I noted the deep marble sinks, stacked with thick towels. Another attendant, standing against the wall, smiled shyly and murmured something encouraging, pointing toward the next door.

Unsure, I followed my attendant and stepped through.

A grand space opened up before me, a pristine hall, soft white marble for the first six feet, then stucco soaring high. The space was softly lit by ruby red glass lamps tucked into niches in the wall and shafts of daylight that pierced the steamy air from above. I craned my neck and saw the ceiling was made up of several domes or half-domes, each pierced through with small, star-like windows, so that, even on a gray day like today, the interior of the baths seemed to glow. Little rivulets of condensation dripped around each opening, marring the perfect white. I squinted and noticed that the biggest, central dome was topped by a glass eye, letting in even more light. I followed the shaft to where it ended on a large, inlaid marble table in the center of the room, an intricate design of squares, octagons, and shooting stars in black, gold, and pink marble. Women lay on their stomachs or backs, some resting peacefully, a big mound of bubbles hiding everything but their heads, others being scrubbed vigorously by young women dressed in halters and sarongs. Still others were being pummeled and pounded, their sighs testament to the thoroughness of the massages they were receiving.

*The navel stone*, I thought, satisfied to have figured it out.

I scanned the perimeter of the room, noticing the deep niches set back from steps, each punctuated by gray-streaked marble basins. Gleaming brass fixtures shone through the steam.

"Here," my attendant whispered softly, guiding me slowly across the floor and up a set of steps. She turned the handles, and water gushed forth into the basin, a new rush of steam rising up. She gestured for me to take off my wrap and sit on one of the low marble benches that lined the room. I hesitated, but she nodded, miming the routines of bathing to spur me on.

I let the towel drop to the floor and shivered despite the heat of the steam room. Her eyes grew soft. She stared frankly at my scarred body, murmuring to herself in words I could not understand.

I bent down to snatch the towel back, wanting to hide, but her hand grabbed mine, stopping me.

I looked up, and her eyes were kind.

"I'll take care of you," she said, rubbing my hand gently until I dropped the towel and settled back into my seat. I let the warmth emanating from deep under the bowels of the room sink into my bones. She smiled quickly, dipping an elaborate golden bowl into a deep sink and motioning for me to drop my head. I did, closing my eyes, letting the heat of the hammam lull me. Hot water trickled down my neck and back, then all over me, as my attendant dipped and poured, dipped and poured, the sounds of the running water and soft swooshing sounds of the furnace soothing me.

My relaxation did not last long, however, as a stream of ice-cold water dumped over my head and ran down my back, shocking me back awake.

My eyes flew open to find my young attendant smiling sweetly. "Shock therapy," she said, shaking off my attempt to end the session right then and there.

She dipped her ladle back into the running water and poured it around my shoulders and all over my body, delicious heat sinking into my tired muscles. I could feel the tension slipping away as she poured the water, again and again, the rhythm of it soothing my body into relaxation once again.

"My name is Ays," she said, pointing to the charm around her neck that spelled out her name in delicate gold. "Now your turn," she insisted, handing me the bowl. "I will be right back."

I snuck a few glances about me as I tried to replicate Ays's perfect rhythm. A few women were tucked up in alcoves like mine, chatting away, mindlessly dunking and dumping their bowls full of water, as they gossiped in quiet voices, every now and then turning the water faucets to refill their basins. I sank deeper into my seat, letting my eyes flutter closed. The clank and whir of the mechanical workings deep in the belly of the hammam punctuated the silence, as did the call to prayer floating out over the square.

I felt a hand tapping my shoulder. I opened my eyes to see Ays, now dressed in a sarong. She winked, taking the bowl from my side and moving swiftly to repeat the dousing with which she'd started. She ran her fingers over my limbs, twisting me this way and that, having me stand and turn before her. Tutting softly, she picked up my hand and led me, like a baby, to the great marble table in the center of the room, where my wrap had already been spread out next to a big silver bucket, gesturing for me to lie down on my back.

My self-consciousness gone, I stretched out on the towel, feeling the heat from the furnaces below seeping into my body, my eyes fluttering shut.

"No scrub. Too tender," my attendant whispered in my ear, her fingers lightly dancing across my scars. "But I will fix you."

I didn't answer. I didn't want to wonder what she thought. I just wanted to give myself over to the steam and the heat. Through the echoes, I could hear my attendant talking to herself as she prepared.

"Very soft," she whispered, and I was conscious of her hovering over my body. "Very soft," she said again, reassuring, laying her hands upon my back.

I heard a soft whirring in the air above me. Then, big dollops of warm suds fell about me. Whir, plop. Whir, plop. She was weaving a long white cloth through the air, then deftly slinging it across my body, never actually touching me but depositing mounds of soap bubbles in her wake until I could no longer see any of my body. When she was satisfied I was sufficiently soaped up, she dropped her cloth back into the bucket and began to work.

Deftly, as if I were an infant, she picked up my limbs and moved me about, wiping away the grime from days of travel. Her hands never ceased, bending me this way and that, rinsing away the soap with torrents of hot water. Swiftly, she whisked away my wet towels, wrapping my clean parts in fluffy new ones, so that I was entirely protected in a warm cocoon of cotton before she moved on to the next part of my body. I sighed, sinking deeper into relaxation, wondering at her skill.

As she washed my body, she began to tell a story.

"The sultan once loved his concubine so much he made her his wife. Very unusual to do this. He stopped visiting the harem, all for love of this wife. He gave her everything. He even built this hammam in her honor, so that all the staff at mosque could come and bathe here. But the wife, Hurrem—you call her Roxelana—she was never satisfied. She wanted more. More buildings. More jewels. More power. Never happy, this Roxelana. The sultan was a powerful man in his own right—some say the best ruler in the all of Ottoman history—but Hurrem wrapped around his brain like a snake."

A dollop of suds fell on me as she continued her tale.

"This sultan had a son by another woman. This son was loved by the people and was to be the sultan's heir. But Hurrem wanted the throne for her favorite son. She whispered in the sultan's ear and convinced the sultan to kill his best advisor. Then she whispered some more, and convinced him to order and witness the death of his own heir.

"Turn over," she whispered. Dutifully, I flipped myself over, easing onto my stomach.

Whir, plop. Whir, plop. She prepared me for the next round of bathing before taking her story back up.

"But still, this Hurrem was not satisfied. No, to be satisfied she had to kill her other son, and his four boys, to be sure that her favorite son was safe upon the throne."

My blood ran cold.

"See?" My attendant asked sweetly, never pausing in her ministrations. "Love can make you do terrible things. It can twist one's mind, so that it is no longer possible to tell right from wrong. It can cause one to destroy what should be cherished. But even such a terrible love can leave behind great beauty," she said, giving me another dollop of soap. "Like this hammam."

She fell into quiet humming, then, folding me this way and that while I pondered her story. Was it a warning? Would I be the thing Michael destroyed? I pushed my curiosity and foreboding away, telling myself there was no deeper meaning in the tale, so that I could surrender to the lull of the bath.

After several minutes, she finished her ministrations with a final wipe of a cloth. I lay there on the hot marble table, swaddled in warm towels and in a state of complete bliss, oblivious to my surroundings. Then, she leaned over and whispered to me again.

"Yes, love does terrible things," she repeated, tracing the scars that criss-crossed my skin as if she already knew the truth of their origin. "But now I will fix you."

Shock rippled through me, but before I could react, she was unwrapping the towels covering my back. I mumbled a slight protest, as she exposed me once again to the wet air of the *hararet*, trying to push myself up off the stone to ask her meaning. Firmly, she pushed me back onto the marble. Then, her hands began fluttering across my skin, barely touching me before moving to the next spot, and the next. The scent of roses, lavender, and rosemary surrounded me, and I breathed in deeply, feeling the ageless peace of the hammam sinking into my soul, pushing all other thoughts out of my mind.

My attendant was murmuring to herself, now, a slight, singsongy sound that rose and fell with the movements of her hands. The rhythm and the heat were intoxicating; so much so that I didn't notice when she began going deeper into the muscle, kneading and pulsing my broken body.

I gasped at the pain as she began to work the knot in my neck and tried to push myself up. She stopped me, laying a steady hand on my shoulder. "Hurt now, better later," she whispered into my ear, easing me back down onto the marble slab. "Trust me. Okay?"

I paused, unsure, before I nodded for her to continue, bracing myself for the pain.

Her skillful fingers began working again, drifting over each part of my body, unerringly finding each knot. She would ease into it, trying to learn the secrets my muscles held, and then coaxing and persistent, would undo the fear, doubt, and regret that lingered there. As my body fought to hold onto its pain, clenching and protesting her touch, her voice would rise into song, as if she could dash away the memories my body held with the lightness of her tune. Each tightly held hurt came undone, chased away by her swift fingers, until she finished, leaving me weeping silently into my towel.

"You will be okay," she whispered, pulling a dry towel up around me and patting my shoulder in a last, comforting gesture before moving away, back into the folds of steam that circled the hararet.

I lay there, wanting nothing more than to curl myself into a ball. While the bath and massage had given my aching body and skin relief, my doubt about Michael had rushed to the surface, leaving me feeling raw and exposed. The twisted logic of the harem and its safety, the separation of women and men into their different worlds, suddenly seemed appealing, especially with the words of my attendant, a warning really—"love does terrible things"—echoing in my mind. I didn't want to leave this sanctuary. But I knew I couldn't stay. Michael was waiting for me, and his warnings about being trapped alone were insistently worming their way to the front of my consciousness, urging me to hurry.

I pushed myself up, clutching my towel close. Mindful of the slippery floors, I shuffled across the open space toward the door. I left behind the magical peace of the steamy dome and slipped through the arched exit, a small sign pointing the way back to the changing rooms. As I did, I caught a glimpse of myself in the mirror.

My skin, once crisscrossed with angry red welts and white scar tissue, seemed different. In the dim light of the locker, I almost had a healthy pink glow. Could it be?

I leaned in closer and wiped the mirror, foggy from the steam, with the corner of my towel.

The harsh reality of my scars had been softened by the steam and mist from the hammam, but it was more than an illusion. My skin definitely looked different. I was healing, faster than I should have been.

I stared for another moment, confused, slipping out the door and climbing, heavy limbed, back to my changing room. Once inside, I sat on the bench and stared at my pile of clothes. I couldn't bear the thought of wearing them again, the stiff cotton sure to rub against my tender skin, but I had no choice. My emotions spent, I slipped out of the towel and dressed myself. Muscles tender, I checked to be sure I hadn't forgotten anything and stole one last glance in the mirror to confirm it had not all been in my imagination. Then, I slipped down the wooden staircase, moving past the tall glasses of tea and water that waited by the cushions. The front desk was empty. I lingered, hoping for the desk attendant to appear, giving me an excuse to delay my return to reality, but after a few minutes it was evident she wasn't coming back. Knowing I had probably taken more time than we'd planned, I gathered myself to meet the others. I crossed to the heavy wooden door and left the confines of the hammam, wondering just what magic had been worked upon me, body and soul.

I climbed the stairs, walking alone around the perimeter of the building back to our designated meeting place. Suddenly, a strong hand clamped my shoulder.

I reeled, pushing my assailant's hand away, afraid that Michael's misgivings had been right and that the Fallen had found me after all. As I stumbled, trying to regain my bearings, I looked up to see the puzzled face of the hammam receptionist.

She held out her hand. "You forgot this, miss." It was my credit card.

Embarrassed, I thanked her and shoved the card deep into my pocket, hurrying to find my band of angels.

~

Nobody berated me for being late. All I got was one sideways glance from Michael as I handed him back the credit card.

"You're okay? Nothing unusual happened while you were in there?" he interrogated me.

I hid how shaken I was by my harmless interaction with the receptionist outside the hammam—better for him not to know how terrified of the Fallen I actually was.

"Good," he nodded, his relief at my safety palpable.

It was past midday by this point. It was late to be restarting our search, but we had to do something to stave off the hopelessness I knew we all felt. So, with a sense of purpose, Enoch spread out the map we'd gotten at the chapel the day before and looked for a place to start. He was dressed like a fisherman now, a thick cable sweater straining against his burgeoning stomach, his gray head topped with a jaunty cap that tilted to one side, its ribbons twisting in the breeze. His shiny aviator sunglasses looked oddly out of place, but then again, he was a complete anachronism.

"Nice getup," I said, the sight of him making me smile despite myself.

"This is a maritime city. I thought it an appropriate homage."

He peered over the map, never letting on whether or not he was actually able to read it with his empty eyes. With a satisfied grunt, he picked up the map and slapped it with his hand. "Perfect. We can get started right now."

"Here?" I looked around the square.

"Not every site on this map was a church dedicated to Michael. There are other things that were sacred to him. One is right here. Isn't it Michael?"

Michael was peering intently through the streams of water that jetted from the fountain's perimeter. He didn't look at us as he answered; he simply nodded across the square before voicing almost reverently, "Ayasofya."

We followed him across the wet pavement toward the old church.

The great wooden doors loomed ahead of us. Michael hesitated at the threshold, reaching one hand to grip the doorway. "She is an old friend, this church. Many memories tread her grand halls. But you wish to see the icons, do you not, Enoch?"

"You know the one we wish to see."

"Very well," Michael said, slipping inside the great door.

He walked with purpose, leaving me to steal little glimpses of the ancient church, as I hurried after him. But when I followed him through another set of vast, wooden doors, it was as if the sky opened up and I had to stop and stare, dumbstruck.

A huge dome spanned the entirety of the nave, easily two hundred feet above me. It seemed to float overhead, somehow supported only by tiers of marble columns that ran the length of the space. The weak sun streamed in from the endless rows of windows, filling the vastness with an ethereal light. Huge black circles, emblazoned with gold calligraphy, hung from the arches of the dome, marking the church—long ago converted to a mosque—for Islam. Shadows crisscrossed the marble floor. Overhead there was a dizzyingly spectacular gold mosaic, covering the ceiling and filling the entire place with a heavenly glow.

I was overwhelmed by the enormity of the place. There was so much to see, I wasn't sure where to look. But then I saw Michael and the others heading out the side. With a pang of regret at not having time to explore on my own, I followed after them.

I caught up with them at the top of the ramp that led us to the upper galleries of the building. We wordlessly passed a mosaic of a man holding a skull and a drawing of a sailing ship, not pausing in our pursuit of the icon Enoch had mentioned. The crowds were thin in this second level, and Enoch's cane, with its distinctive thump, echoed among the marble as we hurried along.

We went through another marble doorway and Enoch whispered, "The Gates of Heaven and Hell."

"What?" I whispered back, confused.

"That's what this archway is called. The Gates of Heaven and Hell. Nobody is sure why."

We turned the corner and found ourselves facing a gorgeous mosaic—resplendent with gold and blue tiles—of Christ, his mother, and John the Baptist. But we didn't stop there, either, instead winding through the halls, past more magnificent art, heading directly toward the center of the church to push ourselves up against the rail.

We were high up, near the base of the dome. Across from me, nearly at the same level now, hung one of the black medallions with Arabic writing. The soft murmur of the sightseers below floated up, muffled and distant. Michael was leaning against the low rail, his lean body draped, so I could see every muscle. He didn't say anything but shifted away to make room for me. I took the spot he cleared for me, aware of the closeness of his body and the heat that emanated from it.

"Look up," Enoch urged, nudging me with his cane.

I looked to where he pointed, at the top of the half-dome that protruded from the main part of the church, and saw an enormous mosaic of the Virgin with the Christ Child in her lap.

"Now, over there," he said, nodding across the way. I looked across the dome and gasped.

A majestic angel, composed of thousands of tiny tiles, was set into the wall, filling the bottom of the arch. Large pieces of the mosaic had apparently fallen away in ruins over the years, but I could still see his mournful, dignified eyes staring at me across the empty space. Half of a golden halo encircled his head. Most of his wings were intact, the greens, blues, and creamy whites of his feathers falling in graceful rows to the very ends of his wings, which nearly dragged to the tips of his toes.

"That's Gabriel," Enoch whispered. "And if you look straight up, above your head, you'll see what is left of Michael."

I leaned out over the rail and strained my head to look. All I could see were a few lonely feathers.

"Is there one of Raph, too?" I asked, looking about. There were pictures of what looked like saints and some weird, six-winged creatures, but nothing else that looked like an Archangel.

Raph snorted. "Not likely. I'm surprised they even bothered to show Gabriel, after all."

I bent my head quizzically. "I don't understand."

Michael answered, continuing to stare off into space. "The people had a special love for me here. That's all."

Enoch interrupted. "You should tell her why, Michael."

Michael sighed and unfolded his body from the railing, turning to speak. "Because the Emperor Constantine credited me with a great victory and built many shrines to me, many people believed the greatness of Constantinople came from my blessings upon him. It is nothing more than that."

"Michael always had a knack for getting all the glory," Raph harrumphed. "And for ingratiating himself to humans." His easy smile was belied by the sharpness of his tone. I looked at his black eyes, flashing with resentment, and wondered whether Michael could really trust him.

"I still don't understand why you dragged us here," Raph complained, pushing away from the railing and stretching like a languorous cat in a beam of sunlight. "There's nothing special to see; you wouldn't even know that was supposed to have been Michael if you hadn't read your guide book. It makes no sense to have him here, anyway, with the Virgin and Child. Gabriel, yes, because of the Annunciation. But Michael, no. Just another sign of the addled human mind."

Enoch's lips moved into the faintest of smiles. "Perhaps not. Does anything strike you, Hope?"

I thought hard, knowing Enoch wanted me to figure something out on my own, but I came up blank. I shrugged and looked down at the marble floor.

"No matter," Enoch continued. "We have seen enough here. Time for us to make our way to the next stop on our tour."

Enoch gestured to Raph and, together, they began winding their way back through the hallways toward the ramp. Michael lingered, gazing at the floor below.

I hesitated before asking, "What are you thinking?"

He turned and smiled, but his eyes were sad. "I was remembering the night the city fell to the Ottoman army. The very last refugees fled here, to Ayasofya, pleading with God to save them."

"You were here," I whispered, searching his face. The lines in his face seemed to deepen with sorrow as he relived that night.

"Yes, I was. But I could do nothing to stop it. God's face had turned from them, so I could only watch."

"I'm sorry," I said, impulsively reaching out to take his hand. He pulled it to his chest, pressing my hand against his heart.

In a flash, his memories flooded my mind. The air was filled with ash, the sconces ripped from the wall turned to torches as the soldiers set about ruining the sacred place of worship. Screams pierced the acrid air; voices begged for mercy in a language I couldn't understand. But the vicious warriors paid no heed. They cut down everyone in their path, the bodies piling upon each other, their work done only when the marble floors ran with blood, the tangy, ferrous stench of it so strong that it even cut through the lingering smoke.

I snatched my hand away, horrified.

He looked at me, his gaze steady, but the strain of his sinewy neck, the tightness around his eyes, told me the storminess of his soul.

"That is what I remember. What it is like . . . "

I finished his sentence, feeling dead inside. ". . . when you cannot help those you should."

I blindly ran from the gallery, swamped with guilt for all the people who were suffering because Michael was preoccupied with me. I knew that their plight plagued his every moment, and I was certain that there was nothing I could say, nothing I could ever do to make up for the pain and horror he would experience—was experiencing—because of me.

~

We traveled in silence from Ayasofya, each of us pointedly staring away from one another, fixating on the endless rows of shops, pretending to be fascinated by the magnets and key chains and evil eye pendants that still managed to twinkle despite the dull sky. Enoch had taken over the itinerary, picking places marked on the map for us to visit, narrating as we walked as if we were simply tourists with no other purpose than to take in the historic glories of the fallen empire. We did not have to go far to reach his first destination.

"That, right there, is the Column of Constantine," he said, pointing down the plaza at a rather dirty marble column, mounted on what looked like an ugly pile of concrete. "They say there is an incredible cache of relics somewhere under or inside the column. These relics include the hatchet Noah used to build the Ark, the stone from which Moses made water flow in the desert, the nails of Christ's crucifixion, and the basket and remains of loaves from when Christ fed the multitudes . . . "

"But no rock, stained by Abel's blood? How unfortunate," Raph scoffed. "Where are you taking us, old man? And why isn't the girl leading the way?"

Enoch ignored Raph's outburst and smiled serenely. "We're going over by the prison gate to the Church of the Pantocrator."

"The Pantocrator. The Church of Christ the Almighty," Michael whispered. "I haven't been there in . . . "

" . . . Centuries? I figured as much," Enoch interrupted. "We'll be there soon," he promised, hustling us toward the platform for a tram. He handed out passes like candy for children, shooing us through the turnstile just in time to see a little train wheezing its way up the hill to us.

Why we were going there, and what we would see, was not discussed. Nobody spoke again until we'd been dropped off back near the Golden Horn, at the base of a wide avenue. We trudged in the direction Enoch pointed. The ruins of the ancient aqueduct were looming in the distance, the walls of an old cistern bulging out toward the sidewalk as we climbed.

"Up here," he directed, pointing his cane up a steep stone path, rutted with age.

I peered up the hill with skepticism.

"It looks like an abandoned construction site," I said, unable to keep the questioning tone from sneaking into my voice.

"Trust me," Enoch said, flashing a smile as he forged ahead, hobbling with difficulty over the rocky path.

The climb was steep, winding us past several walled-off renovation sites and more decrepit wooden houses, leaning and crowding into the alleys as if they were about to collapse around us. "For sale" signs were nailed up against their warped wooden walls, and I wondered who would buy such disastrous piles of decay. We kept winding our way through the alleys, running into dead ends and crumbling walls encroached by brushes and weeds, seemingly going in circles until we found our way past a fleet of driverless trucks to another barricaded work site. My pace quickened. Beyond the tarps and corrugated tin walls topped with barbed wire, I could see the top of a dome, silhouetted against the sky. I began running, my skepticism forgotten. I emerged first from the street, finding myself alongside another stone monolithic church and in front of an abutting restaurant, perched high above the city on a terrace. We walked through the terrace, winding our way through a maze of café tables and umbrellas. A carpet of green grass, punctuated by odd, crescent-topped statues, columns, and shrubbery, surrounded the space. Below it, the Golden Horn was visible. In fact, the entire city of Istanbul spread out before us. It was a crazy quilt of collapse, abandonment, construction, and restoration, sliced through by the blue sparkle of waters where the Bosphorus and the Marmara Sea converged. It seemed somehow out of place to me, like I was visiting a botanical garden, not a church.

But what a church it was.

It was a magnificent pile of stone and bricks, all arches and domes and soaring windows, great bulbous bays protruding from the walls and obscuring its actual heart. It was muscular and massive, commanding my attention.

We followed the packed dirt path around the church walls, looking for the entrance. As we walked, I dragged my hand against the rough stone and bricks, sunk deep into the masonry. I could feel their age, as if the stones were speaking to me of the long-ago time when they were laid, carefully, as a monument to God. I tried to peer through the arched windows, hoping to get a glimpse, but most of them were high above my head, with lattice and steel bars blocking the view and revealing only darkness.

Occasionally we'd see a break in the walls, an avalanche of brick where time had gotten the best of the monumental edifice. Tufts of stubborn grass poked through gaps in the mortar. Elsewhere, gaping windows were covered with sheets or boarded up, and whole sections were embraced with scaffolding that looked just as precarious as the crumbling church itself.

"Neglected," Michael breathed. I gave him a sideways glance, trying to gauge his mood, but his face was placid.

"At least it looks like it is being restored," Enoch said. His limping gait seemed firmer now, and he charged ahead, pulling us forward by sheer force of will.

We turned the corner, following Enoch's lead, and came to a full stop.

"It's closed," I said, disappointment flooding me. I couldn't read the words on the sign in the roped-off area in front of the entrance, but I didn't need to when I saw the heavy chain and padlock on the outside of the door.

"It doesn't matter," Enoch said. "Michael, Raph, can you move the ropes away?"

They glanced about quickly to make sure nobody was watching us before rolling away the ropes. Enoch waddled up to the door. He lifted his cane and pressed it, deliberately, against the giant padlock. It fell open, sinking to the cobblestone, immediately followed by the slipping chains that fell with a clank to the ground.

Enoch pushed against the door, and it swung open, hinges shrieking. He turned, pleased with himself, and gestured at us with his cane. "Come on, then. Let's go inside before somebody sees us."

"Wait," Michael ordered. "It's a mosque now. We should take off our shoes."

Hurriedly, we deposited our footwear, dumping it unceremoniously outside the door before slipping inside. Carefully, we pushed the heavy wooden doors closed behind us, wincing as the hinges protested once again.

"Make it quick, Enoch," Raph complained as we stood, poised, on the edge of the room. "Show us whatever it is you want us to see."

"It's not so much what you can see, as what it is," Enoch answered, his voice echoing against the cold plaster and stone walls. "This is actually three churches. Right now we're in the original Pantocrator. As you said, Michael, it's a mosque today."

My eyes began adjusting to the dim light, and the shape of the church began to make sense to me. It was shaped like a cross, a giant dome spanning the center with a half-dome at the head. The floor of the half-dome was covered in a rich, burgundy carpet. Its upper walls were decorated in ornate calligraphy—graceful white on green, surrounded by swags of gold—delicate flourishes in jewel tones circling the domes and arches, reaching higher and higher toward the sky. A turned wooden pulpit sat at the far end, to the side. I started to walk toward it, but Michael's hand darted out and grabbed my elbow.

"Better not," he warned. "I'm not sure it's safe."

"Hurry up, Enoch," Raph ordered, looking uneasily about him.

Enoch's mirrored sunglasses reflected a tiny sliver of light from the far-off windows as he turned to speak. "This is the Pantocrator, Christ Almighty and Triumphant. Over there, on the far side," he continued, waving his cane to the north end of the building, "is the Church of the Virgin Eleousa, The Merciful. What we came to see is the chapel that connects them."

He turned and began making his way toward a dark arch, not bothering to see if we were following him. Ahead of us, from the shadows, we heard him swear an oath.

"It's boarded up! We'll have to push our way through."

Michael and Raph gave each other a look.

"Enoch . . . " Raph began, a note of warning in his voice. They pushed ahead, forming a wall of angelic flesh before me. I couldn't see past them but heard the creaky protest of boards and the sudden explosion when they splintered. A cloud of dust blew toward me. I closed my eyes and felt a rush of dust, woodchips, and dirt whip about me. My hands flew up to cover my mouth, but not before a fit of coughing shook my body.

"Are you okay?" Michael was at my side. The heat radiating from his body exercised some sort of magnetic pull on me. I wanted to lean into him and rest my head against his shoulder, breathing him in. Instead, I just mumbled something and shook my head.

"You can open your eyes now; the dust has settled."

I lowered my arm and looked. The tiniest hint of light glimmered ahead of us, well past a row of stone arches. We began to pick our way through the broken plywood that littered the floor, heading toward the light.

The passageway opened up into a narrow, but very long, room. The limited light came from tiny windows that punctuated the two oval domes overhead. Pale beams of sun filtered through their dirty glass, illuminating the floating particles of dust and glancing off silvery cobwebs that hung from piers and unlit sconces. The air was stale. At the right end of the room, I saw a half-dome and a raised pulpit that mirrored that of the church from which we'd just come, scaffolding from some forgotten project abandoned up against the dirty marble walls.

"This is the mortuary chapel of the Comneni dynasty," Enoch explained breathlessly, worn out from his escapade.

"That means you're standing on bones," Raph said drily, laughing as I jumped to the edge of the room and backed against the wall.

"Really?"

Michael nodded. "The crypt is underneath us."

The floor was dirty, but when I scraped my foot across the layer of dirt I could see the strange script of an ancient grave marker. A faint pattern of them ran in straight lines across the marble.

"It reminds you of the Martyrium in Jerusalem, does it not?" Raph queried Michael. Michael nodded, distracted, as he walked around in the empty chapel.

"A martyrium? Like for people who sacrificed themselves for God?" I asked, curious.

"Yes," Enoch replied, his voice bouncing off the marble walls. "How interesting, then, that it is dedicated to Michael."

In the dimness, I could see Michael's back stiffen. Without turning, he announced, "It means nothing, Enoch."

His denial was still echoing when Raph snorted derisively. "You would say that, wouldn't you? You, who are the only one of us to whom churches are built and icons are struck?

Michael swung around, then, his face stiffened with irritation. "Your jealousy ill becomes you, brother. I would have thought the millennia would have diminished your pettiness."

Raph crossed his arms as if daring Michael to come closer. "I have no jealousy of your sick love of humans. Did you extend your protection to these dissolute emperors, too? Is that why they bowed and scraped to your name?"

Michael scowled. "Actually, no. I had nothing to do with them. I have no idea why they named their burial chapel for me."

Raph laughed, a harsh bark that rang through the chapel. "Likely story. You, linked as equal with the Virgin and the Savior, with your own church at the center of it all? I would have thought even you would have some shame." With that, he stalked off through the corridor. Behind us, I could hear the giant door of the Pantocrator squeal angrily and then slam shut as he stormed out of the church.

Michael wasted no time before pouncing on Enoch, who stayed uncharacteristically silent through the whole exchange. The throbbing vein in his forehead broadcasted that his irritation was quickly turning into anger.

"What game are you playing, Enoch? Why did you bring us here if not to stir up trouble between Raph and me?"

Enoch backed away, raising his palms in protest. "I meant nothing by it. But you must admit, it is unusual."

"Not so unusual," Michael retorted, biting his words with anger. "Mont Saint-Michel. Castel Sant'Angelo. There are countless churches around the world named for me." He took a swipe at the open map that still drooped in Enoch's hand. "That damned pamphlet is full of them; you said so yourself."

Enoch tilted his head, seeming to be lost in thought. "Yes, perhaps you are right. Perhaps it was a mistake. But to be—"

"That's enough." Michael didn't raise his voice, but he didn't need to. His steely eyes flashed his warning to Enoch. No more.

Enoch shrugged. "Perhaps we can go to the next—"

"Enough!" Michael's voice shook with fury. "We're leaving. Now!"

He pointed through the dark archway and stared at Enoch while the old man slowly folded the pamphlet and tucked it into his guidebook. Enoch took his time before placing his cane firmly in front of him and beginning his strange, thumping walk through the dark.

Michael turned and waited for me to go next, his lips clamped into a firm line.

Instinctively, I defended Enoch and tried to smooth things over. "It's not so bad. What he did, Michael. He didn't mean to cause any trouble." I said, the stillness of the chapel making my voice seem tiny.

*Be careful,* Henri whispered. *He's not thinking rationally.*

I tried to ignore my guardian angel and focused on Michael.

His mouth curved into a frown as he shook his head. "He knows the history between us. He knows how hard it is for Raph . . . " He cut himself off, and I could see the uncertainty in his eyes.

"How hard it is for Raph to help you when he resents you? Or how hard it is for Raph to help me, when he hates humanity?"

Michael's shoulders slumped in disappointment. "You. You see too much. Your mind grasps understanding too quickly. I should have known it was useless trying to hide it from you."

Impulsively, I moved closer and reached out to rest my hand on his arm. I could feel his biceps tense under my touch, but I didn't move away, not even as my fingers began to tingle with the familiar heat. And neither did he.

"You don't need to hide anything from me," I whispered.

"I just . . . " He stopped short again. Frustrated, he threw off my hand and raked his fingers through his hair. He turned toward me, suddenly close, eyes wild.

"If this damn pain would just stop." His tone was almost plaintive, beseeching me to make the hurt go away. He clenched and unclenched his fists, and I swallowed hard, knowing Henri was right. Michael was dangerously close to the edge.

"We need to go, Michael. You said so yourself." My voice trembled, but I kept my eyes steady, gazing directly into his, hoping he couldn't see how scared I was. I needed to be strong—strong enough for the both of us.

My words echoed around me, fading bit by bit until we were alone in silence. Every plane of Michael's face was taut. He looked stretched beyond his limits, and I watched as he took deep breaths, gulping down the stale air until slowly, with great effort, he forced himself to relax.

He let out a big breath and dragged his hand over his eyes, rubbing his temples to chase the last vestiges of his pain away. When he dropped his hand, his eyes looked normal, except for the lines that seemed to be carved even more deeply around them.

"I don't like for you to see me like this. Let's go," he said, his voice emotionless, the moment between us lost.

He led the way, guiding me in the dark over the fallen splintered boards that were scattered in the arched corridor as we moved back toward the first church. Wordlessly, he pushed open the door, which creaked its protest at being disturbed, and waited for me to walk out.

*Phew,* Henri said. *That was too close. You better hurry up and figure out where that rock is. Once he loses control, there's no telling what he'll do.*

My finger snaked up involuntarily to trace the outlines of the Mark, once something I did out of habit. I traced its intricate design, knowing now that it identified me as the bearer of the rock with which Cain had slain Abel—the rock that was, in reality, the key to unlock Heaven's Gate, the thing the Fallen Angels wanted more than anything, so they could overthrow Heaven. If I failed in my quest to find it in time—or if Michael decided to take things into his own hands—this Mark meant my death sentence.

# four

## TURKEY

"I need to go running."

I wasn't negotiating. Simply stating the facts. As far as my angel companions knew, since I'd left Atlanta I'd had no time, let alone opportunity, to run. My muscles were aching from fatigue. My brain was clouded by jet lag. And my skin, though healing, still stung with the pain of the licking flames that had enveloped my body. I was testy and anxious. After yesterday's clashes at the churches we had toured, the tension between us all had simmered and bubbled. There had been no discussion of what to do next, nor where to go. Instead, I'd been cooped up inside our temporary home, Enoch and Raph my watchdogs, while Michael disappeared to do God-knows-what. I had nothing to entertain me and had been forbidden use of the single television in the living room.

Enoch used the opportunity to keep pushing me to think about the Prophecy. I'd pored over the strange words, smoothing out the crumpled piece of paper for what seemed like a thousand times, waiting for inspiration, but nothing came. It seemed just as foreign as before. But this time I had an audience pacing around me, watching me struggle with the ancient text, which only heightened my frustration.

I knew that my previous effort had only failed because I'd stumbled into that protest. The fact that the Fallen had turned up, in a twisted sort of way, confirmed that I was on the right track. If I was going to find the Key, I needed to get out.

I needed to run.

Now.

I had a window while Michael was gone. I had a halfway decent chance of convincing Enoch, which would put him and Raph at a stalemate. And in a stalemate, I might just win. So I crossed my arms and faced off against the two angels who had put me on lockdown inside the old wooden house in the backstreets of the Sultanahmet, daring them to refuse me.

Raph rolled his eyes, yet again, at my seemingly inane request.

"She doesn't get to do anything," he said, speaking of me in the third person as he pretended to read Enoch's discarded guidebook with great interest. "She is not on vacation. She is not on a pleasure tour. Clearly the answer is no."

He'd been this way ever since the blowup at the chapel. He didn't even bother to look up from his book, pointedly ignoring me while he kept turning the pages with a perfectly manicured finger.

I hated him. I hated his impossibly pressed khakis and cotton shirt. I hated his immaculate grooming. I hated his dark, brooding handsomeness. I hated how he goaded Michael. And I hated how dismissive he was of me. It was almost better when he was openly hostile, when he had treated me as if I had been personally responsible for the fall of man.

But if Raph drew me into an argument, he'd win. So I counted to ten and tried again, focusing my efforts on Enoch. While we were staying indoors, Enoch had changed his appearance back to the Birkenstock-wearing hippie guise in which I'd met him. It reminded me that he'd said I was like one of his granddaughters. I could use that, if I could just make him remember it again.

"Enoch," I began, tentatively, uncrossing my arms, "running clears my head. I think it would help me focus on the Key and where we might find it."

I looked up into his round, dark glasses expectantly. But he said nothing and simply grunted. I took that as a sign he was considering it and pressed on.

"I promise, I won't do anything dangerous. I'll stick to populated areas, I won't talk to anybody, and I'll come right back. Twenty, twenty-five minutes, tops. I promise."

Enoch was stroking the scraggly lengths of his white beard. My pleading eyes, distorted into two huge orbs, stared back from the mirrored lenses of his glasses.

"Michael will never know," I offered, hoping this might seal the deal. My fingers snaked up to the Mark upon the back of my neck, nervously fingering it as I waited for Enoch to answer.

"But are you well enough to run?" Enoch asked. "You haven't let Raph heal you. It might do more harm than good for you to exert yourself."

Raph slammed the guidebook shut and sent a sharp look to Enoch. "You can't be seriously considering letting her go, can you? Michael wouldn't allow it."

"Michael's not here. And Michael is not infallible, as you so regularly point out," Enoch responded, stretching out a hand to me. "Come here, my girl."

Obediently, I went to his side.

"Give me your hand."

I offered my hand up to him and he began to inspect it, turning it over to examine the shiny scars that crisscrossed its back and palm. He grunted again, and then pushed up my shirtsleeve with his other hand to see if the skin on my arm was in the same condition.

He didn't let go of my hand. Instead, he leaned back in his chair and regarded me with his sightless eyes. The warmth from his touch radiated against my skin, sending waves of comfort and relief throughout my body.

"All of your skin is the same, is it? No open sores anymore?"

"No sores. It's just itchy and tight. I think it might help to move around a bit more."

He hadn't broken his gaze. I shuffled nervously, worried that I might have misplayed my hand. But my fears were unwarranted.

"You may be right. We need to find that rock. I am willing to try almost anything, if it will help you unlock the mysteries of its whereabouts. But only under one condition: you must let Raph and me run with you, for your protection."

I opened my mouth to protest, but he shook his head almost imperceptibly, as if in warning.

Grudgingly, I nodded. "You can follow me, but only at a distance. I don't want to know you're there. I need some time alone."

Raph snorted, tossing the book to the ground. "Perfect. Just like that, she gets her wish? Enoch, are you out of your mind?"

I flinched at the anger in his tone, but Enoch simply smiled. "She is the Bearer, Raph. Without her, we have no chance of finding this . . . thing. And we must find it," he continued on, eagerly. "If a little run will help her, I am more than happy to oblige." He squeezed my hand, complicit in my scheme. "I think you'll find some things you'll need in your room. Just look in the armoire."

"Thank you, Enoch!" I squealed, throwing my arms about him

and nearly knocking him out of his chair. For the first time ever, he seemed discomfited. He patted my arm awkwardly. "There, there. Go get yourself ready. We'll wait for you here."

I pulled the sheet off the armoire, rolling it up into a ball that I tossed into the corner. I pulled the heavy doors wide. The musty smell of old air and mothballs seeped out of the cabinet. I peered inside to find the entire thing taken up with long coats—some woolen, some fur.

I reached an arm in to jostle among the coats until my knuckles came upon a hidden shelf. Shoving the coats aside, I saw everything I needed for my run, just as Enoch had promised: long tights with reflective stripes, a base layer and running top, even socks and running shoes just like the ones I had at home—but new. I slid into it all, my body already exhilarated at the thought of the freedom I'd experience—at least for a little while—while let loose upon the streets of Istanbul.

The last thing I found, at the bottom of the pile, was a set of earphones and an iPod. I flicked through the playlist and found all my favorites, loaded up and ready for me to run.

I was ridiculously happy.

When I emerged from the house into the cobblestone street, I found myself alone. I looked around, trying to spot Raph and Enoch while I stretched to warm up, but I couldn't see them anywhere.

*Impressive*, Henri said snidely. *I would think it would be hard to hide the kind of girth Enoch carries around.*

"Be nice," I chided under my breath.

I didn't have a map, but I didn't think I'd need one. After all, how far could I go in twenty minutes? I started my playlist and set off down the street, my ponytail tucked neatly inside my hood.

The music kicked in, and I found myself falling into the old, familiar rhythms of my run. The cobblestones were trickier to navigate, however; one false step could mean a sprained ankle or worse. So I reminded myself to watch the road, my steady breaths quieting my mind, so I could think.

I laid out the pieces of the puzzle in my mind. We knew we were looking for the rock with which Cain had slain Abel. The last time Michael saw it, it was here, in Istanbul.

*Constantinople*, Henri sniffed. *Only the nouveau arrivistes call it Istanbul.*

*Fine*, I thought, with an inward sigh. Constantinople. Which seemed to be the seat of some sort of . . . cult of Michael, if the number of shrines and holy places dedicated to him were any indication.

But why was he so popular here?

*Honestly? You don't know?* Henri interrupted again.

"I'm sorry, they didn't offer Byzantine history at my high school," I snapped, irritated at his continuous prodding.

Henri pointedly ignored me, giving me a moment to weave through the crowds of tourists as I cut across another monumental square. I looked both ways quickly before dashing across traffic, continuing to run away from the Westerners into a quieter part of town.

As I got out of the crowds, Henri continued.

*Michael told you that Constantine founded that church you were searching for?*

I nodded. Michael said as much earlier. I waited for Henri to continue.

*Well, originally, it was a temple to Zeus that the Argonauts had built.*

He must have noticed my jaw drop for he continued on, smugly, *Yes, those Argonauts. Not everything you read as mythology is untrue.*

*Yes, after Constantine won his great battle he gave the credit to Michael and rededicated the temple of Zeus to Michael, in thanksgiving. Michael's fame spread from here, through what you now know as the Middle East, and back up through the old Western Roman Empire. There are no churches built to Gabriel, or Raphael, or any of the other angels, unless they are lumped together in a group. But Michael? Michael has cathedrals and monasteries and churches the world over. He has captured the imagination of the faithful, and so they build to him.*

*And here is where it all began. All because Michael chose to defend and bless one human. Mankind blesses him, because he has always chosen to bless mankind. Their stories are inseparable.*

Henri spoke without bitterness, his characteristic sarcasm gone. I let his story roll around in the back of my mind, accompanied by the steady bass of the music being pumped out by my iPod.

"Henri, do the other angels really hate him for his fame?"

*No. They hate him, because he loves man. And because those of confused faith say he is God or Christ himself.*

*You really should turn back, now,* Henri prompted.

I'd been so engrossed in Henri's storytelling that I'd lost track of time. I pulled up short on the sidewalk and checked my watch. With a sinking feeling, I saw that I had been running for quite some time. If I were to keep the privilege of going out of the house, I'd have to return now.

I took in my surroundings. I was halfway up a hill, on a cozy square that had opened before me from the warren of winding cobblestoned streets. Narrow shops crowded up to the curb, several of their doors marked with the telltale talisman of the blue eye. Nestled in among them was what I took to be a church. It was set back from the street within a tiny courtyard, Greek lettering splayed above its doorway. In the courtyard stood a gnarled tree, glass amulets of blue and white trailing from its budding branches, repulsing the wayward gaze of any evil eye. Next to it, one of the shops beckoned, its dusty windowfront stuffed with what looked like knickknacks and objets d'art. Something seemed to click in the back of my brain.

Intrigued, I began to cross the street when I felt a slight tug at my shoulder. I turned around to find myself alone on the sidewalk.

*No time for that now*, Henri admonished. *You need to get back.*

"Maybe just a minute in that shop?" I bargained, its promised secrets proving nearly irresistible.

*Go ahead. I'm sure Michael will be happy to tether himself to you like a watchdog when he finds you snuck out without his permission. That should be fun for all of us.*

Silently I took inventory of the street scene and the dilapidated store, promising myself I'd find a way back. Then I turned and began jogging back down the hill, hoping I'd be home before Michael realized I'd been gone.

My run had exactly the effect I'd wanted. I felt refreshed, my anxiety about our situation relegated to the back of my mind, so I could give my full attention to the dilemma at hand.

Our evening was quiet. We spread out throughout the house, like boxers sent to our own corners to prepare for the next round in our bout. We were all being so careful, now, I thought with a pang of sadness, watchful of our words, of our looks, of the very way we intersected one another's space lest we cause another outburst. We weren't a team, looking for the Key together. No, we were a band of misfits forced upon one another by the uncomfortable truth that everything we cherished might be destroyed if we did not work together. But that didn't change the fact that Michael's feelings toward me could veer from longing to overbearing protectiveness to resentment in the space of time it took for me to catch my breath; that my own feelings toward him were complicated, at best, spurring me on to confront him at the least opportune moments; nor that he and Raph were caught in a deadlock grip of mutual disgust that was more ancient than the city in which we found ourselves.

Our fragile alliance threatened to crumble under the weight of it all—something none of us wanted. The consequences were too dire. We would need to at least tolerate one another until we got what we had come for. So, mindful not to draw too much attention to myself, I claimed the coziest corner I could get, right next to the fire, and laid out in my mind all I had learned about Michael and the rock since we'd been in Istanbul.

Michael was beloved by the people of Istanbul—or Constantinople, I corrected myself, hearing Henri's chiding voice—because it was believed he'd intervened to save their ruler and bring him victory on the battlefield. His followers had spread from here throughout Christendom, bringing him acclaim that had not come to any other Archangel. Some people, Henri had said, even thought he was God or Jesus in another form. The weird juxtaposition of him with Mary and Jesus in the mosaics at Ayasofya, along with his association with martyrdom at his chapel at the Pantocrator, seemed to underscore this false conflation.

Pure jealousy—or anger at the audacity of it all—would certainly pit angels like Raph against him. That and his decision to protect Cain so long ago. That decision, which Michael saw simply as the fulfillment of his role as mankind's protector, permanently split the angels into two camps. The camp we were fighting resented their de facto demotion when God elevated humankind in his image and thought our sinfulness an abomination deserving of extinction.

It all came back to the rock and to Michael's reputation as a lover of humanity. I tried not to think about the way our complicated relationship might be affecting that reputation. It was hard to believe so many angels wanted mankind wiped off the Earth, but the facts were there. I shuddered, knowing that is exactly what would happen if the Fallen were to find the rock before we did.

Was it as simple as that? I wondered. Or was there something more about Michael? Something was niggling at the back of my mind, spurring me to think harder.

I sighed and stretched in my chair, the pleasant ache of my muscles a reminder of my run. As I did, I looked up to find Enoch watching me. His face was impassive, the mirror of his sunglasses blinking back like soulless eyes.

I shifted uncomfortably, waiting for him to look away. When he didn't, I huddled myself back into the chair and closed my eyes, pretending I didn't see him, that I didn't know that all things rested on me and my ability to unravel the mystery before us.

~

My dreams were filled with free-floating images of the blue and white talismans that hung from the tree in the church courtyard. I woke up feeling invincible and filled with a sense of urgency—compelled to go back and explore the entire Greek neighborhood and, especially, the dusty shop. I knew there was something special about that place, something that would clarify our path.

I hurriedly dressed in my running clothes, shoving my feet into my shoes. I looked about the great room. Raph and Enoch were in the same places they sat the night before. Raph appeared engrossed in yet another book, while Enoch, cross-legged, appeared to be meditating, his fat body somehow folded into lotus position, his hands stretched out in front of him as if in supplication. Istanbul was bringing out his new-agey side again. I wondered idly if he ever smoked pot or tried his hand at yoga.

"Where's Michael?" I demanded.

"He left. Needed some time outside of his human form, I imagine, to recharge his batteries," Enoch answered without changing his pose.

"Human weakness," Raph muttered under his breath, never lifting his head from the book.

"So it's okay for me to run again?"

Raph arched a brow. "Why not? You've already broken the rules once. Why stop now?"

I didn't wait for them; I knew they would find and follow me as they must. Instead, I ran down the stairs, noticing only fleetingly how my joints seemed easier, how my skin felt more my own, as I launched myself into another run.

I retraced my path from yesterday, winding my way back to the little Greek enclave. With my attention all focused on what was going on around me, I noticed the mouthwatering smells of baklava and souvlaki drifting out of the shops; the telltale amulets on stoops, warding off the evil eye; the domes and crucifixes scratching against the gray sky, marking the neighborhood as one of the sole Christian holdouts in this city claimed by Islam.

Breathlessly, I pulled myself to a stop at the top of a hill. I'd reached my destination.

The blue and white talismans dangling from the churchyard tree tinkled in the breeze that drifted in from the water and glinted in the weak sunlight. But they were not what commanded my attention. Instead, I slipped across the street and walked to the window of the shop that was once again beckoning to me.

It was covered in a layer of grime and dust so thick it seemed almost deliberately put there to disguise the treasures that lay inside. As I wiped the glass, I could make out the delicate paper and ink tracings of maps; the gilt-edged calligraphy, spread out for admiration; the dull paint of a phalanx of tin soldiers, their uniforms topped by jaunty fezzes, lined up and brandishing bayonets as if ready for battle. Some fantastical mosaic lamps with intricate patterns of green, gold, pink, and yellow floated like jellyfish above the case. The inside of the shop was dim, the lamps unlit, making me wonder if the shop was actually open. I leaned up against the glass, my breath making a little cloud of steam against the window. I wiped a bare finger against it, etching a little smiley face into the condensation as I peered more closely into the darkness.

A rumble of incriminating Turkish or Greek—it was coming too fast for me to be able to tell which—interrupted me. I jumped back from the window to find a severe-looking man standing over me, poised on the steps that led into the store, his finger wagging as he continued to berate me. He looked like I'd interrupted him at some sort of task—he was wrapped in an apron and with something that looked for all the world like a monocle hanging from his neck.

I looked up at him, completely confused.

He frowned, his heavy brows forming a deep V. Sighing heavily to show the imposition, he switched into English. "This is not the kind of shop for young girls. Especially tourists. Nothing here for you. Now go away."

"But I—"

"The store is closed," he declared firmly. Turning on his heel, he went back into his shop, pulling the door behind him. In a flash, a sign appeared in the glass. I couldn't read it, but I was pretty sure its red letters spelled out the Turkish equivalent of "gone for lunch."

I waited, thinking perhaps he would grow tired of me hanging about or worry that he was driving away valuable customers by closing up early. But nobody else came by, the bustle of the streets seeming to completely bypass this little corner of the neighborhood.

Resigned, I began walking down the hill, wondering what was inside the shop he was so adamant was not for me.

*It's probably nothing,* Henri sniffed. *He's probably just an angry ethnic leftover, still counting up all the impositions his people suffered under Ottoman rule. Hate and resentment only intensify when passed down over generations.*

I wondered at how easily Henri dismissed the strange man and his store, and whether he was right about him hoarding the complaints of his forbears, bitterly reliving them even now. My intuition suggested otherwise. It seemed to be on red alert, drawing me to the shop, but I couldn't figure out why. But, then again, I had to admit my intuition hadn't actually been that helpful to date.

"You're probably right," I murmured, more to give myself time to mull it over than anything else as I moved into an easy jog, mindful that my babysitters were somewhere, watching and waiting for my return.

~

I couldn't stop thinking about the little shop, but I knew it was useless trying to wheedle my way in. The shopkeeper had been resolute. If I were going to get in, I needed to have adult supervision. So first thing the next morning, I tried to convince my angel companions to come with me to the shop.

Enoch seemed excited by the prospect. "You sense something,

then? What exactly do you feel?" he probed, peering at me through his dark lenses.

"It's nothing specific," I confided, "but it is the strongest feeling I have had since we've been in Istanbul. We need to check it out. We can go this morning. Just think how happy Michael would be if he returned to find us with a clue, or maybe even the Key itself!"

"No," Raph interjected, his hooded eyes solemn. "You need to slow down, Hope. If it is as you say, it could be dangerous. We need to wait for Michael. Besides, I, for one, would like to avoid having to explain to him how you came to know of this shop. I don't want to have to confess that someone—" he shot a poisonous look at his blind companion, "thought it was a good idea to let you roam the city unattended. You'll have to wait for Michael to come back, and then lead us all to the shop. But find a more subtle way to do it."

I flushed an angry red. "But we're wasting time! And I wasn't unattended! You know that. You were with me the whole time," I asserted, brushing aside the facts of my secret run our first morning here. "And he won't care—not if we manage to find the Key. Nothing matters to him more than that."

Raph gave me a funny look. "You misunderstand his priorities. This is not up for debate. Michael has left us in charge of you. The answer is no."

Enoch began to argue, "But Raph, she has a point. We can scarcely afford to wait, not with the Fallen on our tail."

Raph cut him off. "The Fallen, you will have noticed, have been conspicuously absent. Perhaps without Lucas at their head, they struggle to organize themselves and await his return. Who knows? They are likely even more confused than we are at this point. Unless they have been trailing Hope all along—which I'm sure they haven't, for surely we would have noticed them—we can take the time to build our safety in numbers. No; we wait for Michael to return."

"It's not fair!" I shouted. I knew we needed to get to that shop. I didn't want to wait for Michael. I wanted to do it now.

"The discussion is over," Raph snapped, turning on his heel. "Now find something else to do." He stalked off, swinging the doors to the patio wide open behind him.

"Enoch?" I pleaded. He looked deep in thought.

"Let me see what I can do," he murmured. He thumped across the floor with his cane and drew the door closed behind him as he went after Raph.

I could hear them arguing about me, their voices getting ever louder.

"She has no insight, Enoch. She is simply throwing darts at a board, hoping in vain for a bull's eye. I don't believe for a minute that she knows what she is doing. And I'll be damned if I'm going to confess we've let her run rampant, just so she can drag us all to that shop."

"You don't give her enough credit," Enoch countered.

"Credit? For what?"

I didn't need to hear anymore. Frustrated, knowing that I was just on the edge of figuring something out, I decided to try one more time on my own. In my running gear once more, the rising sounds of their argument behind me, I propelled myself down the stairs and out the door. The cat lurking at the steps stared at me, accusing.

"What?" I demanded, looking fixedly back.

With a flick of its tail and a lazy stretch, it turned and disappeared around the corner. I shrugged and looked down the street.

The city was shrouded in a fine mist, the clash of warm and cold air above the Bosphorus throwing off rolls of fog that blanketed the streets. I shivered inside my layers of clothing, wondering briefly if I would be able to find my way. I felt a vague sense of guilt, leaving without telling my angel jailers. Should I have asked their permission once again?

*No,* Henri's sarcastic voice cut into my thoughts. *You wouldn't want to do something responsible and mature so they don't worry, would you? After all, you've done such a good job of causing trouble—why start behaving now?*

In my mind's eye, I envisioned him rolling his nonexistent eyes at me.

"I'll be back before they even know I'm gone," I pledged, turning into the mist. Even though I couldn't see much, the sounds around me confirmed that I'd awakened early. I could hear the rumble of garbage collection trucks roaming the narrow streets and the shouts of delivery men as they unloaded their wares into the waiting shops. Nobody else seemed to be out. I realized that the shop would not be open at this hour. I had some time to meander a bit before I began my campaign to enter.

I turned an unfamiliar corner, watching carefully lest I run into some unsuspecting pedestrian. As I took the curve, I worried briefly about my ability to find my way back, but rationalized that the fog would burn off soon. I had some cash in my pocket. In the worst-case scenario, I could hire a cab and get back to the Blue Mosque or Ayasofya and find my way home from there.

I stretched out, falling into an easy pace that was perfect for an extended run. I let my mind wander as much as my legs, thinking through the unsettling normalcy that had descended onto our little party. Michael had been gone for two days. Neither Raph nor Enoch seemed to know where he was; presumably, he was restoring himself, back in angel guise, preparing himself for whatever came next. While Raph and Enoch remained watchful, they'd eased up on me, leaving me to think in solitude, trailing me on my forbidden sojourns through the city and not reprimanding me for extending and prolonging my time away. Raph had even let me watch the television news last night.

I hadn't been able to make a thing out in the local Turkish broadcast, but the pictures that filled the screen were sobering and clear enough for me to see that the world was falling apart, bit by bit. Missile strikes in the Middle East—uncomfortably close to where we were. Riots inside of refugee camps that teemed with graft and greed and violence, the lawlessness and disregard for life stunning. Brutal guerrilla groups targeting civilians in Africa. Gunmen shooting down children trapped in schools. It had been overwhelming, the parade of horrors that flickered in high definition, especially the tear-streaked faces of victims, of survivors, blown up large on the screen, their pain laid out for all of the world to see. I shook my head, trying to chase the images out of my mind, trying to forget that if it weren't for me, maybe Michael would have been able to help some of them.

I was glad Michael hadn't been there to see it. It would have torn him apart, their pain compounding his until he erupted. The ferocity when he lashed out at his helplessness was breathtaking. And every day that passed, the intensity of it only increased. The space I had to breathe these last few days while he was away helped me keep my sanity.

Even so, I missed him.

It was hard to love someone and be afraid of them at the same time. To never know if your glance or your touch would be met with gentleness, a rebuff, or even scorn, in return.

But it was probably harder for that person to see you looking at them with eyes full of fear and doubt.

I shivered inside the shroud of fog that still enveloped me.

Yes, I thought to myself. I still love him, maybe even more so after seeing him suffer.

*Suffering doesn't make it romantic, you know.* Henri's voice sounded fed up. *It just makes you both pathetic.*

I felt my outrage rising up. "I'm not romanticizing the situation," I shouted into the air.

*But you are. You think his suffering is noble. Thinking so helps you ignore the fact that you are the cause of it. What is worse, you cling to the idea that your sympathy for his suffering is love. Your mind has twisted the truth, hiding it from you so that you can bear your situation. You rationalize it as if you were one of those nineteenth-century heroines in your precious books. But you aren't Jane Eyre. You aren't Cathy, being tortured by your love for Heathcliff. You're not acting out a comedy of manners and misunderstandings that will magically resolve itself in the end, like* Pride and Prejudice. *You're a simple girl caught up in a deadly race, your only ally someone just as likely to kill you as save you. Have you forgotten?*

"How could I forget that?" I cried, tears welling up, leaving me to run blindly through the already treacherous fog. "I wake up to it every day. My nightmares are filled with it."

My toe tripped over a loose brick. I gasped, sudden pain wrenching my ankle as I collapsed to the slick cobblestone, angry at Henri for distracting me, furious with myself for not watching where I was running. I huddled on the sidewalk right where I had fallen. Carefully, I tested my ankle, trying to bend my foot. Shooting pains radiated up my leg every time I tried to move.

*Henri?* I sent my mind out, probing for his presence. Nothing. He was silent, most likely gone again, if history were any indication.

I turned off my music and pulled my earphones from my ears. As I rubbed my ankle, I peered through the mist to check out my surroundings. I'd definitely wandered into a part of the city I'd not seen before. The signs on the storefronts were Arabic script, not the western letters used for Turkish. The streets seemed closer, somehow, the sad shops crowding close to the curbs where veiled women with small children in tow walked swiftly, looking over their shoulders as if afraid they were being watched.

Instead of cozy, it felt oppressive.

A gust of wind cleared the fog away in a billowy burst.

I was at the head of an alley that wound between two blocks of shops and apartments. Lines of gray laundry hung overhead between the buildings, cracking in the gusts of wind that came shrieking off the water, chasing away the last lingering clouds of mist. Down the alley, a few men sat listlessly on crates, smoking and watching as a pack of stray dogs nipped at what appeared to be a runt from a recent litter.

The puppy yipped as one of the bigger dogs lunged at his hind leg. Outrage flooded my system.

"Hey!" I shouted, my breath still ragged from running. I pushed myself up off the curb and limped down the alley, ignoring the throbbing pain in my ankle.

"Hey! Aren't you going to do something?" The men looked at me blankly, and I wondered if my words had been lost in the snarl of the pack as they circled the helpless puppy. As I came closer, I could see how mangy and hungry they looked.

I looked around and saw a long piece of discarded cardboard. *It will have to do*, I sighed, picking it up to test its heft. It felt flimsy in my hand, but there was nothing else long enough to keep me out of range of the dogs' sharp teeth.

The puppy whined again as the dogs circled it, teeth bared.

I jumped in between the puppy and the pack, swinging the cardboard in front of me as if it were a sword.

"Leave him alone, now! Go!"

The dogs growled, a low, guttural sound that came from them as if they were one. They bared their teeth at me, but I noticed they had stopped moving.

"I mean it! Go!" I waved the cardboard at them, doing my best to be menacing.

The dog at the front of the pack began barking at me, his body jumping off the worn pavestones with the force of each protest. I stood my ground, unsure what the pack would do, while the puppy hid behind my feet.

Abruptly, the pack's leader quit barking and turned, trotting out of the alley as if nothing had happened. The other dogs trailed behind him, leaving me alone with the frightened runt, who was peeking out from between my legs.

"Come here, silly thing," I coaxed, scooping him out and letting myself plop down on the curb. He clambered up into my lap, trying to lick my face but getting tangled up in the wires of my earbuds instead. I laughed, disentangling him, while I checked him for sores.

"Seems like you're okay. Better than can be said for me," I smiled ruefully as I looked at my ankle. It had swollen up to twice its normal size in the few minutes it took to shoo away the stray dogs. The puppy licked my face, and I laughed at the ticklish, sandpapery feel of his tongue.

"You are hurt."

The heavily accented voice startled me. I looked up to see a young, pale woman, conspicuous for her lack of a headscarf and the skimpy clothing that did nothing to keep out the damp. Her dull blonde hair hung in lank chunks around her face. I gazed up at her almond-shaped green eyes, noticing the smudges of black makeup that only made the shadows under her eyes more pronounced. I glanced over her bare arms, stick thin in the tight, lacy tank top that clung to her body, and started. There, on the palest underside of her wrist, an ugly pattern of welts stood out from her skin. A number: 41. She'd been branded.

She noticed my shocked stare and jerked her arm away, hiding it behind her back. I looked at her again—really looked at her—and noticed how her knobby knees stuck out from her legs, saw the bruises that at first melted into the half-light. A flash of recognition ran through me—she was just like those girls in Las Vegas: trafficked girls, girls who had been sold and abused, over and over, and would eventually be thrown away when they got too sick or too old, like a chewed-up stick of gum or a used tissue. She saw I understood and, just for a second, a look of shame and resignation flooded her eyes. Then, just as quickly, she shuttered her eyes, halting our connection as if she were putting on armor and girding herself for battle. She licked her lips and shot a glance over her shoulder, back toward the men who'd been watching the dogfight, before looking back down at me.

"You shouldn't be here by yourself."

"I'm fine," I replied stiffly.

"Fine? I think not." Even though she was slight—really, almost as lean and hungry as the puppy in my lap—she loomed above me, blocking the little sliver of gray light from the sky. "Not good for a girl to be out alone. And now you are hurt, too? Where is your father? Your brothers?"

I bristled at her words but tried to remain polite. "Thank you for your concern. But my friends know where I am. They'll be here to help me soon, I am sure." I darted a look over my shoulder, back up to the street, expecting to see Raph and Enoch coming down the alley toward me, but the tiny passageway was empty. Uneasily, I remembered that I'd snuck away without bothering to even tell them. They may not have even known that I had left.

The girl shifted from leg to leg as if pondering what to do before shouting something back to the men in a language I did not understand. One of them jumped off his crate and came over to join us. Up close I saw the scattering of acne across his forehead and chin and the muscles straining against the T-shirt he wore underneath an army-issue camouflage jacket. His eyes were glassy, his breath shallow, as he looked me up and down.

I blushed, angry at the presumption in his frank stare. I wrapped my arms around my waist, wishing I'd paid better attention while I was running.

He smiled a great, fake smile. His mouth was full of fillings, his teeth yellowed and discolored. "Oksana here has told me of your predicament. My uncle, he has a car. He will take you home. Be a good girl and come now. Okay?" Without waiting for my answer, he reached down to grab me by the elbow.

Instinctively, I jerked my arm away. "I don't need a ride from you."

His face collapsed into a frown as he leaned in menacingly. "Do not make trouble. We try to help you. Nobody here to help you but us, see?" He waved a hand behind him, and I realized he was right. The alley had gone deathly quiet. Nobody else was here to see what was happening.

Nobody.

"I don't need your help. I can make it home by myself." I looked up at the young woman, silently beseeching her to help, but she had retreated, her back pressed up against one of the alley walls as she steadfastly refused to look me in the eye. I turned back to the man and braced myself for a fight.

His eye twitched with barely suppressed frustration. "You will come with us," he muttered between clenched teeth.

He grabbed me under the shoulder, as if to pull me up. Before I knew what was happening, the tiny dog, which had been cowering behind me, lunged at the man and sank his teeth into his calf.

The man dropped me, swinging at the dog in a blind range. The dog darted out of reach, positioning itself between me and the man, yipping its defiance while it darted side to side, marking its territory and daring him to cross its invisible boundary. The young woman shrank back into a dark doorway, leaving me alone to face the bully.

He reached into his pocket. I watched with trepidation as he drew out a knife, which he unfolded with a determined look on his face. Jeering and wild-eyed, he swung the knife out in front of him, flourishing it before me and making a big show of jabbing it at the dog. The pup, unimpressed, went for his ankle, getting in a solid bite before darting back to defend me where I had hobbled to my feet.

The woman was gone, now, but the other man, whom I presumed was the "uncle," still sat impassively across the narrow way, watching us square off. He shouted something to the man with the knife, who yelled and swung his hand dismissively. The uncle simply shrugged and then disappeared inside one of the buildings.

That left my attacker and me. I braced myself as he closed in. Above us, the sun burst from behind the clouds. The sudden light made me squint. I raised an arm to block out the sunlight, fearful of losing sight of him and giving him the advantage. On the gusting wind I caught a whiff of sulfur as a shadow suddenly loomed up, blocking the sun.

"That's quite enough."

A wave of relief swept through me at the sound of Raph's stern voice. The man wheeled, surprised to be interrupted. Raph towered over him by a full head and shoulders, his menacing look unmistakable.

"This is no concern of yours," the man argued, holding up his hands in a show of innocence as he tried to impose himself between Raph and me. "We are just trying to help the poor girl find her way home. Much too dangerous for her to be on city streets by herself."

"I agree," Raph said acidly, pushing past him to take me by the arm. "Come on, Hope." I stumbled, weak-kneed, past the man, as Raph dragged me along. The cloud of tobacco stench that clung to my attacker made me gag as I brushed by, the sneer on his face making me want to vomit. Raph's fingers cut into my arm as he pulled me faster, back up the alley. The man shouted after us, but that only made Raph pick up the pace.

"I had it under control," I protested weakly, wincing from the pain in my ankle as Raph dragged me along.

He shot me a sideways glance. "I see. Well, it's not me you have to convince. It's him." He nodded toward the top of the street. My heart fell as I saw Enoch, apparently trying to calm down a livid Michael who was pacing back and forth across the alley, gesturing wildly.

"Of course," I mumbled, remembering the whiff of sulfur that had caught my attention just moments before.

Raph smirked at my disappointment. "Maybe your friend will help you out."

"My friend?" Raph stopped and turned me around. I looked down to see the puppy, trotting faithfully behind us, chest proudly raised and tongue lolling about. He looked almost happy.

"Please?" I asked Raph. He raised an eyebrow but didn't say anything, so I bent down and scooped up the puppy in my arms. The scruffy dog thrust his tiny tongue out, giving me a wet kiss on the cheek.

When I drew my hand away from petting him, it was red with blood.

"Look, Raph, he's hurt. He must have gotten nicked by the knife while he was protecting me." I held the dog up to Raph, sheepishly. "Would you mind?"

The hard planes of his face dropped into a look of incredulity. "You want me to heal a stray dog?"

"He's not a stray anymore," I insisted. "It will only take a second. Please?"

"You're only delaying the inevitable," he warned, darting a glance up the alley to where Michael and Enoch were still arguing. He looked down to my swollen ankle. "But I'll do it if you let me fix your sprain, too."

I hesitated, not wanting to let him use his angelic powers on me.

Before I could refuse, he cut me off. "Trust me, it will be better for *all* of us if he doesn't find you worse than when he left you."

"Okay," I agreed, grudgingly. "But just the ankle."

"Yes, of course. God forbid I use my powers on anything serious, like, a—"

"Just do it." I interrupted, impatient with his lecture. I held the puppy out to him and he picked it up between his fingers like a dirty tissue.

"You do make odd choices, Hope," he said, wrinkling his nose in distaste. The mutt squirmed, clearly uncomfortable being dangled in the air. "Help me hold it still."

I reached up and cradled the dog in my hands. "Shhh," I soothed. "It will be okay. Just let Raph help you."

Raph spread his fingers wide, covering the pup's entire body with his open hand, and closed his eyes. Instantly, the puppy stopped wriggling. A low, almost purring sound emanated from deep within his throat. Missing tufts of fur in his mangy coat miraculously filled in, and his coat became thick and glossy before my very eyes. I rubbed the spot where I'd found blood and found nothing.

"That's incredible," I whispered, amazed at how easily his touch could heal even the ravages of long-term deprivation.

Raph opened his eyes, his hand still embracing the healed dog. The pup, now smitten with Raph, scrambled up his arm and nuzzled in under his chin, wagging his tail in bliss.

"Ugh," Raph said with a grimace.

"I guess you don't do cute," I said, laughing at him.

"Not on your life," he said. "Get this thing off of me."

I plucked the tiny dog from his shoulder and tucked it in under my own arm. "My turn," I said, warily.

"Sit down, so I can touch your ankle."

I hobbled over the curb and leaned against the wall of the apartment building behind us, sliding my way down to a seated position.

"Here you go," I said, stretching my leg out at Raph.

He slid his fingers under the leg of my running tights and pulled it up to give himself access to my ankle. It was puffy and purple, so swollen that it was barely recognizable as an ankle. I winced when he touched it, ever so slightly.

"Not the first sprain you've had, is it?"

I shook my head. "Hurry," I urged, fearful that Michael would see us over Enoch's shoulder and know something had happened.

Raph smiled. "Yes, ma'am," he answered, his voice a deep but friendly rumble. He felt his way around my ankle, turning it this way and that before resting his hands around it.

A wave of warmth emanated from his hands, penetrating deep to my bones.

"Ah," I sighed, the disappearance of pain taking me by surprise.

Raph didn't open his eyes. But he started talking to me, a stream of constant conversation to take my mind off what was happening. "You were quite brave back there."

"How do you know?"

"Enoch heard you sneak out of the house. We were with you the whole time, not that far behind. But we'd changed out of human form to keep up with you unseen. You can imagine what it would have been like to have Enoch wearing spandex."

I giggled at the thought. "My eyes!" I joked, before a sharp resetting of something in my bones took my breath away.

Raph grinned, his eyes still tightly closed. He let his fingers dance about the delicate bones of my ankle, probing and poking to make sure everything was aligned. "Exactly. Anyway, Enoch convinced me to let you continue, undisturbed, as you rescued your mutt here. And I was impressed enough by your courage to let you handle those men on your own."

"Until you knew Michael was coming."

A sad look passed over his face. "Until Michael was upon us, yes. I didn't want any of us to suffer the consequences of his unmitigated anger. Even though I was quite sure you could have gotten out of that scrape on your own."

He opened his eyes and smiled before looking down at my ankle. It had a healthy pink glow and, except for the burn tissue, looked completely normal. I wiggled it around under his touch.

"Good as new," I said. "Impressive."

"Yes. Impressive," he said, eyeing me with a thoughtful expression. Swiftly, he pulled down my running tights and pulled me to my feet.

I looked back down the alley, searching for the girl who'd melted into the darkness.

"Will she be okay, Raph? That girl?"

He sighed, weighing his words before answering my question. "It's too late for her, Hope. She's damaged. Broken. Physically and emotionally, probably beyond repair."

I gulped. "You couldn't . . . ?" I didn't even have the words to ask him. Couldn't he save her? Couldn't we all save her?

"It doesn't work that way. I wish we could, but we can't. She has to want to be healed for me to be of any help. For any of us to reach her, for that matter. Besides, as noble as your thoughts are, you really should be worried about yourself." He nodded back up the alley.

"Good luck."

He turned to give me a full view of Michael, now unencumbered by Enoch, bearing down toward us. The men in the alley had slunk away, leaving no witnesses whose presence might stay Michael's wrath. I braced myself, expecting a good tongue-lashing.

Raph made a half-hearted attempt to soften him up. "She's fine, Michael. They weren't Fallen, if that is what you are worried about."

Michael ignored him, focusing only on me. He ran his hands over me, checking to be sure I was whole, his touch sending sparks of heat coursing through my body. "Did he hurt you? Are you okay?"

I nodded, unable to speak for the lump in my throat.

He sighed and then stepped back, turning from me, head in hands, as if he couldn't believe his luck. I waited for him to turn around, expecting to see a smile of relief on his face. Instead I was met with cold fury. His jaw was set, his lips pressed together so tightly they were turning gray. It was taking every effort he had to keep his temper contained. He could barely bring himself to look at me, couldn't even stand to be next to me, as he spit out his orders, clearing us out of the alley.

"We're leaving. Now."

He turned on his heel and began marching back to the street. I stared after him, almost disappointed. Raph turned to me and shrugged. "Better keep up," he muttered, pushing me ahead.

We were walking at a blistering pace. If it hadn't been for the way we darted single file in and out of crowds, weaving our perfectly synchronized way like a flock of birds, you wouldn't have even known we were together. Nobody spoke; the only sounds were the blaring horns of the cars rushing by, the chatter of the crowds, and the winds surging up from the water. While I'd been fending off the trafficker, Istanbul had woken up, the pale yellow sun rising in the sky doing nothing to warm the air.

"I thought it was supposed to be spring in Turkey this time of year," Raph muttered to himself, tucking his bare hands under his armpits.

"Maybe hell is freezing over," Michael said sharply in response. That ended any attempt at conversation for several blocks. Every now and then, I'd look back to see the puppy—my puppy—trotting behind us contentedly.

Michael was not leading us back to the house. It was unclear what he was doing, other than trying to punish us with the death march across the city and up its famous hills. As we crested another swell, things began to look familiar. Greek letters were stenciled neatly on the signs outside of each doorstep, the random sign here and there amended with a spattering of English. The domes and crucifixes of a few ancient churches loomed above the buildings—silent witnesses and survivors of the "cleansing" that had converted many to mosques hundreds of years ago. We wended our way back to the very place I'd wanted to be: the old Greek quarter I'd been haunting for the last few days.

Wearily, I stopped in my tracks and gaped. It couldn't be an accident. It just couldn't be.

"Michael," I began. He kept walking up the steep sidewalk. "Michael. Please."

He turned around and crossed his arms, looking at me intently.

"Please. Stop punishing us. We're sorry, okay? I was just trying to clear my head, so I could work on the Prophecy. Enoch and Raph were with me the whole time. I promise."

A dark shadow came over his face, and his blue eyes shifted to steely gray.

"You went into one of the most dangerous neighborhoods in the city."

"I didn't know. It was stupid of me not to have checked a map. I'm sorry."

He looked at me, and I realized he wasn't angry. He was afraid. He let out a giant sigh and lifted a hand to his brow, wrinkled deep with worry.

"Those weren't just any men, you realize. They were traffickers."

"You don't know . . ." Enoch began, shaking his head sadly. Michael raised a hand, instantly silencing Enoch.

"They were traffickers. I know it. Turkey is infamous as a through-point for trafficking foreign girls. Syrian, Ukrainian, Greek. Girls from all over. Girls just like you, Hope." He was grabbing me by the shoulders now, shaking me with each word that left his lips. Even through my thermal running clothes I could feel his heat surging against me, and it was all I could do to stop myself from leaning into him, from tilting my face up expectantly, for a kiss.

"If those men had gotten you . . . if they were allied in any way with the Chinese . . ." His mouth trembled as his fingers dug even more tightly into my arms. I bit my lip, unsure if there were anything I could say to make him feel better.

"But they didn't." Enoch rested a hand on Michael's arm as he intoned the words, his voice steady. Michael visibly relaxed under his touch.

"No. You're right. They didn't." Michael smiled a shaky smile. "They didn't," he repeated, as if trying to convince himself that everything would be all right. He searched my eyes—for what, I couldn't tell.

Raph cleared his throat, and we both turned to face him. Michael's hand drifted to the small of my back, as if he was sheltering me.

"Did you have any epiphanies during your run?" Raph asked dryly. I wondered if he knew what I was thinking.

"Don't push yourself too hard. I always found that things would come to me when the time was right." Michael smiled down at me as he shared his advice, and my heart fluttered. His eyes sparkled, the blue of a robin's egg, all the worry seemingly wiped away.

Why couldn't he always be like that?

*Because of you,* Henri intruded. *That's why.*

I couldn't hide the frisson of self-doubt that struck me. Michael noticed it, too, and frowned slightly.

"I'm not so sure if what worked for you will work for Hope, Michael," Enoch opined. He was barely wheezing now, having taken advantage of our break to recover from walking the difficult terrain of Istanbul. Even so, he leaned heavily into his cane as he made his way up the hill, catching up with Michael and me.

"She may need even more searching. She is unused to her powers, and they are ill-formed. She will need to try harder to make up for it."

Michael scowled. "It doesn't have to work that way, Enoch."

"But it might. And we don't have a lot of time to waste. You know the Fallen will be after us soon, if not already."

Michael threw up his hands in frustration. "Fine, then. What do you suggest?"

I piped up before Enoch could open his mouth. "You didn't let me finish earlier. When you asked me if I'd had any epiphanies. I was about to say I have an idea."

The three angels paused and looked at me, surprised.

"Go on, tell us, then," Raph prompted. He looked serious, but I could detect the start of a smile, a sign of grudging respect, under the grim set of his mouth.

"That is an antiquities shop," I began, pointing across the street at the dusty glass front, packed with odds and ends, that had been my object all along. "Am I right?"

"Yes. Go on," Enoch said, curious.

I thought through how to explain the mysterious pull the shop had on me without giving away the fact that today's errant run through the city was not an isolated incident.

"Well, what we're looking for certainly qualifies as an antiquity. Maybe we can find out something by talking with that shop's owner."

Raph looked at me dubiously. "Now that's logical," he said, rolling his eyes like the old Raph I knew. "What do you propose? Waltz in and ask him if he's seen the rock that belonged to Cain? And he'll just pull it out from under the counter and say, 'Here you go, missy? Is there anything else you'll be needing today?'"

Raph dug his hands deeper under his armpits.

I raised a brow and gave him my best hard stare, silently willing him to work with me. "At least it will be warm inside."

"Sold!" Enoch sang out, waving his cane in the air to marshall us all. "Let's get in there and see what we can find."

We wandered across the street, and I realized what a motley crew we made. Enoch was still in his Grateful Dead T-shirt and a pair of cargo pants. He had a knit cap on his head, the kind with earflaps and ties that really only look right on children under the age of five. Underneath the cap, his gray hair flowed down his back, almost as long as his grizzly beard. His cane had some new bumper stickers—they were hard to read, because they wrapped around such a small surface, but I was pretty sure one read "No Nukes" and another had psychedelic bears.

Raph was the polar opposite. He was dressed in pressed khakis, with a fancy sailing sweater over a button-down shirt that probably cost more than my dad's used car. Our altercation with the men in the alley had not added a wrinkle or stain to the entire ensemble. He looked like he'd stepped out of a men's fashion magazine.

I knew I looked ill-suited for any shopping right now, in my running gear and shoes. And then there was Michael.

He looked older, still. The shadows that had once seemed temporary had settled in permanently under his eyes, giving him a haunted look. His skin looked taut, the five o'clock shadow he'd let grow in over the last few days underscoring that he was more, well, grown-up now. He was wearing a faded pair of Levi's that highlighted every contour of his muscles. The cream cashmere sweater he wore looked like it was molded to his very body.

He caught me staring at him as he climbed the step to the antiquities shop and grinned. I blushed, feeling foolish, and stared down at my feet to compose myself. The shop door's bell tinkled, and I looked up to find him holding the door for me.

"After you," he said, politely, the smile wiped from his face.

I looked to the pup. "Stay here," I admonished, and to my surprise he sat, obediently, at the doorstep.

I climbed the steps and ducked into the store, cursing myself for the lapse that let Michael see my feelings. I could afford to feel sorry for the pain I was causing Michael, but I couldn't afford to let down my guard. I couldn't let him catch me thinking about him the way I used to.

*Like when he sent you that Valentine's Day card?*

I blushed an even deeper red at Henri's needling, remembering the promises Michael had made to hold me in the palm of his hand. But it had been easy for him to promise to keep me safe when he was hidden in the shadows of anonymity. Easy, when he didn't know that I was the Bearer of the Key. I shook my head, reminding myself there was too much at stake for me to indulge in wishful thinking.

My embarrassment was soon forgotten, though, as I took in the treasures displayed inside the store. From the street, the shop had seemed tiny, a space wedged between two larger establishments that took up most of the building's front. Inside, however, the space seemed to unfurl into a maze of twists and turns, each room unfolding into another, all equally packed with shelves and racks full of books, objets d'art, and other curiosities I couldn't even begin to explain. Vases and busts were piled upon what looked like old altars. Statues crowded against candelabra and reliquaries, each more magnificent than the last. The air was filled with the must and dust of old things. I breathed it in, my eyes pulled in a hundred competing directions, unsure of where to begin.

I rested a hand on top of a pile of neatly folded cloths. I picked at the top one, wondering at the delicate embroidery that ran along its edges.

"That is six hundred years old," a stern voice noted with a tone of disapproval. I snatched my hand away from the fabric and turned to see the small, dark man from my earlier visit, dressed formally in a suit and vest, a pocket watch hanging from the front where his jacket hung open. I paused, waiting for him to shoo me away with the same dismissive treatment he'd used on me yesterday, but apparently he didn't recognize me. He waited expectantly for me to say something appropriate in response to his statement.

"It's beautiful. Everything is," I said, hoping my smile might smooth his ruffled feathers. Instead, he grimaced at me, exasperated, over the glasses he'd perched on top of his sharply hooked nose.

"Of course everything in here is beautiful. I have collected it all myself. I only take the very best."

He turned and began making his way through the maze of things. "That altar cloth is much too new for me, but the embroidery was so exquisite, I couldn't resist."

I trailed after him. "Just what is it that you do, sir?"

He turned and looked me up and down before answering me. "You're too young to be a collector. Have you gotten separated from your parents?"

I ignored the obvious insult. "I'm young, but I am still interested in collecting, as you call it. So are my friends. They came in with me—perhaps you saw them as they entered?"

He scoffed. "The oafish, clumsy ones? They aren't collectors, either. I can tell."

"Looks can be deceiving." Michael had somehow appeared at my side. I could tell he was enjoying the banter. "You specialize in antiquities. Of what type?"

The man appraised Michael. "In what type are you interested, sir? Perhaps we can narrow things down more quickly," he sniffed.

"I'm interested in religious antiquities."

"Religious? That is quite broad." The shopkeeper took out his pocket watch, making a big show of checking it and polishing out some unseen smudge on its glass face before snapping its gold lid in place.

"Christian antiquities."

The man eyed Michael speculatively. "Of what era?"

"Very early Christianity. Byzantine or earlier."

The man tapped his fingers together, making a V in front of his face. "Mosaics, perhaps? Chalices?"

"Relics."

"*Deveye hendek atlatmaktan daha zor*," he muttered, flushing purple as he tried to maintain his composure. "I am not a huckster, peddling pig bones as the knuckles of Saint So-and-So. I run a respectable shop here; ask any one of my customers." With that, he turned on his heel, making a dignified retreat to the front of his shop.

"Sir," I called out, chasing after him, "he didn't mean to insult you or imply that you are a cheat. It's just that we are genuinely interested in things that were *believed* to be relics." I saw him pause, considering what I said, and knew that I had him. "If you had any here," I said, "real or otherwise, we would love to see them."

He walked behind his front desk, pulling himself up to his full height. "I only trade in things that are authentic."

"Of course," I said in my best soothing voice. "Of course we know that. A man with your reputation."

"Yes, my reputation." He smoothed his tie out and fidgeted with the chain on his pocket watch. "I am glad we understand one another."

He spread his hands out on the worn leather top of his desk. All four of us had crowded around him, expectant and hanging on his every word.

"You are Westerners, yes?" He waited for our acknowledgment before continuing. "As Westerners, of course, you should realize that there are no relics left in Istanbul."

Michael looked confused. "But Constantinople had the greatest collection of relics in the world. It was famed for them."

The man shifted his round spectacles on his nose and then waved a hand dismissively at Michael. "Had. Was. All in the past. Nothing now. Because of the Westerners who plundered our heritage."

He slipped on gloves and reached under the desk to pull out a heavy book, bound in leather. He laid the book out carefully on his desk and gently turned its pages until he got to one that looked like a map.

"This is the layout of the ancient city," Michael breathed, wondering at the pages before him. They were hand scripted, illuminated in gold, purple, orange, and blue. Streets were not just labeled, they were populated with tiny drawings of the people who lived and worked in them, so that every quarter—the tanners, the bakers, the soldiers, and the various monasteries—was brought to life. Little, hand-drawn buildings loomed at intersections and along great squares. Bigger than them all, Ayasofya welled up off the page.

The man adjusted his spectacles. "Where is it?" He peered through his glasses, searching for something in the map. "Ah, here it is."

He pointed a gloved finger at one of the buildings. "Pick up that magnifying glass; you'll be able to see it better."

Raph picked up the magnifying glass that was perched in a velvet case at the end of the desk and passed it to me. I lifted it to my eye and crouched as close as I could to the map. "What am I looking for?"

He shook his head. "You tell me what you see," the shopkeeper countered.

I bent closer. A drawing that looked like a tiny piece of wood, stained red and dripping, loomed into view in the glass. I could barely make out the tiny script next to it.

"*Sanctum Crucem.* The True Cross," I breathed. I jolted upright, shocked, accidentally head-butting Raph. He grimaced, rubbing his head as I murmured my apology. "It's a picture of a piece of wood labeled 'The True Cross.' Is that what I think it is?"

The man beamed, taking the magnifying glass from me. "What you have is a map of old Constaninople, showing where all the important relics were housed, at least the ones people knew about and could venerate. The piece of the True Cross, discovered by Saint Helen—the Emperor Constantine's mother—was one of the most important ones. But we had hundreds of them."

He shifted the book around to face him and began scanning and pointing. I noticed the signet ring on his finger, a stylized Maltese cross. "Moses' staff. A thorn from the crown of thorns. A piece of hay from the manger in Bethlehem. The Virgin Mary's girdle and her veil. A tear wept by Jesus. They were all here."

His hand stopped and rested on the delicate vellum of the book. We were all eyeing the map, desperately looking for any sign of the rock. Before we could find it, the shopkeeper carefully closed the book's cover and put it away under his desk.

Sadly, he shook his head. "And then the Crusaders came and stole them all away from us."

I stared at him, confused. "What? That doesn't make any sense. The Crusaders marched against the Muslims who had overtaken Jerusalem. Not to fight Christian cities and kingdoms."

The man's face turned bitter as he looked at me. "You do not even know your own history in the West, do you? Yes, Byzantium was Christian. But the greedy Crusaders missed the good weather they needed to sail to the Holy Land and were forced to linger here for months. As they dallied, they were drawn into local politics, backing a pretender to the throne on the promise of reward. They were paid for their efforts, but they were dissatisfied. As my Turkish grandfather used to say—*Kumasini verince, astarini ister*—if you give him cloth, he'll ask for the lining. When the hoped-for additional booty did not materialize, their leader, the Doge of Venice, allowed them to sack the city they had sworn to defend. They slaughtered Christians, the same way they slaughtered the Muslims who violated the holy ground tread by Jesus. And they stole from us. A great exodus of wealth, and of relics, never to be seen again. Carried out of the city on your pilgrimage routes. Spirited away to your monasteries, your libraries, and your palaces. Stolen."

He was jabbing his finger at us now, accusing us of somehow being complicit with this ancient crime.

"That's horrible," I breathed, stunned.

"Does that mean there are truly no relics left in the city?" Enoch asked, ever practical.

The man grunted, disgusted by the story he had told. "Some in the base of that pillar, they say. Maybe a few in a church here or there, or in museums. Nothing like the glory we had. We have the reliquaries," he answered, gesturing about. "My shop is full of the less beautiful, cheaper ones and the ones that were too heavy to carry away. If you want a reliquary, I can sell to you. Everything else is gone."

I looked at Michael and knew we were thinking the same thing. The rock had to have left Constantinople. From here, it could have gone anywhere. How would we ever find it?

"Where were things taken? I mean," I said, stuttering as I tried to analyze my way through the story, "if this was during the Crusades, it was, what . . . the 1100s?"

The shopkeeper grunted again at my poor grasp of history. "It was the Fourth Crusade. The city fell in April of 1204."

1204. The Barbarian raids on Europe were in a lull—I was digging deep into my memories of AP history—so it had been a relatively safe period. Stolen relics could have gone anywhere. I turned to Michael, hoping he had some ideas, but he just shrugged.

"Who knows?" The man continued, angrily wiping at the leather top of his desk. "The Crusaders came from all over. They scattered to the winds afterward, taking their spoils with them. The safest place for such treasures would have been a monastery cut off from all people. A place that Viking and pilgrim alike would struggle to attain. That is, if the thieves cared at all about keeping such a holy object safe. But I doubt that was their aim."

"But if it was your aim? Where would you have taken a relic, if you had been the one to steal it?"

I blushed, embarrassed by my ignorance and boldness as he looked at me with shrewd appreciation, startled by my question.

"*Sormak ayip degil, bilmemek ayip,* as my grandfather would have said. It is not disgraceful to ask, it is disgraceful not to know. Your question is a good one. But I am afraid I would not have done such a thing."

I tried another tack. "Well, let me ask you this. In the early thirteenth century, what were the most inaccessible places that were dedicated to the Archangel Michael?"

His eyes narrowed as he looked at me, confused by my non sequitur. "I don't understand."

I willed myself to be patient as I tried again. "You seem to know a lot more than we do about history. What monasteries and shrines to St. Michael were established by 1204?"

The flattery helped. He paused, tapping the bridge of his glasses while he thought.

"It makes no sense to me to be focused on the angel Michael, you see? For there were no Crusaders fighting under his banner that year."

"But if they had, and they had wanted to hide away relics in his honor . . . ?" I prompted, hoping he'd buy into the scenario.

"If they had, they might have had many choices of where to hide something taken in his name. Already at that time, there was Castel Sant'Angelo, Monte Gargano, Mont Saint-Michel . . ." He paused as a burst of insight seemed to come upon him. He began nodding—suddenly pleased with himself, clapping his hands with delight, the corners of his mouth turning up ever so slightly.

"Yes, that is it. That is where I would hide it away, if I had been a Crusader interested in my soul and fearful that Barbarians would come back."

"Where?" We all asked at the same time.

"The remotest of them all. Skellig Michael."

I felt a strange chord of recognition sounding throughout my body.

"That's it," I whispered. "That's where we need to go, Michael," I said, turning toward him, the shopkeeper forgotten. I was in his arms, pleading, knowing I was right. I just had that feeling.

"You're sure?" He asked, his eyes filled with doubt as he looked down at me.

I nodded, my mouth too dry to speak. I didn't even know where Skellig Michael was, but I was certain it was the place.

He squeezed my shoulder. "Then that's where we will go," he whispered back, his eyes warning me to speak no more of it while we remained in the shop. He turned me around, still keeping me close, while offering his hand to the shopkeeper. "You've been an enormous help. And your shop is fascinating. I wish there was something we could buy, to thank you for your time, but we are traveling light . . ."

The man scowled.

"I do not know what you are searching for, but if it is relics, you have my wishes for good luck. You will need it. As for a purchase, the young lady might like an ancient burka?" he said, snidely. When he found his suggestion met with a stony stare, he continued, "No? Then you can buy this book." He rummaged around under his desk until he managed to find an old paperback. "It talks about the other things stolen from Byzantium by the West."

He held it out, cover first, to face me. "Doorways of Christendom," the title read. I reluctantly took it, knowing it would be on the bottom of my reading list.

"There was nothing like our bronze doors in all of Europe. They forced our craftsmen to sell these works of art for a song, at the point of sword. That is, when they didn't just plunder them right off the front of our churches. They even stole the hinges," he sniffed. "Always thieving, the West. And if not stealing, cheating us out of a fair price. No respect, ever since you split the Church in two."

Michael ignored the implicit invitation to dogmatic debate, pressing some money into the man's hand and thanking him again.

We tumbled out of the shop and onto the street, to find my little dog waiting patiently. The city had grown dark again while we were inside the shop. I was exultant at our discovery and couldn't hide my exuberance as I skipped down the street, laughing, the puppy trailing at my heels.

"Why are you so quiet, Enoch?" I teased. "I thought you'd be as excited as I am to have our next lead."

"Are you sure it is a lead, and not grasping at straws?" Enoch asked somberly. He looked at Michael, who pursed his lips and barely shook his head.

"What do you mean?" I asked, confused and worried they were thinking this was another crazy idea, much like the search for the Michaelion had turned out to be. I wrapped myself in a façade of confidence and continued. "Of course I am! We're just lucky we came upon that shop. See, everything works out in its own way," I smiled, trying to forget all the turmoil of the afternoon. "But where is this Skellig Michael? It seems like you are familiar with it."

"It's off the coast of Ireland," Michael answered vaguely. "It's an ancient monastic site, very remote. We'll have to hire a boat to get there." He shot another warning glance at Enoch and Raph. "We'll figure out the logistics tomorrow. Tonight, we'll celebrate with a good dinner," he said wearily, making me think that perhaps our celebration was premature.

"What is it?" I demanded, turning to look into the skeptical eyes of Raph. "Come on, tell me."

Raph's face had fallen back into that familiar, haughty mask of condescension I found so irritating. "I don't know what you mean," he sniffed, pushing by me to stride up the street. Any understanding between us somehow had been lost.

Enoch scratched his chin. "Dinner will be good, Michael. This human body, for one, needs recharging, as I suspect is the case for all of us. Come, my dear," he continued, looping an arm through mine. "You have done enough detective work for one day. Let's get you home and cleaned up for a proper meal."

We climbed back down the hill, following the tracks of the city tram to make our way back to Sultanahmet, trailing behind Raph who walked in stony silence. I turned the day's events over in my mind, examining each conversation, each word, like a jewel in its setting, trying to ferret out the reality of my situation. Were we prisoner and guards? Victim and protectors? The lines were increasingly blurry as we rushed headlong into our chase for the rock, leaving me feeling confused and exposed—most of all when it came to Michael.

As if he could read my mind, he looked over at me and smiled.

I blushed and looked down at my shoes. I so wanted to believe him. Believe in us. Believe that we could win this race to the finish.

*Ever hear of Stockholm syndrome?* Henri hissed at me as the darkness of night enveloped us. I almost started to argue with him before I caught myself, remembering where I was. In the back of my mind, I heard Henri's self-satisfied harrumph. *Be on your guard,* he warned.

My puppy barked, as if he were in on the conversation. I turned and scooped him into my arms, grateful for the distraction. He wiggled and licked at my throat. I buried my face in his fur, trying to ignore Henri's words for the rest of the way home.

~

Out of thin air, once again, I found a change of clothes waiting for me, laid out with careful precision on my bed. I trailed a finger against the turquoise turtleneck sweater, noting the weight of the cashmere. The long woolen skirt had a fine weave to it, and the riding boots were made of buttery leather. Cozy and appropriate, suitable for a girl going to dinner with her grandfather, I thought, silently thanking Enoch.

I looked at the bed longingly. My new pet was already curled into a ball at its foot, sleeping soundly. I wanted to climb in and join him. I was exhausted, caught between the fatigue of jet lag, my injuries, and the forced march through the city. But I knew I was expected for dinner; indeed, I suspected the whole thing was for my benefit.

Why bother? I thought, giving in to despair and the growing doubts, lovingly cultivated by Henri, which were re-sprouting in my brain.

*Why bother? He needs to keep you close and contented. He needs you to find the rock. You're the Bearer, after all.*

"As if I could ever forget," I whispered back at Henri, my hand moving to trace the tattoo-like pattern that spread across the back of my neck. "But once we find it, what will he do?"

The question hung in the air.

*Once you know where it is, you must not tell him until the absolute last moment. It's the only way for you.*

"Wait? Does that mean it's not in Ireland? What do you know, Henri?" I asked, suddenly afraid.

My question went unanswered, for he had disappeared once again.

If only I could disappear, too, I thought bitterly. But then, where would I go? What could I do? They would always find me—always come for me to take them to the relic they needed to access Heaven's Gate.

I sniffed at myself, absentmindedly noting that I needed another trip to the baths. Resigned to being trapped here, as well as remaining stinky, I pulled off my shoes and began changing for dinner.

When we gathered to go to the restaurant it was evident that the confusion I felt about our situation had overtaken all of us. We stood in awkward silence, unsure of what to say or do, unclear if we were truly celebrating or simply taking a break to stoke the fires of the human machines in which the angels had willingly trapped themselves.

"You look nice, Hope," Michael said, gruffly. His ears turned a little red as he spoke. "We have a bit of a walk, so we'd better get going." Quickly, he moved to the door and led us shuffling down the narrow staircase to the street. As we departed, I scattered a handful of kibble I'd managed to scrounge up for the absent cat, wondering idly if she'd be back to reclaim her territory.

We took the tram and then wound through the back alleys toward one of the main squares, huddling together as we walked into the wind. I'd expected normal people to have been driven inside by the cold, but the streets were packed, clusters and clumps of them pirouetting around tattered umbrellas that struggled to resist the sudden gusts. The sparkling lights stood out against the velvety black sky, creating an almost festive atmosphere that was accentuated by the occasional outburst of laughter drifting over to us across the wind.

"Tourists?" I shouted my question to be heard.

Michael shook his head. "Saturday night."

We turned off the square into a side street that was less congested. The contrasting quiet just made the howling wind seem that much fiercer, its shrieks echoing off the silent bricks and stones. I pulled my rain jacket around me, grateful that Enoch had thought this far ahead when he made his angelic arrangements for clothing. We walked several blocks in silence, the mist from our breath entwining our heads like halos as, bit by bit, the other revelers fell away, leaving us alone in the street.

"Michael!" Raph had trotted up, coming even with Michael. Even the brewing tempest couldn't disguise the warning growl in his voice. "We're being followed."

I looked over my shoulder. There was no mistaking whom Raph was talking about, for there was only one other group behind us. They were brawny men, about a block and a half back, walking four abreast down the street.

I thought I'd only taken a second to glance backward, but in the time I did, the angels had responded to the threat, subtly shifting into defensive positions. Enoch was taking point. Raph had fallen back; he'd be the first line of defense should the men advance. Michael was now right next to me. I looked down as he locked an iron grip on my arm.

"Faster, now, but act as if nothing is going on."

As one, the angels accelerated, pulling me along with them. Enoch was breathing heavily, but that was the only sign that anything was amiss. I, on the other hand, was practically running to keep up with their long, urgent strides.

"Are they Fallen?" I asked, feeling the pit of dread in my stomach growing bigger.

Michael looked at me sideways, shaking his head. "No. They'd be handling this differently if they were. I think one of them may be one of your traffickers from earlier today, but they're too far away to tell for sure. Just keep looking straight ahead."

"They're closing in. Why don't we just deal with them here?"

The urgency in Raph's voice scared me, and I darted a look over my shoulder. They had gained another half block and were jogging. No mistaking, now, that they were after us.

"No." Michael said roughly, his jaw squared. "We can't draw attention to ourselves. There is too much at stake. Eyes forward," he barked at me, yanking on my arm. "Take this right," he commanded, and we all swerved around the corner into another tiny side street. As we rounded, we broke into a full run. Enoch tossed aside his cane, leaving it to clatter against a pair of dented garbage cans as he picked up speed.

The panic welled up inside of me. I could taste it like steel in my mouth. Enoch, Raph, and Michael closed ranks around me, the space between us gone, their bodies a forbidding wall that would protect me from this new threat.

"Down there. We'll go into that club," Michael shouted over the wind. "We'll lose them inside."

Three blocks away, we could see the line wrapping around the corner of the club and hear the throbbing music. I looked over my shoulder again. The men were still a block behind us. We'd never get through the line fast enough . . . if we could even get in at all.

Nobody else seemed to worry about anything but getting there.

I focused on the pounding of my heart, trying not to notice that its beat was echoed by the ever-closer footfalls of the men chasing us.

"On my count," Michael ordered as he pulled us to a sudden stop. "One . . . two . . . now!"

I looked around me, confused. The pounding music from behind the club's doors and the steady murmur of the crowd was making it difficult for me to concentrate. Somehow in that instant I had lost Enoch and Raph.

"Where are they?" I whispered to Michael, turning around as I desperately tried to find them in the line. He just shook his head, pushing me forward. "Keep walking. And smile."

We cut through the crowd of restless teens waiting for entry into the club, who hooted and jeered as Michael steered us to the VIP line. The smell of pot and something else—sulfur, mingled in the air, making me cough.

"But, we're not . . ." my voice trailed off as I looked down. My respectable outfit had somehow been altered. I was now poured into skintight jeans that tucked into thigh-high platform boots. I could feel the leather of my distressed jacket rubbing against the bare skin of my back—a quick peek confirmed I was wearing an ornately beaded silk halter. I stared at Michael, who'd also been transformed into club-worthy clothes—though in his case, they weren't much different than the jeans he'd wear normally.

"We don't have time for questions," Michael muttered. "Keep moving." Behind us, I could hear shouting as the men chasing us ran into the buzz of the crowd, who did not want to let them through. Michael pushed me, and I surged ahead, tripping on the cobblestone into the two leggy blondes in front of me.

"Oh, I'm so sorry!" I gasped. They turned and looked at me with grim expressions I recognized.

"Stop staring and go in," the first one muttered. I gaped, recognizing the impatient tone I always associated with Raph's voice.

"Come on," said the other blonde, who was dressed suspiciously like Stevie Nicks, as she pulled me up to the rope.

"Enoch?"

"Shhh!" The bohemian blonde put a ring-covered finger over her lips, then posed and pouted for the bouncer, who parted the chain and let us through.

The crowd surged behind us, closing the gap we'd left in our wake, as we rushed into the club.

We were in a sea of people, a writhing mass that moved as one with the pulsating music.

"We can lose them in here," Michael reiterated, staring into the crowd. "Let's move deeper in—if we're lucky, they won't make it in at all—or by the time they do, we'll be gone. You two keep on Hope's tail; make sure you block any view of her."

The blondes dropped back and converged behind me as we delved deeper into the club, Michael leading the way. The strobe lights and lasers flashed, cutting psychedelic lines through the clouds of dry ice. Everything about this scene was unfamiliar to me—the thumping music, the twisting bodies dancing with abandon. I was starting to feel lightheaded—because of my fear or the pot smoke that seemed to be completely surrounding me, I couldn't tell.

Michael kept pulling me through the crush of bodies, his hand clamped onto mine. Suddenly the music shifted—the familiar beat of a popular song rising—and the crowd surged, embracing the music. In that instant, Michael lost his grip on me, and I was alone.

I scanned the unfamiliar faces, trying to find him, or the blondes, but I was lost in the mass of jumping, swaying bodies. I was buffeted about by unfamiliar hands. Bodies pressed against me as I tried to find a way off the dance floor.

Behind me, I heard shouting and saw our pursuers pushing their way through, making their way straight for me.

Everything seemed to slow down in the shimmer of the strobe lights. The crowd moved up and down to the beat, arms raised in tribute to the music. In the shadows, I saw the blondes, their figures shimmering and morphing as they left their female guises behind in favor of bodies that seemed more appropriate for bodyguards. Their faces distorted as they changed, their features melting and blending into a strange blend of familiar and foreign.

Then, in the brief flash of a strobe, I thought I saw Lucas standing in the crowd, a rush of sulfur rising above the smoke to assault my nose.

I shrieked, moving backward, spilling drinks out of the hands of angry dancers, not caring in my need to get away. The strobe flashed again and again, but whatever—or whomever—I'd seen was gone.

Not wanting to take any chances, I began pushing my way toward the stage. A strong hand closed on my arm and I turned to fight it off, only to sigh with relief. It was Michael.

"This way," he shouted over the music, steering me through the crowd.

We made our way to the edges and found ourselves at a long bar. We looked back and saw a struggle erupting in the middle of the crowd.

"They're still behind us. Enoch and Raph will take care of them, but we've got to find you somewhere safe to hide."

Michael looked around, his eyes finally settling on the sliver of light that emanated from the kitchen door behind the bar.

"Over here," he insisted, dragging me behind him. He strode purposefully around the bar and pushed his way through the swinging door. A torrent of angry Turkish followed us, but he ignored it, pulling me through the long, almost deserted galley.

The light was too bright in here after the darkness of the dance floor. It hurt my eyes, and I had to look away from the gleaming stainless-steel surfaces. Our walk turned into a run as we moved through the narrow kitchen, looking for a way out. My heart was pounding, my hand warm in Michael's grasp as he pulled me along.

We opened door after door. Refrigerated walk-ins. Freezers.

Washing stations. No exits. Behind us we could hear more shouting and the clang of pots and pans being flung onto the floor.

At the end of the hall, out of options, we opened only door left. The only door behind which we might hide. It was the door to a broom closet.

"In here," Michael growled, pushing me in, then quietly pulling the door closed behind him.

There was no room for us in the muddle of buckets, mops, and brooms. I was pressed tight against Michael's body. I could feel every hard muscle and the rush of his pulse against me as we held our breaths, listening for our pursuers.

I shifted slightly, trying to find a more comfortable position, and tripped backward over a bucket. Before I could fall, Michael caught me in his arms, holding me upright. My hands had nowhere to go but to rest on his shoulders.

A thrill ran through my body at his touch. Confused, I tried to look away.

He pulled me closer. "Shhh. Wouldn't want you to fall."

Unable to resist, I looked up, trailing a hand down to his broad chest. His breath was shallow, and I could feel the throb of his pulse under my palm. His face was inches from mine. He looked down at me, steely eyes shining.

Hesitant, he lowered his face toward mine. I closed my eyes, moving on tiptoes to meet his lips, even though I knew I shouldn't. A small sigh escaped me, anticipating his kiss.

His lips pressed against mine, searching and soulful, then moving with an urgency that took my breath away. He stood me on my feet, pushing my back against the wall of the tiny closet, my hands pinned beneath his, as he explored, insistent. A wave of emotion swept through me—anger, confusion, desire—and I realized, with a gasp, that the emotions I was feeling were not my own, but his, transmitted directly to me through his touch. He reclaimed my mouth, letting go of my hands to run his fingers along the length of my body. I shuddered, weakening as the familiar pulse of heat began to spread through my body.

Suddenly, he pushed away, throwing himself back against the opposite wall.

We leaned apart, the ridiculously tiny space he'd created between us doing nothing to quench the need we felt for one another. Our breathing sounded harsh and foreign to my ears. It was all I could do to drag my eyes away from him in a futile attempt to bring my desire for him under control.

"Did you feel that?" he asked in a whisper.

I nodded, not trusting my voice to speak.

"I felt it, too. Your emotions."

I didn't know what to say. He let the silence settle around us before continuing.

"Why?" he asked plaintively through ragged breath.

"Why what?" I forced myself to look into his eyes as I answered his question. He looked tortured. Not angry.

"Why do you keep pushing me away?"

"I'm not."

"You are. You won't let me in. You don't trust me anymore. After all this, you still don't trust me."

"That's not true!" I protested, feeling the heat of anger and confusion rising in my face. "You're the one who has surrounded yourself with your angelic guard dogs. They don't want me near you."

He sighed a heavy sigh and rubbed his hand against his face, weary.

"You're wrong. They're protecting you from me. I asked them to do it. I can't trust myself around you any longer."

"Why? Because of the fire?" In the darkness, I could see him flinch as I spoke. But he didn't answer. I continued on impulsively. "I believe you, you know. I believe you didn't mean to do it. I didn't know at first. But I do now."

He slumped against the wall. There was more he wasn't telling me, more from which he was trying to protect me.

"Michael," I pressed. "Are you changing?" The question hung in the air between us. When he didn't answer, I persisted. "Are you Falling?"

He stared at his feet. "I don't know," he admitted, his voice full of misery. "Sometimes I think I see the signs . . . but then, I don't know. I don't even know myself."

"No." The word fell from my lips. Now that I had spoken it out loud, I didn't want to believe it was happening, despite all the evidence. I forgot about caution and moved to him, clasping his hands in mine. I held onto them tightly, squeezing hard. "You won't. You can't."

He pulled one of my hands free, placing it on his chest, giving me direct access to his thoughts.

*If I could, I would crack open my chest and keep you there, close to my heart. I'll make sure you're safe, Hope. Even if the danger is from me. I promise.*

I pulled away, my hand trembling.

Outside our door we heard shouting and commotion. Swiftly, Michael pushed me behind him, shielding me with his body. The door swung open to reveal a large man, silhouetted against the light. I held my breath, tensing for a fight.

"They're gone. You can come out now."

We sighed. It was Raph's voice. Relieved, we tumbled out of our hiding place, blinking into the fluorescent light.

Both Raph and Enoch had morphed back into their normal forms. The galley was quiet. We were alone in the back, the sounds of the busy kitchen far away in the distance. Enoch's discarded cane was back, propped up against the wall where Enoch stood flipping through some documents, thick fingers moving restlessly through the pages.

"I grabbed these off one of them," he said, brandishing a little booklet in the air. "Russian passports—not one, but two, with different names. More traffickers, I would bet. Looks like our Chinese friends are calling in some chips."

He shoved the booklets at Michael, who flipped to the photos. I peeked over his shoulder—the sneering face in the snapshot sent a shiver up my spine.

"One of them is the same man from the alley," I whispered, trying to swallow the aggressive wave of guilt that threatened to swamp me. If slave traders had found us, it was my fault.

"But how did they track us down so fast? It doesn't make sense. We've been so careful," Michael said, beginning to pace.

"Who cares?" Raph challenged. Michael stopped his pacing and confronted Raph.

"What did you say?" Michael shot back, his jaw clenched.

"I said: Who. Cares." Raph rose up to his full height, unwilling to back down. "You're neglecting the whole world for the sake of this one girl. The world is falling apart around you, and you are barely noticing. We are not but one step ahead of danger, and still we are no closer to finding this . . . this abomination you call the Key, than we were before. The solution is obvious, but you can't bring yourself to do it."

"What are you suggesting?" Michael snarled, closing the distance between himself and Raph.

"Boys," Enoch warned, trying to step between them. "Raph," he pleaded, his voice full of reason and warning. "You're making it worse. Don't let your jealousy of Michael warp your judgment."

Raph's eyes snapped with fire as he pushed Enoch out of the way.

"Don't speak to me of judgment, old man! Look what he is doing—he leaves everyone open as prey to the Fallen Ones, because he is so certain he is right. It is this same folly that caused him to protect mankind when it should have been condemned. The same foolishness that tore apart the Legion of Angels and allowed this situation to even come about in the first place! He risks Heaven against our better judgment!"

He spat his final words, defiantly, in Michael's face.

They stared each other down. Nobody moved. The only sounds were the sounds of our breath as we waited.

"If you feel that way," Michael stated, coldly and quietly, his face a mask of fury, "then you may leave. I banish you."

Raph scoffed. "*You* banish *me*? You who begged for my help? Very well, then, I will leave you to it."

With that, he turned his back on Michael and, in a flash of light, disappeared.

"Do not come back," Michael muttered, as he stared with unseeing eyes at the place where Raph had been standing. "I can do this alone."

"Michael," Enoch said, cautiously. "You are not yet alone."

"But I am!" Michael roared. He reached onto the stainless-steel shelves that cut through the center of the galley, upending pots and pans in a blind rage. "What have I done? How am I supposed to keep you safe?" he demanded, moving toward me with an anguished look on his face. He slammed his fist against the steel counter, letting the din echo in the night.

He wheeled on Enoch, continuing his rant. "If it comes down to me against you, Enoch, I will overpower you. You know I will. I am the seasoned warrior. I won't be able to stop myself." Shaking with rage and self-pity, he slumped against the wall, sliding down it with his head in his hands.

Enoch's eyes flashed, but he remained calm as he stepped between Michael and me. He looked down at Michael with a severity and authority I had not yet seen from him. "You forget whom you deal with. I was human once. I know better than you your every emotion. I can see it forming in your eyes. I recognize it before you have even registered it. You might be stronger than me, but I will outsmart you. I will keep Hope safe, away from your pain and anger." Michael looked up, disbelief on his face.

"Come, Hope." Enoch pulled me away, grabbing his cane in one swift motion as he made for the door. "We must leave him to compose himself."

Blindly, I followed Enoch as he dragged me through the kitchen. Somehow, we made our way through the crowds and began our silent walk back to the house. I did not feel the cold. My mind was racing, unsure of what to make of the turn of events as I tripped over the rough cobblestones.

"Will Michael be okay?"

Enoch thought for a few moments before answering. "He will be fine. His human emotions are confusing to him, as I am sure they are to you."

"Enoch, what's going to happen to us?"

"We will continue on as we planned. We will go to Skellig Michael, and you will find the Key."

"What did you mean when you warned Raph about his jealousy?" I thought of my earlier conversations with Henri, and my own musings as I'd tried to puzzle out the Prophecy, afraid I already knew the meaning of Enoch's words.

Enoch sighed. "Surely even you have noticed how of all the angels, Michael is the subject of human veneration. It stings to have him singled out above us, Hope. Even Michael's name—'Who Is Like God?'—is vain and wrong."

"He's too proud, too certain of himself. So sure that he is incorruptible." Enoch was getting agitated now, his voice rising and his cane hitting the pavement for emphasis. We had come to a full stop in the street, nothing but the moon to witness our exchange.

"But you know what they say? Pride goeth before a fall. He will learn to suffer the consequences of his choices before this is all over." His eyes flashed with a sudden anger that worried me.

I reached out to rest my hand on Enoch's where he held his cane. He snatched it away, surprised, and then seemed to remember where we were.

"I'm sorry, dear. I just worry that Michael is too blind to his own faults, and someday they will come back to haunt him." He took my hand in his, patting it in an attempt to comfort me, but his words had only unsettled me further.

# five

## GEORGIA

"You two are awfully quiet," Arthur, Mona's driver and friend, commented from the front seat. Normally, Mona would be seated next to him, gossiping and debating the finer points of Georgia football. But the afternoon at the FBI offices had worn her out, and with Don accompanying her home, they'd silently climbed into the middle row of the SUV.

Arthur tried again. "Don, it is nice to see you after all these years. Though, of course, I wish it were under better circumstances."

Don made his best attempt at a smile, a twisted grimace that told Mona how upset he still was.

"That's nice of you to say, Arthur. It's good to see you, too. I still remember the first time we met. Do you?"

Arthur chuckled, peering back at them through the rearview mirror.

"I do, I do. It was crazy, wasn't it? Your car battery had died, and you both had to be at the airport. Little Hope was with her nanny. She must have been, what, a year old? I don't remember how you found me, but that was the first time I drove you."

"You were supposed to pick up our neighbor that morning," Mona reminded him. "And our other car was in the shop. Remember? You were out in the cul-de-sac, waiting, and he came out to cancel on you. I couldn't believe it when you offered to take us. You were a Godsend."

"That's right! After that, you both became regulars for a while."

"Until Don stopped traveling," Mona whispered, remembering what it had been like on those occasional mornings when they'd both had to make their way to the airport. Arthur would stop to pick up coffee for them both, and they'd sit in the back seat, fingers entwined, grinning like teenagers on a date.

Don interrupted her thoughts. "You mean until I lost my job. After I'd lost Hope." He dangled his statement out there like a giant piñata, waiting for her to take a whack at it—at him. It was the invitation to an old argument, one that had healed over with time, but just barely. It was like a scab, itching to be picked, underneath still oozing and raw.

The air got very still. Arthur kept his eyes steadfastly on the road, straining to block out their conversation. Mona sighed, wondering if his self-hate would turn on her, now that she was the one who had lost Hope.

"It wasn't your fault, Don."

"And this time isn't yours, either," he answered, surprising her. She turned in the roomy seat, so she could see if he was serious.

"You mean that?"

He nodded. "Of course. But I need to ask you, what were you thinking, letting Hope see this boy, this boy you seem to know nothing about?"

It was a fair question, she realized. She peeked into the front seat, but Arthur was still studiously ignoring them.

"He seemed good for her, Don," she shrugged. At the time, it hadn't seemed like a big deal. But now it appeared as if everything might hinge on Michael and his real intentions toward her daughter. "He seemed smart and straightforward, not like he had anything to hide. I don't think they did anything but moon over each other, if that makes you feel any better. It was kind of sweet."

She peered at Don. He was trying hard, she could tell, to understand. Trying hard to be balanced in his judgment.

"How did you not know she was upset by all that human trafficking business? That she wasn't sleeping? What if she really got swept into it, like the FBI believe? While you were away . . ." He cut himself off, but the sharp edge in his tone made clear his implication—that she had once again neglected Hope for her career.

Was he right? She stared out the window, choosing to evade his questions.

"Mona? I'm not blaming you, I'm just trying to understand what you were thinking."

"I thought she needed to spread her wings," she whispered, pressing her flushed cheeks to the cool glass of the window, thinking of the timid thing that had come into her home, barely any possessions to her name, and how she seemed to blossom under Michael's attention. She changed every day as she experienced the freedom she'd been denied in the circumscribed life permitted by her father, who feared that the Mark on Hope's neck, indeed, her very abduction, meant she was a target for something bigger than any of them understood.

She teared up, Don's unspoken accusation smarting, her own self-doubt eating at her heart.

Arthur cleared his throat. "She did what she thought best, Don.

Just like you did all those years. Maybe it would be best for you two to just drop this. It won't come to any good."

"No, he needs to hear this," Mona interjected, her voice thick as she turned away from the window to confront Don. "And I don't mind saying it in front of you, either," she added, drawing Arthur into their conversation. "After all this time, you know as much about our messed-up family as anybody does. Don," she continued, leaning across the seat divider, her gestures hard and emphatic, "all these years that you kept her under lock and key, thinking she was at risk: You were stifling her. I couldn't do that to her. And even now, I wouldn't change that. I couldn't. She needs to be a girl, Don, just a young girl. With everything that means—parties and boyfriends and the freedom to make her own mistakes, so she can grow up and be proud of who she is, to know her place in the world, to know she belongs. She needs that."

"But what if she's not just a girl? What if she's meant for something else?"

Mona threw up her hands, a stifled sound of frustration catching in the back of her throat. She collapsed back into the cavernous leather seat, crossing her arms. She was done with this conversation.

They rode the rest of the way in stony silence. Arthur navigated them through the winding roads of her neighborhood. As he commented on the absurdity of the callers on the talk radio station they were listening to, the best either Mona or Don could muster was a mumbled yes or no, despite Arthur's efforts to lighten the mood.

Mona emerged from his SUV, steeling herself once again for an onslaught of reality, reminding herself of the routine, trying to block out the conversation in the car. *You enter through the garage,* she began, thinking it through as she walked up the short drive, slowly acting out each step. *You press the keypad, and the tiny motor roars to life, lifting the barricade for you to enter. You turn the knob on the kitchen door, which you leave unlocked, because really, after all, Dunwoody is such a safe neighborhood. You put your car keys on the hook and press the garage door button, so the door closes behind you. It doesn't really matter if you forget the last step, because nobody else comes this far down the cul-de-sac, but closing up the garage is the right thing to do. Just in case.*

She would just ignore the klatch of reporters that sat like vultures outside her home, shouting her name. She could pretend they weren't there if she focused on her routine.

It was the same routine she'd followed every time she returned home for more than fifteen years. Normally it comforted her, this sameness, this predictability, the oasis of familiarity that she brought to her otherwise chaotic, traveling life. But this time it just underscored how meager and fragile her defenses against the world had been. How things had changed, and how powerless she had been to stop it.

How little she would have left if she didn't find Hope.

She looked down and saw she was holding Don's hat in her hands. She'd brought it in with her, after picking it up off of the passenger seat, not even thinking about it.

She was worn out by their argument . . . and disappointed. She'd thought they had made some progress.

Mona looked more closely at Don's knit cap. She poked a finger through the tiny hole that was emerging near the back. Worn, but still serviceable, especially since it was so loved.

There was a faint knock at the front door.

As if in a dream, Mona moved to the window and peeked out. Don. She had forgotten she'd left him standing in the driveway. The sight of him didn't provoke her anymore; she had grown used to him again, after all those hours in the FBI offices. She had to admit that she'd even grown to look forward to seeing him, in spite of the circumstances. But right now she was hurt by his insinuations and too tired to think about her complicated feelings for him. Shoving them aside, she opened the door.

"I think I forgot my hat in Arthur's car," he said sheepishly.

"It's right here," she said, swinging the door wide and proffering up the hat.

He looked down at Mona's hands. Her finger was still laced through the loose yarn.

She blushed. "Sorry," she mumbled as she disentangled her finger.

He stood there, awkwardly, at the threshold. "May I come in?"

"What? Oh, of course," she said automatically, turning an even deeper shade of red. *What is wrong with you, Mona? You said you wanted him out of here,* she thought as she stepped back, giving Don full entry into the house.

He seemed less comfortable in the house than the last time he had been here. Before, he'd filled the place with his presence. The questioning by the FBI, their failure to find Hope, had deflated him. He was weary, and the gray pallor of his skin showed it. He stood in the formal entry to the house, waiting. She was conscious of his gaze, aware that she, too, was tired.

Tired? She felt old. She tucked a stray piece of hair behind her ear and waited for him to say something.

He shuffled his feet and then pointed halfheartedly toward her. "Um. I'll take that." She looked down to where he pointed and saw she was still holding onto his hat; she had wadded it up into a little ball that she was working nervously. A jittery self-derisive sound escaped her. This wasn't like her, not at all. She pressed the ball of yarn into his hand, their fingers touching. She let hers linger before pulling away.

"I'm going back to Alabama now," he said, watching for her reaction. She had prepared herself for this, had rehearsed their parting in her mind during the quiet time in Arthur's car. They would never go back to the way things had been, and they couldn't stay this way, either. She knew that.

But that didn't make it any easier.

"Do you need anything before you go?" She asked, hoping he didn't hear the quiver in her voice.

"Mona," he began, running a hand through his thinning hair, "that girl said she'd read Hope's Mark. *Read* it. I know you. I know you wouldn't just let her go. What did you tell her when you said goodbye?"

Should she tell him? It seemed harmless. But then again, the more he knew, the more that could slip. The last thing she needed was for Hale to find out she was holding out on him, interfering with a witness.

"I'm her father," Don said, his voice rough. "I deserve to know as much as you."

Mona nodded, knowing he was right, and secretly relieved to have something to discuss that would get him back on her side. "Come in."

He strode to the formal living room and sat down on the edge of the love seat. He'd never looked at home in this room, and today he looked even more uncomfortable. Expectant and nervous, he was fiddling with the hat in his hands with the fervor of a fan watching the ninth inning of a no-hitter, twisting and kneading it while he hung on Mona's every word.

"It's really nothing, not yet," Mona said, sitting next to him and leaning in, eagerly. "I mean, I couldn't question her in there without Hale hearing. So I just told her I had to ask her something privately and to call me. I don't know if she'll do it. I mean, she nodded, but that could mean anything."

Don gripped her hands. "Do you know what this means, Mona? This could be the key to everything," he said, his eyes shining. "I'm just surprised that Hale didn't pick up on it."

Mona nodded, Don's enthusiasm contagious. "He will, eventually. If he goes back to her original case files. But for now, I think he has a lot of other things on his hands. I know he won't understand us keeping it from him, but . . . that Mark. It's part of such an old hurt. I just feel like we needed to hear it ourselves, first."

She looked deeply into Don's eyes. They were complicit in this. She had to trust him now.

"I'll tell you as soon as I hear from Tabby—if I hear from Tabby. But you have to promise me you won't do anything crazy."

Don surprised her by laughing. His eyes were dancing, and he seemed almost joyful. She remembered him looking like that on the day she told him she was expecting Hope. For an instant, his face was as youthful and spirited as it had been then, before any of this happened. Before they fell apart.

"Revelation usually demands action. But yes, Mona, for you, I promise I won't do anything crazy." He squeezed her hands as he made the promise. Suddenly, she felt shy.

"I suppose you should go now," she whispered, withdrawing her hands from his grip.

"I suppose," he answered, his burst of joy disappearing just as suddenly as it had come, the lines etched by years of disappointment resurfacing on his face. "But if you don't mind, I'd like to see Hope's room before I go," he responded, looking at her cautiously.

She didn't speak. Instead, she took him by the hand and pulled him after her, up the stairs. Hope's bedroom door was closed. They stood outside of it, as if waiting for her to emerge.

"I haven't been in since that morning." Mona breathed the

words as if she were afraid that by speaking she would shatter the silent bubble of mystery that surrounded her daughter, making it feel even more real. The room was a cocoon. She could imagine her daughter sleeping safely inside, holding onto that memory until something brought Hope back into her arms. She was loathe to disturb the illusion—had gone so far as to excuse herself the day the FBI searched for clues—but Don had asked, and she didn't know how to say no.

Don held her hand and turned the knob. The door swung open. The afternoon light was filtering through the windows and lighting up the bits of dust that floated in the air, creating an aura of sanctity that passed when a cloud filled the sky.

Mona shook her head, trying to clear the sentiment away. It was just an empty room, she told herself, and walked through the door, still holding Don's hand.

They looked around at the clutter. Nothing stood out as unusual to Mona's keen eye.

Don dropped her hand and moved to the black and white houndstooth hat that was slung over the low post at the foot of the bed.

"Roll Tide," he whispered, picking up the hat and twirling it on a finger. He stopped and fiddled with the rim, his eyes getting misty. Then, he noticed a maroon and gold baseball cap that had been hidden underneath and smiled ruefully. "She would do anything to get under my skin, wouldn't she? Even embrace the enemy." He slumped onto the rumpled bed. "More like anything to prove she was not my daughter. I guess I didn't make it any easier on her, though. Maybe you're right, after all. Maybe I should have let her . . . let her be."

Mona pressed her eyes closed, willing herself not to think of the acrimonious battles they'd waged in courtrooms, the snippets of daily humiliation and isolation he'd forced on Hope—the little bits that Mona knew about, the ones she'd wrested out of Hope. She forced a smile, shaking the thoughts away. She'd take this tiny sliver of admission and focus on the good instead.

"I think this is normal teenage behavior, Don. Even if we hadn't made life difficult for her, she'd still have her rebellions. We're lucky they stopped at her cheering for the Seminoles and the Crimson Tide." She sat down next to him, absentmindedly smoothing over the unmade covers. "She'd kill me for showing you this, but I don't think it can do any harm. Not now."

She burrowed under the stack of pillows and pulled out a ratty stuffed animal.

"See?" She said, holding the plush yellow jacket out to him. "Still a Tech girl at heart."

He chuckled, wiping a tear from the corner of his eye as he took the animal in hand. "Do you remember when we got her this? How big her eyes got when we took her into the stadium?"

Mona laughed, envisioning the little girl, drowning in her Georgia Tech sweatshirt, trailing a yellow and black plastic pom-pom after her. "She had to use her hands and knees to take the steps, but she wouldn't let us carry her, would she?"

"Not our girl," Don agreed. "She never did like to do things the easy way." He looked at the stuffed animal and tossed it lightly in his big hand. "Maybe she didn't hate me after all."

"Doesn't." Mona said, fiercely, taking the toy from him. "She's still here." She stumbled on the word, gesturing emphatically. "*Somewhere*. She's not . . . *gone*." She burst into tears, hunching over, as if she could hold in her sorrow as she sat there, clutching the animal in her lap.

Don shifted on the bed. He lifted one hand, then another,

unsure of what to do, before Mona finally turned and fell into his arms. He wrapped his arms about her and held her until the sobs that wracked her body subsided into tiny hiccups, murmuring into her hair as he stroked her face and comforted her.

They sat together until the sun was low, leaving poppy-colored streaks against the sky, the promise of a brighter tomorrow.

"I keep thinking about last time," Mona whispered against his shoulder. "It's been twice as long, Don. What if we don't find her?"

Don held her tighter and smiled. "She'll come back."

"They always say if you don't find a missing child within the first 48 hours . . ."

"She's still alive," Don said, kissing her forehead. "She'll come back."

Mona pushed away from him, irritated at his confidence. "How do you know?"

Don looked at her, amused. "You don't want to know how I know, Mona. It just makes you think I'm crazy." She opened her mouth to protest, but he interrupted her, laying a finger gently across her lips. "Just this once, let it go."

Mona was too tired to argue. She looked up at him, her limpid eyes beginning to well over again. "I want to believe you. I do."

"Then believe. Just for tonight, forget about what happened so many years ago. Forget about all the things I did wrong, all the things that embarrassed you and that you resented. Forget about your need for rational explanations and proof and just believe."

He sounded logical. He sounded confident and strong. He sounded like the man she'd fallen in love with all those years ago.

He traced the outline of her lips with a light finger. "Believe in me, Mona . . . like you used to."

He bent his head, as if to kiss her. And Mona, wanting to believe, and to forget, did not stop him.

~

Pale light filtering through the curtains gently coaxed Mona awake. She rolled over and groaned. Her body felt like it had been hit by a Mack truck, achy emptiness occupying places that before had been full of tension. She hadn't slept like this since she came home from her trip to find the house empty and thought Don had kidnapped Hope.

Her mind reeled as reality came rushing back in. She turned over to check the other side of the bed. Rumpled. Empty. The impression of another head on the pillow.

She pushed herself up from the bed. What had she done?

She flew to the bathroom and stared at herself in the mirror. Her skin was ruddy, rubbed raw by Don's stubble. She turned on the tap as far as it could go and dashed cold water against her face, rubbing her skin as if she could make the evidence go away.

*Stupid, stupid, stupid.*

She girded herself in her old flannel robe, pulling the belt tight, and shoved her feet into slippers. Already, she was rehearsing what she would say to Don when she found him downstairs: It was a mistake. It should never have happened. You need to go, Don. Go back to Alabama.

She flew down the stairs, speech ready. At the corner before the kitchen, she paused and squared her shoulders before sweeping into the room.

It was empty.

Confused, she ran into the living room.

Nothing.

She walked back into the kitchen. Only then did she notice the aroma of coffee and see the half-empty pot and the note on the counter, propped up against Hope's stuffed animal.

Fingers shaking, she unfolded the paper.

*Gone home. Call with any news. I love you. Don.*

She looked at the note, her brain refusing to accept what she was reading. Slowly she walked to the front door and swung it wide, poking her head out to look around the cul-de-sac. The reporters had already regrouped for the day; Don's pickup was nowhere to be seen.

Disappointment, heavy and undeniable, rushed through her.

She closed the door and leaned her back against it, trying to make sense of what she was feeling. Knees shaking, she sank to the floor and unfolded the note, tracing Don's handwriting over and over again.

Alone on the stone floor, she wept, the ink of his goodbye running from her tears.

# six

## TURKEY

*Was I crazy? Was I falling easy prey to Michael's manipulation?*

I kept turning the questions over in my mind, unable to sleep.

Raph was gone, but I wasn't sure if that was a good thing or a bad thing. On the one hand, he'd been a complete pain in the ass—except for the brief moment we'd had earlier this afternoon, when it finally seemed like he understood me. He did nothing but goad me—and Michael—with his barbed comments.

On the other hand, he might have been the only thing capable of keeping Michael from destroying me if Michael finally was pushed too far by his pain. Or turned.

I shivered in the cold night and pulled the sleeping puppy closer to me. After seeing what happened earlier at the club, I had no trouble imagining Michael being pushed too far.

But, then again, he'd protected me from the men who'd been pursuing me, when it would have been easy to let me fall into their hands. And when we'd kissed . . .

I brushed my fingers up against my bruised lips, remembering the feeling of his hard body pressed against mine and shuddered again.

When we touched, in his inner thoughts, he said he would always protect me. I wanted desperately to believe him. But even Enoch wasn't sure. Besides, Michael didn't even trust himself and said as much.

Frustrated, I pushed the covers away and started pacing the floor, the wooden boards creaking with every step. I needed some air to clear my head. I remembered the old winter coats inside the depths of the armoire. I pulled one out and slid into it, slipped on my shoes, and moved to my bedroom door. I paused before the lock, leaning into the door to listen. Hearing nothing, I turned the key in the old-fashioned keyhole and cracked the door just wide enough to slip out.

Alone on the bed, the dog lifted his head, suddenly alert.

"It's okay. Go back to sleep," I whispered before easing out the door.

Enoch, who'd set himself the task of guarding me overnight, was slumped in a chair, snoring. I tiptoed past him, pausing only when he grumbled in his sleep. Then I tread like a ghost through the house, moving to the French doors inside the old ballroom. I opened the doors wide. A gust of wind whipped the curtains around me before swirling around the dying embers in the fireplace, which gave off a little puff of sparks.

I slipped onto the balcony. The air was sharp, like needles piercing my lungs, as I took a deep breath. When I turned to take in the view, I saw something unexpected: Michael.

He was engrossed in thought, sitting cross-legged inside an empty alcove that once held an urn or statue. Moonlight glowed against his skin, the shadows playing up his chiseled brow, the muscles splayed across his chest and the arc of every perfect rib. His wings were folded behind him, the feathers a million different shades of silver and white—iridescence that shifted as he did—reflecting back the glory of each soft moonbeam that struck them.

I knew I should turn away—give him privacy—but I couldn't. I couldn't tear my eyes from him. He was too beautiful.

As if he could read my thoughts, Michael said, "I'd prefer you to stay with me. If you want to."

Tongue-tied, I nodded. "I'd like that," I finally managed to choke out. I looked around for somewhere to sit and was about to take a seat at the small bistro table, but Michael swung his legs around and patted the space next to him.

"Come here. I'll make room."

I moved to the alcove and jumped up, awkward in my pajamas and coat. I pulled my knees in as tight as I could, tucking my feet in under me, trying to stay warm. The concrete surface was rough, and I shivered in spite of myself. I stared steadfastly ahead, acutely aware of the silence and space between us.

Michael finally spoke. "Couldn't sleep?"

"No," I admitted. "Too much going through my head."

"Me, too," he said, swinging his legs. "I finally gave up and put on these," he said. Out of the corner of my eye I saw him shrug his wings, giving off a shimmer of light. "I thought I'd be fine after the last few days, but no luck. It's funny how it works. It's like recharging my batteries, getting out of my human body for a while. Makes everything better." He sighed, and then whispered almost as if to himself, "Well, almost everything." I heard him settle back deeper into the alcove.

"Michael?" I began, hesitating. "What is going to happen to us?"

"Don't you mean you? What will happen to you?"

I said, turning to face him. "No," I whispered. "I meant us."

He was deep in the shadows now, so I couldn't see the expression on his face as he spoke.

"Through all of eternity I have always been so . . . certain. So certain of the right thing to do. How things would and should work. Everything made sense. God's will, my instincts—all of it was perfectly in synch, all of it focused on the eternal battle. Good versus evil. Protector of the people of God. I never doubted. And I never questioned. Not once did I think about, really think about, who it was I was saving—their hopes, their dreams, the people they loved. Nor did I think about the millions of people who *did* suffer. I paid no heed to the unlucky ones, the millennia of people who were forced to deal with their misfortunes without divine intervention. It was as God had ordained, and I never gave it a second thought.

"Until, in the quiet of the night, I heard a little girl crying in her sleep. I heard you, and my soul leapt at your voice. It was as if my heart recognized you, and I finally understood. Suddenly, humanity was more than just a mass of sinners, beloved by God and therefore warranting, if not deserving, my respect. Humanity was fragile. It was innocent. It was embodied in you, and you were so vulnerable, like a flower in a cesspool. I couldn't let him hurt you."

He paused, taking a deep breath, as if bracing himself before continuing his story.

"The man who abducted you was human trash. He was an addict and had no idea what he had gotten into. He probably had concocted some harebrained idea while he was high of ransoming you for drug money, but he had no capacity for carrying it out;

he didn't even know where to begin. He was panicking. If I hadn't done something, he would have hurt you. I was sure of it.

"So I waited until you fell back asleep in the motel room where he had hidden you. He was pacing, scratching at imaginary bugs and mumbling to himself, trying to get up his nerve to do whatever it was he was planning to do to you. Periodically, he would burst into tears. Then he'd scream at you, blaming you for his circumstances. I knew you were running out of time. I waited until you were asleep, and then I cornered him. I didn't want you to be scared when you woke up, so I forced him into the bathroom."

I thought back to the photos in my mother's album.

"You burned him alive."

"You've seen my sword. Its flame was the instrument of his death. He did not suffer."

I willed my brain to remember, but only bits and pieces of that night came back to me. Like the ravaged mosaics we'd seen in the churches of Istanbul, my memories were only a patchwork. The only thing of which I was certain was that Michael had truly been there. I saw him. It just took me tumbling off Stone Mountain to recognize him.

"Why are you telling me this?" I demanded. He leaned forward, his face emerging from the shadows. His eyes were shining with intensity.

"Because I don't know if you were already chosen to be the Bearer, or if by my helping you, I marked you myself. All I know is that I chose to save you. Because of that, my path has been changed forever, and I have put you in danger—I continue to put you in danger. And yet, I do not know what else to do."

Tears were gathering in eyes. He reached for my hand, blindly, gripping it against his chest.

"I like this—this feeling of being with you—a little too much for my liking, Hope. I could give myself over to it so easily. But I can't. I can't let myself love you anymore. It's too dangerous. For both of us."

Even as he said it, he winced, a visible sign of how his feelings for me brought down God's punishment.

His words cut me.

He stopped talking, letting the winds from the strait and the long, lonely calls of the midnight barges fill the silence. My mind rejected his words and searched for anything, anything at all, to bring him back to me, to make him talk, so we could both forget what he'd just said.

"Did you kill Ana's uncle, too, when you brought Ana and Jimena back to Mexico?" My tone was rough, accusing.

Michael laughed, a harsh, cold laugh that made me shrink back. "He deserved it. But no, I did not kill him. Ana asked me not to."

I gaped at him, astonished.

Michael raised his eyebrow. "What, you think he cannot be forgiven?"

"What he put them through was horrible. And they were family!" I protested, stunned at Ana's request.

"Yes. Family. Perhaps that is why Ana could not bring herself to condemn him in the end. So she asked that I simply teach him—and all the other traffickers—a lesson."

"What did you do?"

Michael grinned, the old wicked grin that meant he was up to no good.

"Go on, tell me."

"Ana told me where to find her uncle, at some seedy bar where he liked to play dominoes and watch dog fights. She brought me right to it. He was there, with a bunch of his cronies, way too flush with cash to be working any legitimate job. I waited for the right moment. When he was right in the middle of telling some big story, really the center of attention, I made my grand appearance. Full Archangel regalia, flaming sword, voice of God, the whole bit."

"I bet that was a hit," I prompted, envisioning the scene.

"It was total chaos," he chortled. "The whole place was tin and bits of leftover wood and cardboard, so in no time flat the entire building was on fire. Everyone darted around, screaming. I stood my ground, glorious as the sun, reciting the litany of pain that will be his to endure as he lives out his destiny, burning in Hell, unless he repents and puts an end to the trafficking. He fell to his knees, praying Hail Marys and promising to do anything I demanded."

"Then what?"

"Well, there is a big square right in the middle of town. At one end of it there is an old church with a giant crucifix on top. I scooped him and a couple of his buddies up and flew them around the square first, just to make sure they were good and terrified. Then I flew to the top of the church and mounted them on the crucifix, leaving them dangling there to think about what I had said. I carved into the stone of the church the chronicle of their crimes, using the flames of my sword to darken the rock, so that all could read and know of their guilt. I'm fairly certain that by the time I left, our trafficking friends weren't sure whether they should be more afraid of me or of the mob of angry townspeople that was going to come after them with their proverbial pitchforks."

"Did you go get the police then?"

Michael's face fell, his glee at recounting his tale gone. He regarded me sadly. "Hope," he said, gently, "the chief of police was right there. He's part of the trafficking ring. I tied him up right next to Ana's uncle."

The world was full of people who disappointed you, I thought bitterly. People you thought you could trust. People you turn to for help when you most need it, who then use your weakness against you, laughing about your gullibility and never hesitating to make the trade: your innocence for cold, hard cash. He probably never even gave it a second thought. At least now Ana and Jimena would know the truth.

I shivered as the blast from another passing ship lightly shook the glass panes of the door.

"You're cold. I shouldn't have kept you out here," Michael reproached. "Besides, Enoch will have my head. He's determined to keep you away from me. For your own good, I might add," he sighed.

"I'm not ready to go in," I protested through chattering teeth while I stifled a yawn. "I'll be fine."

"At least come here, where I can keep you warm." He surprised me by holding out his hand.

I hesitated, wondering how safe it was for me to be so close to him. I didn't have to explain.

"You're protected by your coat. Besides, haven't you noticed? As you've been absorbing my powers, you are becoming immune to the heat of my touch. You should be fine."

He extended his hand farther. I took it and slid across the alcove toward him.

"Come close, now," he instructed, pulling me tight into the crook of his arm. "These feathers are nice insulation." Gently, he folded a wing around me, enveloping me in its downy softness. The heat rising off Michael's bare skin coursed through me, warming me to my core. I was acutely aware of Michael's proximity, even if it was through my bulky coat.

"Go on, settle in," he urged. "You'll feel better."

I burrowed into his side, resting my head against his shoulder and wrapping my arms the best I could around his waist.

"Comfortable?" He asked.

"Mmmmmm. Yes. Though I'd trade the comfort for a flight with you," I added, gazing out over the rooftops. "One where I'm actually conscious. It would be quite a view."

He shook his head slightly. "Yes, it would. This is one of the most beautiful places in the world, with the skyline of the ancient city, the sparkling stars and lights, and the Bosphorus and the sea coming together. But I can't. I'm not sure I'm strong enough. With all the time I am spending in human form, I'm not at my strongest. My powers are a bit unpredictable right now."

Just another reason for me to feel guilty.

"Do you miss it? The flying?"

"I can't even begin to describe it. It is the closest I can ever get to feeling like my spirit form when I'm on Earth. All energy and light. And riding the air currents? Dive bombing through clouds?" A slight smile stole across his face, lighting up his eyes as he remembered his last flight. "There's nothing like it. Maybe someday I'll be able to show you."

I bit my lip, biting back the urge to question his maybe, and nestled in even closer. We sat there together, looking out at the twinkling stars, for what seemed like ages. I started to drift asleep when I felt the dusting of something cold on my nose.

"Snow," Michael whispered softly. "In April." I opened my eyes. Fat flakes were falling heavily around us.

He tilted my face, brushing it with his thumb. Little drops of melted snow followed in its wake.

"This weather . . ." he began, his voice a caress. "The last time I saw anything like it was during the reign of Constantine. The Bosphorus actually froze over. Maybe it's a sign." He ran his hands over my face and my arms, and then he looked at my hands.

"Your skin continues to heal," he said, wondrously. "It's not my imagination."

I nodded sleepily. "I thought so, too, but I wasn't sure. It doesn't hurt very much anymore, either."

I burrowed my head against his chest and sighed. "You never really answered my question," I mumbled.

"What question?" he replied, pulling me in tighter.

"What is going to happen to us?"

He didn't speak. Instead, he pulled my palm to his chest, splaying my fingers over its muscled expanse, covering my hand with his. There, in the beating of his heart, I heard his answer.

*I don't know, Hope. I don't know.*

Istanbul was soon just a smudge of darkness against the sea as we lifted off for Ireland. Michael had been strangely chipper—maybe because of the time and rest he'd been able to steal last night in his original form.

Despite this, Enoch insisted he keep Michael company in the cockpit. He was still miffed that I had snuck past him to be with Michael on the balcony.

"Better to keep you two separated. That stunt you pulled last night was dangerous, Hope. You cannot expect Michael to control his rages, especially since you are the cause of his pain. You cannot be alone with him. I can't keep you safe if you defy me."

"But, Enoch," I began, leaning into him conspiratorially, "I think his changing has stopped. Or maybe slowed down. I've only smelled the sulfur once since we got to Istanbul."

His face softened. Gently, he rested his hand on my cheek. "Dear Hope," he said. "We've been sheltering you from the worst. All the more reason for you to listen to me now."

Chastised and stunned, I plopped into one of the rear seats, alone.

"Besides," Enoch continued, trying to distract me, "you can use the time to work on the Prophecy again. There's got to be more to it than just finding this rock."

I looked at him, confused. "I don't understand why you can't just tell us, Enoch. You know what the Prophecy means. Why aren't you helping?"

My complaint startled him. Flustered, he shot back, "I can't tell you anything. You're the only one who can interpret it. You're the Bearer." When I began to argue with him, he turned and thumped his way down the aisle, back to the cockpit.

I made a face behind his back and grumbled in my seat, drumming my fingers in an impatient rhythm against the tabletop. When nobody emerged from the front after several minutes, I gave up and began rummaging in my ratty bag, looking for something to do.

The first thing my hand pulled out of the depths of the backpack was the book about bronze doors that the antiquarian forced us to buy. I looked at the window and confirmed there was, indeed, nothing to see from this altitude. Istanbul was gone. I felt a stab of guilt at having left behind my little stray. But Enoch and Michael insisted I couldn't bring a dog with us to Ireland, so we left him—and a big wad of cash—with a stranger at the airport who promised to take care of him.

I realized I'd not even given him a name and felt somehow that I'd let him down.

Doubtful I'd find anything of interest, I cracked open my book, the stiff spine resisting my intrusion until it gave with a slight pop, allowing me to flip through its untouched, creamy pages until I found the table of contents.

I ran my finger up from the bottom of the page, looking at the title of each chapter. Casting methods from the Middle Ages to Renaissance. Byzantine Manufacture and Influence. The Advent of Bronze Doors. Church doors and the Theme of the Gates of Heaven.

I stopped. The Gates of Heaven. I thought of the references to Heaven's Gate in the Prophecy. Coincidence?

Hurriedly, I flipped to the chapter and began reading, my eyes flying over the paragraphs, trying to absorb it all at once.

*In early church history, the doors of the church were seen both literally and figuratively as the entryway to eternal life . . . The image of the door as the gateway to the fountain of life and the summit of Heaven dates to as early as the year 1000 . . . Inscriptions carved above and around the doors reinforced this imagination of the church doors as a threshold to Heaven. They warned sinners not to attempt to enter unrepentant, while at the same time reminding sinners that through the sacrifice of Jesus Christ—who declared himself the Gateway into eternal life—salvation could be theirs.*

I flipped deeper into the chapter. Dozens of images of stern, stone-faced churches presented themselves to me. Translations of the doorway inscriptions surrounded each photo:

*This is the gate of the Lord, which is a church founded in honor of Saint Mary . . . How terrible is this place! This is no other but the house of God and the gate of Heaven.*

Each door was surrounded by incredible sculptures—Images of the Virgin Mary, a corona radiating around her head as she blessed those invoking her name. Monsters, gargoyles, and devils taunting the damned. Rows of saints, eyes rolling in agony or ecstasy as they contemplated their sacrifice and the promise of Heaven. Always above them sat a triumphant Christ, seated in Heaven and crowned in glory. The themes were the same, page after page of doorways, always equating Christ himself with the gateway to Heaven and forgiveness.

Then one photo caught my eye. It, too, showed a triumphant

Christ, crowned in Heaven, but it was different than the others. In this one, Jesus was seated near an angel bearing a shield. The angel was positioned side-by-side with Christ at the apex of the door, elevated above all other saints and even the Virgin Mary.

I read the translation: *You who are passing through, you who are coming to weep for your sins, pass through me, since I am the gate of life. I am the gate of life.*

I flipped to the Italianate chapter and began reading. *Taken as a whole, one can discern four major themes of bronze church doors in the eleventh and twelfth centuries, all centered around achieving Heaven . . . Four major pathways are highlighted by these doors' designs, each one offering the faithful a separate route to forgiveness and, therefore, entry through the Gates of Heaven to receive eternal life. These paths are, in turn, new birth in Christ through baptism (the primary route focused upon by most artisans), the intercession of the Virgin Mary and saints, the example of Popes and Bishops, and, finally, the guidance of the Archangel Michael.*

I reread the last sentence, incredulous. Here, in print, was a reference linking Michael directly to the Gates of Heaven. Hands shaking, I turned to the index, feverishly looking for mentions of Michael in doors. It was a short list.

The first church I turned to was Monte Sant'Angelo in Italy. I pored over the photos of the doors dedicated to Michael. They were exquisite, divided into more than twenty panels, all depicting angel-themed events from the Old and New Testament. It was the right-hand door that fascinated me. It focused on Michael's actions after Christ's birth, including various local miracles attributed to him. The text underscored: *The doors in Monte Sant'Angelo open the sanctuary to penitents and pilgrims, symbolically offering up the guidance and example of the Archangel as the path to Heaven.*

I turned to the next church listed—Hildesheim, the Church of

Saint Michael in Germany. I gasped, looking at the close-up photos of each panel in the doors. They seemed alive, in motion, the tension in each scene leaping off the page. They moved first through the book of Genesis—I saw the Creation of Eve, her introduction to Adam. More ominously, brought to life and captured in bronze, was the rejected sacrifice of Cain and his murder of his brother, Abel.

My breath caught in my throat. Michael's association with Cain and Abel was laid out for all to see, captured forever in the doorways of Hildesheim. A thought, still vague, began to form in the back of my mind.

I shoved the book aside and reached for the Bible I'd taken from the motel in Vegas. I knew the verse; I had memorized it as a child and heard it countless times in sermons. But I needed to see it for myself.

I pressed the tissue-thin pages of the book flat and began to read the words attributed to Jesus.

*I am the Gate. Whoever enters through me will be saved. They will come in and go out, and find pasture.*

"I am the Gate." Michael's voice, reading over my shoulder, made me jump.

He swung around the table and sat opposite me, lifting the books from my hands.

"You know, people debated that word, *gate*, for years. They always thought *gate* meant something to keep the bad things—wolves, thieves—out. But Jesus clearly spoke of sheep going in and out. His allegory of the Good Shepherd was meant to help his followers understand that through him, humans could overcome the Fall represented by original sin and ascend into Heaven, regaining God's presence. He took their human form, so he could sacrifice himself for their sins and give them a second chance. He was a gate for coming in."

I sat there, looking at him, unable to speak as I began to understand what all this meant. But Michael didn't notice my stunned silence. Instead, he began flipping through the Bible.

"Hey, I bet there's a book you don't know. See if you recognize this one:

*I was asleep, but my heart was awake. It is the voice of my beloved who knocks:*

*Open to me, my sister, my love,*

*My dove, my undefiled;*

*For my head is filled with dew, and my hair with the dampness of the night.*"

I looked at him, horrified, as he recited the words from Song of Songs. I clasped my hand over my mouth, pushing myself away from the table and stumbling down the aisle, dragging my backpack with me. But there was nowhere to go, nowhere to hide from the ugly truth. Nowhere but the bathroom.

I nearly broke down the door, fumbling to get in. Once inside, I locked the door and leaned against it, trying to block out what I knew.

The disconnected thoughts came rushing at me.

The jealousy of the angels. Michael's name and all its meanings, including the most important one, the one we'd mistaken for a question: *Who is like God?* The confusion expressed by humans over his true identity. The chapel in the Pantocrator, elevating him to equal status with Mary and Jesus and practically calling him a martyr. The churches and the gates, including gates that elevated Michael as a path to Heaven. The strange distinction he had among all the angels.

It was all there, the whole time. I began to shake.

"Hope? Hope, what is it? Are you okay in there?" He was shouting at me through the flimsy bathroom door.

I took deep breaths, trying to calm myself.

"Hope?" Michael's voice was insistent as he pounded on the door, making it shake. "Hope! I'm coming in there."

"No!" I cried. "No," I repeated, more steadily this time. Michael couldn't see me like this. "I'm just feeling airsick. I don't need you to come in." I forced a laugh, trying to sound light-hearted. "See? I'm feeling better already. I just need a little time. And you're wrong," I asserted, my voice trembling as I tried to distract him. "I know how your verse continues."

I closed my eyes and recited the words from memory. At first all I could manage was a hoarse whisper, but my voice lifted with the rhythm of the poetry:

"*My beloved thrust his hand in through the latch opening.*

*My heart pounded for him.*

*I rose up to open for my beloved. My hands dripped with myrrh,*

*My fingers with liquid myrrh, on the handles of the lock.*

*I opened to my beloved; but my beloved left; and had gone away.*"

Tears were streaming down my face. Even the verse he had chosen—even it told me what I didn't want to know, for it mentioned the unlocking of a gate, and myrrh. Myrrh, to anoint the dead.

I huddled on the floor, crying silently, until I heard Michael move away.

*What's all the drama?* Henri demanded.

I didn't respond.

*Are you mooning over him again? Is that what this is all about?*

I ignored Henri, knowing that if he kept to form he'd give up and go away, leaving me to my own thoughts. *Get out of my head. Get out of my head. Get out of my head*, I repeated to myself, over and over as I rocked back and forth inside the tiny bathroom.

I couldn't share this pain. It was too fresh.

The low hum of the engines was the only sound. Even my own gasping breaths abated, leaving me to sit, spent and squashed up against the door.

I knew I'd eventually have to come out of the bathroom. I heaved myself up off the floor and splashed the lukewarm water from the tap onto my face, patting it down with a thin cloth. I stared at myself in the mirror. Even in the dim light, my eyes looked swollen. I picked up my bag and poked my head out to make sure Michael was back in the cockpit. Silently, I stole back to my seat, where I found Michael had left my Bible.

Fingers shaking, I picked it up and turned back to the verse. Again, I didn't really need to read it; I already knew what it said. But I wanted to see it there, on the page, stark and cold as the silent churches of Istanbul.

> *I am the gate; whoever enters through me will be saved. He will come in and go out, and find pasture. The thief comes only to steal and kill and destroy; I have come that they may have life, and have it to the full. I am the good shepherd. The good shepherd lays down his life for the sheep.*

I placed the book facedown on the table and dug in my bag, until my fingers felt the scrap of paper and drew it out. It was wrinkled and worn. I smoothed it out on the table, hoping against hope that the words of the Prophecy had somehow changed. But they were just as I remembered them:

*With this Key, the Bearer shall come and the Gate shall open, spilling out Heaven's glory, and letting those desirous amongst you to ascend once more.*

I started crying again.

Michael is the Gate. He is marked for sacrifice, his death the way the Fallen Angels will regain Heaven—but through redemption, not war.

Michael is the Gate. And he doesn't know it.

# seven

## IRELAND

We'd been in Ireland for three days. For three days, the winds howled and the rain lashed the streets. For three days, we found the tourist ferries shuttered, the visitor center practically deserted. For three days, we haunted it anyway, desperate to find a way to the pile of rock that sometimes, when the rain lifted, would come into view a few miles off the coast.

For three days, I refused to speak to Michael—no more than a few words at a time—because I didn't know what to say. I couldn't possibly bring myself to utter the only thing that mattered.

For three days, I cried myself to sleep.

We were hollowed out, all three of us—jittery, tired, and afraid of what was coming next—be it a trafficker, a Fallen Angel, or simply what had been destined. With nothing else to do, we paced among the displays of the visitor's center, numbly taking in brochures of the island's flora and fauna we could not see, frustrated again by the multiple exhibits that were closed for repairs or otherwise inoperable. I moved mechanically, shoving my desperation deep inside, forcing my mind to fill with meaningless trivia, watchful and alert that I not give away anything, not even—or maybe especially—to Henri.

All the while, through the clouds of mist, the Skellig taunted us, daring us to come.

"There's got to be a way out there," Enoch muttered, pulling at the collar of his too-tight fisherman's sweater. He paced noisily around the room, brandishing his cane as if he might kill someone with it. "It's not right, this weather. Not this time of year."

Even Enoch feels it, I thought to myself as I turned to a display on seals. Even he can sense something is wrong.

*It doesn't take a genius to figure out that sitting in this dump is a waste of time.*

I smiled wistfully. "Good old Henri," I whispered. "Always there to lift my spirits."

"I'm going to talk to the lady in the pub," Michael announced, uncoiling his lithe body from the corner in which he'd been slumped for most of the afternoon. "There's got to be someone who's not afraid to take us out there."

"It's not fear, lad, its common sense," the curator tutted at him from her chair against the wall, never bothering to look up from her knitting. "Storms like this, you won't even get past the rocks outside the bay. Waves have been known to reach out of the sea like bony fingers of witches grasping for your life, rising all the way to the top of the Skellig in a fury of icy water and spray before they dash themselves out on the rocks. Broke the windows out of the lighthouse, they did. T'was years ago, true, but we all remember that, now."

She tucked her needles into the ball of yarn in her lap and folded her work away neatly. Rising up from her seat, she smoothed her prim knit suit with her hand and peered over her reading glasses to skewer Michael with a stern look.

"Only a fool would be takin' you out in weather like this. A fool or a drunk. Wouldn't be doing you any favors if he did." With that, she marched out of the room, her unfinished handiwork tucked under her arm.

"That didn't sound very promising," Michael muttered. "She's probably warned off the whole town not to take us by now."

"Look on the bright side," Enoch said. His eyes seemed to crinkle into a smile behind the reflection of his sunglasses. "There must be a fool, or a drunk, or maybe both, since she was so ready to mention it. Perhaps I can sweet-talk a name out of her."

Michael arched a brow. "Sweet-talk her? You?"

Enoch grinned, forcing himself to take on a sprightly air that didn't quite match the grayness of the day. "Someone's got to do it. Besides, she reminds me of my favorite wife. You go to the pub, and I'll work on her. A spot of tea might make her a little friendlier."

Michael shrugged and watched with wry amusement while Enoch sauntered awkwardly after the curator, a whistle on his lips, his cane almost an afterthought, leaving us to wonder just how many wives he'd had when he was human.

"Are you coming with me, then?" Michael asked so quietly I wasn't sure I'd heard him. I looked up to see him staring at me intently, his icy eyes a cipher. The hot sting of embarrassment crept up my neck, snaking its telltale pink stain across my face. I turned my back to Michael, leaning against the glass case. It was cool and smooth underneath my cheek.

"No, I think I'll stay here," I answered, refusing to look at him.

"And do what?" he asked, irritated.

I kept staring at the glass steadfastly, my eyes drifting down the case to the video where jellyfish and anemones danced in the current, softly out of focus.

"Maybe the projector will be fixed, and I can watch the film in the auditorium. The one about the history of the monastery."

"They said it's been broken for weeks. It won't be fixed today." He'd moved up behind me. He was leaning against the wall, his arm stretched above me, his body so close I could feel his heat radiating and enveloping me. I closed my eyes, breathing in his scent and letting myself imagine, for just a second, that we were in a sunny meadow instead of on this forbidding, wet stretch of seacoast.

"Do you not want to go to the Skellig? Is this not the place after all?"

I closed my eyes even tighter, listening to the thrumming in my body, the pull, like the tides, that was drawing me out to sea at the same time it was urging me to settle back into Michael's arms.

Instead, I just sighed.

"No," I conceded. "It's where we need to go. I can feel it."

"Then I don't understand. Hope," he demanded, placing a firm hand on my shoulder and forcing me around to face him. When I kept my eyes fixed on the time-worn industrial carpet, he took my chin in his fingers and forced me to look at him. My body leapt at his touch while my heart sank. His eyes were hard, unforgiving.

"Why won't you talk to me?"

I pushed his hand away. "I'll come with you," I said, stiffly, and made for the exit of the center. "We'd best go back to Portmagee."

The cold air stunned us both into silence. I kept a brisk pace, not waiting for Michael to catch up. I could feel his eyes boring a hole into the space between my shoulder blades. I could almost hear his mind calculating the ways he could force me to speak. I squared my shoulders and strode on, wincing as the wind chapped my face, focusing on the soft crunch of gravel under our feet, and trying to maintain the distance between us as we walked along the side of the road back to town.

The sky was already dark as we approached the cozy village nestled against the coast. Her buildings formed a bright dash of primary color against the somber backdrop of shadowed emerald hills that rolled away from the water, lights twinkling against the storm. Boats huddled in the port, awaiting a better day. It was here that we were staying, and from here we would depart, if we could ever find someone to take us out to the Skellig.

I paused at the edge of the water, watching the boats bob, their ropes straining as the rough water tested their moorings.

"There, on the other side. That place looks busy enough," Michael shouted above the wind as he brushed by me.

I turned to look. There was a pub mere steps from the pier. Michael was already crossing over to it.

I looked back longingly at the boardwalk that jutted into the harbor. It was deserted, the fishermen and tour guides having fled inside for shelter. I wanted nothing but to sit out among the boats, the shrieking wind and creak of wood my only companions.

Reluctantly, I followed Michael across the street.

The windows glowed with a welcoming light, but the cozy invitation did not dispel the dread I felt as we crossed the threshold into the pub. It was packed, a stream of chatter rising and falling around us. We pushed our way through the crowd to the counter. Michael pushed a stool at me as we took our place at the bar.

"Now what?" I asked, not sure what our plan was.

"We watch," Michael responded grimly. "Watch and wait." He bowed his head over his hands, which he clutched together on top of the bar counter almost as if in prayer. As he perched on the stool, I could see how our quest was taking its toll on him. The shadows under his eyes looked like bruises now. The ropey veins in his neck and hands made his lean body seem gaunt.

I looked away, guiltily, hoping for something to distract me. I was grateful for the steady hum of camaraderie that filled the place. I let it lull me, hoping it would blanket over the never-ending monologue that was running through my head.

*If you leave, he will be safe.*

*If you leave, he will be safe.*

*If you leave, he will be safe.*

I brushed away the tear that was forming in the corner of my eye. If I ran away now, before we found the Key, Michael might be safe, at least temporarily—but at what cost to everybody else?

"What'll you be having, then?" The bartender demanded, interrupting my thoughts.

"Whiskey, straight up, the best you have," Michael ordered without hesitation. "She'll have a cider."

The bartender wiped a glass dry, his massive hand barely able to fit the cloth inside the rim.

"Best I have?" he mused, a twinkle in his eye as he slid the glass under the counter and threw the towel over his shoulder in one graceful move. "We could debate that into the wee hours. But I have something you might like."

He turned away and busied himself among the bottles.

"Whiskey?" I asked, turning to Michael with a skeptical eye.

"I'm of age," Michael answered drily. "In case you hadn't noticed."

"I noticed," I whispered. A smile tugged at the corners of Michael's mouth, as he raised an eyebrow, reading more into my response than I meant. I blushed as he swept me with a rakish look.

The bartender slid a tall glass of pale gold liquid before me, saving me from further embarrassment "Your cider, miss. Not too strong, but it should shore you up. As for you," he said with a nod to Michael, "You'll have to tell me what you think of this."

He stood the short tumbler of amber reverentially in front of Michael. It seemed to glow, its liquid light reflecting off the polished wood of the bar, the facets of the cut crystal twinkling.

Michael fingered the glass appreciatively. "It's beautiful," he murmured. "Look at that color. It's like caramel."

"That she is," the bartender agreed with a knowing nod. "But many a whiskey turns out to be like a beautiful woman, pretty to look at but nasty inside. Taste her and tell me if this one is worth the name of whiskey." He crossed his arms across his broad chest, watching Michael with an expert eye.

Michael picked up the glass and held it to the light. Its glow deepened. He drew it to his nose and inhaled deeply, once, then again, closing his eyes.

"It smells of citrus and honey," he breathed, sighing. "Maybe some apricot."

"Aye, it should," the man nodded ever so slightly, granting Michael a grudging respect. "Now give it a try."

Michael tilted the glass back, gulping some down. I watched, entranced by the working of his jaw as he seemed to chew the whiskey, and then the bobbing of his Adam's apple as he swallowed it down. He made a slight grimace as he slammed the glass down on the counter. A little wave of whiskey sloshed over the edge.

"Sour finish," he said, wiping his mouth with his sleeve. "Thin."

The barkeep nodded sagely. "So they tell me. She is the most premium of whiskeys—the most expensive barrels, the most expensive ingredients—and yet she leaves a bitter taste with all who try her."

Michael picked up the glass, tilting it back and forth, side to side, staring at the amber liquid as if hoping to see something emerge from its depths. With a hint of disappointment, he shrugged and wrinkled his nose, downing the rest of his drink in one gulp.

His body shivered as if to chase away the bad taste. He put the glass down, shoving it away with disgust.

"What is it?"

The bartender whisked away the glass that Michael had drained, giving me a wink, as he replaced it discreetly with our check and began wiping off our spot.

"It's named The Wild Geese. For the Irish heroes who fled our land and took to France, establishing themselves there when desperation left them no choice. A pretty name, but not such a pretty story. That's the plight of us Irish, is it not? The diaspora and all that. But you've not come here for sad stories of Ireland. You look as if you have a sad tale all your own." The bartender fixed an eye upon Michael, waiting for his answer.

Michael seemed to sag under the reminder of his burden. "We need someone to take us to the Skellig."

The bartender busied himself, straightening the garnishes and barware under the counter as he leaned his head, indicating Michael should continue. Michael and I both shifted in our seats, leaning in. Maybe this was our chance.

"We have been waiting here for days. Nobody seems willing to take us," Michael continued.

The bartender took out a rag and began polishing away an imaginary stain on the wood. "It's a dangerous thing, taking a ship out in these waters, under normal circumstances. You mix in this strange weather, and it becomes nigh on impossible."

Michael slumped on the stool. "So we've been told. We just hoped there might be someone willing to make . . . an exception."

The bartender cocked an eyebrow, looking up at Michael with a gentle admonishment. "You're not asking for an exception. You're asking for a risk. A chance. You must have something mighty precious to do if you cannot wait for the storms to subside before you get yourselves to the Skellig."

Suddenly, he shifted his gaze to me, waiting for an answer. I felt my skin deepen into a ruby blush as he pinned me down with his bright green eyes.

"We're . . . pilgrims of sort," I said, apologetically, fighting the urge to look away. How else could I put it?

He nodded wisely, tucking his dishcloth into his apron ties. "I thought as much. A brother and sister, I gather. Probably here to pray for your ma and da, or some such thing. It's noble, it is. Touching. But no one here will brave these seas for you, that I can promise." He looked at my untouched glass of cider, my downcrest face, and he softened.

"Ah, lass, it will happen soon enough. You'll get to your island and say your prayers and the Good Lord will hear them, too, I reckon."

He took the bill from the counter and ripped it up. "This one is on me, then. To your quest. May the Lord hear your prayers." He nodded and left us to tend to his other patrons.

I pushed my glass around on the polished wood, wondering what we should do now. The bartender's promise scared me.

What should I pray for, if God would hear me?

At this point, I didn't know.

The crowd roared, cheering the local team whose exploits were being televised in all corners of the pub. Glasses clinked together in celebration, and ruddy men hugged and shouted with joy. Their heartfelt camaraderie—something that seemed welcoming when we entered the pub only a few minutes before—reminded me now of how isolated I had made myself.

I snuck a glance at Michael. The dark shadows were accusing

stains on his paper-thin skin. He was gripping his hands together so tightly that his knuckles were turning white. I sank lower into my stool, trailing my finger through the tiny puddle of condensation pooling around my cider.

I had to do something.

I couldn't leave—there was too much at stake for the rest of the world. But I couldn't let Michael suffer in pain. I had to do something to get us onto that island and find the Key—but what?

I closed my eyes, willing the answer to come to me.

The bustle of the bar faded away, turning into white noise. Behind my eyes, I could feel it; I could hear it—the buzzing of a thousand whispers, voices that carried the answer in their words. The harder I tried to understand them, though, the more elusive they became. I'd think I'd grasped a word, rising from the hum like a silver fish surfacing in a stream, only to lose my grasp of it as it morphed into shapeless mutterings, twisting away from me to let other, just as meaningless, words rise in its place.

"Hope."

I opened my eyes, startled.

Michael was standing next to me, stilling my hand with his own. I jerked away, confused, my fingers burning where he touched me.

He looked worriedly at me, trying to explain. "You . . ." Unable to find the words, he simply slid his hand away from where it rested on the bar.

There, gouged through the varnish deep into the wood, were three letters: DEL.

"You wouldn't stop. It was like you were in a trance," he said quietly before sliding a napkin over my act of vandalism. "Does that mean anything to you?"

I shook my head, numb. I lifted my fingers to inspect them, finding little bits of varnished wood and grit under my nail.

"Let's get you out of here," Michael insisted, hustling me up from the stool before I could protest.

"Wait," I said, pushing away from him and straining over his shoulders to scan the crowd, unsure of what I was looking for.

The buzzing in my head faded in and out as I glanced around.

He was here, the man who would take us to the Skellig.

Determined, I looked about in earnest. The sounds seemed to be coming from everywhere, now, pulling me forward and urging me on. I pushed away from Michael and through the crowd of drinkers, letting my body follow where the voices took me. The rowdy fans yelled out again, arguing with the television over a bad call, their angry shouts drowning out my voices. I screwed my eyes shut and held my ears, trying to find the voices again in the din.

There. Barely there—only a thread for me to hang onto—but there, nonetheless. I opened my eyes and kept pushing to the back of the building, past the kitchen and the empty music room, out the back door into the cold night air.

The whispering stopped.

A grizzled old man sat by himself, rings of smoke from his pipe encircling his head. He was dressed for the sea in heavy woolens and a well-worn slicker. He leaned back in his hard wooden chair against the side of the pub, arms crossed over his chest, looking as if he were waiting for somebody. He pulled the pipe out of his mouth and looked me up and down.

I stepped forward, letting the wooden door slam heavily behind me.

"I hear you are in need of a boat to the Skellig," he stated, as if it were a known fact, not a question.

I nodded before clearing my throat. "Yes."

He pointed at me with the stem of his pipe while he spoke.

"I'll require double payment, cash, and I won't guarantee you a landing. But I can take you out in the morning. If you're still needin' to go." He raised his bushy eyebrows, waiting for my answer.

I nodded vehemently. "Yes. Very much."

"Good," he grunted, clamping his pipe back in his mouth. "Be at the pier before eight, or the harbor master may not let us slip out." He looked me over again before continuing with a hint of disapproval. "You'll need to bundle up. I presume you'll be climbin' to the monastery?" He didn't wait for me to answer. "Wear layers and rain gear and good shoes. Tell that beau of yours the same."

"He's not my boyfriend!" I protested, glad for the cover of darkness to hide my blush.

He grunted, not bothering to hide his disbelief. "Then why is he hovering there, in the shadows, keepin' an eye on your fair face?" I looked back to the doorway from which I'd emerged and sure enough, Michael was standing there in the dark, just outside the pool of light that spilled from the lamppost, his body tense as if ready for a fight. I didn't have time to wonder how he'd slipped behind me, unnoticed, because the man kept giving me orders.

"Just be there," he continued. "You'll see my boat. Remember, before eight. With cash."

He seemed to be finished then, settling back into his chair with his pipe, a look of satisfaction on his weather-beaten face.

"But, how do I know which boat is yours?" I asked, confused.

Another cheer roared out from the pub behind us. His gruff voice cut through the noise as he answered.

"Her name is the Wild Goose. And I'm Del."

~

We gulped our coffee down on the way to the dock the next morning, holding the steaming cups in our wind-chapped hands, grateful for the bit of warmth. We piled on as much clothing as we could to ward off the chill. I had a wad of cash stuffed into my pocket, ready to hand it over to Del, so he could get us on our way.

As adamant as I'd been that we needed to get out to the island, the instant I stepped onto the pier, I felt like I was walking a gang-plank. I looked over the edge; the gray water boiled around us, whipped into a frenzy by the unrelenting weather.

"Nice day," Enoch mumbled to nobody in particular as he juggled his coffee and cane.

We passed row after row of cruisers and ferries, designed to carry tourists in relative comfort over the treacherous waters for a glimpse of the seals and birds that basked around the Skellig. Spacious and sturdy, they looked fit enough to face the roughest seas. Surely, the Wild Goose was among these.

But no, as our boots trudged up and down the docks, there was no sign of her. The longer we looked, the more I began to fear that safe, modern transport was not to be our lot. And when we finally found the Wild Goose, my heart sank.

She looked like a fishing trawler, worn and dingy. There was no heated cabin with coffee service; indeed, there probably was no heat at all. Above decks, in fact, there was almost nothing beyond the dilapidated, leaning pile of wood and Plexiglas that seemed to serve as the captain's quarters and hold a bunch of nets and ropes.

*Wild Goose. More like wild goose chase*, Henri muttered, and I cringed.

Del poked his head out of the shack. "I was wonderin' if you'd changed your minds. Come aboard, then, quickly." He waved us on, pointing out the plank as he bounded out of the shed.

We scurried on, careful of the scattered things we found on deck.

The engine was already running in coughs and spurts. Del

pulled the plank aboard behind us, slamming the gate and rushing about to untie the ropes that held the Wild Goose to the dock. With alarm, I realized there were no other crew members.

"There will be some papers you need to sign. You'll find them on a clipboard in the wheelhouse. Tuck your payment under the clip when you've finished, and we'll be off."

I glanced up at the sky—roiling with black, angry clouds.

"Hurry now, missy," Del added impatiently, pointing me toward the shed. "Hurry or you'll be missing your chance to leave."

Wordlessly, Michael and Enoch followed me into the wheelhouse. We slammed the door shut behind us, and the little building trembled. I realized the walls, ramshackle as they might be, did an effective job of blocking out the wind. I looked around for the papers Del wanted us to sign. His charts were spread all around, along with a compass and a few other instruments I didn't recognize, all heaped upon a rickety table.

"Old school," Enoch nodded appreciatively as he looked around the tiny space. "He'll be able to handle this kind of weather."

"I don't know," Michael responded warily. He looked over the instruments. "He doesn't seem to have much modern technology on this boat. No radar, no depth finders."

A gust of wind ruffled the maps as Del stepped back inside to join us. "Don't need it," he asserted, tapping his head. "Have it all up here. I was born on these waters, have made my whole life on them. If I can't guide you safe, nobody can." He reached under one of the charts and pulled out his clipboard, thrusting it toward me.

"Sign these now, while I steer us out."

The clipboard was stacked with waivers. I pulled out the pen that was tucked under the clip and started scanning the clauses.

Not guaranteed for landing. That one he'd already mentioned. The others gave me pause: Not responsible for death or injury from falling overboard. Not responsible for crashing upon the rocks in foul weather. Not an actual guide to the Skellig . . . so therefore not responsible if, through poor footing, avalanche, or other mishap, we plunge from the rocks.

*Is this really necessary?* Henri's exasperated voice suddenly filled my head. *This is a worse idea than that desert hike you took in Las Vegas. It might rank up there with visiting those Chinese gamblers. Or kissing Michael,* he said archly.

*Leave me alone*, I thought to myself, my lips jutting into an irritated pout. *Go back to wherever you came from. It's not like you're in any danger*. I signed my name with a flourish, shoving the wad of bills under the clip before passing it all to Enoch.

*Suit yourself,* Henri shot back, amused. *Just don't expect any help from me. You'll have to rely on lover boy over there. Oh, but he's not quite himself these days, is he?*

Exasperated, I turned to the tiny door. "It's too crowded in here," I announced. "I'm going to wait on deck."

Before anyone could protest, I threw myself out into the cold.

We'd already cleared the shelter of the harbor and were headed out to open sea. The waves tossed the boat, which seemed even smaller now that it was alone on the water. Ahead of us, a cluster of black rocks jutted up. White-capped waves swirled and crashed around it, sometimes completely engulfing the entire mass.

The boat rocked, falling into the troughs of the waves, then laboring up a new crest. I lurched, grabbing onto the rail to keep myself from tumbling overboard. Over and over again, we plunged and climbed, riding the waves, leaving my stomach behind with every movement.

The pile of black rock was closer now, and it seemed as if we would crash right into it, shattering the tiny boat into splinters as the waves spent themselves upon the harsh stone edges. It was so close now it seemed impossible to miss it. But at the last minute, Del turned the boat and we skimmed by, another surge of water pushing us past the treacherous pile.

I turned back and scanned the shore behind us. We were far away from the pier now. I squinted ahead into the gray sky, scanning the horizon, but despite the distance we'd made, the Skellig seemed no closer. It stood, resolute, daring anyone to violate its isolation. Its smaller companion—an inhospitable fortress, never occupied by humankind—rose to the side, almost as foreboding.

I made my way down the deck, clinging to anything I could find to hold me steady. The spray of the waves was soaking me through, but I needed to get out here. I needed to be as close as I could to the Skellig.

"Hope!"

I looked over my shoulder to see Enoch leaning hard onto his cane, one hand on the side of the boat, struggling his way down the deck toward me. His face had a green tint to it. Sensing he had my attention, he stopped and waved me in before cupping a hand around his mouth to shout.

"Del wants you inside. Now!"

He stood there, clutching some old pulleys and gear, waiting for me to walk back. Reluctantly, I started lurching my way back to the wheelhouse. When I got close to Enoch, he wrapped an arm around me and bent in to explain.

"He wants to plan our landing and needs all of us to listen."

I nodded, imagining that getting the boat to dock in this weather would not be an easy task.

Inside, Del had stripped out of his top-most slicker. He had a waterproof jacket on, its sleeves pushed up high. He was flushed—probably from the mini heater he'd propped up in the corner.

"Good, now I'll only have to say it once," he said, noting my arrival with a nod. "See here?" He pointed on his chart to what looked like the backside of the Skellig. "There are three places we could land on the Skellig, but in this weather, the only one we can chance is this here. It will be nasty, with these waves. We'll need to catch the dock just so, or we'll end up a pile of timber on the rocks. And there will be no one there to help us. I'll need you to crew while I guide her in."

"What do you mean?" I asked apprehensively.

Del explained patiently. "You'll all three need to be on deck with the ropes, so we can lash her tight. Might need you to jump right over the side to do it. It's a dangerous task, it is, but with no other aboard we have no choice."

"I'm not so sure that's a good idea," Michael began. He was looking at Enoch, no doubt imagining our portly friend falling between the dock and the boat as he attempted to jump ashore.

"We'll do it," I interrupted, shooting Michael a silencing look. "But Enoch will need to stay on the deck. It will be too hard with him and the cane. Michael and I will handle the ropes."

Enoch shrugged, apparently just fine with staying off the wind-strafed deck during our landing.

"Good lass," Del said, approvingly. "I know you will do it just fine." He reached into a little tin and began repacking his pipe with tobacco, one hand still somehow managing to balance the wheel, his eyes never leaving the horizon.

"'Tis a pity you're not here in better times. Strange weather this is; started just before your arrival, if I understand your travels properly. Normally, this would be the start of the spring season. The entire Little Skellig would be covered in gannets—so many of the birds that the island itself looks like a glowing expanse of white marble. But look at it now. Dead. Black. Nothing to be seen, not even a wisp of spurrey popping up between the rocks. I'd wager the puffins will be missing on the big Skellig, too, but we'll find out soon enough."

He was chewing on the stem of his unlit pipe, every once in a while giving the wheel a violent turn to balance the tiny boat atop the whitecaps.

"You'll be climbing to the monastery, won't you?" He continued, never taking his gaze from the waters ahead.

Michael looked at me, questioning. I nodded, but it barely mattered. Del was launching himself into a tale while he had a captive audience.

"The monastery is an amazing place, that it is. D'you know how it came to be there, perched high on the rock? Monks sailed from the mainland in a tiny boat made out of animal hides. They were on a quest, a quest of the spirit, and they let the boat carry them where it may, allowing the whims of the currents and tides to steer the boat to whatever God had in store for them. They had no goal in mind but to sacrifice themselves, martyrs to a person, martyrs in a self-imposed banishment from the green and lush land on which they'd been raised. They were cast upon the Skellig, surrounded by fog and wind and not much else. They thought it a most wondrous sight, I imagine, a lonely place, perfect for their prayers and fasting. So they set about building upon the rock. They even had to carve out their own stairs to reach the top, and only then could they build their tiny home, clinging to the cliffs, shrinking away from the howling wind, shrinking away from all worldly things."

Cast about, directionless, waiting for the fate God had in store for them. I thought of my mom and dad, waiting for me back home, and felt a strange twinge of recognition as Del described the ancient monks' journey.

"It was a lonely existence. No ships sailed here to replenish their wares. They had to scrabble the rock for the little it would yield and pull what bounty they could from the sea. It was a good thing, I think, that they were a fasting band of brothers, given to strictness in their Order, for the less stout-hearted might not have lasted. As it was, for centuries they lived there and died there, embracing the loneliness and praying for our souls. Praying for the Good Lord to take them away, too, I reckon."

He paused for just a moment to manage the boat while it lurched into a big trough of sea. We grabbed the sides of the shelter and leaned back for support, feeling queasy.

Del continued, unperturbed. "They had their excitement, though, I daresay. There were shipwrecks aplenty, with poor souls to save and goods to pull from the water. The occasional penitent on pilgrimage, sent to the good brothers to seek forgiveness and salvation. And then there was the apparition of the blessed Michael."

My ears perked up. I shot a glance to Michael, but his face betrayed nothing. He just continued to listen intently, keeping a watchful eye outside on the sea.

"I cannot recall when that was, but when the angel appeared, the monks built a special font in his name, a font for the holy water. And it was from then on that the island was known as Skellig Michael."

"Del," I pressed, intrigued. "How do you know that Saint Michael appeared?"

"As I know all else, girl. It has been handed down to me through the ages by my people. It is common knowledge enough, I would say, though there is some debate as to whether he actually appeared or perhaps just sent a sign." Del brushed aside my question and kept on with his story. "Either way, it was a change to the routine of the monks. And more change came later, when the whole coast came under attack by the Viking horde. Their longboats sailed the rough seas at will, seemingly unstoppable in their quest for gold and slaves. Soon, even the Skellig, thought to be impenetrable, was attacked. More than once it happened, each time bringing the monastery closer to its end. It is written in the Annals of Inisfallen that the marauders even kidnapped and starved the prior, Etgal. They left him standing alone on a rock in the middle of the sea, where all the monks could watch him waste away.

"And so it was, bit by bit, that the monastery began to send its brothers away, along with the little treasure it had, to keep it safe, until sometime in the eleven or twelve hundreds the last of them slipped away. They left their gravestones and their buildings, abandoning their home to the puffins and the wind."

I shivered. What if the sign attributed to Michael wasn't a sign at all, but the arrival of the rock—the rock that Cain used to kill Abel—the very relic we were seeking? Would it still be here? Or had it been taken for safekeeping along with whatever other treasures the monks had spirited away?

"The Skellig has a fascinating history," Del said, winding up his tale. "She would just as soon chew up your boat and spit it out as she would shelter the birds and the men who clung to her for life. You cannot know which Skellig you get on any given day. As for us, we will find out soon enough, for we're nearly there. Look."

I peered through the Plexiglas to where he was pointing. The boat was headed for a sheer cliff wall that blocked everything else from view.

"Aye, there she is. A monster rock. If God is good, we'll be able to get you ashore. You two bundle up and put on your life jackets," Del added briskly. "You'll be needed on the deck in just a moment."

We began piling back into our outerwear, preparing ourselves for the spray and wind that would lash at us. As I leaned over to tuck my pant leg into my boot, I whispered to Michael.

"You didn't tell me you'd shown yourself here."

His forehead crumpled derisively. "That's because I never did. He's just spreading old wives' tales."

My heart thudded as I stood up. It had to have been the rock that came to the Skellig and set off the tales of old. I just knew it. I turned and pressed myself against the Plexiglas to peer at the stark, bald stone that jutted up from the sea, and my body seemed to thrum in anticipation. This is it, I thought. This is where we'll find the Key.

As if he were reading my thoughts, Michael gently interrupted me. "First, we'll need to get safely off this boat."

I nodded and pushed through the door, back onto the deck, Michael coming behind me. "You stay here and shout out what Del needs us to do. I don't want him to get distracted from his navigating," Michael told Enoch over his shoulder.

The wind had shifted. It was a gale now, driving us away from the tiny bit of shore that had been carved out of the stone. We felt a lurch as Del shifted the motor into a higher gear, trying to power our way in.

We leaned into the storm, slowly making our way toward the bow, the puffy life jackets making us awkward and slow, like toddlers taking their first tentative steps. The ropes were coiled, waiting. I braced myself as the boat rose and fell between white-capped waves that crashed against us, daring us to come any farther.

"Ready now," Enoch yelled, leaning out from the wheelhouse door. "He's going to ride the next wave into the dock and put the engine in reverse, so we don't crash. You jump ashore and start tying us off, if you can."

I eyed the dock warily. Its wood looked like mere matchsticks compared to the force of nature we were dealing with. But we had no choice, if we wanted to get to the monastery.

"Now!" Del shouted.

All at once, the steady thrum of the motor shifted and cut out.

We were atop a wave, perched for an instant high above the dock. Before I could think, I wrapped the rope around my hand and flung myself overboard.

I landed with a thud, rolling onto my side on the water-slicked wood. Michael fell next to me. We scrambled up.

The engines throbbed to life, pulling the boat away from the dock just as the waves were crashing it in. In the balance of time, we wrapped the rope around the metal hooks, lashing them as tightly as we could. The Wild Goose crashed against the boards, throwing up icy water and causing the dock to give out a great groan, before she settled in next to it.

"Get back," Michael said, pushing me behind him as if he were unsure if the boat would stay put. Annoyed, I stepped aside.

"It's fine, Michael. We did it. The boat is safe and so are we." I didn't wait for his answer but carefully picked my way down the tiny pier to the Skellig, keeping an eye out for gaps in the worn planks.

Behind me, I heard the engine cut out, this time for good. The men shouted, but the wind muffled their sound, so I couldn't hear what they were saying. I didn't care, though. I was listening in awe to the shrieking gale and staring up at the bleak pile of rock, imagining what it would have been like to live here, knowing you would never, ever leave. Stairs had been carved into the sheer face of the island, beckoning pilgrims upward. I knew from the visitors' center that the climb was long and steep. I was eager to go, the pull of the Skellig insistent, demanding that I forge ahead.

I started toward the steps, shrugging out of the bulky life jacket and letting it fall to the ground. A heavy hand on my shoulder stopped and turned me. "Together," Michael insisted. "We climb together."

I looked over his shoulder. "Where's Enoch?"

Michael grimaced. "Del insisted they both stay. He's afraid

Enoch is in no condition to climb, and he's worried about his boat. So they will stay here and make sure the boat is safe while we go up to the monastery." He gave me a grave look. "Hope, it is very dangerous up here. Some of the trails have collapsed, and the steps themselves are only inches deep. A single gust of wind could knock you off the edge. You have to give all your concentration to the climb. And we have to stick together. Agreed?" He squeezed my shoulder tightly, concern for me shadowing his blue eyes gray.

I nodded, his gaunt face a reminder that I was running out of time. I turned to lead the way up the steps.

Almost immediately, a light rain began falling on the Skellig, adding its misty mix to the wetness left behind by the hammering waves. The steps were slick, not porous enough to drain the water. I carefully reached ahead, using my hands to balance as I began to climb.

We'd not gone far when I saw a strange sight. Not far from where we stood, a set of parallel steps had been carved into the rock. But they started in the middle of nowhere and ended, just as abruptly, with no landing or escape.

"Stairs to nowhere," Michael muttered behind me.

I looked away, the sight of the mysterious staircase unsettling me. I quieted my mind, focusing on the cracks in the dark stone as we pushed ahead. We were creeping now, careful not to slip, clinging to the rocks when the winds gusted. When I dared to steal a glance about me, I saw nothing but more rock. No plants. No birds. Nothing. It was utter desolation.

The quiet rain eventually stopped. We climbed our way around the island for what seemed like hours before finally emerging onto a little terrace. Man-made walls of stone loomed out of the earth, funneling us toward a slight opening. Lower walls ran out like guardrails, offering those who stumbled scant hope of avoiding a fall to their death. I lowered my hood and peered down over the low rock walls. We were thousands of feet above the sea, the boat no longer visible. I stepped back, closer to the rock, my head spinning.

"Here's the gate into the old monastery, just where Del told me it would be," Michael said, gesturing to the gap in the stone wall before us.

I gulped hard, steadying my racing heart. I kept one hand on the rock face behind me as I edged toward the arch, only letting go at the very last moment when forced to step through. I emerged from the darkness of the arch and blinked against the pale light.

Disbelieving, I stopped, my feet rooted to the rocky, barren ground.

Stones.

Everywhere.

Everything was made up of stones. Compact beehive-like huts dotted the enclosure, each one made of stones, some bigger than I could hold in my hand. The walls, the pathways, the outbuildings—everywhere—stones. Piles of abandoned stones stood in the dirt. Little, broken stones drifted like snow, trailing away from collapsed walls and buildings.

Enough stones to shelter hundreds of monks through the ages. More than enough stones to kill a man.

I sank to my knees. How would I find the one I was looking for amidst them all?

I felt my body heave with angry sobs and tasted the salt of a single tear as it rolled down my face.

"God's whim," Del had said. *God's cosmic joke*, I thought to myself bitterly, as I thought about the impulse that had driven me here like a fool. A hysterical laugh escaped between my sobs.

Michael knelt beside me, wiping my face with his thumb. He

tilted my chin up and looked gravely into my eyes. "Did you not know then, that this is what you would find?"

I shook my head vehemently, not trusting myself to speak. I realized, now, that this had been the source of his and Enoch's misgivings from the very beginning.

"I supposed not," he continued, "since the exhibit was closed at the visitors' center."

He cradled my cheek and looked at me sadly.

"You don't feel it, anymore, do you? The pull?"

I closed my eyes and waited for the familiar thrumming, waited for it to signal me that I was in the right place, waited for it to guide me to the singular stone amongst the multitude we faced. But I felt nothing.

A strangled cry left my lips, and I collapsed in frustration into Michael's arms.

"It's okay, it's okay," he crooned into my ear, his lips moving against my hair.

"It's not okay!" I argued heatedly, trying to push him away. "You don't understand. Nothing will ever be okay!"

He grabbed my arms, holding me tight.

"Of course it will, Hope. This is just a setback. We've gotten through worse than this already. We'll figure it out."

"I don't want to!" I said, wriggling to get out of his grip. "I don't want to be a part of this Prophecy. I don't want to find the Key. I can't! Let me go!"

His face darkened, and he tightened his hold on my wrists. "You can't back out. We need to find the Key or nobody will be safe. I can't find it by myself. I need you, Hope."

"You're going about it all wrong," a voice rang out over the wind.

Walking through the warren of beehive huts was the most beautiful woman I'd ever seen. Even though we were here, on the top of a storm-shorn cliff, she wore flowing robes of pure white. The wind barely seemed to touch her—it caressed her hair and her gowns with no more than a gentle breeze. As she turned around one of the buildings I caught a glimpse of wing.

An angel. Fear stabbed me through.

Michael dropped my hands and rose to his feet, positioning me behind him as he did so.

"Gabrielle," he greeted her, his voice uncertain.

She smiled warmly and came to a stop.

"Michael, my brother." She opened her arms, beckoning him close.

Michael hesitated, just for a moment, before bracing himself and striding purposefully toward her. She beamed and embraced him, kissing him once, then twice, on the cheek, resting her graceful hands softly upon his shoulders. I felt a twinge of jealousy as I glanced from her pristine beauty to myself, sitting in a disheveled heap.

"What are you doing here?" He said tersely, his right hand unconsciously forming a fist. "Did Raph send you?"

She bent her head quizzically. "Raph? No. Raph did not send me. I came as I always come, with a message."

Michael drew his brows into a fierce point. "For me?"

"No, of course not," Gabrielle smiled gracefully. "For her." She pushed past Michael and extended her hand toward me, bidding me up.

I scrambled to my feet, confused.

"What would you have with her? How do I know you're really Gabrielle?" Michael said, uncertain, subtly moving between the angel and me to shield me with his body. "Whatever you have to tell her, you can say to me."

"You know I cannot give my message to anyone but her for whom it is intended," Gabrielle gently admonished. "It is a message for Hope. Only she can hear it."

"You didn't answer my question. How do I know it is you? How do I know you aren't one of the Fallen, come to trap us? How do I know we can trust you?"

She laughed, a tinkling sound like ringing bells and singing birds. "Raph said I might find you confused. Very well, then. Shall we settle it like old times? I think you'll know me then."

Michael glowered at her. "As you wish. Prepare yourself."

He turned, closing the space between us with a few paces, then hustling me over to the ancient stone wall. He leaned in close to whisper his instructions. "If anything goes wrong, if you see anything at all that makes you think she is one of The Fallen, climb down as fast as you can to the boat and let Enoch care for you. Trust no one else."

"What's happening?" I asked, panicked.

"Just promise me, Hope." He stared into my eyes, insistent.

"I promise," I whispered, frightened by the intensity of his gaze.

"Good," he said, closing his eyes with relief. "Good."

He turned back to face Gabrielle, but she was no longer there. Instead, a muscular youth, shorn of wings and stripped down to what amounted to a loincloth, was pacing the stony ground in bare feet.

"Are you ready, brother?" the youth demanded, a cocky grin lighting up his face. "I thought it might be more sporting if I started out in male form, just like you."

Michael tore off his clothes, hastily, leaving all but the last layer in a heap on the ground. I was startled at how thin and pale he seemed, as if he were wasting away. "I'm ready," he growled, never taking his eyes off the boy.

"We wrestle to see who is who, then. Like old times."

They squared off, wheeling about, slowly pacing as they sized each other up.

"You beat me last time, I recall," the youth called out pleasantly. "But it took until dawn."

"I don't have 'til dawn. Whether or not you are Gabrielle, I shall beat you quickly this time."

"We shall see," the boy answered, crouching, the muscles in his legs tensing. Before Michael could answer, he launched himself toward Michael. As he crashed into Michael, the boy's body shimmered, the air around him seeming to bend as his body contorted into that of a majestic lion. The beast wrapped its paws around Michael, giving an ear-splitting roar that even the winds could not drown out as the animal threw its full weight against Michael.

They fell to the ground, tumbling and twisting as I watched, terrified.

Michael strained to break free of the lion's hold. He seemed tiny next to the animal's golden brawn, yet somehow he managed to twist his arms free so he could trap the lion's shaggy mane in a headlock. The lion growled in protest, rolling to its side, dragging Michael down into the rocky dirt with it. They crashed into one of the huts, sending stones tumbling from the roof. For a split second, the lion seemed incapacitated. Michael hauled on its mane, banging its head against the wall, his sinewy body rippling with the strain.

The lion roared in anger and in an instant shifted into the form of a wolf. The sudden change forced them both off balance, sending them tumbling in a death grip across the yard. The wolf shook Michael free and regained its feet, growling low as Michael forced himself up to face off again.

Michael was breathing heavily. Blood dripped from a gash in his forehead where he'd fallen against a rock. The wolf, too, seemed spent, its tongue lolling from its open mouth while it ever so slowly circled Michael.

"Michael, be careful!" I shouted, but I was too late. He tumbled backward, tripping over a fallen stone. The wolf lunged, seeing its opportunity, and sank its teeth into Michael's thigh.

Michael grunted and began kicking, trying to shake the wolf loose. He landed a blow to the wolf's belly. The wolf let out a high-pitched whine, as it sailed over the hard-packed dirt, landing on its back up against a stone wall, before sliding to the ground.

Michael hurled himself on top of the wolf, clamping its jaws shut and using his entire weight to trap the animal against the wall. In rapid succession, the wolf morphed into different animals—a leopard, a fox, and a viper—trying to shake Michael off with the sudden changes. It wriggled and snapped in frustration at Michael. But Michael held fast, only tightening his grip upon each beast, in turn. In desperation, the animal shifted to eagle form, flapping its wings and scratching at Michael with its talons, tearing apart the flesh on Michael's brow. Michael snatched its clawed feet in one hand, keeping its beak trapped with the other, while it frantically flapped its wings, trying to escape.

"Give up," Michael ordered with ragged breath as he dragged himself to his feet, struggling under the weight of the mighty bird. "You've been beaten, fair and square." Blood poured from his wounded leg and forehead. I moved to go to him, but he shook his head, warning me off.

"Show yourself, Gabrielle," he ordered sternly. "If it is, indeed, you."

The eagle cried out in defeat, flapping its heavy wings, until slowly, they took on the shimmer of the setting sun. Its shape shifted, flickering and glowing until gradually, it took the solid form of an angel once again, its vast wings spanning out to block our view of the dark sky. She stood impassively, her struggle over.

Still, Michael did not release his grip on the angel's wrists and face.

"Did you notice anything, Hope?" Michael demanded, his jaw tense. "What did you notice about our visitor, here?"

I thought hard about the shape shifting that had occurred during the wrestling match. "There was no smell of sulfur when she shape-shifted. I think that means she really is who she says she is and not a Fallen Angel."

Michael nodded, approvingly. "Good girl."

He released Gabrielle and stepped back, pressing his lips into a grim line while he watched her straighten her robes and dab at the red smear of blood that marred the pristine white. She rubbed her ear where Michael had twisted it, making a face at him as she did so.

We knew she was truly who she claimed to be.

"But it still doesn't explain why she's here," Michael continued, a stern warning in his voice.

Gabrielle straightened up, shaking her wings impatiently as she attempted to regain her dignity. I realized with a shock that she was actually taller than Michael—at least in her angelic form.

"I already told you," she said, shooting an amused look at Michael. "I have a message for Hope. Will you hear it, Hope?" she asked kindly, turning to me.

I looked at Michael. He was scowling but said nothing.

"Do I have a choice?" I asked.

She cleared the ground in a few graceful strides and took my hand in hers. "You always have a choice," she said gently.

I looked to Michael for guidance, but he was determinedly staring at the dirt.

"All right," I conceded. "I'll hear your message."

"I'm so glad," Gabrielle said, smiling warmly as she took my arm. "Let us walk for a while."

"But what about Michael?" I asked, looking over my shoulder to where he stood, waiting. "He's wounded. He needs help."

"Michael will heal without your attentions." I shot one more backward glance at him, hoping she was right, as she pulled me out of the monastery compound, and we began to climb. He was dabbing at his injuries with a T-shirt, paying us no attention.

"Are you sure he'll heal?" I asked, concerned. "He isn't . . ."

"As strong as he used to be? I noticed. For a moment there I thought I was going to beat him. That would have been a first," she said wryly. Before I could comment, she continued. "He is weakened by all that has happened. But he isn't *weak*. He still has depths of power upon which he can draw. His human body will recover soon enough."

I hung my head, shame flooding through me once again. "It's my fault, isn't it? It's because of me that he is losing his powers. I've stolen them from him."

"Did you choose to take his powers, Hope?"

"No."

"Then how can you be to blame?"

The question was so simple, but I found myself unable to answer it.

"We are responsible for our choices, Hope. Only that. You cannot take responsibility—whether blame or credit—for the choices others have made. You can only recognize their consequences and deal with them as best you can." She steered me around a rock in our path, waiting for her words to sink in as we climbed ever upward.

"It just seems so unfair," I said bitterly. "And right now, neither one of us is strong enough to find the Key."

"Hope, you know that is untrue. Together, you are strong enough."

My eyes swam with angry tears. "You say that as if it were so easy. But every moment he spends with me is excruciating. He's in constant pain, Gabrielle. You see what it has done to him—what it is doing to him. He can hardly stand it any longer. How can we work together when God is punishing him for even being with me?"

Gabrielle stopped and took my hands in hers. Her eyes were deep with sadness. "My poor child. The guilt you carry is a heavy burden, and an unnecessary one. God does not wish you parted from Michael. Quite the contrary."

A solitary tear ran down my face. I wiped at it angrily with my sleeve, not believing my ears.

"That doesn't make any sense. Of course God is punishing us for being together. Why else would Michael be experiencing such pain? It's God's way. Michael told me."

Gabrielle sighed and pulled me down to sit on a boulder.

"What Michael doesn't understand about God's will could fill volumes. It is true of all of us. But I can assure you, on this matter, Michael is mistaken. And I think you know why."

I shivered where I sat on the rock. Gabrielle tucked me under her wing and dabbed at the tear on my cheek with the sleeve of her gown. "You know why, Hope," she reiterated. "You must face what you know."

I looked at her blankly. "I don't know what you are talking about."

She looked at me with probing eyes and smiled indulgently. "You know what Michael is, do you not? You've known it for some days now."

My heart stopped. Of course I knew what she meant. But I didn't want to talk about it. I shifted against the uncomfortable rock, wishing she would go away.

"You must talk about it, child," she scolded me, as if she could read my thoughts. "Ignoring it won't change the truth you have discovered."

I pulled my hands away from hers and busied myself, picking at a loose thread on my jacket. "Yes," I admitted. "I know what he is."

"You must say it out loud and acknowledge it."

I hesitated. Saying it would make it real. And if I spoke it out loud, then Henri might hear me.

"You can speak freely with me. Your Guardian Angel is not here," she prompted.

"But how . . . ? I questioned her, puzzled.

"You needn't know how. Just trust I have found a way to keep him occupied elsewhere. Go on, now, tell me what you know."

I sighed. She had an answer for everything. I kicked my toe at a rock in the dirt path.

"The good shepherd lays down his life for the sheep," I said, feeling like the words were being dragged out of me.

"The good shepherd lays down his life for the sheep," she repeated, compelling me on with her melodious voice.

"He is the Gate." I stared at the dirt, barely able to breathe the words.

"He is the Gate," she repeated, reverently. "He is the Gate, it is true. But do you really understand what that means?"

I closed my eyes, following the threads I had drawn together until I could see it in my mind's eye and articulate the answer.

"It is through him that the Fallen will regain Heaven. But not as conquerors. They will be redeemed. And Michael will be the instrument of their redemption."

"Yes!" Gabrielle said, her voice thick with emotion. I opened my eyes and saw hers were shining with joy, gazing into space at something that, clearly, I could not see. "The Prophecy says those who wish to, will return. Many of the Fallen despair of their evil ways. They wish to be reunited with the Father once again, but for that to happen, someone must redeem them. The Gate must open for them to enter, just as Christ opened it for humankind. Michael is the Gate, the shepherd of the angels who will save the lost sheep, the savior of the angels, just as Christ is and was mankind's." She squeezed my hands tightly in hers, and I could feel her trembling.

"Can you imagine what it will be like? Can you imagine the rejoicing that will fill the Heavens when they return? The endless centuries of pain, the gnawing hunger of their separation from God, gone, in an instant? Not all will make the choice, of course, but many will. Heaven will be theirs once again."

I couldn't imagine anything. I was numb, screaming on the inside.

Gabrielle turned to me again with urgency. "You understand, then, what it means for Michael to be the Gate? For Michael to redeem the Fallen Ones?"

I nodded.

"You must say it, child. To acknowledge it, you must speak it aloud."

I pressed my eyes closed again. The words were torn out of my very heart. "He has to die. He has to sacrifice himself."

"Yes," Gabrielle whispered, grasping my hands tightly. "Yes. He must, so they may live again."

"It's not fair," I keened, my voice cracking with grief.

"My dear," Gabrielle rebuked me with the gentleness of a mother correcting a young child, "how can you speak of fairness? Do you think God only loves his human children? Do you think only mankind merits forgiveness? Do you think the Heavenly Father will let even the least among his creation suffer for their sin, with no hope of salvation? He will send a shepherd after them, too, just as surely as he sent a shepherd after you."

I tore my hands away and rubbed at my face, irritated by her logic, angry there was nothing I could do about it, and ashamed I would want to stop it.

"That still doesn't explain Michael's pain," I argued, irrationally hoping to win some part of the argument.

"You already know it, Hope. You have already used the word."

I looked at her blankly.

"Sacrifice," she whispered, the wind carrying the word away from her lips. "Sacrifice. As you say, Michael must sacrifice himself to save the others. But if it is easy for him to do so . . . if giving over his body to death is merely a matter of obedience, as he has always obeyed God, over and over through the millennia, it is not really a sacrifice."

I frowned. "I don't understand."

Gabrielle placed her warm hand on my cheek, her face grave. "For Michael's death to count as a sacrifice, he has to really regret what he is leaving behind. He has to not only love you, Hope, he has to accept that he loves you. Only when he acknowledges his love for you—when you both stop fighting it—only then will he experience the real loss that is required for sacrifice."

I felt like she had kicked me in the stomach.

"I'm here to make it hurt," I said, all of it making sense in a sick, twisted way.

She nodded. "He is in pain, because he resists you, resists his fate. That is all. He has been resisting his love for you since the very beginning. That Mark upon your neck?"

I nodded, my fingers drifting up to it.

"It appeared there after Michael chose you for himself, that day he saved you as a child. Even then, he ran away from you, confused by his choice to single you out. But his choice marked you as his forever, marked you as the one who would fulfill the words of the

Prophecy. Michael will continue to feel pain until he stops fighting his love for you. Only then will he be following God's path."

Sudden nausea overtook me. I pushed myself away from the rock and vomited until there was nothing left but acid burning my throat. I bent over, clutching my stomach and shaking, refusing to believe what I'd just heard.

"Are you okay?" Gabrielle was behind me, pulling my hair away from my face, her voice full of concern. I felt her tracing the outline of the Mark with her finger as she held my hair.

"Of course I'm not okay," I snapped, pushing her hand away. I wiped my mouth and forced myself to stand and face her.

"Is that it?" I demanded, my voice cold. "Is that what you've come to tell me? That the one person on Earth who understands me, the person I love, has to die?"

"Oh, Hope," Gabrielle sighed. Her wings drooped. "I had believed you would understand."

"I understand that this sucks," I snorted, brushing by her.

I started stomping up the path. We were higher now, and I wasn't exactly sure where I was, but I had to get out of here. I pulled my jacket tightly around me and began climbing.

"Hope, wait!" Gabrielle called after me, but I ignored her. I focused my eyes on the rocky path before me, determined to get away.

I turned the corner and there she stood, slightly higher than me in the middle of the trail, blocking my path.

"I haven't finished delivering my message," she stated, her eyes flashing like flame.

I stopped in my tracks, frightened and mesmerized all at once.

Gabrielle didn't wait for me to respond. Instead, she spread her wings so wide that she filled the entire path and launched into her message.

"Without love and pain, there is no sacrifice. Nor is there sacrifice without foreknowledge. Michael cannot redeem the Fallen without assent. He must knowingly go to his death. You must tell him what you know for the Prophecy to be fulfilled."

Anger rose up like bile in my throat.

"And if I refuse?"

She looked down at me with an unreadable expression. "There is always a choice. You are marked as the Bearer. It is by your hand that Michael will feel love and loss, as well as betrayal and death. But even though it is foretold, you still have a choice. If you choose poorly, the Fallen will be condemned forever."

I stood there, paralyzed by the decision I had to make, confused by her words. How could anything I ever do amount to betrayal? How could Michael die at my hands? I would never kill Michael. If it were in my power, I would fight to the death to prevent it.

But could I condemn the others?

I brushed aside her words, struggling to voice my feelings.

"I've just been a pawn in your game of heavenly politics," I argued. "I have no choice."

Gabrielle chided me, her eyes decidedly frosty as she gazed down at me. "You could have left at any point, Hope. You never even tried."

"They would have come after me," I parried back.

She arched a perfect brow. "You can fool yourself with your excuses, but not me."

Desperate, I lashed out, tears clouding my vision. "I could go now! I could run away and then the Prophecy could never come true!"

She took a step closer, stretching out a hand to me. "Now that the Fallen know who you are, they will stop at nothing to get you. The thought of their revenge will spur them on, even if they have no idea what it is that they are chasing."

Frustrated, I flung myself down onto the ground.

"I don't know how to tell him, Gabrielle," I cried plaintively, my tears sinking into the moss and stone beneath me. "I can't. I could barely even speak to him these last few days."

Gabrielle floated down the path and sank down to me, surrounding me in the protective shelter of her wings. "There is a way," she murmured, holding me close. "You have noticed by now, surely, how you can feel each other's emotions, read each other's thoughts, when you hold one another close?"

I nodded.

She gave my arm a squeeze. "Your powers are growing."

I lashed out. "Growing at Michael's expense."

She diplomatically ignored my outburst. "You move toward equilibrium, you and him. You become stronger, he becomes weaker, until you find stasis. Until you are equals in all things, as God intends you to be. Use the power he gives you. Open your thoughts, and your heart, to him. Sometimes it is easier than speaking aloud the words that cause us so much pain. You will find that Michael will understand the things you keep in your heart—that you may even draw strength from each other. If you give him a chance."

She rose up and stepped away from me, gazing on me with something that amounted to awe.

"Be strong, Hope Carmichael. All Heaven awaits your decision." She closed her eyes and folded her wings in about herself. The winds gusted, and in an explosion of light, she vanished from the path.

I sat on the hard ground, watching the empty space she left behind.

Sacrifice. Love.

Choice. Fate.

Which of these was most powerful? Or were they simply different sides of the same coin? I wrapped my arms around my knees and rocked, unable to face the decision that, one way or another, I was bound to make.

The crunch of gravel behind me alerted me that I was no longer alone.

"Hope?"

Michael's voice was tentative.

I wiped my cheeks, hoping he wouldn't notice I'd been crying.

"I'm here," I answered.

"I was worried. You'd been gone so long. Did Gabrielle leave you alone?"

I pushed myself up from the path and wiped my dirty hands against my pants. I took a deep breath before turning to face him.

"She left a little while ago." I hoped he didn't hear the tremor in my voice as I spoke to him.

His look was inquisitive and concerned at the same time. "Did she give you her message?"

I looked at him—looked at him really hard, realizing I could never look at him the same way again. He was as disheveled and worn out as I felt, the wounds from his wrestling match still fresh. His handsome grace was being eaten away by worry. His eyes were dull, almost lifeless, from constant pain and lack of sleep. His face had been whittled down to its bones by guilt and distrust.

I was the reason. And yet, I had one more blow to deliver.

I shook my head, unable to hold back the sobs that were wracking my body. I wasn't ready. I couldn't talk to him—not yet, not now. Blindly, I turned and began running up the path, feeling my way along the rocky wall of the Skellig as I tripped along rocks and stones.

"Hope! Wait!"

I ignored his cries, picking up the pace to increase the distance between us.

I mounted the crest and found myself in a grassy, windswept

knoll, the wide expanse ending abruptly in a sheer cliff. A narrow stone formation forming a doorway through the cliff was the only way out. I ran over to the gap and peered in, then down. It was a tunnel. And it had no bottom. I kicked a pebble, sending it careening over the edge, and watched it fall until I could no longer see it.

"Wait!"

I looked over my shoulder to see Michael. Without thinking, I eased my back, then my feet, up against the walls of the rock tunnel and began climbing, carefully sliding my feet and shoulders against the walls to push myself slowly up the twisting corridor away from Michael.

"Are you insane?" Michael called after me, his voice echoing against the stone walls. "Get down from there!"

I laughed hysterically. *Yes, I am insane*, I thought, pushing myself ever higher. *I am in love with an angel. Every minute I spend with him keeps him away from the ones he should be protecting, the ones he is sworn to guard. And every minute I am with him brings us closer to the moment when I must deliver him unto his death.*

My foot slid a little against the rock and I froze. Slowly, I looked down. I saw the dizzying slice of gray sky and sea spiraling away far below me and nearly fainted.

*It would be so easy*, I thought as my body tensed. *So easy to just let go.*

But instead I climbed, higher and higher, squeezing my body through the thin gap of rock that proffered my only chance of escape. Pushing ever harder against the smooth, slippery rock, I refused to give up.

By the time a light opened up at the top of the tunnel, I was shaking with the strain of carrying my body weight. Sweaty and weak, I barely hoisted myself over the lip of the tunnel onto the hard stone cliff.

Gasping, I pulled my body out of the gap and lay on the stone to catch my breath. The rock was rough and cool beneath my cheek. Around me I could hear the whipping winds.

I was alone.

I pushed myself up and looked around. A small shelter filled the bulk of a tiny cave. Nothing but a neat, hand-lettered sign reading "Caution" marked the site, which jutted out in a narrow promontory into the dark sky.

I heard scuffling behind me—the sounds of Michael climbing after me.

"Stay away!" I turned and shouted into the hole from which I'd just emerged. "I want to be alone!"

"It's not safe, Hope," he yelled back. "I'm coming after you."

Tears stung my eyes. He was coming to save me, when there was nothing I could do to save him.

I backed away from the mouth of the stone tunnel, willing him to go away. When he emerged, puffing from the exertion, I stepped onto the promontory.

"Don't come any closer," I warned him as he pulled himself out of the hole and stood up. I stepped over the "Caution" sign, as if daring him to follow me.

He froze, eyeing me cautiously.

"This isn't the place for you, Hope," he said, shouting to be heard above the wind.

"You don't know," I shouted back. "You don't know anything. Just leave me alone!"

He raised his hands, spreading his fingers wide as he cautiously stepped forward. "I know how this place came to be," he said, gesturing about him at the tiny shelter. "I know what happened to the monk who lived here. He refused the help of his brethren. He allowed himself to sink under the weight of loneliness and isolation. Whether he fell or jumped, he plunged to his death, dying alone."

He made a move toward me, and I took a step back, inching closer to the ledge.

"Careful," he warned, his eyes growing dark as the sky.

I looked behind me. My sneaker was a mere inch from the edge. Little bits of gravel and dirt were falling away from the rock, plummeting into the wild sea that churned and frothed below us.

"Come to me, Hope," Michael pleaded, holding out his hand. "I'm tired of this wall between us."

I looked at his hand, tears running down my face.

*For God's sake, step away from the ledge,* Henri hissed. *You'll be no good to anyone if you're dead.*

I wiped my face, willing Henri away as I chanted to myself, *Get out of my head, Get out of my head, Get out of my head.*

A gust of wind shook the cliff, and I froze, afraid to move.

"It's okay," Michael coaxed, moving closer to me with outstretched arms. "Just one foot in front of the other. I'll be right here, ready to catch you."

My knees were shaking as I forced myself to move. My feet felt heavy as I shuffled them, one at a time, moving away from the ledge, bit by bit, until I passed the "Caution" sign. As soon as I did, Michael dashed forward and grabbed me by the shoulders, wrapping me in a big hug.

"Don't ever do that again," he murmured against my hair as I collapsed into his arms. His warmth cut through the layers of my clothes, heating me to my very core, as we stood holding one another under the stormy sky. I wanted this to be all there was. Just me and him, holding each other tight, but I knew it could never be that simple. Not for us.

He pushed me away to search my eyes, holding my shoulders fast. I braced myself for an onslaught of questions, but he surprised me.

"With these winds, I'm afraid to stay here too long. Are you strong enough to descend? Can you make it, Hope?"

I hesitated. The very thought of climbing back down made me exhausted, but I shuddered at the thought of sheltering in that cave. I knew we had to get down before night set in. I nodded, grateful for his kindness.

"Good girl," he said, stroking my face. "We'll go down together. Just take a moment and catch your breath."

As soon as I was ready, we began the descent. Slowly, we inched our way back down the rock tunnel. I was tired and sore, but the effort of focusing on the climb distracted me from the bigger fears that were looming in my head and heart.

We emerged unscathed and kept climbing down to the boat, walking in silence down the path, through the empty monastery, and back down the rock steps cut into the walls of the Skellig. Michael led the way, making sure the path was clear and safe as we descended and blessedly leaving me to brood in silence. He began questioning me only after nightfall, when we were well on our way down the rock-hewn steps.

"Did Gabrielle tell you where to find the Key?"

"No," I said, surprised in retrospect that it hadn't even come up. "Should I have asked her?"

"It wouldn't have mattered if you did," he answered. "She tells what she is supposed to tell. No more. No less. If she didn't tell you, she means for us to find out on our own."

I didn't comment on his observation. I supposed we would wait for something to strike us, some insistent pull or flash of insight that would reveal to us where we were to go. For now, we were running blind.

"I don't blame you, you know," Michael continued, his voice gentle. "I mean for not finding the Key here on the Skellig. We were obviously meant to come since she was waiting for us. Her message must have been very important."

I felt my throat constrict as I remembered all she had shared with me.

"I can't talk about it now," I said, my voice hoarse.

There was a long pause. "That's all right," he said, his voice flat with disappointment. "We're almost to the boat."

"Michael?" I asked, hesitating. My mind returned to the moment I'd stood frozen at the edge of the cliff.

"Yes?"

"What happened after the monk fell?"

"The monastery made a rule that monks could not remove themselves from community. They learned the hard way that it is not good to bear one's burdens alone. Don't make the same mistake, Hope."

His soft reprimand echoed in my ears as we descended the last few steps and emerged by the dock. We'd been gone too long. The sun was low in the horizon, nearly set, and darkness was pressing in from all sides.

Del was sitting on the dock smoking his pipe, an abandoned crate his makeshift chair. He cocked an eyebrow at the cuts and bruises on Michael's face and gave us a good once-over before speaking.

"Can't leave in the dark. Double charge for overnighting," he said without malice. "We'll be wanting to leave as early as possible in the morning. I already radioed into Portmagee to let them know. Wouldn't want them sending out a search party for naught. I don't have accommodations for you all onboard," he said, sweeping his hand behind him in a grand gesture. "But I do know where to find the key to the old lighthouse. You can sleep there overnight."

I was too drained to argue or ask questions, grateful to have someone take charge. I followed obediently as he gathered us up and began leading the way.

Enoch scuttled over, pulling me away from Michael as we trekked back up the Skellig the short distance to the lighthouse. He lingered behind, waiting for Michael to be out of earshot before peppering me with alarmed questions.

"What happened up there?" he asked. "Did you encounter the Fallen? Are you hurt, too? And why isn't Michael healing?"

The barrage only made me wearier. "No, we didn't find Lucas or any of the others. As for the rest, you'll have to ask Michael," I answered despondently, pushing away from him and leaving him to struggle alone up the rocky path. More climbing. I trotted, puffing out warm clouds of breath into the cold night air until I caught up with the others. Del shot me a sharp look, but kept his counsel as I rejoined them.

When Del had said "old lighthouse," I'd expected a spooky relic, abandoned and worn. Instead, as we approached the cliff, I saw a more modern structure shooting out its beam of light, a beacon of warmth in the cold, sterile night.

"Fully automated now," Del huffed as we climbed closer. "Used to have whole families operating this one or, even earlier, the one on the other side of the island. Now it is all done with a switch from the mainland. The only keepers to come out here now are the ones coming out for prescheduled maintenance. But the rooms are still there and will keep you dry and warm as you sleep. Better than bunking down on the Wild Goose."

We'd gotten to the base of the lighthouse. The wind was whipping all about us, the cold cutting deep into our bones. We were in for a long, wet night. Del dug around behind a staircase and presented a key with a flourish.

"Don't be telling your neighbors about this key," he said, winking. "Or they'll all be wanting to spend the night at the lighthouse."

He hastened to the door, which opened with a gigantic creak. "In you go," he ordered, nodding to me to do the honors.

Cautiously, I stepped over the threshold. It was so dark inside I couldn't make out anything but a vague sense of the room's dimensions. Michael followed closely on my heels, and then Enoch, panting from the effort of climbing the hill.

"Here, this should help," Del said as he came inside. He flicked on his flashlight and shone it around the circular space. The room was small and tidy, a thin layer of dust covering all of its surfaces. A ladder that ran up to the second floor cut the room in two.

"The beds should be on the next level," Del informed us. He flicked some light switches on and off, to no avail. "I wouldn't go up beyond that or you'll risk messing with the equipment, which will make you none too popular with the safety commission. There are probably some kerosene lamps in the cupboard over there. Be careful with them—would hate to lose you in a fire." He cracked his fingers and held them out. "Heat's not on, but the upstairs has a wood stove, which should help. You know how to light a fire, I gather?"

He didn't wait for our answer as he prepared himself to leave.

"I'll be going now. Need to keep an eye on the Goose. May be some rough waters with the tides tonight. Enoch, will you be staying here or joining me to spin some yarns in the wheelhouse?"

Enoch looked toward me, then at Michael, a strange expression on his face, his true thoughts hidden behind the dark lenses of his sunglasses. "I think it's a good night for stories, Del," he responded, a gruff note to his voice.

"Good man," Del chortled, slapping Enoch on the back. "I knew I could count on you. I've got some whiskey on board; we'll make an Irishman of you yet. You kids okay here?"

We nodded.

"Good enough. We'll be off, then. We'll come get you in the morning if you don't show up. Keep this flashlight, just in case, and remember to be careful on those steps," he concluded, setting the flashlight down on the tiny table that seemed to take up half the room.

With that, Enoch and Del pushed their large frames through the door, leaving us alone.

"I guess we'd better get that fire going," I said, unable to stand the silence they left in their wake. I grabbed the metal rail of the ladder and began climbing up to the second floor.

The room was small and tightly packed. An ancient wood stove stood on one side of the ladder, a small stack of wood piled neatly next to it. A double bed, unmade, was pushed up against the opposite wall, a trunk at its foot.

Michael clanged up the ladder behind me. I stepped aside, conscious of how close his body was to mine as he stepped away from the ladder, filling the room.

"I'll make the fire if you make up the bed," he bargained, his voice carefully neutral. I nodded and went to the trunk while he busied himself laying the logs in the stove.

The sheets were laid out at the very top of the trunk. I dragged a light hand over them—soft and worn, they bore witness to years of loving care. I picked one up and snapped it out, unfurling it over the bed. Swiftly, I made up the bed, being careful not to think about the question of who would sleep where.

The crackle of the burning wood broke the quiet. I smoothed out the blanket I'd laid on top of the bed and sat down on its edge.

It was so dark now I could barely see Michael's face.

"Do you want me to get a lamp?" he asked, politely.

"No," I responded. "I think I just want to go to sleep."

There was a long pause.

"Do you want me to leave you?"

I fingered the edge of the blanket nervously.

"No," I whispered, grateful for the darkness. "I want you to stay."

In the shadows, I saw him begin to turn away. I reached out and grabbed his hand, pulling him over to the bed. Quietly, I kicked off my shoes and socks. He watched me, intently, his eyes shining in the dark. Quickly, I dropped his hand to pull off my outerwear. I began to struggle out from my layers of clothes. Without saying a word, he began to help me, peeling one item off, then another, being careful not to touch my skin as he helped me out of my clothes. My body called out for his touch, the tension between us palpable, but still he remained the gentleman, quietly folding each piece of clothing as he pulled it away from me. When I was down to a T-shirt and underwear, I slipped under the cool sheets and turned over on my side, staring at the wall, waiting for him to join me.

I listened for a few moments to the soft sounds of fabric pulling away from his body. Then, silently, he slid in behind me, coming as close to me as he could without actually touching me, the worn mattress sagging softly with the weight of him, conspiring to drive us closer together. I could smell him. I could feel the warmth rising from his skin and my mouth going dry at the thought of him next to me.

Cautiously, he slid his hand up my thigh, leaving it to rest on my waist. I sighed, sinking into the mattress as he pulled me tightly next to his chest, emboldened by my response.

He rubbed my hip bone with his thumb, tiny circles, lulling me into a calm state. I could feel his breath on my neck, could feel the familiar surge of his heat as it coursed through my body. I turned into his arms, facing him in the dark as I pressed my hand to his heart. I was close enough to see his face. Close enough to see the weariness in his eyes.

*I'm scared, Hope.*

I heard his thoughts, as clearly as if he'd spoken them aloud.

"I'm scared, too," I answered.

His eyes glinted.

*But I don't know if I'm scared for the same reason you are. I'm scared I'm losing you. You're pushing me away, and I don't know why.*

I started to protest, but he laid a finger gently over my mouth, quieting my words before I could speak.

*Please, let me finish.*

I nodded my assent, and he moved his hand behind my neck, gently caressing away all the tension.

*You know I won't hurt you.*

I nodded quickly, ashamed that I'd ever doubted him.

*So I can only surmise that there is something else of which you are afraid. Something from Gabrielle's message.*

I closed my eyes, closing my mind, shutting off his access to the truth.

*Please, Hope,* he pleaded, pulling me closer, leaning his forehead against mine. A stirring of lust rose up in me, and I shuddered.

*Just tell me,* he coaxed, stroking my back. *Whatever it is, it can't be that bad. It can't be something we can't work out, together.*

I bit my lip, holding back a sob. Silently, I pushed away from him and turned over, pulling my knees close against my chest. Instead of getting angry, he simply draped his arm back over me and pulled me in to the shelter of his body.

"I love you," he whispered into my ear. Slowly, tenderly, he kissed the back of my neck, then my shoulder, then the hollow spot of my clavicle. His lips lingered on each spot, soft and sweet. I dissolved into tears. I turned back into his arms, wrapping my legs around his, holding him close and letting myself sob against his chest.

My tears fell against his skin, their rivulets evaporating in a rush of steam. He pulled my hand to his heart once again.

*I won't pressure you, but when you're ready, I'll be here*, I heard him thinking as I fell asleep in his arms. *I'll always be here.*

~

We woke, our bodies tangled among the sheets. The ghost of first light was filtering down from the lighthouse's windows on the upper stories. My head was still resting on Michael's chest, my hair splayed out around me.

He was tracing my Mark, drawing his finger over its delicate lines, knowing them by memory. He did it intently, as if by the act he could unravel its mystery.

"Good morning," I mumbled, pressing a kiss onto his chest.

"Good morning," he replied, a smile in his voice. "It's still early. We have hours before Enoch and Del will be expecting us."

I lifted my head to look at him, propping my chin up on one hand. The shadows under his eyes appeared lighter, and though he had more than a five o'clock shadow, he looked more well-rested than he had in weeks. The gash on his forehead was completely gone, not even a scab to indicate where he'd gotten scraped up in his wrestling match.

He looked at me watching him and smiled, pushing a stray lock of hair out of my face.

"You look happy," I stated.

"I feel happy," he replied. He took my hand and kissed the

knuckles, his fingers lingering on each bone. I felt woozy and alert, all at the same time.

"Michael," I asked, this time with urgency. "Are you in pain?"

He didn't let go of my hand. "Not a bit," he said, turning my palm over and kissing it deeply.

*No!* I thought. *This can't be happening. He can't accept it. He can't love me. Not now.*

I pulled my hand away and jumped from the bed, trailing the sheet behind me as I paced.

"What's wrong?" he demanded, leaping to his feet behind me.

I stared at the wall, forcing myself to be rational. "What you said last night—did you mean it? Do you still mean it?"

He pulled me around to face him, his hands on my shoulders as he looked deeply into my eyes.

"I meant it then, and I mean it now. I love you, Hope Carmichael."

I pulled the sheet up to my face to stifle my mangled cry.

*Without love, there is no sacrifice.*

There was so little between him and death now. So little.

He looked at me, confused and hurt. Immediately, I was flooded with remorse. Even inadvertently, I kept hurting him.

"I love you, too, Michael," I whispered, tears streaming down my face, once again, as I rushed to reassure him.

"Then please, help me understand," he pleaded. I bit my lip. Frustrated, he stepped away from me, holding his head in his hands.

He stood in the middle of the room, wearing nothing but boxers that were too big at the waist. I closed my eyes and could see every curve of every muscle, the breadth of his shoulders, the way his chest narrowed to a V at his hips. I could see the way he looked at me, hungry and needy, and I wanted to love him back.

"Come here," I said, stretching out my hand. He closed the distance between us with one stride, clasping my fingers in his. I pulled him in closer, pressing my forehead against his and clasping his hand to my heart, which was beating like a hummingbird's wings.

"Listen," I commanded quietly, letting my tears flow. We stood in the middle of the tiny room, holding each other close, as I opened my heart to him, watching his reactions.

His emotions flit across his face like fireflies darting in the night.

Elation, as he understood how deeply I truly loved him.

Remorse as he felt my confusion at his mood swings, the pain I felt at his coldness when he'd tried to push me away.

Anger toward Raph, as he felt the disdain with which Raph had treated me behind his back.

Then a stumble.

A fall to the floor, pulling me with him, as he understood the depth of my grief and the reason for it.

He clung to me, his jaw slack with shock, as he saw all the pieces of the puzzle fall into place, just as they had for me. His eyes raced ahead, looking for an alternative, searching in my memories for something that would disprove what he'd only now come to understand.

He looked up at me, pulling my palm to his heart, his eyes questioning.

*I am the Gate?* His blue eyes brimmed with unbelieving tears.

I gathered him in, holding him in my arms, weeping, the sheet billowing out around us. I clutched his hand to my chest, so I wouldn't have to speak the words out loud.

*You are the Gate.* I repeated, over and over, rocking back and forth. *You, my beloved, are the Gate.*

# eight

## GEORGIA

Mona looked around. She was in the middle of the produce section at the local Kroger. It seemed nigh impossible to get out of her house without being seen. Even though there had been no word in her daughter's case, the press swarmed about her house, insatiable in their hunger for a word, a sign, a clue. She had to break down and cry and ask them to let her do her grocery shopping in peace to manage this meeting.

She wasn't above pretending she was weak to get her way, not when it came to her daughter. She made the mistake of showing her strength once before, when she thought her high-paying job would be an asset, yet Don used it against her to gain custody of Hope. She wasn't about to let it happen again.

Still, lingering amidst the fruits and vegetables, a long scarf wrapped around her head, dark glasses perched on her too-straight nose, she felt silly, like she was playing spy. But it wasn't a game. She had to find a way to meet Tabitha Franklin. Hopefully, her daughter's friend would show up.

It was an odd time of night to be shopping. She and Don were the only ones in that part of the store. Did the store have cameras, she wondered? Probably. Knowing there was a good chance they'd be caught on film, she squeezed an imported avocado and pretended to consult her list. Don, unsure of himself, pretended to be busy reading the labels on packages of nuts. He made the drive back from Alabama when she told him what she was planning and met her right in the parking lot.

She pushed the cart listlessly from one display to another, randomly adding items to the basket, as they waited. As she did, she stole a few glances at Don. Their meeting had been awkward, neither one of them sure what to do after their night together and Don's abrupt departure. Butterflies? Hell, Mona had a whole zoo trampling around in her stomach. The problem was she couldn't pinpoint whether it was the giddy nervousness of rediscovered love that was making her so useless, or the overwhelming sense of fear that she'd made a horrible mistake. She wasn't one to fool herself with unrealistic optimism, but she found herself hoping she was starting to mend her broken world—that this thing with Don could be real, that maybe after all this time he was coming around, that they were on the verge of finding Hope . . . That they could bind themselves back together and, like a reknit bone, be stronger at the breaks when it was all said and done.

"Psst. Mrs. Carmichael." The whisper came from around the corner, in the international foods aisle.

Mona slowly steered her cart, Don trailing behind her, skipping that aisle, to avoid being obvious, and landing in the baking section.

She waited for a few minutes, carefully reading over the descriptions of the gluten-free flours, until Tabitha and her father turned into the aisle and headed toward her. Mona drew her eyebrows together, pursing her lips. She'd expected Tabitha to come on her own.

"Hello, Tabitha. Dr. Franklin," Mona said with feigned surprise. "How nice to run into you this way."

"Yes, indeed," Dr. Franklin responded. His voice was deep and sonorous. Mona could imagine him preaching, how a sermon delivered by such a voice might touch a listener's soul. With one hand, he gently pushed Tabitha ahead of him, closer to Mona. "How fortunate that we are both late-night shoppers. Tabby mentioned she had a hankering for brownies and ice cream, so I decided to come with her."

He looked sternly at Mona. His eyes seemed to say, *don't you dare draw my daughter into this any deeper.* Mona sighed. The minister nodded at Don, not registering any surprise at his presence.

"Tell her what you came here to tell her Tabby, so we can go home." He moved down the aisle and picked a box of chocolate brownies from the shelf, placing it in his basket. He crossed his arms, waiting.

Tabitha squirmed, shifting from side to side in her black biker boots. She was wearing pink and white polka-dotted pajama bottoms under her leather jacket, her face freshly scrubbed under her faux Mohawk. *Caught between worlds*, Mona thought to herself as she waited for Tabitha to speak.

"The night that Hope stayed over at my house, we were getting ready to go out when I accidentally got a glimpse of the tattoo on her neck. She was really freaked out that I saw it."

"I can imagine," Mona said, dryly, picturing Hope's reaction.

"I thought it was cool, but she was all worked up about it. Then she seemed to calm down when I told her what it meant. I still can't figure out why she'd get a tattoo that she didn't understand. Even though it does look pretty good."

Mona breathed quietly. She had to be careful not to rush it. Tabitha paused, and Mona nodded, saying, "Go on, Tabitha. How did you interpret her . . . tattoo?"

Tabitha's face became animated. "It was written in Aramaic. That's the ancient language in which a lot of historical documents in the Christian faith were initially recorded. Even early books of the Bible. My dad studied Aramaic in Divinity School. He used to teach it to me. That's how I recognized it." She looked down at her feet demurely, shoving her hands deep into the pockets of her jacket, as if embarrassed to admit she knew something so scholarly.

Mona looked at the girl, then her father, with newfound respect. "Tell me," she urged. "What did it say?"

"It didn't make sense to me," Tabitha forewarned her. "But I'm pretty sure I got it right. I mean, I wrote it out today for my dad, so he could see if I translated it properly."

Dr. Franklin nodded, the expression on his face unreadable.

"It just said 'Bearer of the Key.' I guess that means she, Hope, is the person who carries the Key. Whatever that is. Do you know what it means?" She added, her eyes sparkling with hopeful curiosity.

Mona shook her head. "No, I'm afraid I don't." She frowned, turning over this new bit of information in her head as Don shifted beside her. "Did Hope tell you how she came to have these markings on her neck, Tabitha?"

Tabitha looked glum. "She didn't tell me very much about herself, Mrs. Carmichael. She was a very private person. So no, she never explained why or how she got the tattoo."

Don muttered under his breath, "I don't understand why no

one recognized the script as Aramaic before. Especially at the FBI. They have linguists on staff."

Dr. Franklin looked at them, intrigued by Don's reference to the FBI. "Most people think Aramaic is a dead language, even though there are entire villages all over the Middle East where it is still spoken. I would imagine the FBI linguists are more focused on modern languages. Today, with the anti-terrorism focus on Iraq and Iran, they might be more likely to recognize it, but even a few years ago, it would have been unlikely. They might not have even recognized it as a language at all, the way it was arrayed inside of the Greek motif." He paused, considering how to put his next words. "Whatever you were trying to determine, what you needed was a biblical scholar, or a student of ancient Semitic history, not the linguists of a modern crime-fighting agency."

An old man wheeled into the aisle, a bum wheel on his cart rattling. Dr. Franklin looked over his shoulder and waited for the man to pick out his goods and leave. Once they were alone again, he continued, placing an arm protectively around Tabitha's shoulders.

"Why do I get the idea there is more to this story—and Hope's tattoo—than you are telling us?"

Mona pressed her lips together, silently damning Don for slipping up.

"There's nothing to tell," she stated flatly.

Dr. Franklin looked at her skeptically, crossed his arms in front of his chest. "If you say so. Come on, Tabby. I think we're finished here. Unless there is anything else you want to share with Mr. and Mrs. Carmichael?"

Tabitha shook her head. "No, that is all I had."

"Very well, then." Dr. Franklin stood tall, pulling Tabitha closer to his side. "I hope you got what you were looking for." He began to walk toward checkout.

Mona was filled with a sinking feeling. There was more they could learn from Dr. Franklin. They'd learned more about Hope's Mark from five minutes with him than they'd found in ten years. But she'd angered him, and now he was leaving them in the baked goods aisle.

"Wait." Don's voice called after the Franklins. They stopped and turned.

"I'm listening," Dr. Franklin said, nodding to acknowledge Don.

"There is more," Don continued, looking about nervously. "But here is not the place. We need to find someplace safer. Quieter."

Dr. Franklin stared hard at them both. "Is any of this going to put my family in danger?"

Mona's thoughts flickered briefly to the traffickers. There was no way they would ever connect the dots between Hope to the Franklins. Not when all they were talking about was the Mark on Hope's neck. She brushed away the faint uneasiness that was wrapping its tentacles around her brain.

"No, you're in no danger. I promise you."

"Then meet us at our house. I trust you know the way?"

Mona nodded. "Behind the church. Right?"

"We'll meet you there in ten minutes, then," Dr. Franklin said, steering Tabitha out of the aisle.

Mona watched them go. Tabitha looked over her shoulder before they moved out of sight, giving a slight wave before she disappeared toward the checkout lanes.

*The Bearer of the Key.*

What did that mean? She abandoned her cart and began making her way to the door. If anyone would know, it would be Don. She was eager to talk with him, out of earshot of any nosy shoppers.

She climbed into the car. Mona punched Don's number into the speaker phone, launching into her speech as soon as he picked up.

She didn't bother to hide the note of excitement in her voice. "She identified Hope's Mark, Don. She *translated* it."

"I always knew it had to mean something. And in a biblical language," he murmured, awestruck.

She nodded, forgetting for a moment that Don couldn't see her. "They said it says 'The Bearer of the Key.' Do you have any idea what that means?"

There was a long pause. Mona could hear Don's breathing, heavy, over the line.

"Don," she prompted, fear spidering up her spine, "Whatever it is you know, you have to tell me. Hope's life may depend on it."

She heard him gulp in air, shuddering, before he spoke. "Let's wait until we get to the Franklins' home. I don't want to jump to conclusions. I'll follow you over." He hung up, his truck pulling behind her. Frustrated, she began the short trip to the Franklins' house.

Mrs. Franklin opened the door to them, not waiting for them to knock. She was wrapped in a plush robe, apparently ready for bed, just like Tabitha had been.

"My husband told me you were coming. I've got coffee brewing. Please, come in," she said, swinging the door wide.

She led them from the entry to the dining room. Dr. Franklin and Tabitha were already sitting, waiting for them. Mona and Don joined them as Mrs. Franklin disappeared into the kitchen.

They sat, staring at one another, listening to the loud *tick, tock* of the grandfather clock. Mrs. Franklin reappeared, bearing a tray laden with steaming cups of coffee. She passed the cups around, saving a glass of juice for Tabitha. Mona wove her hands around the handle of her mug, breathing in the aroma, staring into the inky depths of the coffee to avoid looking at the Franklins' waiting faces. She looked up at the sound of a scraping chair as Mrs. Franklin took a seat next to her husband. They were arrayed there, in a row opposite her and Don, looking like a jury waiting to judge them.

"So." Dr. Franklin looked at them expectantly. "Tell us."

Mona cringed. She'd spent the last ten years trying to forget about Hope's abduction. And now, he was asking her to go back to the very beginning, sparing no detail. She couldn't see any way around it.

Don's hand snaked up to take hers in his, startling her. He gave her a little squeeze. "Let me," he said. Mona sank, relieved, into her chair.

"The tattoo you saw on Hope's neck really isn't a tattoo. We're not sure what it is."

Mona caught the spark of curiosity in Dr. Franklin's face. It was a look she recognized. Those doctors from long ago had it. The FBI agents had it. The reporters, especially, had it.

"You see," Don continued, "when Hope was a little girl, just four years old, she was abducted by a stranger."

Mrs. Franklin clutched at the neck of her robe. "My goodness."

"I was with her, at the park, when it happened. You know that park with the playground and the dog run? It was that one. I used to sneak off of work every now and then and take her there in the afternoons. It was her favorite. She liked the slides, especially. She liked to scare me, going down them in the most acrobatic ways possible, daring me to stop her."

Mona looked at him out of the corner of her eye. He was pale, his Adam's apple bobbing, as he swallowed back the memories that were threatening to engulf him. He took a deep breath and kept going.

"That day, well, it was just like any other day, but we'd had a big system go down at work. A plant had shut down production and my boss kept calling me, asking me if I could check this and check that. I wasn't paying attention to Hope. After all, we'd been there so many times and it was Dunwoody, for God's sake. Dunwoody. I let her wander out of my sight. I lost her."

Mona had never heard him tell the story like this. In court, their lawyers posed questions to which they always answered a simple yes or no. She knew he'd blamed himself, but for some reason she hadn't recalled this note of anguish in his voice. Even now, after all this time, she realized with a start, he was hurting.

The Franklins squirmed uncomfortably in their chairs. Mrs. Franklin drew Tabitha in close; Tabitha reached searching fingers across her mother's lap until it found her mother's waiting hand.

"That's before we lived here, isn't it, Daddy?" Tabitha questioned her father, her voice grave. Dr. Franklin nodded back at her.

"If you'd lived here you would have remembered. It was a media circus," Mona interjected, giving Don a respite. "People kept claiming to have seen a stranger, a man, hanging about the park, but nobody told the same story; nobody could describe him. It was as if she just vanished into thin air."

"But someone called in a tip and we found her," Don picked up the tale. "We found her, unharmed, thank God, holed up in some motel not far from here. But what we found there with her only deepened the mystery. Her abductor was dead—inside the motel bathroom. Hope was not molested," he said between gritted teeth, "but we found her with that symbol—or I guess, those words—burned into the back of her neck. It was like a brand when we first saw it, raw and angry, and we thought she'd been marked as property by some human trafficker or a gang. But the symbols didn't match anything the FBI could link to any crime ring. And as time passed, the burning quality faded, and it looked more like a tattoo."

"We could never get rid of it. We tried tattoo removal and all sorts of things, but all it ever did was hurt Hope more. The Mark never went away. And no one could identify what it meant.

Eventually we gave up," Mona added. "We just wanted our little girl to have her life back, to have some normalcy."

"That can be hard on a marriage," Mrs. Franklin murmured sympathetically. "I can't imagine."

Don spoke up before Mona could answer. "It was. But not because of Mona. She never blamed me, not once. She never held it against me, that I was the one who lost Hope. She stood by me the whole time."

Mona turned so she could look more fully into his face. His eyes were still heavy with the same remorse she remembered from all those years ago. She tangled her fingers in his more tightly.

"It was me who couldn't let it go. Mona's right. She wanted Hope to settle back into her routine, to put it all behind her. And there was a good chance it could have worked. After all, she was only four. She had already suppressed all memories of what happened during the kidnapping. So there was a good chance that it would fade into the background."

"Like wallpaper," Mona whispered, remembering their old arguments. Her face turned hard. "It was other people who kept it alive, with their stories and speculation."

"It was me, Mona," Don answered, shaking his head. "I just couldn't let it lie. I was convinced the Mark and Hope's abduction were not a coincidence. That there was something more to it."

"Why would you think that?" Tabitha added, looking quizzically at them both, her dark eyes sparking with intelligence. Her father looked at her sternly. "Sir," she rushed to add.

"That's a good question, young lady." Don drew his cup of coffee to his lips and took a deep drink. Mona noticed his hands trembling, a trickle of coffee sloshing over the edge of his cup as he set it down on the table. Whatever he was about to say was weighing on him.

"During the brief time we were searching for Hope, I leaned heavily on my faith. We hadn't really been churchgoers up until that point, but I was desperate and terrified. Not to mention helpless. Hitting my knees seemed to be the one thing I could do."

He shifted in his chair, untangling his fingers from Mona's, so he could twist his hands together.

"I remember being there, alone, just me and a bank of candles, listening to the choir practice for an upcoming mass. It probably was a day and a half after she'd gone missing. I was there, alone, for I don't know how long, when I was suddenly filled with this incredible sense of peace. And in my mind, I mean, directly in my mind, I heard this voice say 'She is of the angels.'"

Tabitha's eyes grew wide.

"Of course, at first I thought I was imagining it. But the voice got louder and kept repeating that. 'She is of the angels.' I looked around, but I was still alone. Finally, the voice told me, no, ordered me, 'She is of the angels now. It is time for you to leave this place.'"

"You never told me this," Mona stuttered, bewildered.

"Are you kidding?" Don answered, turning to face her where she sat. "I thought I was going crazy," Don responded. "I ran out of there so fast I could have made the Olympic 4x400 team. I didn't want to have heard anything. I was convinced it meant she was dead. How could I share that with you? How could I ever be the one to deliver that news? Besides, I didn't want to believe it myself."

"You said that was a little over a day after she went missing?" Dr. Franklin prompted.

Don nodded. "It was. It was later that evening when they found her in that motel."

"Interesting." The minister simply nodded, his hands steepled together on the polished dining room table. "Did your voices come again?"

Don nodded. "Later on, a few weeks after we had Hope back, I went back to the church. I felt I needed to say thank you. You know, thank God for bringing our Hope back to us. As I was lighting a candle the same voice began whispering to me: 'She is of the angels, and her story is not done. You must prepare her.' The more I ignored the voice, the stronger it became. It stayed with me, even after I left the church. It was like it was haunting me, torturing me to get me to act. I could barely keep myself together."

"You didn't keep yourself together," Mona said quietly, finding a surge of sympathy in her heart for him. "You became obsessed with protecting her. No wonder you were so convinced it was God's doing. You should have told me this, Don. You never told me any of these details."

"I didn't know how," Don shrugged in his chair. He snorted a derisive laugh at his own predicament. "We were Tech grads—trained in rational, logical thinking. This was about as far from my personal beliefs as I could get. I was confused and scared. But I couldn't deny it was happening to me. I even went to a psychiatrist to have my head examined. The pills he prescribed didn't help, though. Nothing made it go away. It only stopped if I was with her, constantly watching and protecting her. It flew in the face of everything I believed about rationality, about science."

Dr. Franklin interjected. "Actually, there is a long history of scientific inquiry being linked to angelic studies and visitations. Even the great Dr. Dee, advisor to Queen Elizabeth I, claimed to have discourse with angels while he was compiling his natural histories. You are in good company, Don. I take it, Mona, that you did not sympathize with his views or behavior?"

"His convictions are what eventually drove us apart." They didn't need to know the details, she rationalized, feeling strangely defensive of her husband.

Mona gripped his hand even more tightly.

She cleared her throat. "So you can imagine how . . . disturbing we find her latest disappearance. And the fact that you actually could interpret her Mark after all those years of fruitless searching, well . . ." She left her sentence unfinished.

The Franklins were staring at them now, dumbfounded by all that they had heard.

"And now that you know what it says," Dr. Franklin prompted, "what do you think it means?"

Mona looked at Don. He had some idea, she knew. It might be harebrained, but by his reaction earlier on the phone, he had a point of view.

"I'm not sure," he wavered.

Dr. Franklin stared at him, hard. "I know from Hope's time here that she has quite a handle on the Good Book. I have to believe that comes from you." He darted an apologetic look at Mona. "No offense, but you don't seem like the religious type."

"None taken," Mona conceded. "Don, go ahead. Say what you think. You're in friendly company, if I'm not mistaken."

Don hesitated.

Dr. Franklin challenged him. "Isaiah."

Don drew a deep breath. "And the key of the house of David will I lay upon his shoulder; so he shall open, and none shall shut, and none shall open."

Mona frowned. "I don't understand."

Dr. Franklin threw down another citation. "Matthew."

This time Tabitha answered. "Chapter 16, Verse 19. I shall give you the keys to the kingdom of heaven. And whatever you bind on earth will be bound in heaven, and whatever you loose on earth will be loosed in heaven."

"Revelation," Don parried back, the tremor in his voice

unmistakable. “I am he that liveth and was dead; and behold, I am alive for evermore, Amen. And have the keys of hell, and of death.”

Mona glanced around the table. Everyone else looked pale, in shock. All she felt, though, was confusion. It was as if she’d dropped into a dinner party where everyone was speaking Mandarin. She had no idea what had just happened.

Frustrated, she slammed her palm against the table. “All of you, stop speaking in riddles. What are you saying?”

Don looked at her before pulling his hand away. “You won’t believe me. You never have.”

“Stop it! We don’t have time for this. Are you telling me Hope is in danger?”

“It’s not possible,” he stated, his voice full of wonder. “She can’t be. There were no other signs. They never said, Mona. They said she was meant for something special, but never this.”

“Can’t be what?” Mona was shouting, the Franklins forgotten, willing Don to tell her what he knew. Her fear was so strong that she was bathed in sweat.

It was Dr. Franklin who answered her.

“Those verses are all about resurrection, Mona. Resurrection and death. The second coming of a Messiah. The apocalypse.”

Don interjected. “Don’t you understand, Mona? If Hope bears the keys of death . . .” He was talking so fast now that it was hard to make out what he was saying, his words tumbling forth from him with the power of a rushing waterfall or a gathering storm—unstoppable, unrelenting, undeniable; a force of nature.

“Then she’s the Messiah? You’ve got to be joking.” Mona was angry now, gripping the edge of the table so hard her hands hurt. She pressed her fingers to the bridge of her nose, wishing her impending headache away. “Don’t, Don. Not now. Please, not now.”

"Maybe not the Messiah. But in service to him. Part of the End," he breathed. "Think about it, Mona. What else could it be?"

Disappointment flooded through her system. She'd hoped he would have a realistic answer. But she should have known she'd been hoping in vain. She'd been a fool to think he could change, a fool to think that he was anything but the crazy conspiracy theorist he'd turned into more than ten years ago. This latest idea just proved it.

She choked back a sob, pushing the memories of their recent night together far into the recesses of her mind.

"It's not just me, Mona. Look, even the Franklins see it."

She looked around. Tabitha's wide eyes were darting back and forth between her parents' faces. The fear in her face was unmistakable. Mohawk or no, her tough exterior had fallen away, abandoned like a snakeskin, so that she looked like a child half her age. But there was still a hint of skepticism, her fear quickly dissolving as her face folded into a look of intense concentration. The minister and his wife looked shell shocked.

"Do you?" She demanded of them. "Is this the only explanation you see?"

Dr. Franklin chose his words carefully. "It is an explanation. One that certainly fits with the scriptural references. There could be others," he conceded. "But I must admit, the possibility is intriguing. How else do you explain the Mark? The fact that she was taken not once, but twice, under mysterious circumstances?" She looked into his eyes. They were beginning to shine with the zeal she recognized from years of arguing with Don.

"Don't be seduced by it. Don't," she pleaded.

"Don," the minister pressed, "Do you have any other reason to believe this to be the case?"

Don leaned into the table, ignoring Mona.

"The angels that visited me warned me to prepare her. For what, they never said. But why would I need to prepare her if it weren't for something great? For something dangerous? And now the voices have stopped. They stopped around the time she asked to move in with you, Mona," he added for her benefit.

Her dawning sense of disappointment only deepened. Nothing had changed, after all. "So that's why you barely put up a fight? Because the angels were telling you to let her go?"

He nodded. "And then there is this. I'd almost forgotten about it."

He dug into his pockets and pulled out some papers, crumpled and yellow. He laid them out on the table, smoothing them over carefully.

"These are the program notes from the choir that was singing in the church the first time I heard the voices," he said. "I guess I'd grabbed them on my way in to pray and had tucked them away. I'd forgotten them until recently. Look at what they say."

He moved to pass the papers around. Tabitha took them swiftly from his quivering hands.

"*Missa de Angelis*," Tabitha read. "Mass of the Angels. You were listening to Gregorian chants about angels?"

"Apparently so. Now read the translation of the chants. They are printed near the bottom of the program."

Tabitha squinted and continued. "You were sent to heal the contrite of heart."

Her mother reached across to take the papers from her. "Please, let me." She turned to Mona and Don, adding by way of explanation, "I studied liturgical music while Roger was getting his PhD."

She held the sheets up closer to her face, pulling her reading glasses down on her nose to get a better look. "The program says this was followed by a *Misereris Omnium*. If I remember correctly, that work begins with 'Your mercy extends to all things, O Lord; you despise none of the things you lovingly made.'"

"Wisdom 11," Roger Franklin whispered. "As well as Psalm 56. It is a redemption story. Poetry about God's unending love for his creation. All of it."

"It's too many coincidences," Don said, rubbing his face with his shaking hands. "Too many—all pointing to the same thing."

"What? That Hope is the second coming?" She said dismissively, ignoring the cold fingers of fear gripping her heart. "Give me a break. It could be anything but that, Don. Anything but that," Mona said, each word dripping with weariness.

Abruptly, she pushed herself away from the table and stood. "Your theories are interesting, but you're ignoring the simplest explanation. We have proof that she was taken by traffickers this time. Hard evidence," she added for emphasis.

"Evidence that keeps disappearing as if it never existed," Don countered. "How do you explain that away?"

"Not by heavenly intervention!" She had shifted into the cold professionalism in which she cloaked herself every time she strode into a boardroom. Her mind rejected the mystery. She could only deal in facts.

"You're all wrong," Tabitha interjected, cutting through the mounting tension. The recriminations evaporated from the air as they stopped arguing and all swiveled, as if marionettes on a string, to stare at her.

"You're all wrong," Tabby repeated, swallowing hard and squaring her shoulders. "Look at the evidence."

Her father peered at her over his glasses. "Go on."

"Everything keeps pointing to angels. You, Mr. Carmichael,

heard voices saying Hope is of the angels. They keep telling you her work isn't finished. The choir you heard when she disappeared was singing about angels."

"So?" Don leaned into the table, wondering what Hope's friend was getting at.

"And the lyrics of that sung mass, they were about forgiveness. About God loving *all* his creatures. All of them. Don't you see?"

Her father's brow crumpled in puzzlement. "I'm afraid I don't, Tabitha. What do you see that we don't?"

Tabby raised her chin, almost anticipating they would reject her idea. "Hope isn't part of the Second Coming, or the Apocalypse. She's here to save the Fallen Angels."

She felt them staring at her and crossed her arms. "It's obvious."

Her father pushed away his coffee cup, bemused. "That's an interesting theory, Tabitha, but I'm afraid . . ."

"Roger—" his wife shook her head, cutting him off. "Not now. Now is not the time for another theoretical debate. I have to say I agree with Mona. The evidence points to the traffickers. Time is running out. We need to find Hope, and the traffickers seem to be the key to it. From what Tabby has said, I suspect this boy, Michael, was part of it, too."

"Mom!" Tabby burst out, jumping up from her chair. "Michael's not a trafficker! He's an angel, I'm sure of it. If he was here to protect Hope, it all makes sense. And it explains why all signs of him have disappeared, too!"

"Tabitha Marie, that is enough." Mrs. Franklin's tone was sharp. Tabitha looked around the table, shocked that, for the first time she could remember, her inquisitive mind and sharp intellect were being shut down instead of stoked by her doting parents. She choked back a sob and ran, knocking over her chair.

Mona's eyes trailed after her as she ran up the stairs. She shook her head. "I'm so sorry. This must be hard for her, too."

She addressed the rest of her words to the Franklins.

"I'm sorry—perhaps this was a waste of your time. Dr. Franklin, I can't see things the way you do. Nor you, Don. I do appreciate you letting Tabitha share more of what she knows about Hope's disappearance, but I'm not sure we have any more concrete idea of what to do than we did before." She could feel the panic snaking its way to her heart, making her sweat.

Roger looked at her with what she swore was pity.

"You might need to keep an open mind," Roger nudged, not unkindly.

"Let her be, Roger," his wife retorted gently.

He sighed heavily before letting his head sag into his chest in a resigned nod. "Fine. Fine. Then we are happy to have met with you. But, Mona, from now on, if you have anything else you need to talk to Tabitha about, please come to her mother or me first."

Mona stared at her hands, clasped tightly on the table, chastened. Of course, he was right. She would have felt the same way if their roles had been reversed. She nodded swiftly. Then she steeled herself to part from her husband, ignoring the impulse she felt to draw him to her, to kiss his troubled brow.

"Don," she said, squaring her shoulders. "I assume you'll head back to Alabama tonight. Good night," she added, not waiting for him to acknowledge her implicit rejection not only of his ideas, but of him.

To her surprise, he simply smiled. "Yes. If I am right, there is nothing more for me to do here. Hope's path is laid out for her, and the best thing for me to do is to get out of the way. Of God's plan, or the investigation. Either way." She ignored the hollow feeling that filled her at the thought of him actually leaving her alone, again, in Atlanta. She ignored the urge to scrabble after him, begging him to stay with her while they waited for their daughter to come home to them. She realized, then, that perhaps her disappointment was all the deeper, because she still loved him. After all this, and all these years, she still did love him.

She left them sitting at the table as she let herself out. Once outside, she sat for a moment in the drive, thinking. A tiny voice spoke inside her head. *Are you dismissing their explanations too easily? Are greater mysteries than your daughter's disappearance winding their way through your world while you sit, blind to them?*

She shook her head and pushed the questions away. Slowly she shifted the car into drive, leaving her doubts behind on the weathered surface of the Franklins' cul-de-sac.

She spent a sleepless night at home, alone. She felt like a caged animal, the days of endless waiting—unable to do anything—weighing on her, and her complicated feelings about Don made things worse. As morning approached, she made up her mind.

She would go into her office and distract herself. She texted Arthur to arrange a pickup.

Her movements were almost mechanical. Hair pulled tightly back. Lipstick and blush to cover her pallor. She faced the row of nearly identical suits hanging in her closet and pulled one out; she pushed to the back of her mind the awareness that it now hung too loosely on her frame, that the stress of the wait had whittled her body down to nothing.

She sidled into the front seat next to Arthur, taking comfort in the mundane. Arthur took one look at her and whistled low.

"Mona. You look like hell. What are you trying to prove by going into the office? You know there's nothing for you to do there.

You said yourself, Clay shifted your caseload to other partners so you could focus on the investigation."

She ignored the flutter of guilt that she felt at his mention of Clayton.

"I need to distract myself, Arthur. This waiting . . . it's getting to me."

"Obviously," he agreed as he shifted into gear and began backing out the driveway. The reporters swarmed about the vehicle, like bees searching for nectar, until he managed to burst through, leaving them to wait for something new to happen.

Mona sighed, sinking back into the leather seat. "Arthur. Don is bringing up his old theories again. His theories about Hope's disappearance being part of some master plan of God's."

"That bothers you?"

"Of course it bothers me," she retorted, feeling defensive. "We don't have time for wild goose chases like that. We need to focus on things that can actually bring her back."

Arthur didn't take his eyes of the road. "Is that what bothers you? That if Don is right, there is no way to bring her back?"

She felt the cold fingers of doubt and fear trailing through her insides, winding their way up to twist themselves in her brain.

"She has to come back," she whispered.

"Mona," Arthur continued. "Just because God has a role for her doesn't mean she is lost to you."

"But he's saying it's the End Times. He's implying she is part of it, Arthur. If I were to take him seriously, how could I possibly think she is coming back?"

"Do you take him seriously?"

She thought about his question. She thought about the resolute conviction that she'd been met with last night as they talked things through with the Franklins. She thought about the strange series of coincidences, each a marker on a trail that led in one direction. And yet, too many things were unexplained by her husband's theory. There were just too many questions left unanswered.

"I think he is serious. But no, I do not think his explanation fits the evidence."

Arthur nodded, thinking over her response.

"What if you thought there was a chance he was right? Maybe not in all the details, but in the big-picture sense that this is all happening for a reason. Would you do anything differently, Mona?"

His question startled her. She hadn't expected him to take such a balanced view of the situation. Then again, he had been a friend to Don, too, and his equanimity was one of the things she valued in his friendship.

"I'd stop hanging out at the FBI office."

"To do what instead?" he prompted.

"To pray," she whispered, a spasm of real fear shaking her to her core.

Mona arrived at work. She'd been so engrossed in her conversation with Arthur that she couldn't really recall the details of their drive in from Dunwoody, nor the ride up the elevator to the floor her firm occupied, high above the city. Even though she was early, more than a few people were already deep into their work, and she was vaguely aware of their curious stares as she moved past them, down the hall, to her corner office.

She walked in and closed the door behind her. It was just as she had left it; piles of reports and memos were strewn across her desk. Books fought with one another for space on her crowded shelves, spilling over into piles on the floor. A diagram filled her whiteboard, forgotten by whatever project manager had last met with her here. It was sterile and impersonal; only a gallery of photos showing Hope's progress through the years gave any indication that a real person occupied this office.

Mona picked up Hope's latest school photo and wiped away the layer of dust that covered the glass. It pained her to see how self-conscious her daughter seemed, her neck wrapped in a scarf and her eyes peeking through her hair, which she always hid behind. She was so young. Too young. Too vulnerable. Certainly not the leader of some biblical movement.

"You shouldn't be here, Mona."

She turned to find Clayton looming in her doorway. She'd been so deep in thought she didn't hear the click of the door as he entered. Automatically, she stiffened. She hadn't spoken with Clayton since the incident at the FBI office. The ease she'd always felt with him was gone, replaced by the awkwardness that inevitably came along with her rejection of his advances.

"Clayton," she answered, looking away as she carefully placed the picture frame back on the desk with the others.

He closed the door behind him with an emphatic click.

"You shouldn't be here, and you shouldn't have done what you did, Mona." He looked at her, accusation in his hurt eyes.

She felt herself flush. How could he know about Don?

"I . . . I don't know what you mean," she answered hesitantly.

He shook his head. "Just because the FBI said you were no longer under suspicion doesn't mean that they stopped watching you. For God's sake, Mona, they've tapped your phone. They know you held back information from them. And what's more, you've tampered with a witness."

She felt a simultaneous wave of relief and anger as she realized he wasn't talking about Don. He was talking about her meeting with Tabitha.

"All I did was get more information out of her," Mona protested. "I didn't do anything wrong."

"When were you planning to share that information?"

She stared at him defiantly, refusing to answer his question.

Frustrated, Clayton ran a hand through his hair. "I can't help you now. There is nothing I can do to intervene."

"What do you mean?"

"They've labeled you 'uncooperative.' They're shutting down your access to the investigation. You'll have to wait for news on their terms."

"No!" Mona cried. "They can't do that. They know I'm not involved. Neither one of us!"

"Us?" Clayton folded his arms across his chest and pinned her beneath his sharp look.

She stammered. "Hope's father."

"Yes," he murmured. "Hope's father." He continued to stare at her, the hurt and anger in his gaze undeniable. She felt the heat of shame stealing across her face as she realized that he knew everything.

"You've made your choice," he said softly as he turned to go. "I can't help you anymore. I'm sorry, Mona."

The click of the door closing behind him seemed final.

"I'm sorry, too, Clayton," she whispered as she watched him walk down the hall, shoulders hunched in defeat.

# nine

## IRELAND

*I won't let you do it. I won't let you die.* I clutched Michael's hand to my heart, sending my unspoken words to him in a fierce burst of love. We were huddled together on the floor, our limbs entwined—unable to stop touching, unable to let go of each other, as if by clinging together we could stop our fates. I had climbed into his lap, wanting there to be no space between us now that we both knew the truth.

He took my hands in his, looked up into my eyes and smiled weakly, brushing aside my bold words.

"All this time . . . all the accusations the other angels made, saying that I set myself apart, or even above them. That I wanted to be worshipped by man, that I wanted the churches and the saints days and all of it—that I wanted to be elevated like Christ. How could their barbed words come so close to the truth? How could they know that when I didn't even know it about myself? How could I go through eternity not knowing who I really am?"

I rubbed my thumb across his knuckles, knowing I had no explanation.

"It's ironic, isn't it?" he continued. "They always said that I loved humans more than I loved our own kind. It was at the heart of their jealousy; it rankled and soured in their very hearts. The reality was that while I admired humans, I protected them as my duty. I didn't love them. How fitting that now that I have found you, my life is forfeit." He pressed his lips together into a grim line, as if bracing himself before continuing. "That's what I must do, to free my fallen brothers and bring them back to Heaven, because I love them still, despite their crimes.

"And I will do it. It is inevitable," he began, saying the words slowly and deliberately. He had a look I had come to recognize—the look of forced distance, with hooded eyes and a set jaw. He was preparing himself to push me away. "The Gate must open. The pain is gone because I accept that I love you, and despite that love, I must leave you and give up my life. But I will do everything I can to keep you safe. You have to go."

He winced as he said it, a rush of pain reminding him of what we both knew. It wasn't possible for me to leave, even if I was willing. I had to find the rock that first brought murder into the world. And I had to deliver it—an instrument of death—to the ones who would take Michael's life.

I shuddered, blocking out the rush of bloody images that came to mind.

"How can God be so cruel?" The accusing question flew from my lips as more hot, angry tears spilled from my eyes.

Michael wiped away a drop that rolled over my cheek.

"Remember when I said He was jealous? He isn't jealous after all.

But He wants more than my obedience. He wants my love. A sacrificial love. Why should it be any different than it was for Abraham?"

I clutched at a wild hope. "An angel stayed Abraham's hand before he slaughtered Isaac."

Michael tucked a lock of my long hair behind my ear and gave me a wistful look. "I was that angel," he whispered. "I was the one who sent the animal that would replace Isaac on the altar. Nobody is going to come and defend me, I'm afraid. There is no one who could." He frowned. "Maybe none of my angelic brethren would, even if they were capable."

"But your army?"

He shook his head. "They won't do it except at my command," he said curtly. "And that is one command I will never issue." He pushed me from his lap, depositing me gently on the hard floor, and stood up. He reached out a hand, pulling me to my feet next to him. In the strengthening light I could see the tracks of his tears, staining his weary face.

"I don't understand," I cried. "Why would God lead you down this fruitless search? Why bury His will in a Prophecy? Why wouldn't He just tell you what He wants from you?"

His lips twisted into a bitter smile.

"Because he wants me to choose, Hope. Not obey. I thought if anything you'd understand that by now.

"It's a good thing, Hope," he whispered, his voice breaking as he said my name. "It's a good thing that the Fallen will have a chance at redemption. You must remember that when the moment comes. Promise me." He pulled my hands, still wrapped inside his, up to his lips and pressed a kiss to my knuckles as if to seal a vow.

I squeezed his hand as if in agreement, but my heart revolted. *I won't do it.* In my mind, the words were clear and strong. Never mind that my knees were trembling.

*Won't do what?* Henri asked.

I froze, horrified. How much had he seen and overheard? I couldn't bear the thought of his snide commentary intruding on our private pain.

*Go away*, I ordered silently, my muscles clenched in apprehension, hoping he'd obey.

Michael looked at me quizzically. "What's wrong?" he asked.

"Just dreading going down to meet Enoch and Del," I answered quickly, sinking against his shoulder to avoid his probing gaze. I glanced up at the sunshine that was now filling the lighthouse, flooding down from the windows above. Hours had passed since we first woke up. It gave me an excuse to change the subject and keep our newfound knowledge from Henri while I could.

"I don't know how to keep it from Enoch, Michael, but it doesn't feel right to burden him with it. Do you think he knew all along?"

Michael shrugged, caressing my shoulder, every touch sending another wave of comforting heat through my body. "Perhaps. Does it matter?"

"I guess not."

He shifted slightly then and pulled my fingers to his lips, turning my hand over to kiss the thin skin of my inner wrist. A shiver ran through my body. He trailed his lips along my arm, past my shoulder, to nestle into my neck. I closed my eyes, reveling in his touch. The horror of what we would face once we left this island did nothing to diminish my need for him. All I wanted to do was give myself over to this pleasure and forget about everything else.

"You're still healing," he whispered against my skin. "But look at me, now. You've left a mark of your own."

He pulled away and pointed to his chest. Over his heart lay the clear imprint of my palm, marked in red, like a rash.

Tears filled my eyes. I had to look away. Michael pulled me in close, murmuring to me as he planted kisses in my hair.

An expectant silence filled the room. Our time here was over, I knew, but I didn't want to leave. I clung to Michael, wishing it all away, but I knew it was no use. Eventually, we'd have to leave and face reality. As if reading my thoughts, Michael finally spoke.

"We'd better get going, or they'll be coming up after us."

Reluctantly, I extracted myself from his embrace. It was all I could manage to let go of his hand.

Methodically, we pulled on our clothes. In silence, we went about the room, unmaking the bed, folding the sheets and blankets, straightening up, careful to leave no traces of our stay. I focused intently on each task, wanting the monotony of the simple tasks to fill the empty spaces of my mind, crowding out the knowledge of what was to come. Michael, too, seemed preoccupied, giving inordinate attention to tamping out the fire. When we were sure the flames were out, we headed down the ladder and pushed through the heavy door to greet the day.

It was like a new world. The sky was bluer than Michael's eyes—a bright, expectant color that spoke of birth and renewal. The sun, still rising, shone brightly. The few clouds that were scattered across the sky were like gentle puffs of cotton, floating harmlessly above. Instead of the harsh winds of yesterday, a gentle, warm breeze fluttered across the hilltop. Somewhere, I could hear the twitter of birds. Life had returned to the Skellig.

My heart was dead to it all.

We walked wordlessly away from the lighthouse. Our feet were leaden as we moved down the rock. The path, which seemed so short the night before, now stretched endlessly before us, the distance to the boat a yawning expanse. When we finally came down the last flight of steps toward the dock, we saw Enoch and Del staring at us, knowingly, as we clutched our hands together, but we didn't care. We just held each other more tightly and slipped silently onto the boat's deck, ignoring the significant look that Enoch was shooting us from behind his dark glasses.

"It's like another sea altogether today," Del said as he busied himself preparing the boat for departure. "Strangest thing I've ever seen. But I'm not one to look a gift horse in the mouth. We'll be leaving now, while the weather is still with us. Help me, Michael, with these lines."

Michael gave my hand a tiny squeeze before moving quietly to Del's side. He busied himself listening to Del's instructions, seemingly absorbed in the discussion of knots and tides and proper technique. Quietly I slipped away to Del's little lean-to, wanting a moment alone to compose myself.

The shack bore the evidence of a hard night. An abandoned hand of solitaire was strewn across the table. An empty lunchbox had been left in the corner along with a flask—empty, too, I presumed. I was still taking in the scene when the springs of the door squealed in protest. I turned to find Enoch walking into the room. He pulled the door closed behind him and came closer. His presence, and voice, overpowered the tiny space. I felt awkward, cornered, as he leaned in, my own distorted reflection flashing back to me from the lenses of his sunglasses.

"What happened up there last night?" he demanded, his voice full of concern as he hunched over the table. "We were just about to come after you."

"Nothing," I said evasively, busying myself with sliding the playing cards into their box, then stacking the numerous maps piled in front of me. "Nothing at all."

"Did you spend the night together?"

He was so blunt it caught me by surprise. I looked up. He was peering at me intently through his mirrored glasses. It felt for all the world like he was leering.

"No! Of course not!" I stammered. The heat of a blush crept across my face. Desperately, I tried to ward off his curiosity. I held out a hand and pushed up my sleeve, making a sudden realization. "No burns."

Indeed, my skin showed none of the aftereffects of Michael's heat. Gabrielle had been right—we were reaching equilibrium.

He scowled, frustrated. "Then what is going on? Something happened on top of the Skellig, and I want to know."

"You're imagining things, Enoch," I said, refusing to look him in the eye.

Enoch thumped his cane, and I jumped.

"You know better than to lie to me, young lady," he said, raising his voice. He slammed his free hand down on the table for emphasis. Maps and papers scattered from the force.

Enoch? Angry? This was new. His face was almost purple, his eyes still hidden behind his sunglasses. I looked at him steadily, trying to remain calm despite my confusion.

"Nothing happened, Enoch. We went to sleep right after you and Del left last night. We woke up this morning and cleaned up the lighthouse and then came down. End of story."

"But something happened yesterday," he said, coming around the corner of the table closer to me. "I demand to know what it was. That huge gash on Michael's forehead didn't get there by accident."

He was leaning too closely to me, little bits of spittle flying from his contorted lips.

"Enoch," I said, stepping backward. "Calm down. You're scaring me."

Shock, then embarrassment, dawned on his face.

He took a step back and looked away, composing himself. Eventually, his gaze seemed to settle on the table, where his hands fumbled to clean up the papers he'd knocked awry.

"I'm sorry, Hope," he mumbled as he straightened and restraightened the pile. "It must be this crazy chase we're on. The paranoia must be getting to me. Maybe that and a little of last night's whiskey." He smiled ruefully. "It's just that . . . I've come to think of you as a granddaughter of sorts. I felt like we understood each other, perhaps when no one else could."

He took off his glasses. His blind, white eyes were welling with tears. "I couldn't bear to think you were hiding something from me. Not after all we've been through."

He fumbled with his glasses and slid them onto his face, hiding his disappointment.

I was swamped with guilt. Even if we hadn't exactly been hiding something from him, we didn't go out of our way to tell Enoch what was going on. After all he'd done for us, he deserved better. Chastened, I placed my hand on his rough knuckles where they rested on top of his cane.

"I'm sorry if we made you feel that way, Enoch. Of course I trust you; you've been a rock for me this entire journey. If it hadn't been for you, I would have gone crazy long ago."

He nodded. "I just did what I could," he said gruffly, staring at the floor.

He paused expectantly.

I took a deep breath and exhaled.

"Gabrielle came with a message. Michael got the wound on his head when they wrestled. Some way of proving Gabrielle's identity, I guess."

"Of course it was her," Enoch said excitedly, squeezing my hand in his, his hurt forgotten. "Nobody else would be foolish enough to confront Michael in one of his own sacred places, especially one as desolate as this. What did she say?"

The door screeched open again, interrupting us.

"Make way," Del shouted as he burst through the door. "Michael's about to release the mooring. I need to take the wheel, or we'll crash on the rocks."

"He didn't tell me," I answered Enoch, pulling my hand free and darting out the door before he could question me any further.

The boat lurched as Del gave the motor gas. I grabbed the side and made my way up the deck to where Michael was sitting among nets and crates.

"It seems so different today, doesn't it?" he asked without turning.

Giant flocks of white birds were returning to the Little Skellig. The waves were calm, lapping against the boat just enough to leave spray in their wake. Just like that, the sea was transforming to its springtime guise. But I knew it wasn't the weather that Michael was talking about.

"Yes," I said simply, resting my hand on his shoulder.

"Enoch suspects something," I continued quietly.

"He would," Michael replied, nodding. "He's just as intuitive as the next angel."

"I couldn't bring myself to tell him, Michael. I just . . . couldn't."

Michael reached up to hold my hand. The familiar flow of heat connected us, giving me solace.

"I think we should. After all, he'll need to take care of you . . . after . . . I'm gone. I'll tell him when the time is right. Once we know where the last stand will be."

We stared at the water in silence, nothing left to say. I knew both of us were wondering what we would do now. We knew what we had to do, what the Prophecy demanded, but our clues and hunches had run out.

If we had to find the Key, where would we go?

Deep down, I didn't want the answer. I wanted to stay right here, riding the currents with Michael, until the end of time.

The boat shifted into open sea, Del giving full throttle to her as we climbed the rougher waters. I looked at the endless waves, hoping they'd mesmerize us into forgetting our pain.

"I know you say you aren't sweethearts, but you sure seem to be so." Del unceremoniously plopped himself down on a crate next to Michael. "'Tis none of my business, to be sure. But you should know you cut a pretty picture, the two of you together."

I smiled weakly. He couldn't know how his comments cut me to the core.

"Del," Michael said, shouting to be heard over the boat's raucous motor. "What happened to the monks who left the Skellig? Where did they go?"

"Oh, they went all over Europe, they did," Del said, pulling out his pipe and settling into his story as if he'd never stopped. "Many stayed in the inland, in Ireland, to be sure. But most were not satisfied to do so. They'd come to the Skellig for their martyrdom, or at least the closest they could get to it. They'd not be satisfied until they'd punished their bodies and souls with the weariness of travel, the hardships of living on foreign soil. A fair number went to France, they did, forming monasteries of their own if there were none they could find." He drew hard on his pipe, sheltering the tiny flame in its bowl from the wind. "Some just deposited their relics in churches along the way, I suppose. Probably melted into the crowd, never to be seen again."

A spark of excitement, of recognition, fluttered in my breast. France. Even as I thought it, I wanted to deny it; I wanted to drown out the very idea of it. I wanted to cry.

Michael leaned in closer to Del. I could tell from the expression on his face that he felt it, too.

"Where in France, in particular, did they go, Del? Does history tell us of their journeys?"

Del crossed his legs and stretched his arms behind his head, pipe clamped in his teeth, enjoying his riveted audience.

"Those were the times of the Crusades, still. They say they went on pilgrimage routes, hoping to bless the Crusaders and the pilgrims who accompanied them. They believed the relics they carried would assure victory in the Holy Lands. But those are only rumors," he scoffed, sucking hard on his pipe. "Imagine that. All those men, their very names lost to the world, their destinies a mystery only God's eye can pierce. Only silly tales left behind by which to remember them."

He slapped his knee and stood up.

"We'll be in port soon. I'd best return to my post before things get rough again. Ready yourselves for the landing."

He strode off toward the little lean-to to retake the wheel.

"France?" I asked Michael.

"France." He frowned, thinking hard. "Like the Wild Geese. And this time, I think I know where."

~

Later that night we parked ourselves in the town's tiny Internet café, huddling over the computer.

Michael spoke as he typed some words into the browser for the search.

"There were four main Crusader routes out of France, starting at Lyon, Marseille, Toulouse, and Metz. There were an additional four pilgrimage trails leading out of France to Santiago de Compostela. In all of these places, there are only two churches dedicated to me. One in Marseille and one in Le Puy-en-Velay."

He tilted the computer screen to give me a better look. The search for his church in Marseille showed what looked like a traditional cathedral in the middle of an urban setting. Two orderly spires reached into the sky, a crucifix between them. I looked at the photograph and felt nothing.

"Now look at Le Puy-en-Velay," Michael prompted, clicking the tab to bring up his other search.

I gasped.

It was a tiny chapel, perched high atop a craggy rock that jutted dramatically into the sky. The photographs showed it silhouetted against dark, angry clouds, making the scene all the more striking.

"It sits atop a basalt needle, all that is left of a volcanic plug. In ancient times, well before Christianity, it was recognized as a sacred place." He paused before adding grimly, "The original dolmens used for human sacrifice are incorporated into the chapel walls."

Sacrifice.

My soul knew—this was the place. I looked at Michael, and he nodded.

I continued clicking through the photos onscreen. The rock upon which the chapel sat rose nearly 270 feet, leaving the chapel perched high over the town of Le Puy.

"268 stone steps," Michael murmured, reading the accompanying text over my shoulder. "And a niche in the wall where relics found underneath the altar are on display."

We didn't say anything; we just stared at the screen, letting it sink in. To me, the pretty little church on the screen seemed like a gaping black hole that would suck us in and destroy us. A quiet thrumming filled my brain as I peered at the photo.

"You're sure?" Enoch asked.

I reached over and took Michael's hand.

"We're sure," Michael said.

He grasped the mouse and with a click shut down the browser.

It was settled, then. Tomorrow we would fly to France.

# ten

## FRANCE

Paris. Lyon. From there, we abandoned the plane and began the drive to Le Puy-en-Velay.

Through the hills. Winding. Turning. Climbing.

Every mile bringing us closer to Michael's death.

I froze with dread as we mounted each hill, thinking the end lay just over the summit. But each mount gave way to yet another curve, yet another hill, and still we climbed in silence.

I clung to Michael's hand from the front back seat, unable to bear any distance between us. Our bodies throbbed with a shared energy that could no longer hurt me, but simply passed between us in a constant current.

Too soon, the pretty town of Le Puy-en-Velay spread out before us, its warren of stone buildings and cobblestoned streets a monument to the rocky soil on which it stood. A statue of the Virgin and

Child soared above one end of the city. A few miles away, opposite the statue, loomed the Chapel of St. Michael.

I squeezed Michael's hand hard.

"It's early," Enoch said. "Do you want to go straight to the chapel?"

I tried to speak, but my mouth had gone dry. Michael answered for us instead.

"I don't think we should go while it is open to tourists. Why don't we settle in somewhere and have dinner?"

Michael navigated us through the maze of streets to a tiny hotel. Enoch had done his best to adopt our somber tone, even down to his attire. Gone was the jaunty fisherman or laid-back hippie of days past. Now, a respectable and grave grandfather-type took his place, swathed in gray and black, beard shorn close to his chin, the only colorful touch in his ensemble a beret perched high on his head. He seemed to know to take charge, speaking flawless French with the concierge, managing our papers, reserving us only two rooms.

He handed a set of keys to me and Michael, keeping the other for himself and saying nothing.

"Hope, can you settle us into the room? I'd like to take a walk with Enoch."

I nodded in response to Michael's question, dashing away the tear that sprang to the corner of my eye. He was going to tell Enoch. Picking up his duffel bag, I headed up the stairs.

Our room was tidy and plain, almost antiseptic. I went to the lace-curtained window and looked down on the gray stones of the street below. Michael and Enoch were walking there in the square, slowly, Enoch leaning heavily on his cane as always. Michael was gesturing as he spoke, his normally proud, erect body seeming to sag from the weight of fatigue and foreknowledge. The wind caught the thin cotton of his shirt, sending it billowing out behind him; all around them, people clutched their jackets close against the cutting chill of spring, but Enoch and Michael didn't seem fazed. Around the square they went, Enoch bending his head, listening intently as Michael continued to speak.

Then, for an instant, Enoch stumbled. Michael caught him before he hit the stones, bearing his weight until he could steady himself.

Enoch clung to Michael's arms, shaking his head in denial. He stepped back, gesturing wildly, seeming to argue with Michael. Michael waited patiently, saying nothing.

Then Enoch sat down on a park bench and began crying into his hands, broken, like the old man he pretended to be.

So now he knew.

Michael waited while Enoch composed himself. Tenderly, like a son, he handed Enoch back his cane and helped him struggle to his feet before pulling him on to continue their talk, tucking the old man's free arm in his as they slowly made their way. I let the curtain fall back into place, knowing what Michael would want to discuss, once Enoch had accepted his news: how to get me out of here, once Michael's sacrifice was complete.

I sat down on the edge of the bed and smoothed out a wrinkle.

Michael may have already accepted his fate, but I was not quite so ready.

We'd been hunted like animals. I'd even been branded like one. But corner a wounded animal, and it will do more than bare its fangs. When there's nowhere left to run, it will turn and fight you with every ounce of strength it has.

It was my turn to fight.

I may have been ordained to be the Bearer, but that didn't mean I had to play nice. I refused to sit by, passively accepting what already seemed decreed. Ancient words on a scrap of paper were not going to stand in my way. My fate was my own, and I was going to seize it back with both hands. They couldn't take Michael away from me—not if I had anything to do with it.

My mind raced over the possibilities. I couldn't simply disappear now—not without the rock. But what if I got to it first? What if I got to it and was able to destroy it? Then Michael would be safe and Heaven unassailable.

It was the only way.

And it would have to be tonight. It was my only chance.

I lost track of myself as I feverishly began to plan how I might safely slip away from under Michael and Enoch's watch. I had to be ready when the moment presented itself. Everything had to go flawlessly if I were to pull it off.

Suddenly, there was a soft brush of knuckles on the door, a jingle of keys. Michael.

He mustn't know.

I willed my mind blank and looked up at him expectantly as he came through the door and closed it softly behind him. He stood stiffly before the door, his customary grace leaving him as he fumbled with the keys. Hesitantly, he dropped them on the small side table before turning away from me, leaning against the door. His shoulders heaved, a silent sob wracking his body.

I flew off the bed and wrapped my arms around him.

He pulled away, as if he would hide, but there was nowhere he could go. Before he could escape, I slid my hand down his arm, past the rope and sinew of his straining muscles, and tangled my fingers in his, pulling him back to me like the moon coaxing the tide. I leaned into his broad back, resting my cheek in the hollow between his shoulder blades.

"Let me help you," I whispered. "Let me be strong for you."

He reached around for my other hand, wrapping it around

his waist. There was no distance between us now. I could feel the staccato of his heart, could feel the surge of life in his veins, could hear the whoosh of air escaping his lungs and leaving his lips in a heavy sigh.

"You can't. This cup is mine to drink," he said, his words tinged with bitterness. "I wish I—"

"Shhh," I whispered, squeezing his fingers more tightly. "It's ours. Yours and mine. Together."

His voice cracked. "I was supposed to protect you."

"And you did."

"But how . . ." His words trailed off.

"How will you protect me when you're gone?" My voice cracked. I could hardly say the words out loud. "I don't want your protection. I want you."

Beyond the thin wood of the door we could hear laughter, the sounds of a suitcase bumping along, a mother scolding her child, voices fading as they moved away down the hallway. We stood there, letting the sounds of the world wash over us, wishing the normalcy could hold back the inevitable.

Michael turned in my arms, reaching down to lift my chin. His eyes shined, one tear welling over and running down his cheek.

I reached up to wipe it away, letting my fingers linger. He caught them in his and pulled them to his lips, kissing them softly, his eyes never leaving mine.

"You have me."

He turned my hand over, stroking the tender skin of my palm with his thumb. He bent his head, pulling me closer as he drew my wrist to his mouth and began trailing his lips across it.

I gave an involuntary moan and leaned into him, unsure of my own feet.

He looked at me, eyes questioning.

I stepped away, catching his hands in mine as I began walking to the narrow bed behind me. When the back of my knees bumped against the soft chenille bedspread, I stopped, pulling him to me.

"I—"

"Shhh," I interrupted, placing my finger on his lips. "We don't have much time now."

I eased myself down onto the bed. Carefully, he came down after me, propping himself up on his elbows as if he were afraid to crush me.

"I'm not made of glass," I said, smiling at him nervously.

He smiled back with sad eyes. "Of course you're not," he said, brushing a lock of hair off my forehead. "I forget sometimes how tough you are."

I forced myself to look at him, really look at him. I wanted to memorize every inch of his skin, the glint of sea and sky in his eyes, even the shadows that seemed to hollow out his face. I needed to remember it all, just like I needed to drink in the smell of fresh hay, honey, and leather on his skin and feel the warmth of his breath on my face, imprinting it on my soul.

He closed his eyes and smiled ruefully before leaning his forehead to mine. "I can't let you do this," he whispered, his mouth not even an inch from mine. "Your grief is getting the best of you."

"This isn't grief," I whispered back before stealing a kiss. I let my mouth linger, savoring the taste of salt. Insistent, I nipped at his lips.

He kissed me back, hard, parting my lips as his hips thrust into mine. I stretched my arms above my head, arching into him as his tongue explored my mouth.

He pulled away, breathing hard. Roughly, he twined his fingers in mine, then took my hand to his heart. His eyes were dark, almost black, as he looked at me.

*This is the last time I will kiss you,* he said as his heart spoke to me.

I turned my head away, but he was faster, lowering his head to meet me with a kiss, slowly dragging me back to his thoughts as his free hand wrapped mine tight, and forcing it once more to his heart.

*This is the last time I will touch you like this*, he thought, as his hand snaked down to my hip. He pulled my blouse out from my waistband and let his fingers stray across my stomach.

My body quivered under his touch, and I began to cry.

*This is the last time I will be able to chase away your tears*, he thought, covering my face with tiny kisses, gentle as a butterfly's wing. His tears mingled with mine, hot and desperate.

Then nothing. Nothing but his breath coming in ragged bursts as he leaned his forehead against mine. Hesitating, he groaned before kissing the tip of my nose.

"I can't do this to you, Carmichael."

He pushed off of me, swinging his legs over the side of the bed. Before I could say anything, he'd stalked away, slamming his hand against the hollow wooden door in frustration.

I pulled my knees up into a ball, sobbing that he would push me away when my need for him was so great.

But all the while, even through my frustrated, angry tears, I clung to my little triumph. I had managed to protect my secret, hiding my thoughts from him even in our most intimate moments.

He still doesn't know what I am planning to do.

~

I rehearsed it over and over in my head, the thought of it carrying me forward as we lay there, curled together on that bed, marking the hours until dinner.

The tiny bistro Enoch had found for us would have been perfect in other circumstances. It was packed with locals sitting so close together it was impossible to tell who was dining with whom. Their chatter, rising and falling, filled the dining room. Light glanced off of gleaming brass and polished glass, warding off the descending darkness. It was supposed to feel warm and welcoming, I knew. But all I felt was a hollowness from which I couldn't escape.

"This way," Enoch murmured, gesturing after the host.

We wound our way through the tables, toward the back of the restaurant, and up a narrow staircase. At the top we walked into a tiny room in which a single table, set for three, was waiting. A fire was lit and crackling in the fireplace, awaiting our arrival.

"Messieurs, mademoiselle," the man said, guiding us to the table. Michael slid out my chair and helped me to my seat, giving my shoulder a squeeze. I bit my lip as his hand lingered there, holding back a cry at the familiarity in his touch. Enoch, struggling to sit down with his cane, didn't notice. The waiter handed us each a menu and pointed to the chalkboard on the wall, on which the evening's specials had been carefully written in curly script. Then he ghosted away, leaving us alone in the upper room.

I stared at the menu with unseeing eyes.

Enoch, too, seemed unable to concentrate, quickly placing the creamy white card down on the table.

"I'm not really that hungry," he mumbled, pushing the place setting away from him.

Michael looked at us both sharply.

"Nonsense. We all need our strength."

A server interrupted him mid-speech, bringing a basket to our table before disappearing down the stairs again.

"Besides," Michael continued, adopting a false joviality as he unwrapped the cloth that hid the warm bread in the basket. "We're here to celebrate our time together, are we not? Plenty of time for our planning later." He pulled a crusty baguette out and broke off a hunk with his hands.

"Here, take it," he said, holding it out to me.

I couldn't break bread with him, pretending nothing was wrong. I couldn't break bread knowing that we were preparing ourselves for his broken body. I recoiled, sliding my chair away from the table.

"Michael, we are not celebrating a last supper here," Enoch reprimanded him. "Show some sensitivity, please." He reached out his hand to me and I clutched it blindly through my tears.

"That's exactly what we're doing," Michael said mournfully, dumping the bread I'd rejected unceremoniously back into the basket.

I stood up. "I refuse to pretend that I accept any of this," I stated flatly. "I refuse to let you feel sorry for yourself when you could—should—be fighting this. You finish your dinner. I'll wait for you both back at the hotel."

Enoch scraped his chair across the wooden floor as if to come with me.

"No. Let her go, Enoch," Michael asked, putting a hand on Enoch's arm. "She'll be fine, and I need company tonight."

Enoch settled back in his chair. I wiped my eyes with the back of my hand and stumbled down the staircase and through the restaurant, out into the cold night air. Couples walked by, arm in arm, while the occasional car motored past. The world was moving, inexorably, when all I wanted it to do was stop.

I waited on the corner, watching the puffs of my breath disappear into the darkness, biding my time until I could be certain they hadn't followed me. The brassy tinkle of the bistro's bell as the door swung open dashed my hopes. I looked over my shoulder to find Enoch thundering with his cane down the sidewalk toward me.

"I want to be alone, Enoch," I began arguing before he even reached the curb, and I began to walk away.

"Hope, wait. I know what you're doing, and I want to help."

I stopped and turned to face him.

"I don't know what you're talking about."

Enoch's face was unreadable. Damn those glasses, I thought, not for the first time.

"You know as well as I do that the only solution to this mess we are in is to get to the rock tonight. Alone. Before Michael has a chance to get there himself."

I held my breath, not sure if I could trust him.

*He can help you. He is the only one*, Henri's urgent whisper spurred me on.

I walked closer to Enoch.

"Say more," I prompted, crossing my arms.

"We know where it is. But the Prophecy is clear. You are the Bearer. You are the one destined to retrieve it. And you can do that alone. Tonight. With my help."

I peered into his aviators. They were black, reflecting back the night.

"What help?"

"Michael will worry about you being gone, don't you think?" In the shadows cast by the streetlights, his face looked sinister, leering. "After all, you two seem closer than ever."

I blushed, embarrassed by his innuendo. Still, I didn't have time to waste. I brushed away his comment, irritated. "Michael's going to come after you any moment. Get to your point, Enoch."

A little muscle in his face twitched.

"I can keep him busy," he continued, "keep an eye on him, while you fetch the thing. We can dispose of it together, later. He'll never know."

I darted a glance over his shoulder, watching the bistro door.

"He can't know, Enoch. You can't say anything to him that will make him suspicious."

Enoch's face split into a grin. "You underestimate me. But even so, you don't have much time. Now go. Take my car. Bring the rock back to me, and I'll find a way to dispose of it." He hobbled closer and extended his free arm, inviting me in. I stepped into his embrace, trying not to choke on his cologne.

He held me close, leaning in to whisper in my ear. "Don't come back until you have the rock. I'll be waiting."

I stepped back. "With Michael?" I asked, needing his confirmation.

He smiled, his teeth flashing white in the dark. "Of course." He squeezed my shoulder. "I should go up now, before he comes after me." He dropped his arm and fished inside his pocket, then patted himself down, perplexed. "I can't find my keys."

"Don't need them," I answered. He shrugged, pushing his hands back deep into his pocket before turning and, leaning into the cane, weaving his unsteady way back to the restaurant. I waited, watching until he'd faded into the crowded tables. Finally, when I was convinced he'd returned to forestall Michael, I squared my shoulders and began to walk.

I wasn't going to wait for some miraculous intervention. I was going to be the intervention and put an end to this, once and for all.

I'd memorized where we'd parked the car. I'd marked the turns, noting the street signs as I wound my way back to it. Enoch had left it unlocked, as was his habit. I slid into the front seat, grateful to my father for teaching me what seemed a useless skill at the time—how to hot-wire a car.

"Thanks, Dad," I mumbled to myself as the tiny engine roared to life. I shifted the car into gear and pulled away from the curb.

All of my father's crazy lessons, all his wild beliefs, didn't seem so crazy now. I felt a touch of shame as I remembered how much I'd resented his lessons, how embarrassed I'd been by him. "I owe you an apology, Dad. As soon as I see you, you'll get it."

I didn't need a map. Michael's chapel loomed above the town, lit from below so that it glowed, like a beacon, against the deep navy of the night sky. I pointed the car toward it, beginning the ascent. One-way streets kept forcing me to turn from the path, but I was able to keep it in my sights so that it seemed I was circling toward it. My body buzzed with excitement, purpose, and dread as I wound my way closer to the church and to the Key.

As I approached the sheer cliffs, the stone buildings swallowed up my view. With a few blocks to go, I slid the car into an open spot on the street. I would walk from here. I fumbled under the seat, pulling out the backpack I'd stashed away, and left the car.

I emerged from the cluster of shops and houses to face the base of the rock. It jutted dramatically toward Heaven, its tower scraping against the moon. The basalt needle was interrupted by moss and greenery, life forcing itself through the barren stone.

I kept walking past an ornate crucifix on a pedestal and a small, octagonal building decorated with the same black and white mosaics I saw elsewhere in the city. The buildings fell behind me until I was facing the wide stone stairs that were laid into the rock, winding their way up to the church. A heavy chain was strung across the steps, a sign in French warning me that the chapel was closed.

I looked behind me. The street was empty. Somewhere, I could hear a radio or television blasting into an alley, its sounds staving off someone's loneliness.

I stepped over the chain. Then, I grasped the iron railing and began the climb, knowing I had no time to spare.

I moved quickly, the rough stone wall to my right giving me

some sense of security as I climbed higher and higher into the night. I avoided looking over the edge toward the town. I avoided doing anything at all, focusing instead on the sound of my breathing, getting heavier and heavier, as I counted each step.

One hundred and one.

One hundred and two.

One hundred and three.

The light reflecting off the church itself was dim, but the steps were smooth. I focused on the cracks between the stones and imagined the men who labored to lay each one, forging a path to the sacred site above, so they could, in turn, carry other burdens of stone to build the church.

One hundred ninety.

The buzzing in the back of my head was getting stronger.

I kept climbing, ignoring the inviting rest stops with their picturesque views. My thighs screamed in protest, but I just gripped the smooth railing tighter, pulling myself up each step, never slowing down.

Two hundred and twenty-five.

I looked up and could see the rocky walls of the chapel. My heart, already racing from the climb, skipped a beat.

I began running, desperate to get there now that I was so close.

Two hundred forty.

Two hundred forty-one.

Two hundred forty-two.

My backpack hit me with every stride, reminding me of the punishing pace. I gulped at the cold air, my lungs aching as I raced ahead.

The staircase widened, and I threw myself forward, abandoning the twisting iron rail in my rush to the top. I ran headlong up the remaining steps, hurtling over the stone walkway to the base of the chapel. I leaned forward, palms against the rocks, heaving to catch my breath.

I turned around and pressed my back against the rough-hewn walls, only then bothering to look at my surroundings.

Beyond the stone walls, Le Puy-en-Velay spread out below me, its lights twinkling in the dark, individual buildings and streets lost in the embrace of night. Across town, the statue of the Virgin Mary glowed, a silent observer of my fevered climb. From here, I could not see the expression on her face as she stared across the chasm toward me. Was it placid and loving, thinking of the babe in her arms? Or had grief stolen into her eyes, the aftermath of an angel's whispered foretelling of the fate of her son?

I didn't have time to think about it. I couldn't think about it. I had to keep moving.

A sudden fluttering echoed across the pavement, and I looked about wildly, shrinking against the walls of the church.

Nothing. There was nothing there.

Nothing but the wind.

I moved along the outer walls, trailing a hand behind me, looking over my shoulder to be sure I was still alone. I barely registered the outward bulge of the walls, round instead of straight, or the way laid stone merged into natural rock, paper-thin tufts of grass forcing their way through the masonry.

Another climb lay before me—the final stairs up to the chapel's door.

I took each step slowly, no longer eager to gain my prize. From here I could see the ornateness of the chapel: red, black, and white mosaics, intricately carved stone arches gracing the portal. I paused at the top, taking in the detail, the rush of imagery confirming that this was, indeed, the place.

At the very top of the wall, five niches filled with statues stood guard. At the center was a figure I recognized as Christ Triumphant, with the Alpha and the Omega. To one side, veiled, stood his mother. To the other, a winged angel—Michael. The triple arch above the door centered on a bas-relief carving of the Lamb of God, the words *Agnus Dei* confirming the image. At the base of the arch, the stone faces of men opened their mouths wide and spewed forth rich vines and foliage that became a tangle of carving spreading like a rainbow over the door. Hidden in the foliage, birds plucked at seeds. Other men, entangled in more leaves, stood to the right and left of the Lamb of God.

"Green men," I murmured, straining hard to remember the term from my art history class. A symbol of rebirth, a sign of the cycle of life turning to spring.

I looked more closely at the capitals atop the pillars on either side of the door. Another green man graced the one to the right. On the left, a bird spread its wings, recalling the phoenix emerging from the ashes.

Death and resurrection, everywhere I looked.

I registered the sirens over the door, their naked bodies seeming out of place. I didn't have time to puzzle over them, though. I leaned on the door and, finding it open, walked in.

Immediately, I was plunged into darkness. I fumbled in my backpack and pulled out the iPod that Enoch had left with me during our days in Istanbul. I pressed it on and used the glow from its tiny screen to light my way.

I was making my way through a corridor, headed into the church. The floor was uneven. I reached ahead of me, blindly, touching the cold walls for reassurance. My shuffling footsteps echoed through the church, bouncing off stone and returning to me, magnified.

I kept walking until I emerged into a narrow space punctuated by slender stone columns. I brandished my iPod up to the ceiling, trying to make sense of the space. The columns' capitals were covered with carvings of animals and more foliage, giving way to a barrel-vaulted ceiling. Instead of soaring, though, the ceiling felt close and claustrophobic. I glimpsed snatches of fresco here and there. I turned my light to the walls and saw I was in an irregular walkway that had nine bays at intervals around the church. Its walls curved away—the slight round shape I'd observed outside, an accommodation to the unusual restrictions of the site, no doubt. Scattered benches sat alone, waiting for a penitent. For the most part, the entire chapel was empty, solitude etched in stone.

The tiny windows in the outer walls let a little of the exterior floodlight into the church. Grey rock, worn smooth by centuries of pilgrims treading its surface, lay like a carpet below my feet. My eyes followed the cracked and pitted surface of the floor up to a short series of steps that gave way to a smaller space.

The sanctuary.

I moved instinctively toward it, the humming inside my brain turning into a full roar as I navigated the uneven floor and mounted the steps.

It was a tiny, square space, its low walls moving into a pyramid-shaped vault. The light was even dimmer here, but in the reflection from my screen I could make out faint frescoes, richly colored. Christ in Majesty, flanked by the sun and moon, was arrayed to fill the shrine's ceiling. Above him, this time, was Michael, depicted in full Archangel regalia and attended by seraphim. Medallions of saints and angels finished the corners. Man and angel, joined as one in worship of the two who would sacrifice everything to redeem those who had failed.

I glanced around quickly at the walls of the sanctuary, the light flickering off the paintings. Images of the resurrection of the dead, Heaven and Hell, angels and saints stared back at me, wide-eyed, the flatness of their medieval likenesses seeming even odder in the half-light. I scanned quickly, knowing what I was looking for.

There, in the right wall of the sanctuary, was the niche.

It had no door or cabinet; it was really just a gaping hole in the dark.

The roaring in my head was overwhelming now, urging me on.

I moved across the stone floor, unable to hear the echoes of my footsteps any longer, until I was standing directly in front of the opening.

I lifted a hand and noticed that my fingers were trembling. I closed my eyes and thrust my hand into the niche, feeling around inside until I felt something rough. I wrapped my fingers around it and lifted. Instantly, the images I'd seen before in my dreams—the man's hand gripping the stone, its surface dripping with blood, came racing back to me.

"Hope! What are you doing?"

I wheeled around, eyes flung open, and saw Michael standing between the columns, breathing heavily.

He looked at me in the face, his eyes searching, before letting his glance drift down to my hand. He stopped, eyes widening.

I looked down and saw that I had it.

In my hand, I had the Key.

It was smaller, somehow, than I'd expected. I ran my thumb over an edge and felt the sharpness of it, how easy it would be for flesh to give way under its violence.

"Don't come any closer!" I shouted, pulling the rock behind my back and backing up to the niche. I glanced over Michael's shoulder, looking for Enoch, but he wasn't there. Michael was alone.

"Hope." Michael's voice was like a caress, bridging the space between us. "You can't do this," he reasoned, his voice utterly calm as he inched toward the first step. "It's not the way it's supposed to happen."

"You don't know that," I pleaded, the rock feeling heavy in my hand.

"We both know it," he said, taking another step toward me.

"Don't come any closer," I warned, moving away from the niche toward the altar in the middle of the sanctuary.

"Carmichael," he whispered, and I gave a little sob to hear the way he said my name, the tenderness in his voice. He stretched his hand out to me. "Don't make this any harder than it already is."

I shook my head, biting my lip to hold back the tears.

"Please," he said, his voice hoarse, as he reached one trembling hand out to me.

*Go to him.*

Henri. Good old Henri.

"Always there for the drama," I whispered to myself, wiping my face.

I took a step toward Michael, then another. I began to run to him, my eyes never leaving his.

But then, out of nowhere, I felt a push, hard, in my back.

My ankle twisted, and I fell down the steps. I hit the rough stone, my hands splayed out to break my fall, and the rock flew from my hand. I watched, shocked, as it skidded across the floor before coming to land at the base of a column.

Michael moved swiftly to my side.

"Are you okay?" he asked, crouching down beside me. I looked up at him and saw something I hadn't expected to see in his eyes—disappointment.

Confused, I nodded, pushing myself up.

He offered me his hand and helped me sit. Sadly, he tucked a piece of hair behind my ear, his fingers lingering against the skin of my neck. I closed my eyes, letting the familiar warmth of his touch flood my senses once again as he kissed the top of my head.

"You should have told me Henri was still here with you." His voice held the slightest hint of reproach.

My eyes flew open wide. He was looking at me, his gray eyes serious.

I opened my mouth to deny his accusation but stopped, unsure of myself.

Michael's eyes were wistful but kind, his voice laden with regret. "Only a guardian angel can break the plane between Heaven and Earth to interfere in the physical world. Only guardians and Archangels," he added. "He pushed you down the stairs, Hope. He's been tricking you all along, waiting for you to lead him here. He must be working with the Fallen. I'm guessing the others will be here shortly."

His words were like blows to my middle, stealing my breath.

Betrayal.

Gabrielle had warned me. *It is by your hand that Michael will feel love and loss, betrayal and death.*

"No!" I shouted, pushing Michael away to scramble on my knees over the rough stone floor after the rock. I grasped it in my hand and then backed up, propping myself up against a column, clutching the rock to my chest. I remembered how puzzled Michael had been that the Fallen had let us escape in Las Vegas, how worried he'd been that our journey to chase the Key had been too easy. His bewilderment when we'd been tracked so quickly in Istanbul. Now it all made sense.

They hadn't needed to chase us; they'd had one of their own in our midst.

"I trusted you!" I shouted into the air, squeezing the rock even tighter in my hands.

*Then you chose poorly,* Henri whispered into my mind, the venom in his voice unmistakable. *And he should have known better than to challenge the order of things. I had to punish him for his interference. He thought it was so easy to dismiss me, didn't he? Now he'll see.*

I sobbed in frustration. All this time, I'd been leading them straight to us. All because I hadn't believed in Michael.

"You didn't know what you were doing," Michael soothed, as if he could read my mind. He moved toward me, then stopped, frowning, to peer into the corners of the church.

"They're here," he said.

There was a rushing sound. The tiny windows of the chapel were suddenly filled with dark writhing shapes, plunging us into complete darkness.

"Michael!" I screamed, but I couldn't see him, couldn't hear him above the mounting roar.

The shapes darted about; they floated like smoke, wrapping themselves around stone and mortar, settling into the far corners of the church. The sickening stench of sulfur wafted across the room in their wake, confirming what I already knew.

I was too late.

In the corners, the shapes began to solidify, taking form. Slowly, they emerged from the shadows, almost seeming to emanate their own dark light.

One. Two. Ten. Twenty.

More Fallen Angels than I had ever seen before, dressed in armor as if for battle. Their black wings seemed alive, coiling and burning like molten lava as they unfurled, shimmering like broken glass, the edge of every feather crisp and sharp.

I cringed, pushing myself up against the stone, looking wildly about for my escape. But there was nowhere for me to go. They were everywhere, the darkness of the night seeming to disgorge them from every corner, their bodies multiplying before my very eyes.

One of them emerged from the pack, his dark wings spread majestically as he strode toward me. His eyes were hard, and he looked at me with disdain, his lips curled in disgust as if I were mere refuse, as he stretched out his palm.

"There's no point in resisting us. Hand over the Key, daughter of Eve. It is written."

I looked up to where he towered above me. Defiantly, I lifted my chin. "I won't give it to you."

My voice was shaky, but even as I said the words, I grew more confident. I pushed myself up, using the column for support, and stood gingerly on my hurt ankle. From across the gallery, Michael frowned and shook his head slightly.

The Fallen Angel smiled, his lips morphing into a sinister grin. "Then we shall have to take it from you."

Flames burst around the edges of the church—ancient torches, hung intermittently on the stone walls, bid to life by the Fallen. As their tongues of fire danced, the torches cast strange shadows among the pillars of stone.

Knowing the theatrics were meant to scare me didn't make them any less frightening.

The dark angel moved toward me, circling as he approached as if hunting his prey, when we heard an unexpected voice.

"Don't you think you should pick on someone your own size?"

The angel spun around. Swiftly, the tip of a cane stabbed him in the middle of his chest.

"Enoch!" I gasped, relief flooding my body as he emerged from the darkness of the ramp, walking the angel, who now appeared less confident, away from me.

Enoch looked smug behind his sunglasses, moving with

assurance even without the assistance of his cane. He looked for all the world to me like a misfit musketeer, brandishing his walking stick like a sword, jabbing the angel's armored chest as he forced him back, back, ever back from where I stood, speechless.

Of course, I realized, in his aged and out-of-shape condition, Enoch had been slower to climb the stairs than Michael. But he'd kept climbing, never giving up. Even in the dim light I could see the sheen of sweat on his face and detect the heaviness of his breathing. He may have been slow, but his timing was impeccable.

Carefully, he forced the Fallen Angel up against a stone wall.

"Unsheath your weapon. Drop it on the floor—here, at my feet."

The angel stood over a head taller than Enoch. I could see his face contort with contempt, then rage, then disbelief as he realized none of his comrades were coming to his aid. Petulantly, he opened his mouth, but before he could speak, Enoch slid the tip of his cane against his throat.

"Now. I mean it."

The angel glowered and clamped his mouth shut. He grabbed the hilt of his sword and withdrew it from its scabbard. Angrily, he threw it down upon the stone floor. The clang of metal against rock echoed around the chapel.

"That's better," Enoch said with a harrumph. "Don't make me use this on you," he warned his captive as he half-turned to face the crowd, keeping a watchful eye on the angel. "That goes for all of you."

The Fallen Ones shifted uneasily.

"You gave us a good chase, missy," Enoch chided me, giving me his full attention. In the shadowy corner where he stood, I couldn't really make out his face, just the slight glint of light bouncing off his sunglasses. "See all the trouble you've caused."

I gulped back my tears, confused. "But, Enoch, you—" His curt shake of the head cut me short. He didn't want Michael to know we'd conspired. "I was only trying to get the Key before anyone else could."

"I figured as much," he answered, thrusting the point of his cane a little harder against his prisoner's neck as he spoke, lest the angel get any ideas. "Still, it was a foolish thing to do. Brave, but foolish. And now you and Michael are in a pickle. Lucky I turned up when I did, hmm?"

"We can't fight them, Enoch," I said, looking about the church at the throng of dark angels. They were hesitant, but I knew it wouldn't last for long. They'd been taken by surprise, but once they recovered we would be no better off than before. "There are too many of them."

"That's true," he said, lowering his cane and leaning heavily into it. He nodded and stroked his long, grizzled beard, giving some thought to our predicament. He gave the angel a stern look and turned to face me, rocking on his heels as he continued his rumination. "But they have to take it from your hand, do they not? This Key must be borne to them by you, for you are the Bearer. If it should come to someone else—someone a little older and wiser, perhaps, we would have an impasse. Would we not?"

My jaw dropped open. It was an elegant, simple solution. "Brilliant!" I gasped.

"Hope," Michael warned, but I was already hobbling forward on my twisted ankle, hands outstretched, to thrust the rock into Enoch's hands.

I didn't notice that none of the Fallen were moving to stop me.

I didn't notice that Enoch seemed too eager to take the rock, abandoning his cane to come swiftly toward me with open hands.

I didn't notice, until it was too late, that the overwhelming smell of cologne no longer clung to his body, replaced as it was by the stench of sulfur.

Enoch's fingers closed around the rock, snatching it away from me. He threw his glasses to the ground, his blank eyes staring reverentially at the thing he now held in his palm, the fingers of his other hand shaking with excitement.

Enoch lifted his face and looked at me with a sneer. There, in the empty whiteness of his eyes, I saw a spark.

He shimmered, and his body seemed to melt before me. It shifted and whirled into itself like a vortex, folding itself round and round the Key, unleashing a storm-like roar. I stumbled back, the force of the wind unnerving me, as I watched the change. His cane twisted and stretched, turning into a sword and leaping up from the floor of its own accord to join the swirl that had become Enoch's body. The winds shrieked—a lonely, guttural sound that spoke of heartache and suffering—as the tornado grew denser, darker, beginning to take shape. Through it all, Enoch's empty eyes stared at me steadily, his gaze never breaking as his body—a different body, taller, broader, unbroken by age or infirmity, a strong body bound in muscle and sheathed in armor—reformed about him. He stared at me full in the face, all that was left of the Enoch I had known, until the white blindness fell away—the vacancy of his stare now filled with greed and hate.

They were eyes I knew all too well.

"Hope, Hope, Hope."

His voice emerged before the body had settled into its final shape, before the fury of wind and sound that had accompanied his transformation had fully died down. I choked back a cry as I recognized it.

I shook my head, refusing to believe what I had done, feeling the last bit of hope drain away from me as I shrank back against the cold stone column.

Enoch was no more. The one who took his place unfurled his

dark wings and flapped them impatiently as he waited for me to acknowledge him.

"Lucas." My voice was flat.

Lucas reached out, clearing the distance between us in an instant and grabbing me by my hair, jerking my head back, hard.

"The Bearer of the Key!" he proclaimed, his voice full of contempt. He twisted my arm behind me, forcing me to walk ahead of him as he paraded me before his fallen compatriots. "She thought she could deny fate. She thought she could outwit us, didn't she, my brothers? But instead she has handed it over to us, as we knew she would."

Out of the corner of my eye, I saw him thrust his fist into the air, biceps straining as he held the rock high in triumph. He held me tight against his body, and I had to fight the urge to vomit from the overpowering smell of sulfur.

"The Key!" He shouted, jostling me again, and the crowd of Fallen Angels roared, their taunts and jeers assaulting my ears.

"When?" I demanded, struggling futilely against him. "When did you take his place?"

"Does it even matter?" he questioned, enjoying my torment as he pulled me closer against his chest. "Yes, I suppose for a little girl like you, a girl whose petty human mind must make sense of everything, it would matter a great deal. I will grant you this favor and tell you, then. We were watching when you met Enoch in the desert. We saw that he had given you the Prophecy."

I remembered the cold shadow that had fallen over me when Enoch had disappeared in the desert and the uneasiness that had settled around me when I couldn't place it.

It had been them all along.

"When we paid him a visit ourselves, and he did not give us the answers we sought, we defeated him in battle, sending him to wait out his time in the depths of Hell. When Michael later called for Enoch's help, it was only too easy to slip myself into your midst. Your snitch, Henri, made it even easier, sowing fear and doubt at every turn.

"You thought yourself so smart, playing both sides in case Michael became too dangerous, didn't you?" He twisted my arm harder and ran his free hand up my neck, leaning in close. He inhaled deeply, burying his nose in my hair. I lashed out, aiming an elbow at his ribs, but he dodged out of the way and hiked my arm more tightly behind me. I winced in pain, but I refused to cry out. I would not give him that satisfaction.

"The smell of sulfur could have given me away, but you were both so frightened we managed to make you think that it was Michael turning, when all along it was me, rematerializing to play my role. You hid your thoughts from Michael, but you could not keep them from Henri. You practically whispered the mysteries of your heart right to me. Every secret, every discovery, was ours as soon as it was revealed to you.

"Everything you did, you did because I wanted you to do it," he boasted. "We played you like the stupid human that you are."

Shame washed over me when I realized how easily I'd been manipulated.

"Let her go, Lucas."

My heart was pounding, but Michael's voice was calm, unwavering, as he continued challenging Lucas. I twisted in Lucas's grasp, straining to see Michael. He was standing alone between two pillars, fists clenched.

"This isn't about her. It's about me. Let her go, and you can do with me what you will."

"I don't need your permission!" Lucas barked. "Don't you see you are surrounded? There is nothing you can do to stop me. All your preening superiority? All your love of man? What will it do for you now? Who will stop us from killing you? You who dared to let yourself be raised on a pedestal. Blasphemy—against God and the angels! Are you like God, as your name proclaims? If you are like God, save yourself, now!"

Michael did not even flinch. He simply gazed steadily back at Lucas, his eyes sad. "My name is what it is. As for blasphemy, it is you who say it, not I."

"Michael," I begged, struggling against Lucas's iron grip. "Forget about me. Defend yourself. Take your angel form; at least then you'll have a fighting chance." All the air in the chapel seemed to contract, as if the suggestion alone could upset the balance of the world.

"I can't," Michael said quietly. "I am too weakened now. Even if I wanted to change, I'm trapped in my human form."

The raucous laughter of the Fallen Ones echoed off the stone vaults of the church.

"See, daughter of Eve? You've betrayed him with your body, too. You've drained him of the last power he had. Now when we fight, we fight to the death. When we defeat him, he will stand no more as the Gate to Heaven, blocking our way. His mortal body shall be his eternal prison and we, the Fallen, will regain the realm from which we were banished. We shall succeed, this time, and it is all because of you."

"You don't understand! It's not what you think!" I fought against Lucas, wanting to make him listen to me.

"I know enough to be certain that you played your role, Bearer of the Key. Because of you, Michael will die."

I felt sick, knowing he was right. Those moments that had meant so much to me—the stolen kisses, the lingering touches—they'd given me intuition at the expense of Michael's own strength. Just not enough to know what was really going on.

"Lucas," Michael began, his voice ringing out as he squared his chest. In the little light that had penetrated the chapel, I could see the vein on his forehead pulsing in anger. "Let her go. It serves no purpose to force her to witness this."

I felt Lucas's hot breath on my neck as he laughed.

"But then who will tell of our glory if none is here to witness it?" He murmured against my neck—a feeling of a thousand spiders crawling—making me cringe with disgust. He jostled me on my feet as if to punctuate his every statement. "Who shall explain to the stupid masses of humanity why their world is upside down, why God does not answer their pleas for help? No, she shall stay. But I am feeling generous. I will let her go when I am finished with you."

"I want your oath." Michael's fists clenched tighter as he waited for Lucas to answer.

"I swear it." Lucas solemnly intoned. Suddenly he seemed grave, as if the prospect of victory after millennia of waiting was overwhelming. He shook his head, chasing away whatever thought had captured his mind.

"The time has come," he barked, shoving me aside with grim determination. He looked around the shadowy church. "Someone hold her. She must see it through to the end."

Rough hands took hold of my arms, pulling me tightly between two massive Fallen Angels.

I tried to twist away, shouting across the vaulted space. "Michael, please, don't let them do this to you!" The angels just held me fast, snickering at my weak attempts to break free. "Tell them the truth! Tell them the truth about the Gate!"

Michael looked at me with furrowed brows from the other side of the chapel, shaking his head ever so slightly. The flickering torchlight showed his eyes full of tears. Wordlessly, he turned away to face the seething crowd.

"I give myself over to you," he said, holding his arms out to one of Lucas's henchmen.

The throng of angels seemed to pulse with excitement. From the shadows, someone produced a length of rope. Quickly, Michael's wrists were bound, and he was lashed to one of the columns, his arms spread above his head, leaving him vulnerable.

"More," Lucas ordered. Two more coils of rope were produced. Michael's ankles were tied, spreading his legs wide as they pulled the ropes around the post. Someone tore open the front of Michael's thin cotton shirt, leaving it hanging in rags about his shoulders. He shivered in the cold, his chest heaving with labored breaths.

Lucas tested the ropes, which held fast.

"Can you feel it?" he taunted Michael, loud enough for us all to hear. He held the rock up to the firelight. "It pulses with life. Can you hear it, Michael, screaming for blood? It was God's mistake that allowed this bloodlust to come into the world. It was your mistake that mankind was allowed to live on, when all Heaven cried out against it. The rock that claimed blood then shall claim yours now."

Faster than we could see, he lashed out at Michael's face, slashing it open with the sharp edge of the stone. Michael cried out in shock. Blood welled and spurted, dripping down his face.

I gasped at the cold, calculated precision of it, realizing that Lucas meant to relish his kill. Instinctively, I reached for Michael, surging against my captors' arms. The angels yanked me back against them, holding me even more tightly.

"Die, my brother." Lucas slashed at Michael's face again, opening up an oozing line over his cheekbone. "Die, knowing that there will be no one left to protect the innocent here on Earth." He lunged at Michael's body, and a red bloom of blood spread like an oil slick across his chest.

"Die, knowing that the Gates of Heaven stand unguarded, and we will stand triumphant over the Throne in mere days."

With a flick of his wrist, he opened a vein in Michael's arm and blood spurted everywhere.

I tried to look away, but the angels twisted their hands in my hair, forcing me to watch as Michael sagged against the ropes in agony.

"Die, knowing you die because of the hand of the woman who you loved," Lucas said with a sneer, "the very woman who betrayed you in the end. Die now."

Lucas raised his hand high above his head, brandishing the rock.

"Stone him!" Someone yelled from the back of the crowd.

"No!" I shrieked, struggling against my captors.

Lucas brought the rock down onto Michael's skull. A horrible thud echoed through the chamber.

Everyone stopped, struck dumb by what they'd just witnessed.

Slowly, Lucas stepped back from the column where Michael's body slumped against the ropes. Suddenly, he whirled, thrusting the bloody rock above him in a sick sign of victory.

A howl of madness ran through the angels. One of them strode up to the column. Mustering all his strength, he kicked Michael in the abdomen. Michael's body twitched against the ropes. Not satisfied, the angel kicked again and again until, spent, he walked away, a sneer of satisfaction on his face. Another angel took his turn, batting Michael about the head like a cat playing with a toy. Then, as if released from a spell, they all fell upon Michael's body, engulfing it in a swarm of violence.

The angels holding me threw me to the ground, their charge forgotten in their desire to join the bloodshed. I couldn't see Michael any longer, but I didn't need to. The throng was three-deep now, angels fighting for a chance to strike their own blow. They'd torn him from the column, throwing his body onto the stone floor, so they could better kick and defile it. The sickening sounds of breaking bones mingled with cries of pain and the screams of violent pleasure as the Fallen Ones took out their millennia of anger and frustration on Michael.

I crawled up the steps, sobbing, to hide behind the altar, waiting for my chance, trying to block out the sickening thuds, the sounds of retribution as they had their way with Michael.

Eventually, the orgy of bloodshed petered out as the Fallen Ones sated themselves with revenge. Bloodied and spent, they stepped away, leaving Michael's body collapsed on the stones. The torchlight flickered, reflecting off the bloody gore that splattered their armor, as they huddled in groups, breathless, almost disbelieving what they had done.

Lucas shoved his way through the clusters of soldiers. "Where's the girl?" he demanded, wiping his brow. He still held tightly to the rock, his talisman, his Key to Heaven. He looked around the chapel, scanning for a sign of me. I shrank back behind the altar, praying he would overlook me in the shadows.

He kept looking, peering into the night as he licked his lips. His eyes were excited, aflame with bloodlust. I could see their whites, gleaming crazily in the half-light.

"No matter," he said, dismissively, turning his back to my hiding place. Carefully, I watched, pressing myself to the ground.

"She is insignificant now that Michael is dead. Yet she annoyed me with her resistance. One day, I will claim her and complete the degradation of our enemy. Let her live in fear, knowing that the protection of the angels is no longer with her. But right now we have more important things to tend to. Tonight is ours, my friends!" He shouted, flinging his arms wide in the air, the slight light glinting off his armor. The fallen angels chanted and hollered their approval.

"The Earth is ours! Let our mayhem be a sign to Heaven that its reign of injustice is over. Away!"

With a scream of vengeance, the Fallen Angels rose like one. As quickly as they'd come, they vanished into smoke and shadow, forming a violent whirlwind in the center of the chapel. The cloud pulsated as, shrieking, it turned into a flock of crows. The birds swirled and darted around the columns, crowing their victory before streaming out the windows and abandoning the church to descend upon the unknowing town below them.

Silence settled around me.

I waited, afraid it was a trap, fearful at the sound of my own heaving breath. When I was certain we were truly alone, I flung myself down the stairs to Michael. He was huddled on the floor, face down. I knelt beside him in a pool of sticky blood, afraid to touch him. Gently, I placed my hands on his broken body. I cringed to feel him shudder at my touch. Carefully, barely touching his shoulders, I rolled him over.

I choked back a cry.

His face was swollen and misshapen, the flesh raw from the beating he'd taken. His forehead was collapsed in; tiny bone fragments clung to his matted, bloody hair.

I ran my hands over his body. Dark purple bruises were already welling up, his taut skin barely able to contain the hemorrhaging. A broken bone, jagged, stuck out of his arm. Everywhere there was blood. Everywhere.

"No, no, no," I murmured desperately, ripping off my sweatshirt and pressing it against his arm to staunch the flow.

He moaned, and opened his eyes. The whites were speckled with red. He looked at me and smiled beatifically.

*Oh my God*, I thought with horror. *He's still conscious.*

My sweatshirt was already soaked, his damaged heart still weakly pumping out blood in fits and starts. The tangy smell of it assaulted my nose, leaving me gagging. I tied the arms of the shirt around his wound the best I could and ripped off my next layer, frantically wiping his face, trying to stop the bleeding.

He reached up and grabbed my hand, stilling me.

"Shhh," he said, his eyes rolling shut. He pressed my hand to his chest. I could feel his heart beating weakly.

*You must let me go.* His words seared themselves into my brain.

"You're not dying," I insisted, twisting his fingers in mine as I fought back the tears. "They left you for dead, but you're alive. You will live."

*Hope,* he chastised. *All God's children must have their chance, even the Fallen. Don't begrudge them their chance. They know not what they do. And neither did you.*

I spread my fingers wide over his chest. Beneath my palm, I could feel his heartbeat getting weaker. A sob escaped my lips. Desperate, I pulled his other hand to my heart.

*Please don't leave me,* I thought. *I don't know how to be without you.*

A tear dripped from my nose and fell onto his face, clearing a tiny rivulet through the blood. He winced from the sting of the salt.

*Hope Carmichael,* he said, sighing my name like a prayer. *Belief. Expectation. Heart of my heart.* His body convulsed, caught in the grip of pain as his eyes rolled back in his head. *I could have spent all eternity with you and been happy. Until I loved you, my sacrifice was unworthy.*

Under my hand, his heart skipped a beat, then faintly stuttered back.

"No," I said out loud. "Not yet." I gathered him up in my arms, cradling him in my lap. He coughed, a fresh stream of blood welling up and running from his mouth.

"No," I repeated, wiping away the blood with my hair. I ran my fingers along his brow, brushing his hair out of his eyes, desperately wishing away his pain. "No."

He opened his eyes. They were clear. Untroubled.

"It is finished," he whispered.

Beneath my hand, his heart contracted, then stopped.

Frantic, I ran my hands over his body, as if somehow I could chase the last fleeting pulse of life, could keep it from leaving his body, could will it back into his limbs. My fingers fluttered over his broken bones, wishing him whole, willing my hands to knit him together. Even as I touched him, I could feel the cold seeping into his flesh, could feel his life slipping away.

I stopped, my fingers hovering over his heart.

*Michael?* My soul sent the question out as I waited in the shadows for him to answer.

A torch sputtered and expired, followed by another.

*Michael?*

There was no answer.

I gathered Michael's body in my arms, the keen cut of grief slicing me through as I realized he was really gone.

I huddled over it, washing him with my tears, as one by one, the torches snuffed themselves out, plunging me back into darkness. I held him tight, rocking, refusing to let him go. I curled up to him like a wounded animal, desperate to protect the shell that was his body, grief-stricken by the knowledge that I had betrayed him. I had been the instrument of his death, however unwitting.

In that moment, nothing existed for me. My world was nothing but the dead weight of him in my arms and the guttural cries—the foreign sounds ripped from my own throat—that bounced off the stone walls, mocking me.

*Hope.*

My heart surged, then recoiled with disgust as I realized it was not Michael's voice I was hearing. It was Henri's.

*Hope.*

Somewhere outside, far below the chapel, I heard the breaking of glass and the plaintive wail of a car alarm.

*It isn't safe here. You must go.*

"No," I said, stubbornly clinging to Michael's limp body.

*You must leave him. It was his last wish that you be safe.*

I paused. "It's not safe?"

*If you linger here much longer, it will not be safe for you. Now, you must flee.*

A sudden weariness overtook me. It would be so easy to just lay down here. I could lie down next to Michael and wait for everything to end.

I felt a sharp pinch in my arm.

"Ow!" I shouted, rubbing at the spot. "You're not supposed to be able to do that."

*I'm your Guardian. I can always break the plane between our worlds to intervene when necessary. And right now it is necessary. Get yourself up. Say your goodbye. You must go. You must do it for him. For Michael.*

"Don't you speak his name!" I shouted, the spittle flying from my mouth as I turned, sheltering his body behind me. My breath was coming in great heaves, my fingers shaking as I clutched at his bloody, broken corpse. The sounds below were growing louder. As angry as I was with Henri, I realized he was right. I couldn't stay here. It was time to go.

"Leave me," I ordered, my voice raw with emotion. "I want to say goodbye alone."

*Very well. I'll wait outside the door. You have five minutes.*

I waited what seemed like long enough for Henri to move out of the chapel, realizing I'd never know it if he was still watching me. I laughed, a hysterical guttural sound, as I realized I'd trusted him, even now, when he was probably the least deserving of my trust.

He and Enoch had both been unworthy of my trust, I acknowledged, bowing my head over Michael, giving myself over to my grief. I slipped my hand across his bloody chest until my palm came to rest over his heart.

*Forgive me,* I thought, willing my thoughts through the night to find him, wherever he might be. *Forgive me for not believing. Forgive me for leaving you here, alone.*

*But more than that,* I prayed, thinking of the frescoes overhead, clinging desperately to their promise, *come back to me.*

*Death and resurrection,* I thought, taking a deep breath as I imagined the image of the phoenix, rising from the ashes, over the chapel door.

*Three days,* I thought, clinging desperately to the notion of an Easter-like awakening. *Come back to me in three days. I'll be waiting.*

I bent over and pressed my lips to his bloody brow.

Carefully, I slid his heavy body to the ground. I wrapped my sweatshirt around him the best I could, as if it were a blanket and he were simply asleep. I touched a hand to my lips and pressed my fingers one last time to his silent heart.

Struggling to my feet, I backed away, limping, until I could go no farther. Then, I turned, picking up my backpack.

From behind a column, a looming shape emerged.

A Fallen One.

I gasped and stumbled back.

He followed me, stepping into the weak light that was trickling in from the window so I could see his face. His eyes were shining, his dusty cheeks marked with the trails of tears. With a shudder, he pulled his sword from his scabbard.

I cringed. So this is how it would end.

The sword dangled there in his fingertips, swinging idly at his side. I watched as he gripped and regripped it, his hands twitching. I could not look away as he wrapped his fingers firmly about the hilt.

He lunged forward, tossing the sword away to clang and clatter against the cold floor, throwing himself at my feet.

I was too scared, too confused, to move.

I watched as he dragged his body across the rough stones. Slowly, reverently, he raised his head, eyes closed, to kiss the tip of my shoe.

A new flurry of tears slid down his face.

"Thank you," he whispered, backing away on all fours.

His form flickered. I watched, stunned, as his black armor fell away, replaced by snowy white. He drew himself up to his knees. Face filled with wonder and joy, he broke into a smile. His body started glowing, then pixelated into a million starry points of light before collapsing in on itself, disappearing.

I stared at the empty space where he had been.

*The first to claim his redemption,* Henri whispered. *The first to understand what the opening of the Gate really means. Now you see for what you suffer.*

I wasn't angry to find him at my side; my surprised scream had probably brought him to my aid. I couldn't find any words to answer him, so I just turned and hobbled away down the ramp and out of the chapel.

The night was black, starless.

*You'll have to move quickly,* Henri urged. *There isn't much time.*

My twisted ankle protested as I began my half-running, half-hopping descent down the rock. The steps seemed endless now, my journey pointless.

*Not pointless,* Henri interrupted. *We have to get you home safe.*

Home. The concept seemed foreign, now. But I felt a flicker of need; need for my mother and father, both; need for the comfort and love and unquestioning acceptance that I knew would be mine if I could find my way back to them.

As we descended, winding down the rocky steps, strange sounds began floating up to me. The screeching of metal grinding together. The tinkle of broken glass. Screams.

*It has begun,* Henri explained. *The Fallen are in a frenzy of bloodlust. It will sweep the Earth, and you away with it, if we aren't careful.*

I stopped and hung myself over the outer stone wall, clinging to the iron rail for support, and looked down. In the streets below I could see cars crashed into walls and into one another, left as smoking heaps against the sidewalk. The road was lined with vandalized homes, doors broken in and windows completely smashed, the crisp, lace-edged curtains that had hung so daintily in them this afternoon now hanging in shreds. Wailing sirens cut through the night, whining *waa waaaah* as the ambulances and *gendarmes* crisscrossed the other parts of town.

The only person I saw was lying in the street, either injured or dead.

"It's a rampage," I whispered in stunned awe.

*It is the beginning of what they think is the End. Even though they have fulfilled the Prophecy, they do not understand it. They think they have won. They think Heaven will yield to force. They cannot comprehend that the Gate has already opened to them, if they only ask forgiveness and mercy. This is the start—their celebration before they fling their armies against the doors of Heaven.*

*Come, you have little time.*

I moved faster now, ignoring the pain in my ankle as we wound our way down the rock. By the time we reached the bottom, Le Puy-en-Velay was in a full riot, screaming crowds running through the streets, opportunists taking advantage of the disarray to plunder from vandalized stores.

*They sow fear and destruction in their wake. The worst impulses of humanity quicken at their touch. Whether driven by greed or cowardice, mankind's violence shall shatter the peace of this night. Quickly, now.*

Henri steered me into the narrow street, back to the car. It seemed so long ago that I'd left it behind, parked against the curb. But, miraculously, it had gone through the night unharmed. I slid behind the wheel and fumbled with the wires, bringing the engine to life.

I gripped the steering wheel. My fingers were tacky with blood, sticking to the vinyl. "I don't know where to go," I said out loud, my vision clouded with tears.

*It doesn't matter. Just drive.*

I blinked my tears away, forcing myself to focus. I did a three-point turn in the narrow street, unwilling to head any closer to the riot. The wheels screeched in protest, but eventually I was racing back up the hill, toward the hotel and away from the dark chapel that stood proud and lonely, its secrets safe, atop the basalt needle.

*I'm fleeing a murder scene*, I thought. When they found the body, Michael's death would be classified as another unfortunate part of the nighttime melee, its mysteries left unsolved.

*Don't think. Just drive.*

"Why are you even helping me?" I asked, baffled by his hanging on, still angry at his betrayal. I hated myself for being grateful that he was here to help me now and was more than a little suspicious that he was steering me into trouble.

*Maybe things didn't turn out the way I expected them to,* he answered, before settling into silence. *In my haste to punish Michael for his prideful interference, I chose my allies poorly. Maybe I, too, misunderstood the Prophecy until it was too late.*

I ran into an improvised blockade: a pile of furniture, an abandoned baby stroller, an upside-down piano, and a burning car in the middle of the street. I took a side street, making a wide berth around the crowd that was sweeping toward me from farther down the block.

The smell of smoke was beginning to seep inside the car. I looked around me and could see fires dotting the rooftops around the city. I sped faster, hoping to outrace the flames—headed to anywhere but here.

The neat, white signs in intervals at a roundabout spelled out my choices. I drove in a circle, considering my options, feeling for all the world like I was playing a game of Russian roulette, the rampaging Fallen Angels closing in behind me.

In my headlights the sign beckoned: Paris.

The airport.

Home.

I careened around the corner, following the arrow, headed back the way I'd come just earlier that day with Michael and Enoch.

I glanced at the gas gauge. I would have to stop, probably soon, or I would risk running out of gas on the open road. I stepped on the gas, willing the little Peugeot to go faster while I kept my eye open for a filling station.

Nervous, I turned on the radio and fiddled with the settings. Urgent French, rapid fire and staccato, jumped out as I skipped around, looking for something I could understand. Every now and then a snippet of old disco or accordion music filled the car. I kept turning the knob until I found the sonorous voices of the BBC:

> *. . . Unexplained, mass riots sweeping through cities around the world. Occupants of Shanghai and Beijing already woke to devastation this morning local time, with mobs ripping entire construction sites to the ground, shopping malls leveled, and open-air markets decimated by fire. Hundreds are dead in scenes that are being reported with eerie similarity elsewhere. No groups have claimed responsibility for these acts of terror. Indeed, the most frightening thing about them is they seem almost spontaneous . . .*

I clicked the radio off. I didn't need to hear how bad things were.

*They want everyone to know that their age has dawned*, Henri intoned. *The age of terror.*

I shuddered, not wanting to think about what it would mean if they got their wish. The road narrowed, signs warning me to slow as I entered a town. I dropped to a crawl and made my way through the winding streets. Everything seemed deserted. A tiny gas station, brightly lit, beckoned.

I pulled next to the pump, right behind another car. I tried to work the credit card machine, but it wouldn't accept my card. Frustrated, I walked toward the station building to get the attendant's help.

I pulled the door handle, but it didn't move. I shook it again and realized it was locked. I peered through the glass.

"Hello?" I called.

I looked again and noticed the pair of legs sticking out from behind the counter. Another pair stuck out at awkward angles from between the shelving, a tiny trickle of blood seeping toward the locked door.

I backed away, frightened.

I climbed into the Peugeot and locked my doors. I twisted the wires together to start the car. It sputtered to life, but not without me noticing how close to "0" the gas gauge had crept.

I looked at the car parked ahead of me. The pump had stopped, and the car stood waiting for a driver who would never emerge from the station.

I opened my door and slunk over to the waiting car, trailing my backpack behind me. The door was unlocked, and the keys were dangling in the ignition.

I slid behind the wheel and tossed my bag into the passenger seat. With one hand I slammed the door shut while I turned the key over. The engine sprang to life, the needle of the gas gauge bouncing to "Full."

I pushed the image of the owner's body back in my mind and pulled out of the station, ignoring the speed limit signs. Soon, the little hamlet was a speck in my rearview mirror and I was alone, speeding through the night. Here and there, along the Autoroute, I would pass the smoking ruin of a car. Otherwise, the roads were empty. I wasn't sure if it was because it was so late, or because people were too scared to leave their homes.

Henri had gone quiet again. I had become accustomed to his unannounced comings and goings, but now that I knew that his departures had likely been on occasions he was reporting on me to Lucas, his disappearance left me uneasy. I wondered how often he had actually been away, or whether he'd been lurking there, eavesdropping, more often than I realized.

*I'm still here, you know. Still listening.*

I flushed, caught in the act of thinking ill of him.

"I shouldn't have to apologize for doubting you now. Not after what you did. You lied to me."

*I know. For what it's worth, I didn't realize that they would kill him.*

He sounded almost wistful.

I gripped the wheel, staring into the green glow of the dashboard. My thoughts drifted back to Michael, lying all alone on the cold, stone floor. Who would find him there when morning came? Who would wash away the blood and stitch his wounds before laying him to rest in some unmarked plot?

"Henri?"

*Hmm?*

"He'll come back, won't he?"

There was a long silence.

*The Prophecy didn't say anything about resurrection, Hope. It only talked about the opening of the Gate. Michael's death.*

The road blurred as I began to cry. I wrapped my hands more tightly around the steering wheel and forced myself to focus.

There can't be death without resurrection, I insisted, bargaining with myself. There can't be all those comparisons to Christ, all the parallels, all those symbols, only to leave out the most important part. In three days, he will come back. I just know it.

I stared at the road, letting the rush of pavement in front of the dim white light of the headlights lull me into numb resignation. I couldn't think about it now, I told myself. I just had to make it to the airport.

The hours dragged on. Every now and then I'd turn the BBC back on, but the reporting was always the same or worse. The violence was spreading, like a great stain upon the Earth, so that as the planet turned its face to the sun, the entire world was waking up to horror.

In the early morning light, I began to see signs for the airport, as well as electronic signs that kept flashing the words, "*l'incident `a Paris.*" The smoldering wrecks of abandoned cars became more frequent, as did the occasional band of dazed survivors, wandering the landscape, looking for shelter. I shut all the vents, but still the smoke seeped in, filling the car as I came closer.

My gas gauge was getting low as I took the exit toward Charles de Gaulle. Cars littered the roadways, some folded in unnatural shapes around light poles, here and there a shuttle bus tipped over on its side. Whole chunks of asphalt were ripped out of the streets, piled with the burned-out bodies of abandoned vehicles and refuse into makeshift blockades. Beyond the fence, I could see the source of the thick smoke: Two planes had collided in the middle of the runway. The one nearest me looked like it had the top peeled off of it like an opened tin can. Black smoke billowed out of both of them as emergency crews tried, in vain, to extinguish the flames. As I wound my way through the debris in the road, a tank with a huge gun mounted on it grumbled by, quickly followed by a camouflage-painted truck filled with troops. From whom or what the place needed protecting was unclear, but the entire place seemed under siege. I nudged the car through the wreckage until I could get no farther, pulling off to the side to park.

"Henri, what do I do now?"

*Whomever you find, remember to tell them you're American. That still counts for something in some places. Good luck.*

"What do you mean, good luck?" I said, panicking. "Aren't you coming with me?"

*I have an appointment with the court*, he responded mournfully. *I was lucky they granted me this reprieve, so I could get you this far.*

I slumped in my seat, resting my head against the steering wheel. "They're going to punish you."

*Yes. And I deserve it. But at least I got you here, safe.* He paused, letting me process this news. *They won't dispatch a replacement until after my trial. So the rest is up to you.*

I felt a lump growing in my throat. "I don't want a replacement." Despite everything he'd done, the thought of losing someone else now seemed unbearable.

*That will be as you wish. But you don't have to decide that now. It is time for me to go. As it is for you,* he added gently.

The car door fell open as if of its own accord. He was kicking me out, a mama bird pushing her baby from the nest.

*Godspeed, Hope.*

"Goodbye," I whispered. When he didn't respond, I slid from behind the wheel, pulling my backpack from the seat, and took in the situation.

The fence that separated us from the airfields was long. As far as I could see, black crows clustered along the top, murderous spectators of the scene. Grimly, I hitched my backpack up.

Don't think about them, I told myself. Maybe they're just regular birds.

Don't think about Michael.

Just focus on getting home. You can wait for him to return to you there.

I picked my way through the smoking rubble toward what remained of the terminal entrance, keeping a close eye on the birds as I went. The extent of the violence wasn't apparent until I got closer to the building. The doors had been blown off; exposed wires and steel beams dangled loose in the cratered cement. Stone-faced soldiers were patrolling up and down the sidewalks, Dobermans straining at their sides. A platoon ran double-time past me, machine guns in hand, but nobody stopped me. It was as if I didn't exist. I clutched the strap of my backpack tighter and kept walking until I slipped inside the ruins.

I flinched as the severed cables hissed and crackled above my head, giving off sparks. Abandoned luggage was strewn across the floor, a trail of clothing spilled out across the terminal. All of the electronic signs were disabled, blinking information for the same flights, over and over. The ropes and chains that once managed orderly lines of patient fliers were knocked over, lying twisted and useless against the dirty floor. Displaced travelers were huddled against walls and in corners—filling every possible open space. Mostly, they were quiet, their dead eyes staring, unseeing, at the wreckage around them, their fingers absently plucking at imagined loosened threads. Many still clutched their passports and tickets, as if this were only a temporary delay, a simple inconvenience. Here and there a harried mother soothed a crying child, using a last bit of cookie or a desperate story as a distraction. Soldiers patrolled, machine guns poised to challenge anyone who caused too much trouble. Waves of dissatisfaction rolled from the far reaches of the refugees, grumblings that vanished just as soon as they surfaced, their shifting presence suffusing the entire place with a continued threat.

I started moving faster, sticking close to the walls, afraid of what had happened here. If the crowds were surly, the soldiers barely able to keep them under control, good enough. I could creep through the chaos as if I were invisible. I kept to myself, scanning the unfamiliar airline signs until I found one that listed an Atlanta flight.

At first, I thought the counter seemed abandoned. But then I saw a flash of movement, a dark shape darting behind the desk.

"Excuse me," I called, walking around the length of the counter. I came around the back to see a lone flight attendant cowering against her printer. Crouched on the floor, she looked like a cornered animal. Her once impeccable uniform was filthy, giant rings of sweat staining the underarms of her starched shirt, the sheen on her forehead and her wild hair giving away the trials of her day.

She looked up at me, her eyes growing wide with alarm as she began scrambling away on her hands and feet. I glanced down and realized with a start that I was covered with blood and dirt. I lifted my hands and saw the sticky grime on my fingers had dried to a dark rust color.

I felt another pang as the memory of it all washed over me anew.

The flight attendant looked wildly about, but she'd trapped herself in a corner. "Dis flight has been grounded," she pronounced with a precise French accent, drawing on all the authority her uniform and years of experience could muster. But her voice was trembling slightly.

I dug my passport out of my backpack and slapped it down. "Then put me on another flight. Any flight to the United States."

She shook her head, scrambling to her feet and looking about for help. "Dat is not possible. All flights are grounded. Dere will be no travel out of France today." Warily, she stepped up to the counter and pushed my passport back toward me with one outstretched, perfectly manicured finger—barely touching it—as if the papers were infested. "Perhaps you can come back tomorrow."

Without thinking, I reached out and grabbed her by the lapels of her uniform. She gasped and tried to pull away, but I simply curled my fingers tighter. My hands were shaking as I began reasoning with her. "You don't understand." My voice sounded loud, even to my own ears. "I have to go. I have to go now. I have to go home. He won't know where to find me if I'm not there."

"*Terroriste*!" someone shrieked. "*Policier*!"

I heard the crowd surging to life, hours of frustration and impatience finally breaking through to the surface as the crowd watched the incident playing out before it. But I ignored it.

"I have to go home today!" I wailed, my grip on the agent's lapels growing ever tighter.

Rough hands pulled me away. "*Arrêtez!*"

The crowd erupted into screams of panic. The ticketing agent broke free, her hands flying to her neck as if to check if she were still in one piece.

"*Arrêtez-vous!*"

Cold steel clamped down on my wrists. Handcuffs. I was spun around to confront a large man in military uniform, waving a gun.

I froze in place. What had Henri told me to do?

"*Je suis américaine*," I intoned slowly, the French words welling up from me unbidden, as I backed up. "*Aidez-moi, s'il vous plaît.*"

The policeman raised the gun, pointing the barrel in my face with shaking hands.

He mumbled something garbled at me and swung the gun. "*Allez.*" He shook the gun insistently. "*Allez! Marchez.*"

"My passport," I pleaded, looking over my shoulder to where I'd left it on the counter.

"*Non.*" With a brusque shake of his head, he ruled that out. "*Marchez.*"

I looked around. Where he wanted me to go, I had no idea, but with the gun pointed at my head, I turned away from the counter, abandoning my passport and backpack, along with any chance I had of getting out of here, and began walking.

The crowd parted before me.

Somewhere above me I heard a bird screech. I looked up and saw a crow, flying about the inside of the airport, its wings spread like a black flag of victory.

Something inside of me slipped apart. I laughed, a crazy sound that mixed with the cries of the bird and my own sobs, a sound that was absorbed into the cacophony of the airport so that no one heard it.

It was the sound of my heart breaking as I entered the first day of waiting, alone.

# eleven

## ALABAMA

"The world is going crazy," Don said, shaking his head as he ran through the store's closing procedures in his head. His district manager had sent an urgent message, telling everyone to shut down early for the night. Something about gang violence. Nothing they'd ever had to worry about here before, but from the flickering images on the television in the dining area, he could see that the spasm of destruction that seemed to be swirling, mob-fed, around the world was making its presence felt even here in quiet Alabama. He couldn't see it yet here, but orders were orders, so they were closing up, just waiting on the last diners to leave before turning out the lights.

He handed Jared, one of his new crew members, a mop. "Start in the back. You can finish the front after that table leaves."

Jared looked at him sullenly, his swirly hair hanging in his eyes, before taking the mop and slowly beginning to move to the kitchen.

Don sighed, watching him meander away. He didn't understand young people today. Hope had been different. Then again, he'd pretty much kept her that way.

He went back to the drive-through station to tidy up, pausing over the register. Taped to the wall was a picture of Hope, her school photo from last year. He picked it up to give it a good look.

Did she look the same now? He strained to remember how she seemed the last time he talked with her in Atlanta, but it was hard to picture her features now. Everything about her seemed fuzzy, almost as if God, in his mercy, was preparing him for the loss of her, the sharpness of grief already being worn away by fading memory and time.

Not so his memories of Mona.

He closed his eyes, briefly allowing himself to linger on the image of her swollen lips, lips he'd kissed too fiercely in his need and love for her. He had waited ten years to see the look he'd seen in her eyes that night. He knew, now, that he might not see it again—that his admissions that night at the minister's house might have closed the door once again on any chance he had to win her back.

But he wouldn't give up.

A horn startled him. He opened his eyes and looked into the video monitor. A lone car, a long black sedan, was parked in front of the drive-through order unit outside. Don looked at the clock. Normally, they'd still be open. He knew he'd been ordered to close up, but he hadn't counted his money and shut down the register yet.

Another blare of the horn broke the quiet.

He tucked Hope's photo into his pocket, picked his earphones off the counter, and turned on the microphone.

"Welcome to Taco Bell. What can I get you this evening?"

There was a long pause. "Just a Coke."

"I'm sorry, sir, we serve Pepsi products here. Is Pepsi okay for you?"

He always hated it when this happened. It seemed wrong to be serving Pepsi here, so close to Atlanta, the birthplace of Coca-Cola. Every good southerner knew there was only one Coca-Cola. *The Real Thing*, that's what they'd called it in the commercial. Sometimes he had half a mind to sneak in his own stash of the red cans, so he could give them to the disappointed customers who would frown and say, no thanks, they'll just have water. But corporate would disapprove. He had enough rebellion in his life, without having to worry about the company coming down on him. He needed to keep this job, to prove to Mona and Hope that he could change, that he could be relied upon.

"Sure. Whatever."

Don nodded to himself. From out of town, then. No accounting for taste, but fair enough.

"What size, sir?"

"Biggest you got. Easy on the ice."

"That'll be $1.99. Pull around to the window."

He ducked out into the dining room after he put the cup on the machine to fill. The customers had left, but Jared was leaning against a table, mop propped up in a corner.

"Jared, you can lock it up now." Jared slid off the table, slumping his way to the front door. Kids today, Don thought, shaking his head as he watched Jared moving so slowly it seemed he was under water.

Don walked back behind the counter. The sedan had pulled around and was waiting at the window. He quickly checked the drive-through camera to see if anyone else was in line and noted the screen had gone all fuzzy, full of static—he'd have to note that on his clipboard, so the day manager could check it out before the lunch rush. He swiped the cup off the machine and carefully pressed the lid down, sealing off the edges. He opened the window to pass the cup, paired with a neatly wrapped straw, through.

The windows of the sedan were dark and still closed.

"Sir?" Don called.

The driver slowly lowered the blackened glass. He was Asian, dressed up in a fancy suit and tie. He stared coolly at Don, appraising him.

"Sir? That'll be $1.99." Don pushed the drink farther out the window. The man took it and settled it into the cup holder next to him.

Don tried to make small talk while he waited for the man to pay him. "You're lucky to have caught us open. There's something funny going on; all the stores are shutting down early tonight. You haven't heard anything about it, have you?"

Don shifted uncomfortably in the silence, waiting for the man to answer.

The man looked at him, no expression on his face. Instead, he reached around to his side—Don thought for his wallet—and pulled something dark and heavy out of its hiding place, pointing it right at Don's face.

It was a gun.

Don stared at it, frozen, unable to process what was happening.

He blinked, his throat constricting.

Two words cut through to his consciousness.

*Hope.*

*Mona.*

The gun fired, a popping noise that was much quieter than Don expected.

The car idled in front of the window for a moment. When the

driver was sure the job was done, he pulled away, taking a long pull on the straw of his Pepsi, black windows ensconcing him in anonymity once again.

Don heard the whirring of the machines—the refrigerator, deep fryer, and lights now a symphony, so loud he could barely hear himself think. The tile was cold beneath him. He shifted, trying to free his hand. His arm flopped awkwardly, his fingers trailing across the floor.

*Sticky*, he thought. *Is that grease or blood*, he wondered idly, as if he were assessing something disconnected and unrelated to his broken body. *I'll have to have Jared clean it before he goes.*

With effort, he heaved his arm back around so that his fumbling fingers could reach his pocket. Carefully, not wanting to get blood on it, he pulled out the picture he'd stashed away.

"Hope," he whispered, trailing his thumb across her photograph. He'd not noticed before how much she looked like her mother in her eyes. Knowing eyes. Eyes that really saw people.

He had always loved that about Mona.

He smiled, thinking of his wife, and let his eyes flutter closed, just for a minute.

He coughed, a trickle of blood running out of his mouth as his heart gushed, spilling his life out onto the tacky floor of the kitchen.

Somewhere, far away, he heard someone scream, a high shrieking sound.

He opened his eyes, smiling at his daughter's, and his wife's, eyes.

*Mona was right, after all.*

"Be free," he murmured, his words a whispered gurgle as he choked on his own blood. His eyes, unseeing now, rolled back in his head. His hand fell to the floor, still gripping Hope's photograph, a bloody thumbprint now marring the image of her face.

# twelve

## GEORGIA

Mona snapped the newspaper.

It was the seventh time she'd read it, trying to decipher the meager bits she could glean from it. It, along with the coverage of the television reporters who hovered around her house like vultures, was her only source of information since the investigators had shut her out of the details in her daughter's case.

It was her own fault, she knew. She'd gone over the line, contacting witnesses directly. And she'd alienated Clayton. But still.

She sighed and shook the paper again, willing the wrinkles away.

Yesterday's paper had contained no updates on the search for Hope, but it had featured, way back with the human interest stories, an article about a little town in Mexico that had been harboring a great network of human traffickers.

Mona had read and re-read that story, searching for clues. It was the same town the FBI had mentioned—it had to be. It even quoted a young girl who claimed to have been abducted and taken to Atlanta, then Las Vegas. Was this the Maria that Tabitha had spoken of?

She trailed her finger, already stained with ink, under the lines of it now. "Without hope, I would have been lost," the article quoted the girl, whose name, much to Mona's disappointment, appeared to be Ana, not Maria.

*Without hope, or Without Hope?* Mona wondered.

She looked out the window. The sun was up now. It had to be past seven o'clock. Her obsessive refreshing of the various online news sites had yielded nothing of interest pertaining to her daughter. Just alarming reports of a wave of violence sweeping the globe—terrorists and protestors and gangs, corrupt police forces and the angry dispossessed. There was no rhyme or reason to it, but somehow, something had finally gnawed away the restraining ropes of civility and law so that all at once, the grievances and greed that simmered beneath the surface had finally risen up, unrestrained and insistent. It was spreading from city to city, as if by unspoken agreement the rejected and hurt and lawless of the world had responded to a signal, spurring each other on to unstoppable violence.

Today's paper—her last chance for more news of Hope—was probably lying in the driveway. She hadn't dared to go out to retrieve it, not after the police had been stationed at the entrances to her neighborhood and the mayor had sent out the message to stay indoors.

Mona tucked her feet into her slippers and went to the front door, wondering if it was safe to duck out to grab the paper before any of the media arrived. She cracked the door open to peek out.

A man in police uniform stood at the door, hand raised as if to knock. He looked startled to see her there, embarrassed even.

"Excuse me, ma'am," he said, looking discreetly down at his feet.

She clutched at her robe, pulling it close about her neck.

"You startled me, officer," she said, pulling on her most genteel southern manners. "But I thank you for the courtesy of checking in on me. I can assure you, nothing unusual has happened overnight. Nothing has disturbed me or my neighbors, as far as I can see."

The man shifted uncomfortably. He looked up briefly, just enough for Mona to see the panic in his eyes before he returned his gaze fixedly to his polished dress shoes.

*Bless his heart*, Mona thought to herself as she took in the peachy youth of his cheeks. *He is probably scared*, she thought with sympathy, *this is likely his first real emergency as an officer.*

"I'm . . . I'm glad to hear that, ma'am. Some of your neighbors have had power interruptions, but other than that, it seems all of you have remained safe overnight."

She beamed, hoping this would reassure him.

He lifted his face. His eyes were full of anguish. Desperately, he looked back over his shoulder to the waiting squad car.

The door to the car opened. A man in a dark suit—not a uniformed officer—emerged and began walking toward her front steps. He nodded at the officer, who turned back to Mona.

The officer shuffled awkwardly, and reached up to remove his hat. He looked at his hands, as if unsure what to do, and began shifting his hat from one hand to another.

She watched his hands, discomfited by his nervousness. Why is he still here? She wondered.

Only then did she notice that the other man had joined the officer, waiting at the foot of the steps for her to acknowledge him.

It was Special Agent Hale, his face somber.

Her mind reeled.

An officer. In dress blues, his shoes shined to a polish. Taking off his hat, looking down at the steps again, as if he didn't know what to say.

She'd seen this look before. It was the same look the police had when they came to her office to tell her that four-year-old Hope was missing.

A spasm of fear ran up her spine.

"I'm sorry, ma'am," the young man began, sounding as if he were going to cry himself. Mona backed farther away until she was pressed against her closed door, refusing to hear the news he had come, heavy-hearted, to deliver.

"No," she gasped, struggling for air.

"Mona," Hale began, climbing up the steps toward her. "I'm so sorry."

"No!" She screamed the word, forgetting about her bathrobe and disheveled hair, not caring if her neighbors heard or saw, not caring about the crowd of reporters that was slowly beginning to gather, their video cameras trained on her face, their flashes popping in the dim light of early morning.

Hale was stretching out his arm now, trying to comfort her.

She flew at him in a rage, her fists pummeling him.

"No! No! She can't be dead! She can't be!"

He absorbed her blows, gently reigning in her flailing arms until she collapsed in his embrace.

She was barely aware of the pale policeman, watching her, helpless, or the gathering crowd of reporters and neighbors pressing closer to her front steps, shouting questions.

"Let's get you inside. You there—" he shouted to someone she couldn't see. "You're a neighbor? Call her lawyer. And get the press out of here, if you can."

Numbly, she let herself be hustled inside the house, her mind refusing to accept what was happening. She could not understand what they were saying to her, was only aware of the murmur of voices, a concerned hum that wrapped her in its cocoon, sheltering her mind from the horrible reality of her daughter's death.

She was seated, a blanket wrapped around her shoulders, when someone pressed a cup of coffee into her hands.

She looked up, startled to see her neighbor, Mrs. Bibeau. The woman, at a loss for words, simply squeezed Mona's shoulder.

Mona looked around. The police officer and Hale were waiting, sitting awkwardly on her settee.

She peered at the black coffee and took a sip, steeling herself.

"How?" she croaked, knowing she had to hear the details for her to accept it, for it to be real. She pressed her lips into a grim line and willed herself to look at the two men who'd been sent to confirm her loss.

"Mona, you don't understand," Hale said, a note of gentleness in his voice.

She looked at him harshly. "What's there to understand? You came to tell me you found my daughter, and she's dead. That's the only reason an officer in blues would come to the door. Anything else and it would have been a phone call."

Hale closed his eyes and shook his head.

"That's not it. We have no further breaks in your daughter's disappearance. That's not why I'm here."

Her eyes darted back and forth between them, confused.

"Then what is it? I don't understand."

The young officer swallowed hard, his Adam's apple bobbing in his skinny throat. She stared at him, demanding he divulge his reasons for being here, but he simply looked away.

"I wish I didn't have to tell you this," Hale began. "If you'd taken us up on our offer of protection, we might have been able to prevent it."

"What are you talking about?" Mona demanded, uncomprehending.

"I'm not here about Hope," he continued. "I'm here about Don."

"Don?" She repeated, still confused.

The young officer cleared his throat. She looked at him and only then noticed that the insignia on his uniform indicated he was from Alabama. Not Georgia.

"I'm very sorry to tell you, ma'am, that last night at about 9:30 p.m., Don Carmichael was shot dead at his workplace, the apparent victim of a drive-by shooting."

"Or a hit, ordered by Triad," Hale added softly. "I'm so sorry."

Mona felt the coffee cup sliding out of her hands. She watched as its contents seeped into the Berber carpet, the stain spreading like the dark emptiness that threatened to overtake her.

"He was holding a picture of your daughter in his hand at the time of his death," the officer added, as if somehow this would help.

This little detail, this tiny fact, made it real.

A keening wail rose around her. She couldn't tell it was coming from her own lips.

Then, mercifully, she slumped forward in her chair, giving in to the nothingness as she collapsed in a faint.

# thirteen

## FRANCE

The metal door clanged as it swung open behind me.

I barely shifted against the rough, pilled sheet. It didn't matter what they asked anymore. I'd told them the little I could. Nobody would believe me if I told them the truth, anyway.

I pulled my knees in tighter as I huddled on the cot, waiting.

Somebody cleared his throat.

I'd wasted a whole day, I thought dully. A whole day, locked up in the bowels of the airport, a prisoner of aviation security.

"Miss Carmichael," the man addressed me. He was the first one to speak to me in English. "Miss Carmichael, I've come to help you get home. You'd like to get home, to Georgia, wouldn't you?"

He had my attention, now.

"Yes," I answered, opening my eyes to confront the cold painted cinderblock of my cell wall.

"Can you turn around, so I can talk to you?"

My alternative was to keep replaying Michael's death in my head, over and over. So I sat up on the cot and turned myself around to face my visitor.

He was trim and official-looking in a navy suit and red tie. His hair was swept across his forehead in a neat, conservative cut. Deep smile lines were carved around his eyes and mouth.

The man looked at me with kind eyes. "You look like hell, kiddo. Didn't they let you clean up?"

I looked down self-consciously. My clothing, hair, and skin were still crusty with dried blood. It was everywhere. Every movement I made released the coppery scent of blood, invading every breath and reminding me over and over of that night. I shook my head.

"Whatever happened to you, it's over now. You're safe. I know the airport personnel thought you were a threat, but you have to consider what was going on at the time. And how you must have looked to them when they were already worried that the place was going to blow up. Figuratively and literally."

I didn't say anything. None of it mattered any more.

The man continued on, coaxing me to speak. "It's a good thing somebody thought to check Interpol, otherwise they might not have called the embassy. They almost didn't anyway, given your passport was completely blank. Not even a photo, no identification. Don't you think?"

I had no idea what he was talking about.

There was an awkward silence. Finally, I spoke. My voice was ragged, raw from crying and disused to speaking. "Are you from the embassy?"

He nodded. "I should have introduced myself. I'm Robert Frazier. I'm affiliated with the immigration desk. I'm actually a special attaché, assigned to deal with human trafficking issues." He held out a hand.

I looked at my own. They were stained brown, dried blood congealed under my fingernails. Hesitantly, I reached up to shake.

Without even a flinch, he clasped my hand and pumped it vigorously.

"I just want to go home, Robert," I said, pulling out of his grip to tuck my hands under my arms.

He touched his fingertips together, his eyebrows coming together in a look of concern. "And we'd love to get you there. But we need a statement from you, or the French officials won't release you. You know the French," he said ruefully, shrugging and smiling as if we were sharing some private joke.

"I've told them everything I can."

"Yes," he said, looking a little confused. "But I think something got lost in translation. I wanted to find out, in your own words, how you came to be here. Looking like that."

I shifted on the cot.

"I was in an accident. Someone was hurt."

"Who? Who was hurt?"

I bit my lip. "I don't know."

He arched a brow. "So it was a stranger, then?"

"Yes, a stranger," I responded, grasping the easy excuse, my heart aching as I did so.

"Where was this accident?"

I stared down at the floor and shrugged.

"I don't know."

"How did you get to France?"

"I don't know."

The questions were coming faster now.

"Were you alone when you arrived?"

"No."

"Who were you with?"

"I don't know."

"But you acknowledge you were with someone."

"Yes."

"Was Michael Boyd with you at any point during your disappearance?"

The mention of his name hit me like a blow to the stomach. It was all I could do to whisper, "No."

"Do you know where he is, Hope? He seems to have disappeared at about the same time you did."

"I haven't seen him since the afternoon I left school," I lied, every cell of my being protesting as I denied him. I pulled my knees up under my chin, curling myself in tighter. Robert continued peppering me with questions.

"Whoever you were with—did they force you to come with them? Were you brought here against your will?"

It should have been an easy question to answer. Had anything that happened been my choice? Gabrielle thought so.

I shrugged noncommittally.

"Did they hurt you?"

I wiped away a tear, nodding once.

"How did you get a passport? And how is it that it came to be like this?" He held the booklet in front of me. I took it from his hand and leafed through it. Each page was pristine. Empty. There was no record of my arrivals or departures, as if I'd never been to Turkey or Ireland or even here, in France. I flipped to the front and did a double take as I looked at the place where the photo should have been. Before, it showed a woman so disfigured by burns that it was impossible to tell her age. Now, it was empty. I looked down at my arms. Underneath the blood, they were smooth. I touched my face. No scar tissue.

As if none of it happened.

Everything erased from the record, swept away by Michael's departure. I knew now that there would be no records of our time in Las Vegas, no proof of anything. The truth was safe, locked inside of me.

I handed him back the passport.

"I don't know. The people who took me had a passport for me."

"The people who took you? Who were they, Hope? Were they traffickers? Did they take you from Atlanta? Would you recognize them if you saw them again?"

It was the easiest thing for them to believe, I knew, and probably my only way out of this. I nodded, avoiding his eyes.

"Okay, honey," he said, his voice thick. He was imagining his own daughter, or niece, or neighbor, I knew—imagining them caught up in the horrific human trade and forced to do something unspeakable. He was wondering what I'd gone through, wondering just what I'd done to manage to escape, and wondering if the blood that covered me from head to toe was no accident at all. He clasped my shoulder in his big, strong hand, leaning over me protectively.

"I know this is tough. The good news is we've got you now. There were a lot of people looking for you, a lot of people worried about you. Your case was especially difficult. There are very, very few people trafficked out of the United States. It was like your entire case was backward—you had all the patterns of a typical case, being moved around to multiple countries, fake paperwork, but moving in the wrong direction. Most of these cases culminate with people coming across the border, maybe from Canada, into the US. But none of that matters now. You're here. You're safe. I'm sorry you're stuck here—" he gestured about the prison-like surroundings, "—but they're still figuring out how to handle victims as we pick them up. There are some other girls down the hall in similar circumstances, but from other places like West Africa and Eastern Europe. All of you in the same boat. We'll get you cleaned up with some new clothes and all that. I'm going to send a doctor in to examine you, to make sure you aren't in need of medical attention."

"No doctors." I stated it emphatically, still refusing to look him in the eye.

He paused, calculating what he could say that would convince me to go along with his bureaucratic duties. He leaned back on his heels, clasping his hands lightly in front of him. I noticed that he hadn't brushed them off after we shook hands.

"I understand why you might not want to see a physician," he said quietly, "but it may help speed up your departure. I don't want to pressure you, but I do want you to know that things will be easier for you if you go along with the local procedures."

I gripped the edge of the hard bed. "No doctors. I'll only see my own doctor at home."

He sighed, nodding to himself. He stood up to pace around the tiny cell.

"How about a nurse?" he asked, his voice full of hopeful compromise. "Just a quick once-over?"

He stopped, waiting for my answer. I nodded swiftly, once.

"Great!" he said, clapping his hands together. "I'll take care of that right away. I'll need to file some petitions to get you out of here, and then we'll have you on the first plane back to Atlanta. Sound good?"

"How soon?"

"Probably a matter of hours, if we're lucky, and we can get you on your way."

"Do my mom and dad know that I'm here?" I blurted, finally looking up to search his face. It was a nice face, earnest and kind. "Are they coming to get me?"

He paused just a moment too long, weighing his answer.

"We've been authorized to fly you home solo. I'm sure you'll be met at the airport when you land. It's still a little crazy out there," he added by way of explanation. He began packing up papers, shoving them hurriedly into a well-worn leather briefcase that he'd left sitting on the floor. "Is there anything you need now? Food? Something to drink?"

I shook my head.

"Then I'll see you in a little bit, okay?" He slipped out the door and turned to say goodbye. "I have to close you in, Hope, but it's just for now, I promise. The lawyers are already working on it." He slid the door over with a firm click, locking me behind bars once again.

I watched him walk away, his smart shoes tapping against the concrete and echoing down the hall.

He wasn't telling me the truth. Or at least not the whole truth. I stared after him anxiously, wondering what it was he was keeping from me.

The cold efficiency of bureaucracy kicked in after that. I was washed, inspected, and wrapped up again like a piece of meat. The nurse limited herself to taking my temperature and blood pressure and looking me over for any obvious signs of damage. Other than my ankle, the nurse could find no injuries; even the scars from my burns had melted away. My own clothes were torn away and thrown in the trash. I was given a nondescript pair of sweatpants and a T-shirt in their stead and asked to wait in my cell, the door left open now that I had been labeled a victim instead of threat.

After what seemed like hours, an embassy escort whisked me through the cavernous shell of the airport, taking me directly onto the runway to board my flight. I barely noticed the armed guards at the stairs and the camouflaged jeeps darting about the runways. He rushed me up the steps, darting glances over his shoulder as if he were afraid we might be ambushed. On board, my escort handed papers to the flight attendant and then settled into the seat next to me to accompany me home.

I curled up in my seat for the entire flight, resting my head against the window to stare out at the nothingness of the sky. I was exhausted but could not sleep. If I closed my eyes, my mind would fill with images of Michael, laying in a pool of blood, his life slipping away. I'd relive the whole thing—the army of Fallen Angels materializing, the horrible moment when I realized that Enoch wasn't really Enoch—that Lucas had been tricking us all along. I'd hear the crush of broken bones, smell the tang of blood in the air, hear Michael's last, wheezing breath leave his lips.

No, it was better to stay awake and focus on what was yet to come.

"What's going on out there?" I asked my companion absently.

"Do you really want to know?" he demanded.

I turned in my seat to look at him, really look at him. His skin was gray with weariness, the bags under his eyes heavy. He looked exhausted, and I'm sure accompanying a kid on an international flight wasn't helping things.

Guiltily, I nodded.

"The riots you saw in France? Well, they were everywhere. Only calling them riots doesn't do them justice. Whole cities turned into outright battlefields. It seems almost unfathomable that the damage done wasn't done by an organized military force. Yet nobody knows how or why it started. All sorts of kooky groups—cults and terrorist organizations and God knows what else—have come out of the woodwork claiming responsibility, but none of the claims are credible. And the freak accidents on top of it? Tornadoes and floods and house fires? It was crazy. A wave of devastation swept the world in twenty-four hours and then poof! Just like that, everything started calming down again. The damage left behind is huge, but the violence itself seems to have dissipated. It's not all back to normal, yet—most big cities are still under martial law or have patrols sweeping around constantly—but the worst seems to have passed. You're lucky we got you out of Paris; we really had to pull some strings to get a flight approved."

I mumbled my thanks and turned back in my seat, pressing my forehead against the cool glass of the window.

So, the Earth had gone quiet. That meant the Fallen had taken their battle to the Heavens. And, in the meantime, we were approaching the close of the second day. Two days nearly gone since Michael's soul had slipped away.

I drifted into an in-between state, neither sleeping nor awake, as the plane hurtled us across the sky. The rattle of the beverage cart, the slight tinkling of glass, and the occasional ring of a passenger's call button against the backdrop of the artificial air circulating through the cabin lulled me, almost fooling me into forgetting. But I couldn't forget. I didn't want to. And if I slipped, I would stare at my hands and see the bloodstains that no amount of soap and water would ever eradicate.

As we approached Atlanta, the terrain below me began to take shape. Little patchworks of freshly tilled soil and early crops made tidy grids along the earth. Ribbons of dirt and asphalt snaked through the lush green of trees and red clay soil. Slowly, the green gave way to rows of houses and fields of parking lots, the roads filled with cars so tiny they looked like toys.

Home.

Our arrival was a whirlwind. We parted from the crowd before Customs, my escort's flashed badge signifying none of the rules were for us. We ducked down a long, lonely hallway and then into an elevator. As we descended, he turned to me.

"Sorry about this."

"About what?" I asked, but the doors were already sliding open, revealing a wall of cameras and reporters. The crowd surged as if to swallow us. Instinctively, I threw my hands up over my face, hiding.

"Hope, can you tell us about your ordeal?"

"Hope, how did you escape your captors?"

"Over here! Hope, look over here!"

My guide clamped his lips down into a hard line. "Don't answer them. Come with me," he muttered, clamping onto my arm and pulling me close with one hand while he shielded my face with the other. "Out of the way!" he yelled into the mob, as we began pushing our way through to the cart that was waiting for us.

We were barely seated when the driver hit the gas, leaving the reporters in the dust.

"Hang tight," the driver shouted over his shoulder to where we sat. "I'm taking you to a private exit."

"Will my parents be there?"

He ignored my question. We flew through the hallway, turning into a tunnel that seemed to cut through the length of the airport. I clutched my backpack and began to strain, eager for my first glimpse of my mother and father, pushing my feet against the floor of the cart as if I could make it go faster by sheer will.

We were approaching a dead end. The cart slowed, then settled into a firm stop.

The man from the embassy stepped off the cart and held out a hand to help me off. I pushed it aside and jumped down, looking around. There was a single door, an emergency exit protected by a keypad.

The cart's driver walked over to the keypad and punched in some numbers. The light above the door began flashing its red light of warning.

"They're waiting for you outside," the man said, but I was already pushing past him through the door and onto the sidewalk.

A dark SUV was parked against the curb. A muscular black man stood waiting, leaning against the vehicle.

"Hope?"

I looked around, confused. We were alone, except for my embassy escort, who hung back, wary.

"Who are you?" I demanded, eyeing the man with unease. "Where are my parents?"

"I'm Arthur." Relief flooded my body as I recognized his name.

"The guy who drives my mom," I said. "Is she in the car?"

"She is," he smiled, but his eyes were sad. He swung the door wide, and I ran to the car, climbing in to where she was waiting for me.

I threw myself into her arms. We clutched at each other, both of us bawling like babies, neither one of us able to stop ourselves from inspecting each other as if to make absolutely certain that this was real, that I had truly found my way home.

Arthur pulled away from the curb, discreetly leaving us to our homecoming in the middle seat. Mom gripped me fiercely, holding me close as if afraid she would lose me again.

"Thank God you are safe," she said, kissing the top of my head.

"I don't want to talk about it, Mom, not any of it," I gasped between sobs. "I just want to be with you and Dad for now. Okay?" I mumbled against her shoulder.

A spasm shook her body, and she pulled me in tighter. An anguished cry, like a bird taking flight, escaped her.

"Mom?" I pulled away from her grasp. She was trembling, a new vale of tears flooding her face. For the first time, I noticed how ravaged her face looked, how thin and drawn she'd become. Streaks of silver had sprung up in her rich chestnut hair. She shook, forcing her eyes closed against obvious pain.

"Mom?" I asked again with dawning fear, shaking her shoulders. "Mom, where's Daddy? Why isn't he here with you?"

"Oh, Hope," she said between choked tears. She opened her eyes. They were ringed red from too much crying. "Those men in Las Vegas, they were very angry with you. They thought that your father . . . at first we all thought your father was the one who'd taken you. And those men, they didn't know the difference . . ."

"Mom, what are you saying?"

She held my hand, just a little too tightly. She was crying so hard I could barely understand her. She managed to choke out her words.

"Your father was killed, Hope. The night that all the rioting started. Whether it was random, or the Triad syndicate targeted him, it doesn't really matter. He's gone, Hope. Gone."

She pulled me in close, as if she could comfort me. I felt numb, unable to process what she'd just told me, my mind registering only the wracking sobs that shook her body.

Gone? Killed?

She said it didn't matter what had happened—random violence from the rioting or a planned murder by the traffickers. And she was right. Either way, it was my fault. We'd laid our tracks deliberately so that anyone investigating would know that, despite all appearances, it couldn't possibly have been my father who had taken me. But we hadn't figured on the Chinese hunting him down. Nor had I known that the violent celebrations of the Fallen would reach across the world, snaking their way into a little town in Alabama.

My chest constricted. I couldn't breathe.

"Stop the car." I said.

My mother just pulled me closer. "I know. It's too much to take in all at once, but . . ."

"Stop the car!" I screamed shrilly, pushing away from her. "Stop the car, Arthur, now!"

He was pulling over, not even parked, when I threw the door open and jumped out. I ran to the weedy edge of the road where I hunched over, trying to force the air in and out of my lungs.

Don't think about it, I told myself. Just breathe.

The air was acrid and stung my throat. A fit of coughing overtook me. I looked up to see the burned-out shell of Turner Field. I looked around and realized that I was standing in a wasteland, an urban desert the Fallen had left in their wake.

"Hope, it's not safe out here. There still might be people roaming the streets." Arthur had followed me out of the SUV. He placed a gentle hand on my arm. "Come back into the car."

"It's not fair," I argued, shrugging away his hand and turning to face him. I could feel my self-control slipping away. "This wasn't supposed to happen."

"I know, sweetie, I know," he said, taking my hands in his, "but your mother needs you now. She's taking your father's death really hard. It's a miracle that you came back to her when you did. God must be watching over you both."

I cracked. How could I be there for my mom? I needed to tend to my own wounds, to fight off the darkness that was pressing in all around me.

"I need my dad," I demanded. "He isn't dead. He can't be. Take it back!" I swung wildly at Arthur's massive chest. It was like hitting a brick wall, but I didn't care. I kept swinging. "Take it back! Take it back!"

"Shhh," he soothed, catching up my hands in his. "It will be okay. I promise." He pulled me into a bear hug and held me until, like a rag doll, all the fight left my body, leaving me strangely deflated. His body heat seemed to sink into my bones, relaxing me into a strange, disembodied state of denial. When he thought I'd calmed down enough, Arthur led me back to the SUV, each step mechanical, my mind barely able to handle the simple task of walking. I climbed back into the middle row next to my weeping mother, who sagged against her seatbelt straps. Arthur buckled my own belt, checking it was secure, before quietly closing the door on us.

We were silent the remainder of the drive to Dunwoody. My mother, exhausted, fell into a troubled sleep on the seat next to me. I watched her, her eyelids dancing as she struggled against her nightmares, knowing what was likely causing her fitfulness.

The same thoughts kept going through my head.

My father was dead.

Because of me.

My mother was heartbroken.

Because of me.

It was too much to bear.

I kept an eye on the scenes flashing past the dark windows of the SUV. The Fallen—or the rioting crowds they'd inspired—had cut a swathe through Atlanta, leaving destruction and vandalism to mark their trail. From the anxious looks Arthur kept darting about and the sounds of helicopters monitoring from above, I realized that the uprising perhaps was not yet finished, that the city might still be in the grip of violence.

Because of me.

"They were supposed to enter Heaven in peace," I whispered to myself as I leaned my head against the window. "Forgiven."

What did the violence mean? Did it mean that the Fallen had rejected Michael's sacrifice? Was Heaven's army—leaderless now—fending them off at this very minute, trying to prevent their storming of the gates?

Were all our sacrifices to be for naught?

I clutched my hands together tightly, refusing to accept it.

One more day.

If Michael were to rise, it would be tomorrow morning. Then, I would know for sure.

We exited the freeway and weaved our way through barricades to enter the town of Dunwoody. There was less damage evident here—more like simple vandalism than the utter chaos and destruction I'd seen downtown. I looked at Arthur, about to ask him why, when he began to speak.

"The Atlanta police force turned on itself. Seems that it was rotten at the core. In the heat of the moment, the bad ones thought their time had come and rose up, bringing it out into the open. People around the stadium and on the South Side had to form vigilante groups to defend themselves. We were lucky up north to have our own police system. Our guys held the line and kept Dunwoody safe."

We whizzed past one subdivision after another. Arthur was keeping a close eye on his watch.

"Have to get you home before curfew," he said, never taking his eyes from the road.

Curfew. So it had come to that. I looked apprehensively at the gates in front of the neighborhoods as we drove by. Would gates keep us safe now? I shrugged in my seat. I might not ever feel truly safe again.

Arthur guided the car into our neighborhood, flashing his license at the guard who had been temporarily stationed at the entrance. We weaved around curves and side streets, not stopping for stop signs, never slowing until we eased into our cul-de-sac. We pushed through the small crowd of reporters that had been waiting, like vultures, for a sighting, before pulling into the driveway. Arthur idled the engine and looked up at me in the mirror.

"Are you ready to take your mom in?"

I looked at her, slumped in her seat, and realized I would need his help. I jumped out of the car and ran to the keypad to open up the garage, shielding my face from the snapping cameras. I ran in, giving him a wide berth to pull his SUV in next to mom's Audi. When he was in, I pushed the button, closing out the world, at least for now.

Together, we half carried my mom out of the car and up the stairs to her room. Mom's doctor had prescribed her something to help her sleep, so we coaxed her into swallowing the little pills and some water and settled her into bed, hoping that now she could get the dreamless rest she so desperately needed.

I wanted the same.

I wanted to go to sleep and for one night, forget that any of this ever happened. Forget the horrible things I'd witnessed in Las Vegas. The abuse that had been heaped upon Ana and Jimena. The slick blood running over the stones in the tiny church in France. The violence that was still gripping the world.

But tonight was my night to keep watch; my night to wait for Michael to return.

I pulled the covers up closer under my mom's chin and turned off the light.

Quietly, Arthur and I walked downstairs, winding through the rooms back toward the kitchen. I noted the piles of mail; the pillows and blankets pushed aside, haphazardly, on the couch; the stacks of dishes in random places throughout the house. Trash tumbled out of an unemptied can. My mom's whole world had turned upside down. All you had to do was look at the shambles that had become of her normally organized house to see it.

"Hope," Arthur said, standing with one hand on the back of a kitchen stool. "This wasn't the kind of homecoming you wanted or deserved. And I know it must feel strange to have me here, but you know," he said, his voice cracking with the effort, "I knew your mother and your father since just after you were born, when Mona had to start traveling again. Every week she'd recite to me your latest accomplishments. I remember when you lost your first tooth. When you learned to ride your bike. When you learned to read. You were such an itty-bitty thing, and she had to pretend to be stern with you when she caught you reading under the covers. But she was busting at the seams, she was so proud of you. Reading, at age three." He closed his eyes, gripping the back of the stool even tighter.

"I remember when you were stolen away, and when the Good Lord brought you back, safe and sound." He paused, taking a deep breath to compose himself. "It tore me apart to see what it did to your mom and dad, back then.

"Since then, we've gotten even closer, your mother and me. Mona is like a sister to me. And I don't think I'm exaggerating when I say I don't think she could have survived this latest blow if you hadn't come back to her." He looked at me, teary-eyed. "I guess what I'm trying to say is that you feel like family to me, even if I don't feel like family to you. So I'll do anything you need, anything at all. If you want me to stay the night, I will, even if it means sleeping in the garage in my car. If you want me to call and check on you both in the morning, I will. You just say the word. I'm here for you."

I smiled, grateful for his kindness, happy to know that someone had been here to take care of my Mom.

"I appreciate it, Arthur, but you don't have to stay. Maybe just run over some of those reporters on your way out."

He laughed, a hearty laugh that filled me with warmth. "You've got your dad's sense of humor."

I looked at him, puzzled and saddened. I had no memories of my father laughing. He was referring to someone I'd never known, someone who'd been lost to us all, many years ago, well before his death.

"Come here, girl," he said, opening his arms wide. I fell into them, burrowing into the warmth of his embrace, letting myself take the little comfort I could, knowing that for what I needed to do, for the vigil I would keep, I preferred to be alone. He squeezed me again, and I felt a strange pulse of heat. Startled, I stepped away.

"What is it?" he asked quizzically.

"Nothing," I said, shaking away the fleeting question that had come and gone. "Nothing at all." He shrugged and, turning, began to make his way to the back door—the friend door, my mom had always called it.

"Hey, Arthur . . . ?"

He stopped and turned. "Yes?"

"Maybe you can come over tomorrow. You know, when it's convenient. Just to check on her."

He smiled a gentle smile. "I'll check on her every day until you tell me not to, young lady."

After Arthur left, I went around the house, performing the kind of security check that would have made my father proud. Satisfied with my lockdown, I looked in on my mother one last time. Her body lay still beneath the covers, only the slight rise and fall of the blankets reassuring me she was alive.

My room was where I would wait. When I turned on the light and took it in, it looked strange and foreign to me, even though everything was exactly as I had left it. The schoolbooks that lay scrambled on the floor, the clothes that were strewn here and there—none of it seemed familiar, let alone important.

Then I glimpsed something tucked against the foot of the bed. My stuffed Georgia Tech Yellow Jacket. Someone had dug it out. I reached down and buried my face in its plush. My throat caught as I imagined my father here, worrying about me, maybe even comforting my mother as they struggled through, for a second time, my disappearance.

I sighed and put the toy back where I found it.

If I were going to wait all night, I needed to be comfortable. I slipped into a T-shirt and my flannel pajama bottoms. The soft fabric slid against my unmarred skin. I let my hands trail against my hands, my arms—the familiar ridges of smoothed skin, burned and scarred, were gone. A sudden panic seized me, and I ran into the bathroom. I pulled my hair away from my neck and strained into the mirror to see.

The Mark was still there, untouched. To be sure, I took out the hand mirror and checked it again, then a third time. Relief washed over me. If I was still Marked, I still belonged to him.

I put the mirror down and turned off the light. Then I slid under the covers of my bed to wait.

It felt odd.

It was an unfamiliar feeling. Emptiness. Anticipation. Even boredom, as I realized that for weeks I'd spent every waking moment working over the Prophecy, trying to figure out our next move, worrying about my safety, or trying to pick apart my complicated feelings for Michael.

But as the stars grew brighter and made their progress against the inky sky, marking the passage of the night, I fell increasingly under the competing grips of dread and hope.

He had to come back to me.

He just had to.

When there were a few hours left until dawn, I grew restless. I prowled about my room, looking for something to distract me. My eye fell upon the box where I'd stored my treasures, ever since I was a little girl. I picked it up and smiled at its childish simplicity. It was a shoebox, wrapped in tissue paper and decoupaged with pictures of the things that had once been important to me: puppies and rainbows and horses and hearts. Lots and lots of hearts.

I couldn't believe my mom had kept it.

I pulled off its lid and began sorting through my memories, one by one. There, tucked under everything at the bottom of the box, was something more recent, something I hadn't realized I'd been searching for.

A valentine.

I pulled it out of the box and slid the card out of the red envelope. The card had been crumpled in anger, and though I'd done my best to smooth it out, it still looked a little worn, the surface uneven under my fingertips. I looked at the lettered verse on the card. It was different now, knowing Michael had written it, and reading it with the benefit of hindsight.

*I will keep you as the apple of the eye,*
*Hide you under the shadow of my wings.*

It was a promise of protection. His promise. He'd proven true to his word, over and over again, even when I hadn't believed him.

And it was a forever promise. You don't break a forever promise.

Certainty flooded back to me. He couldn't protect me if he wasn't here, I reasoned with myself. He has to come back.

It was while clinging to this confidence that I drifted off to sleep, the card still in my hand.

As I slept, I dreamt I was at sea, alone in a tiny lifeboat. It was cold; my clothing was soaked through, and every breath I took made my lungs feel like sharp needles were stabbing them. From the debris floating around me, I could tell I had survived a shipwreck. Bobbing in the ocean were the other survivors. Some I couldn't recognize, but among them were Michael and my father.

They were on opposite sides of my boat, beyond the reach of my oars, struggling to keep their heads above the icy water.

"You must choose," someone whispered in my ear.

How could I choose?

"If you don't, they both will die," the voice urged me on.

Picking up the oars, I hesitated. "Save yourself," my father yelled across the water. "Forget about me."

"There's no point, Hope. I'm already as good as dead," Michael called out from where he was treading water.

"No," I shouted back, determination lighting a fire within me. "I'll get you both."

I dug my oars into the water. Each carving stroke felt like I was pulling through setting cement. It was so cold—too cold. I didn't have the strength to get there fast enough.

They were slipping away, starting to sink under the surface. I pulled harder, faster, waiting to make my choice until the last minute. But I waited too long. A giant wave surged beneath my boat, casting me far, far away from both of them.

I threw myself against the side of the boat.

"Goodbye, Hope," my father's voice carried across the sea.

"Goodbye, Hope," Michael echoed before he slid beneath the waves.

The swelling waves carried me farther and farther away from them until I woke up on the floor, my face pressed hard into the carpet, which was a soggy mess. I tasted salt; it took me a moment to realize it was from tears, not from seawater.

I rolled over, wincing. My entire body ached, reminders of the days of abuse to which I'd subjected it. Even my hands hurt, as if I'd really been gripping the oars I'd dreamt about. I let my eyes adjust to the light. The floor was dappled with sunlight as the early morning rays streamed through the leafy apple trees in my front yard, and I realized with a start that it was morning.

It was the morning of the third day.

I jumped to my feet and turned around, peering into the corners of my room. I expected to find him there, an amused look on his face as he waited for me to wake up.

But there was nothing.

I raced from my room, flinging myself down the stairs. He had to be here. Where else would he be?

I searched the far corners of our house.

Nothing.

I ran into the garage, thinking maybe he'd wait in my mother's car.

Empty.

Had he awoken in France, alone and abandoned?

I moved to the computer station in the kitchen and called up the local news for Le Puy-en-Velay: article after article describing the destruction from the unexplained rioting that had gripped the region. A death count. And there, at the bottom of the death toll, the number of unidentified victims. Michael was sure to be among them . . . but was he still dead?

Frustrated, I kept refreshing the news, thinking surely there was some mistake.

Frantically, I started typing in the search bar.

*Really, do you expect there to be coverage on CNN? Coming to you live from the second resurrection? Really, Hope. I thought better of you.*

It wasn't Henri. It was the Replacement.

"Go. Away." I demanded between clenched teeth. "I don't even know who you are, and I really don't have time for this right now." My fingers fumbled their typing while I cursed.

*Don't be so juvenile. You won't find it there. You won't find it anywhere. There's nothing to find, Hope.*

I scanned the news site, then another. Then another. Everywhere the world was still caught in fits of chaos. Everywhere, it seemed man was turning against man. But it couldn't be. Michael's death was supposed to free the Fallen—not set them loose to destroy the Earth. Something was wrong.

*He's gone.*

I hovered over the keyboard.

"Gone." My voice broke as I repeated the word.

*Gone*, the Replacement said gently. *You never had any chance to save him. It was meant to be.*

"But, the green men and the phoenix on the chapel . . . all the symbols of rebirth . . ." My voice trailed off.

*Perhaps they were a coincidence.*

My heart hardened to his words. It couldn't be.

"He promised he would watch over me! I can't lose him now! I can't!" I blurted into the air, as tears flooded my eyes.

*He belonged to mankind and to the angels. He was never yours to lose.*

My father and Michael, both slipping away under the waves. Away. Forever.

"No!" I screamed. My arms swept the keyboard and mouse away. I pushed the computer off the edge of the desk. "No!" Frantic with denial, I fought against my invisible foe, the messenger whom I would never forgive, never accept.

"No!" It was a howl now, ripped from my soul as I cast about the room, railing against anything that I found in my path.

"Hope!" My mother had rushed to my side and was calling me, trying to break through, but I was too far gone. I fought against her, pummeling her with my fists, until, exhausted, I collapsed into her lap, where she held me and crooned as if I were an infant all over again.

"I know, baby. I know," she whispered against my hair.

But she had no way of knowing what I was going through. She would never know—she couldn't know—that my grief was doubled by the loss of Michael.

I gave myself over to her ministrations; to the cool washcloth against my forehead, the tightly tucked covers of my bed, and the doctor's pill, now speeding me on to my own fitful sleep.

~

Gone.

The word haunted my mother and me. It defined our days and kept us awake at night.

We took turns giving in to our grief, living out our days and nights like zombies, unable to feel, unable to engage with anyone else.

My mother resigned from her firm. She typed her letter and emailed it in, not deigning to even talk to anyone else before she did so. And no one tried to stop her. In celebration, she dumped her closet-full of elegant black suits into a garbage bag and left them at the curb for someone to scavenge.

"That life is over now," she murmured, her lips set in a hard line as she turned on the last vestige of her career.

She kept me home with her, staring down the truancy officer who visited our house, daring him to defy her when she said it was too soon for me to return. She turned Tabby away at the door, demurring that I was too weak to see visitors yet. She ignored the calls from the social worker and psychologist who'd been referred to our case. She was a tigress protecting her cub, defending me to the death.

Until it became too much for her to bear. Then I cared for her.

With nothing to root us—no routine, no relationships—we floated through our days, only our own desperate acts marking one day from the next. I gave full reign to my obsession with the news, tracking the petering out of the global rioting, then giving myself over to observing the minutiae of every war crime, plane crash, boat sinking, or natural disaster that took place, anywhere in the world. I searched unceasingly for any reports of strange sightings of angels, of unexplainable phenomena that could only be accounted for as miracles. I tore stories out of newspapers and magazines, printed out articles from the Internet, taping them carefully on my bedroom walls, believing that if I just studied them long enough, the pattern would emerge, and I would finally understand where Michael was, and why he was there, and not here with me.

But there was nothing.

My sleep was haunted by nightmares—wild images of bloody battles, brutal angels eviscerating one another without mercy. And Michael was there, on the front lines, urging on his army and taking the brunt of the violence. Every night I woke, panting and sweating, having seen what I was sure was the blow that would prove fatal to him—a second death, a heavenly death that would keep him from me forever. I would wake from one nightmare to the reality of a world without him and feel the loss all the more keenly.

We continued on like that for months, our only interruption the daily visits Arthur unfailingly made, until one day, my mother announced over the scalding cup of black coffee that had become her routine breakfast, "I'm moving your father's remains."

I looked at her, not knowing what to say.

She was clear-eyed and even a little excited. She looked at me, and a flash of recognition, followed by concern, went through her eyes.

"You cut your hair," she murmured, drawing her eyebrows together into a sharp point.

I pulled my fingers defensively through the short fringe of my bangs. I'd taken scissors to it a few days earlier. I was tired of hiding behind it. And there was no point covering up my Mark any more. Let the whole world see it; I didn't care. In fact, I wanted to show it like a badge, proof of what I'd been through, proof that I still belonged to Michael. It was the only thing I had left. So I'd defiantly hacked away the long tresses, leaving them in a heap on the floor of my bathroom. Nervously, I fingered my neckline, afraid of what she would say next.

"I like it," she announced, ending all discussion on the topic.

From that morning on, Mom focused almost exclusively on her project to move Dad's body from the gravesite in which he'd been hastily deposited in Alabama. She wanted him closer. She wanted to be able to visit him whenever she wished, and she wanted me to keep his memory alive.

Besides, she'd reasoned, "Atlanta was always his home. His real home."

The opportunity to tangle with lawyers again ignited a spark in her. Her eyes brightened, and she almost became cheerful. Soon, the whirlwind that had been my mother returned, sweeping away the stacks of unopened mail, returning the unanswered phone calls, and writing out thank-you notes in her careful, schoolbook-perfect cursive writing.

My father's parents were long gone, his own parents having followed their desire to be cremated, their remains scattered at sea. But as far back as he could recall, my father's people had all been buried in a tiny cemetery on the edges of Dunwoody, a simple garden that had been engulfed as suburban sprawl expanded the footprint of the little town. It was protected by a historic preservation society now, and nobody had been buried in it for over twenty-five years. Somehow my mother had negotiated her way to a little plot for my father, finally managing to bring him home.

New Hope Cemetery, it was called. Ironic.

My mother's preparations sometimes took her out of the house as she sought licenses and allowances, and it was on one of those days that I found myself alone to answer the loon-like call of the dying doorbell.

I swung the door wide. "Tabby!"

My heart swelled as I saw her waiting, hand on one jutted hip, head-to-toe black despite the heat of the summer day. She shoved her cat-eye sunglasses up over her pink ombré hair, pinning me with a fixed stare under one perfectly arched eyebrow.

"Your mom is a pit bull when it comes to guarding you. Are you going to let me in, or what?"

I pulled her arm, dragging her into the foyer to envelop her in a hug. Her stiff standoffishness melted as she squeezed me back, hard.

"Honestly, girl, I have been so worried about you." She stepped back, carefully apprising me, her mouth twisting into disapproval. "You can't disappear. You can't disappear into this house. And you can't disappear into yourself," she said, poking me in the ribs for emphasis. "What are you doing? Starving yourself?"

I wrapped my arm around my waist as if I could hide. "I'm not. I just haven't been hungry."

She pushed past me, the heavy soles of her combat boots beating a familiar stomp that made me grin like an idiot. "Tell it to someone who will listen. We're eating breakfast, now." I noticed the white paper bag swinging from her hand. "I wasn't taking any chances."

She folded herself into a kitchen chair, pointedly looking at the chair opposite her until I reluctantly sat down, too. Satisfied, she shoved the bag across the table to me.

"You promised me when you were in Vegas. So I thought I'd make it easy on you."

Intrigued, I tore open the bag. Wright's cupcakes. Strawberry pink, encased with loving care inside their plastic containers like engagement rings in blue Tiffany boxes.

I teared up, my fingers clutching the edge of the crumpled bag.

"I would have bought them. I didn't forget, Tabby. I promise."

She reached across the table to squeeze my hand. "I know, Hope. But I thought I needed to remind you that you're not alone."

I blinked back the tears and looked up at her. "You're right. But it's hard to explain. I don't know if anybody could ever understand."

She nodded as if my statement were imminently reasonable. "Of course not. Not if you're keeping it to yourself."

She pulled back her hand and crossed her arms, refusing to look away. "Unless, that is, you're thinking only Michael could understand."

I stammered. "That's not . . . I mean . . ."

I gave up, lamely, as her unspoken accusation sucked all the air out of the room.

"He's not the only one who understands, Hope."

"How do you know?" I whispered, looking down at the table, trying hard not to cry.

"I understand more than you realize," she asserted. "Look at me, Hope."

I dragged my eyes from the table. Her brown eyes swam with kindness. "He was with you the whole time, wasn't he?"

I nodded, unable to lie any longer.

"Did he die? Did he die to save the Fallen Angels?"

The dam of ice that had been protecting my heart began to crack and burst. A sob tore itself from my throat.

Tabby sat back, a satisfied look on her face. "I knew it."

I looked at her through my tears, confused by her callousness.

"Not that I'm happy," she fumbled, rushing to explain herself. "I mean, I'm happy that the Fallen have the chance to return to grace. I just knew that had to be it. But that Michael was the one to do it . . . aw, Hope. And you were there, weren't you? I bet you saw the whole thing. Poor girl." She came around the table and wrapped her arms around me. I leaned into her, giving into the grief that seemed fresh all over again.

"I couldn't stop it. I tried, but I couldn't save him, Tabby. And he hasn't come back."

"Poor girl," she whispered again, holding me even tighter as each violent sob shook my body.

When my tears were spent, she kissed the top of my head.

"Let me show you something," I whispered, pulling away. I led her upstairs to my room. Nobody had seen what I was doing, not even—no, especially not—my mother. I paused as I cracked the door open.

"You promise you won't judge me?" I looked at her, wavering.

She rolled her eyes. "When have I ever judged you? Besides, nothing would surprise me at this point. Bring it on."

I strode through the door, pulling her behind me. I stood in the middle of the room, gesturing at the walls.

Tabby let out a low whistle.

"You did this?" she questioned, moving closer to the walls to inspect one of the hundreds of articles and photos I'd carefully taped up.

I nodded, unsure if it was a good idea to have shown her.

She spun around, taking it all in.

"It kind of looks like a crime scene investigation. Or like a crazy hoarder's room. But it's cool. You're trying to find him, aren't you?"

I sighed, relieved that she got it. She circled the perimeter of the room, peering at each article in turn.

"Honduras. Wales. New Zealand. Guinea. I'll give you one thing, you're thorough. But I already knew that about you." She pulled up short. "I'll help you, of course. This is too much for one person to do on their own." She stated it as a given, so matter-of-fact that I had no choice but to accept. She shrugged off my thanks.

"He wouldn't want you to give up, you know. If this helps, then I'm all in. There were a lot of things I didn't like about Michael, but one thing he and I agree on is you. We both cared about—*care* about—you, Hope. I'm pretty sure he wouldn't want the end of his life to be the end of yours, too. You need to live. For his sake."

I peered intently at her knowing eyes.

"How did you know? How did you figure it out?"

"I pieced it together when your dad told us about your first abduction. But none of the adults believed me." She harrumphed. Her mention of my father shot me through.

"You talked to my dad?"

She squeezed my shoulders again. "He was with your mom. They were trying to piece everything together, so they could find you. He was so excited to finally know what your Mark meant! He was ready for you to be free—free to fulfill your destiny, whatever that meant. Don't cage yourself up again now. Not after all you've been through."

I sniffed back the vale of tears that threatened to erupt at her mention of my father.

"I feel like it's my fault."

"What? His death?"

I nodded. "You know, Michael posed as him. He can make himself look like anybody in the whole world. So when he took me to Las Vegas, he made himself look like my dad. He was trying to give my dad an alibi, but I think it backfired. I think it made him a target."

Tabby frowned. "A target for whom? The traffickers?"

"Maybe. Maybe for some Fallen Angels. I might never know. But I can't stop thinking that if we hadn't used his identity he would still be alive."

She sighed.

"Don't, Hope. You can't second-guess yourself, or Michael. There were forces greater than anything we know at work. You did what you could; Michael did what he thought was best. And when you're ready, you can tell me all about it. All about Michael, all about what you went through—everything. But for right now, we need to get you back to the land of the living."

I managed a weak smile. "Land of the living. Complete with cupcakes."

She laughed and gave me a big hug. "Cupcakes for breakfast. A sacred bond between friends. Now, let's eat."

Tabby stuck to me like a shadow after that. Once there, she was hard to dislodge. And my mother barely even tried, recognizing in her own way, I guess, that Tabby was right: We needed to return to the land of the living. But before we did, we needed to bury our dead.

We went to pay our last respects to my father in the fullness of summer, near dusk. The soft whirring of insects competed with the nearby traffic in the background. The green grass of the cemetery was scarred by gashes of red Georgia clay—the tracks of storm damage and who-knows-what. In the back corner, fresh earth and a creamy white monument betrayed the arrival of a new inhabitant.

My father.

We crossed the field, being careful of the broken pieces of stone that littered the grass. A lone workman trimmed the hedges around the fence line, our only witness.

I clutched the peonies I'd cut from my mother's yard more tightly in my fist and swallowed, hard, trying to force back my tears. Mom took my other hand and squeezed it as we continued walking toward his grave.

We stopped at the edge of the dirt. "Don Carmichael. Husband. Father," it read, the words carved deeply into the marble. I pulled my hand out of my mother's grasp and laid the flowers across the top of the headstone.

Leaning close, I whispered, "You were right, Dad," low so that my mother wouldn't hear. "All along, you were right. I'm so sorry I didn't believe you."

I didn't know what to do. There was no last embrace, no cold cheek to kiss.

I rose from the stone and stood back, looking at my mother. Her eyes were shiny with tears.

"I'll leave you to your privacy," I said, squeezing her hand. She nodded and then let me go. I watched her turn to face his gravestone, her hands absentmindedly rubbing the soft curve of her stomach, the early stages of her pregnancy only evident when I saw her in profile. I wondered again about this unexpected gift, a living reminder of some happier moment and memory of my father, which my mother would now be able to treasure forever. She would never speak of it, I knew. But the happiness this baby gave her was evident in the softness that had overtaken her lined face and in the quiet humming that had overtaken her moments of contemplation. My mother, despite everything, was happy; this last moment with my father would be bittersweet.

I began wandering among the headstones, pretending I couldn't hear her crying. I forced myself to read the names on the grave markers, wondering to whom they belonged, and what had happened to them. Cheek. Booker. Ward. Martin. Duke. Each stone painstakingly carved with curling vines or crucifixes or doves in flight. And then there were the countless little lambs, perched on the backs of heartbreakingly small headstones or toppled onto the grass, the only lingering memory of tiny children sacrificed to fever or stillbirth or any of the maladies that had ripped them from their parents' arms.

It wasn't fair.

Just like it wasn't fair that my mom had figured out, too late, that she still loved my dad. Just like it wasn't fair that there was nowhere I could go to mourn for Michael and no way I could share my grief with anybody else. I began to weep—slow, silent sorrow seeping even further into my bones.

My head ached from it all.

No, I realized with a start. It wasn't aching. It was buzzing—buzzing with the faint awareness that once led me across Europe, proving an unerring guide to the bitter end in our search for the Key.

I turned, just in time to catch the caretaker turn away.

The buzzing grew louder.

I began walking toward the man, who returned to clipping the shrubbery, folding himself over to stay close to his work. I drew closer to him and noticed that he was cutting at nothing, the leaves already neatly shaped into a boxy shape with even edges.

"You were watching me." I accused, as I angrily wiped my tears away, waiting for him to answer.

He stopped clipping, rising to his full height. As I watched him standing, motionless against the hedge, something in my heart caught as I scanned the broad shoulders that, though hidden under the baggy coveralls, seemed strangely familiar.

It was too hot for coveralls, my mind registered.

"I'm sorry, miss," the man said, his voice gruff. "This has always been such a quiet place. It's not very common for us to have visitors, and I couldn't help but notice you crying."

He stood still, as if waiting for me to explain. The air between us shimmered in the summer heat, invisible currents steaming up from the earth. Before I could stop myself, the words came tumbling out from me.

"I'm crying for someone I lost. He's lost to me, and I don't know where to find him."

He inclined his head, ever so slightly, to acknowledge me. "You needn't look, and you needn't weep," he responded. His voice was strong and certain, as if making a promise. I watched, stunned, as he turned and began making his way toward the cemetery gate.

"Wait!" I cried. "Don't go!"

He only lengthened his stride as I began chasing after him. He was moving too fast for me. I stumbled in the pitted ground.

"Please," I pleaded after him as he rushed through the wrought iron doors. "I need to know if it's really you."

The gardener paused, his back strong.

"Turn around, so I can see your face," I demanded, trembling.

He took a deep breath. "Now is not the time," he answered.

I pulled myself up and ran after him. I reached the gate just in time to see a car pulling away. It was slung low to the ground, its body a patchwork of mismatched panels, the dull gray of unpainted metal unmistakably familiar.

Michael's car.

I stared after it, helplessly entwining my fingers through the delicate scrollwork of the cemetery gate as the car spun around the corner, tires squealing.

Hot tears of frustration fell to my cheeks.

How had I missed it before? Or had it even really been there? And if it was real, if that had been Michael, why was he hiding from me? Why had he abandoned me?

A hand on my shoulder startled me. I turned, wiping my eyes, to face my mom.

"Ready to go?" she whispered. Her own eyes were red and puffy.

I nodded dumbly, not trusting myself to speak.

Arm in arm, we walked through the gate, its weathered iron screeching in protest as we headed toward the parking lot.

We clung to each other, numbering our wounds, but refusing to give them voice. We silently acknowledged them, but then, as if by agreement, we left our losses behind us.

We had our own reasons to look toward the future.

Mine was a simple conviction that Michael was still out there. He was alive, and one day he would come back to me.

He just had to.

My mother had the promise of bringing a new life into the world.

Yes, we had our own reasons, but at that moment, we made the same choice. We both chose to put our broken lives back together, and—on shaky legs—we chose to walk in hope.

# ACKNOWLEDGMENTS

This chapter of Hope and Michael's story was a real exercise in serendipity. So many coincidences and chances conspired to bring all the details of their journey to life and to bring richness to the fabric of the Prophecy.

A big thank you to *la famille Pauthe* for suggesting my family spontaneously travel to Le Puy-en-Valley on our way to visit them, way back in 2012. The instant we walked into the chapel it was magical, and I knew right then it was the perfect setting for the crucial entrapment of Michael and Hope. The details of the architecture and its history, which I only really understood later, were the icing on the cake.

An equally big thank you to Kemal Cetin for being my Istanbul accuracy cop. That you also took the time to read *Dark Hope*, so you understood the story, critiqued the entirety of the manuscript, and appreciated some of the "steamy parts" (I quote) was unexpectedly generous. The device of your Turkish grandfather should have your copyright every time I use it.

I am also grateful to my colleagues in Istanbul, who generously hosted me when I did eventually make my way over for research purposes. Hale, Karim, Marwa, and Mutlu, my friends, your hospitality and advice was amazing. *Teşekkür ederim*!

Arthur, thank you for letting me write you into the story, texting me real-time with your reactions as you read early drafts, posing interesting questions that made me rethink my plots and characters, and for your continued friendship. A shout out to Dr. Shami Feinglass for responding to my detailed questions about physiological responses to severe beatings and trauma without really knowing what was going on in the book—and stifling your curiosity long enough to give me medically sound answers. Additional thanks to Lorraine Houle, Jake Houle, Kathy Florence, Dr. Shami Feinglass (again), Beth Melendez, and my daughter, Reagan, for reading and critiquing early drafts of this book (sometimes repeatedly!).

Thank you to the good folks of Greenleaf/River Grove books for their continued excellent support—particularly Corrin Foster, Amber Hales, Diana Ceres, Scott James, Tyler LeBleu, and Chelsea Richards; the good people at Spotify, who made making and changing playlists as my writing mood shifted easy; Street Grace and ECPAT-USA for their partnership; my colleagues at the Street Grace Speakers Bureau, who are so dedicated and inspiring that I am humbled and honored to have the opportunity to work with you; and my colleagues at Coca-Cola for their endless support and encouragement.

I offer my gratitude to my fans. Your demands to know what happened next and your appreciation for this quirky little story with its mash-up twists and turns spurred me on. I hope this book is worthy of your enthusiasm. Particular thanks to Jane Gilles and Linda Heinze, who have been rock star creators of so many radiating points of contact to get the word out about human trafficking through *The Archangel Prophecy* series.

Last, but most important, I thank my family and especially my husband, Tom. None of this would be possible without your unwavering support, including your generosity in giving me uninterrupted writing time and finding a way to get me to Istanbul. I love you.

I consulted many sources for background research before I began writing. These works were incredibly useful, and I drew great inspiration from their descriptions of Turkey and Ireland, especially. They include: John Freely, *Istanbul The Imperial City*; Hilary Sumner-Boyd and John Freely, *Strolling Through Istanbul;* Orhan Pamuk, *Istanbul: Memories and the City*; Des LaVelle, *The Skellig Story: Ancient Monastic Outpost*; Geoffrey Moorhouse, *Sun Dancing: Life in a Medieval Irish Monastery and How Celtic Spirituality Influenced the World*; Thomas Cahill, *How the Irish Saved Civilization: The Untold Story of Ireland's Heroic Role from the Fall of Rome to the Rise of Medieval Europe*. I additionally found insights from National Geographic Traveler's guide to Istanbul & Western Turkey, Insight Guide's Turkey, and Eyewitness Travel's guide to Istanbul, as well as the many pinners of Pinterest who contribute so generously of their talents. I have on occasion chosen to collapse geographic distances and take creative license for the sake of the story. Any inaccuracies about these fabulous, historic, and breathtaking places—and the adventures to be experienced at them—that can be found in *Dark Rising* are wholly my own.

# ABOUT MONICA McGURK

Monica McGurk loves nothing better than to craft thought-provoking, multilayered stories, showcasing strong girls and women overcoming big challenges. Already a fan favorite, she received the 2013 TwiFic Fandom Undiscovered Gem award for *Morning Star*, her alternate ending to the *Twilight* series, written before the release of *Breaking Dawn*. Her first novel in The Archangel Prophecies trilogy, *Dark Hope*, was published in 2014. *Dark Rising* is the second novel in this series. The final installment, *Dark Before Dawn*, is expected in 2016.

Readers can learn more about Monica's work and passions on her website at www.monicamcgurk.com.

# READER'S GUIDE

# *DARK RISING*
# BY MONICA MCGURK

Upon moving in with her mother in Atlanta, sixteen-year-old Hope Carmichael dreams of being free and able to shed the past of her mysterious abduction as a small child, but those dreams are shattered by a series of shocking discoveries. The emancipated teen with whom she has developed an intense friendship that borders on romance has turned out to be the Archangel Michael. The tattoo-like mark on Hope's neck—the only physical evidence of her earlier kidnapping—brands her as part of an ancient prophecy concerning Fallen Angels. And in the rush to beat the Fallen to find the ancient artifact that could open the Gates of Heaven, throwing the entire universe into chaos, their search brings them into the center of the twisted world of human trafficking, putting Hope in more danger than ever.

Michael and Hope's relationship is complicated by factors beyond their control. Are they meant to be together, or has fate thrown them into this chase for a higher purpose alone? Can Hope trust Michael—or will he be forced to sacrifice her in order to fulfill his duties as the Guardian of Heaven? Hope's story connects the powerful emotions and desires of a teenage girl growing into her own with present day human sex trafficking and an epic battle of good versus evil. The mythic love between Michael and Hope is played out on a global stage as the characters race against time, traveling from Turkey to Ireland and then France in their search for the missing relic that could spell life and death for Hope—and for the world.

# QUESTIONS & TOPICS FOR DISCUSSION

What do we know about the role of the angels, Enoch and Raph, in the course of the quest for the Key? How do their histories with Michael and with human beings shape their views of their mission? Of Hope? How did you view their interactions with Hope, and with each other, during their time in Istanbul?

During a typical "hero's journey," the main character is often helped along their quest by a guide. Who plays that role for Hope? In what ways do Henri, Enoch, Del, and Gabrielle each serve as a guide at various points? Does the fact that they each might have ulterior motives impact their role as guide?

Consider the changing relationship between Michael and Hope in the book. Is there any justification for Michael's brusque and controlling treatment of Hope during their time in Turkey? For his unpredictability? Is Hope's response to it reasonable? What finally triggers Michael to open up to Hope?

At the beginning of Hope's time in Istanbul, she remarks that the angels "served as a wall—a wall of flesh and bone, meant to keep me away" from Michael. Why?

Sultanahmet was the heart of ancient Byzantium and Constantinople. Is there any significance to the fact that this is where Michael chooses to lodge?

Hope makes several decisions to disobey Michael's wishes, sneaking out on her own to explore the city of Istanbul and escaping from dinner in Le Puy-en-Velay. What are Hope's motives? Is her risk-taking justified or foolish? Would you have done the same thing in her shoes?

At several points in Istanbul, Hope feels caged, like a prisoner. Is she being held captive, or is she a willing participant in the quest? In what ways is her situation and reaction to it similar to that of a victim of human trafficking? In what ways is it different?

The woman attending to Hope in the hammam tells a very involved story about the history of Roxelana, the slave turned sultan's wife for whom the hammam was built. Why does the author spend so much time on this story? What does it have to do with Hope?

Hope is able to rescue the puppy she encounters in the Istanbul back alley, but not the Eastern European sex trafficking victim. Why?

Why is the Greek antiquities dealer so dismissive of Hope and the others?

Did Michael's recounting of his return of Jimena and Ana to Mexico surprise you? In what ways?

Mona and Don's relationship changes dramatically during the course of Hope's disappearance. What has it meant that they never formally ended their marriage? Was their night together a signal that they still love one another, or just a symptom of their shared grief?

What did you think of the fact that Mona is not entirely forthright with the investigators? Would you have immediately shared the import of Tabby's news—that she had managed to translate Hope's Mark—with the FBI? Why did Mona and Don keep it to themselves?

Mona and Don were educated at the same place, trained in highly logic-driven and fact-based disciplines. Yet they diverge significantly in their willingness and ability to embrace the mystical and unexplainable. Why?

We see three very different "versions" of Tabitha in the course of *Dark Rising*. How does Tabitha's persona and demeanor change from the time of the questioning in the FBI office, the meeting with Don and Mona at her home, and her visit to Hope near the end of the book? Why? What does this tell us about teenage identity?

What was your reaction to Hope's entry into the monastery on Skellig Michael, when she finds herself surrounded by rocks?

Are there other "jokes" God plays upon Hope and Michael in the course of their journey? How do these events shape your view of the God portrayed in this book?

Is Gabrielle right—that sacrifice can only be real if it hurts?

What is the import of Michael's story of the lonely monk who threw himself from the cliffs of Skellig Michael?

Reflect upon Hope's interactions with the diplomat at the airport in France. Did it surprise you to learn that the US Government is dedicating resources to fight human trafficking around the world? In what other ways are governments and non-government organizations taking action to end trafficking and help victims?

Why did Hope chop off her hair after returning to Atlanta? Why is it significant that she did so?

What references—explicit or implicit—to other literary works or Bible stories did you notice as you read? What struck you about these references?

How is the theme of identity woven into the story? How are Michael and Hope both symbolic of the quest to define and understand one's identity? Are their identities and fates in their own hands? How do the characters of Henri, Enoch, Gabrielle, and Tabitha stand for the changeability of one's identity? What do Mona's dramatic life changes at the end of the book say about one's identity?

Betrayal and forgiveness play significant roles in *Dark Rising*. Did Hope, as Gabrielle prophesied, betray Michael? In what way? What other betrayals took place in the story and why are they significant? What does the story tell us about forgiveness, acceptance, and choice?

Do you think Michael is coming back to Hope? Why or why not?

# AUTHOR Q&A

*Q. In prior interviews, you have talked about wanting your protagonist, Hope, to face real consequences for the choices she has made as opposed to having an artificial "happily-ever-after" ending. In what ways does* Dark Rising *do that?*

MM: I think it is woven throughout the book. Whether it is getting caught up in a riot when she slips away from the angels, accidentally playing into the Fallen Angels' hands due to her distrust of Michael, or finding out that her father is dead—possibly targeted due to her involvement with human traffickers—Hope has to deal with the real consequences of her choices all the time.

*Q: You seem to enjoy giving little nods to religious stories, history, and other literary works in your writing. Can you share some of those tributes found in* Dark Rising *with us?*

MM: Of course, references to Cain and Abel and the angelic traditions of multiple religious traditions continue to surface throughout the book. Part of the reason I chose Istanbul and Skellig Michael as settings for *Dark Rising* was their rich histories. The sacking of Constantinople by Crusaders in the 1200s and the bloody rise of Roxelana both fascinated me as stories, and I wanted to find a way to weave them into the plot. Irish monasticism and its role in preserving knowledge during the Dark Ages was also something of keen interest to me; as I explored that period I stumbled into the story of Skellig Michael and its lonely monks. Another reference keen readers might notice includes a salute to C.S. Lewis's *The Lion, The Witch, and the Wardrobe*, one of my favorite books of all time. It was a shoutout, stemming from admiration, but also serves to underscore some important themes in *Dark Rising*—betrayal, sacrifice, and forgiveness.

*Q: Tell us how and why identity surfaces as a theme throughout* The Archangel Prophecies.

MM: Readers might remember that when Hope meets Enoch for the first time in *Dark Hope* he makes a big point of mentioning that the names of things and people are important. This plays out in significant ways for Hope and Michael—both as we learn the real import of Michael's name and all the associations with him over time and as Hope struggles to define herself as something separate from and greater than the Mark on her neck. We see shifting identities in multiple characters: Tabitha, Gabrielle, Enoch, and Henri, for example. Even Michael and Hope need to engage in a bit of role play back in *Dark Hope* when they try to infiltrate the Chinese trafficking ring. The importance of this theme to *The Archangel Prophecies* is twofold: first, it mirrors the experience of young adult readers, who are going through rapid growth and change, trying on and growing into their own identities—which can be scary. Second, it underscores that identity is a choice: Any one of us can change who we are, for the worse or the better, by the actions we take each and every day.

*Q: You take* Dark Rising *to some pretty exotic locations. Did you actually visit these places as you wrote the book?*

MM: By chance, I had actually already been to Le Puy-en-Velay during the early stages of drafting *Dark Hope* and had noticed what a perfect setting the chapel would make for the confrontation with the Fallen Angels. I didn't realize just how perfect until I started researching its history and the meaning of all the architectural devices with which it is decorated! I made a special trip to Istanbul to visit all the locations I'd chosen for *Dark Rising*. I only visited after I had done a significant amount of research and had already written a full manuscript. It is an amazing city, and I long to go back. Though I have been to other parts of Ireland, Skellig Michael remains on my bucket list. I thought it was cool that, as I was writing, J.J. Abrams chose the Skellig as one of the locations for his upcoming *Star Wars* movie. Someday . . .

*Q: During your research trip to Istanbul, did you experience anything similar to what Hope experiences in* Dark Rising?

I did manage to make it to every setting in the book, so I had the same opportunity to be awestruck by the golden, airy spaces of Ayasofya, for example, to drudge myself around the crowded square outside of the university, to even experience the beauty of the very same hammam I write about. Some of my observations are actually written into the book—I really saw the woman hanging out of the window of her high-rise apartment, washing windows. I really did see cats everywhere! I did not get caught up in any riots while I was there (though there was one just a week or so later at the university in Ankara), but I did have a sort of awkward experience in Fener (the site of Hope's confrontation with a trafficker) when I realized that I was the only visible woman for as far as I could see. Nothing threatening at all, though.

*Q: At some stages, Hope seems to make questionable choices—stealing away from the protection of the angels in Istanbul, for example. Why did you make her take such risks?*

MM: It was important to me that Hope not be viewed as a victim, nor that the story be driven by choices solely made by other characters. I always wanted to position Hope as having agency. I also felt that her responses might be considered rational if viewed through the lens of a teenage mind. There is a great body of neurological research that suggests teens view risk differently, and they view risk to relationships as being as real and potentially more important than risks to their physical well-being. Hope's relationship with Michael and her credibility with the angels is on the line in Istanbul. She needs to prove herself and discover the location of the Key. Her choice to escape and explore is all in service of that goal, which ultimately will keep her safe and perhaps improve her situation with Michael. Her repeated decision to stay with the angels and not run away is a rational reflection on her situation: She will be hunted down by the Fallen Angels and by Michael's band because she is central to the Prophecy. Until she finds the Key, she remains in danger. Her decision to not let Raph heal her skin is a little bit of rebellion, among the only things she can do to continue to assert her independence.

*Q: What can you tell us about the title Dark Rising?*

MM: It is meant to reflect the fact that by the end of the book, we feel somehow that evil has overwhelmed Michael and Hope—even though they managed to succeed in the higher mission assigned to them—but also signal that the story is not yet finished. There is more to tell in this battle of good versus evil, as well as in the story of Michael and Hope.

*Q: Human trafficking seems to take a lesser role in this stage of your story. Why is that?*

MM: The plot at this stage is really driven by the angels' search for the Key, the battle for Heaven, and the relationship between Hope and Michael. The trafficking subplot is more subtle at this stage. It is an omnipresent threat in Istanbul, coming to the forefront when Hope has her run-in in the backstreets of Fener and again when Michael recounts his experiences in Mexico. It remains relevant to the story of Mona and Don. It will be much more front and center in the next and final book of the trilogy, though.

*Q: Why did you spend the time to have Michael tell Hope what happened when he went to Mexico to return her friends to their hometown?*

MM: Partly it was because readers kept asking me about Maria/Ana and Jimena—what happened to them? They had come to care about them and really wanted to know the complete end of their story. Partly it was to revisit some of the truths about human trafficking—things like the potential complicity of law enforcement, particularly in places where the rule of law is more of a suggestion than a reality. It serves the theme of betrayal and forgiveness to remind readers of the involvement of the girls' uncle and the police and to reveal that Ana did not wish to have Michael kill her uncle. It also seemed like a natural thing Hope would want to know. She cared about her friend enough to go after her in Atlanta and Las Vegas. She would want to know that things ended up okay for her.

*Q: Tell us about some of the new characters featured in this book.*

MM: I introduced readers to Gabrielle and (in more depth) Raph, both archangels. In one sense, they fulfill the roles assigned to them in various religious traditions: Gabrielle is a messenger, so she gets to provide some clarification of Hope and Michael's quest in classic *deus ex machina* style, while Raph is a healer. But they are both challenging to Michael and his authority, introducing new sources of tension into the story. And they will each play a significant role in Book 3. The other minor characters I introduced—Del, the Greek antiquities dealer, the trafficker and his victim, and the diplomat in France—mostly acted as plot devices. The antiquities dealer, though, in particular, was quite fun to write. He is such an erudite snob, still nursing the wounds of history! I loved him and the entirety of his surroundings. I got a kick out of researching old Turkish aphorisms that he could spout off as he lectured them all from his dusty showroom.

*Q: You spend a lot of time describing the architectural and decorative details of many of the buildings the characters visit in the course of* Dark Rising. *Do you have a special love for architectural and art history?*

MM: The details of the buildings and their histories are meant to both transport the reader to the setting but also to provide clues to the unraveling of the Prophecy. But yes, I do love art and architecture. I actually considered being an architect at one stage and even attended a design program during one of my summers as a college student.

*Q: What can readers take from the seeming equilibrium that emerges between Michael and Hope?*

MM: It is equilibrium on two fronts: physical equilibrium, in that his touch is no longer threatening to her and they can equally sense one another's thoughts and feelings when they touch, and an equality of powers in the sense that Hope has gained some of Michael's intuition. I wanted to find a way to put them on more equal footing, in general, and of course find a way to make it possible for their romance to advance. The idea of a transfer of powers from angel to human as a consequence of intimate contact can be found in some ancient religious traditions.

*Q: Do you have any favorite scenes in* Dark Rising*?*

MM: I love the scene where Michael and Hope are nestled together on the balcony in Sultanahmet. I had envisioned that scene very early and loved bringing it to life. I also loved writing everything that happened on Skellig Michael. It was so nice to finally get Michael and Hope on the same side, understanding one another and being open about their feelings! As hard as they were to write, I also loved Hope challenging the trafficker in the Istanbul alley and the scene in the chapel in France.

*Q: You really seemed to develop the characters of Mona and Don much more fully in this book. Can you tell us a little about that?*

MM: I thought it would be interesting to explore their reactions to Hope's disappearance, whether Mona comes to believe Don's theories at all, and how their relationship is affected by their worry and grief. The loss or potential loss of a child can either drive a couple closer or tear them apart. The fact that Mona had never really cut her final tie to Don was intriguing to me and suggested they might go down a different path. Their relationship and its inadvertent outcome provide the platform for much of the plot in the next book.

*Q: How do you think Hope matures in* Dark Rising*?*

MM: She definitely has become much more assertive than she was at the beginning of her relationship with Michael. She questions and challenges him and the other angels more regularly and more frequently pushes beyond the boundaries they have set for her. She maintains her independence, even in small ways, like with her refusal to be healed by Raph. She also becomes more attuned to the interpersonal relationships between others—picking up on the tensions between Raph and Michael, for instance, or having a new understanding of her mother and father's true feelings for one another. And she learns some painful lessons, particularly about seeing beyond the surface of someone's demeanor to understand their real motives and actions, and the importance of trust in relationships. These insights are essential lessons on the road to adulthood, even if they are earned in painful ways.

*Q: There was a lot of discussion of Hope's love of food in* Dark Hope *but the characters never really seem to eat much in* Dark Rising. *Was this deliberate?*

MM: (Laughing.) I just couldn't fit it into the story that well. I think Hope probably lost some weight on her trip. She'll have to double up on the Wright's cupcakes to get back to her healthy weight.

*Q: Some people might find the literary references in your sneak preview of* Dark Before Dawn *odd (p. 385). Can you explain them?*

MM: Certainly. Aurora, or Rorie, is named for her father, Don, but on the sly—aurora originating from the Latin word for "dawn" or "goddess of the dawn." So her name is a play on words, a rhyme. Her name also suggests much needed renewal or new beginnings for Mona and Hope, as the Goddess Aurora used to fly across the sky every morning announcing the return of the sun. The excerpt included as a sneak preview of the final installment of *The Archangel Prophecies* is also is a tweak of the old stories written by Giambattista Basile, Charles Perrault, and the Brothers Grimm—ultimately memorialized in the Disney film, *Sleeping Beauty*. Aurora is the name of the princess featured in the movie—the one whose fairy godmothers bless her but ultimately cannot protect her from the evil doings of Maleficent. She needs her Prince to come and rescue her from eternal sleep. Our Rorie has warrior angels for her blessing and protection. They bless her with insight, strength, and bravery, as opposed to the blessing bestowed in different versions of *Sleeping Beauty*—things like beauty, grace, and perfect dancing skills. It is quite a contrast. And our Rorie won't be waiting for a prince to save her in Book 3. So the reference is a tongue in cheek riposte to the "princess awaiting rescue" trope that too often pops up in literature aimed at girls of all ages. It is consistent with my vision of providing readers with a strong female protagonist.

Q: *Did you change anything in your writing process as you tackled* Dark Rising*?*

MM: I probably did much more of what I call "desk research"—reading books, looking things up on the Internet—than I did with *Dark Hope*, as the settings were much less familiar to me. I probably asked more "specialized" readers to read the manuscript at earlier stages and to read for very specific things. For example, a friend of mine who is a doctor advised me heavily on the medical accuracy of Michael's injuries as I described them. Another friend who grew up in Istanbul read for the accuracy of my descriptions of the city and my use of Turkish. I think the complexity of the story in this book was greater, and so I had many more iterations of the manuscript than I did for *Dark Hope*—hopefully it pays off in a better read! I continued to build playlists for inspiration; I continued to interview people with special knowledge of the issues or settings upon which I was focusing; I continued to paper the walls of my office with images of each setting, gleaned from Pinterest and other places online. I kept on using my typical mix of notebooks, iPad, laptop, and even the backs of receipts for my actual writing. So in those respects, it was a similar process.

Q: *Many readers might be upset by where you end the book. Can you explain why you chose to end it with such a cliffhanger?*

MM: Well, I originally intended to end it even earlier—at the chapel in France. Then I felt like the story needed to keep going and I wrote quite a bit of additional content. In the end, my editors and I decided there was too much happening at the end of the book, too many changes coming too fast, so we chose a happy compromise. Hopefully readers will be excited to know what happens next for Hope and Michael and pick up the third book when it is released!

*Q: Do you already know how Hope and Michael's story will end?*

MM: Oh, yes. I have it all plotted out and have run this final chapter in *The Archangel Prophecies* by my teen daughter. She approves, by the way!

*Q: How have you expanded your efforts to combat human trafficking and domestic minor sex trafficking since the release of* Dark Hope?

MM: One of the efforts I am most excited about is the development of a reading curriculum more closely centered around the elements of human trafficking depicted in *Dark Hope*. I have worked with specialists in the anti-trafficking and anti-DMST movement, as well as middle school teachers, to develop a reading guide that can be linked to Common Core standards. The curriculum is being piloted with several nonprofit agencies that work extensively with middle- and high-school-aged girls. Best of all, it is available free of charge to any organization or teacher wishing to use it in their own clubs or classrooms. Anyone interested can find it on my website, http://monicamcgurk.com.

Turn the page for a sneak preview of

# *Dark Before Dawn*

*Book Three of the Archangel Prophecies*

# one

They'd left the window open. The gauzy, Swiss-dot curtain billowed and danced on the spring breeze that filtered through the screen.

It was twilight. The baby had been put down for her evening nap—still on the seemingly endless cycle of sleeping and eating that cut up the day into three-hour increments—giving her mother a precious few hours to nap. Her mother was just down the hall, the baby monitor transmitting each rustle of blanket, each little coo, so that the weary woman's subconscious mind could stay alert to any deviation in the peaceful noises of her sleeping child.

The curtains billowed again, but this time, it was different.

A wisp of shimmering smoke rode in with the breeze, another, then another. They buffeted the delicate fabric of the curtain, writhing and twisting as yet another delicate filament ghosted in to join them. They danced together, merging in a flash of brilliant light that, for a split second, illuminated the darkness that was beginning to fill the room with the setting of the sun. The pulsating mass floated over to the head of the crib, a slight electric tang filling the air as it settled and began to flicker.

One by one, the smoky shapes separated out and took up their forms. Bone. Flesh. Wings. As they took shape, another figure stepped from the corner of the room to join them.

Muscle-bound and armor-plated, the angel sentries stood before the crib and peered in. They had hard-planed faces, chiseled by worry and war, but soft eyes that melted as they gazed on the sleeping babe.

One shook out his wings, releasing a soft rush of wind that would sound no different than a gentle breeze over the baby monitor.

The angel at the head of the crib shot him a dirty look, then looked pointedly at the baby monitor. The offending angel, Arthur, rolled his eyes and extended his wings again, unfurling them just to make his point before turning the knob on the monitor to "off."

"Really, Michael. Mona's not going to notice a thing," Arthur argued. "She's exhausted. She's so afraid of missing something—keeps saying she wants to take advantage of every moment. I just sent her and Hope both to catch some sleep. Rocked Rorie to sleep myself."

The Archangel Michael ignored him, turning back to the crib.

"Aurora," Michael breathed, leaning over the railing to get a better look at the child. "Our Rorie."

Michael had laughed as Arthur—who now more than ever was Mona's confidant—explained to him the agonies Mona experienced while choosing her baby's name. Mona wanted something to honor her late husband, Don but didn't want it to be so obvious. The play on words and rhyme she'd come up with—Aurora, meaning dawn—was clever, just like Mona. Michael wondered if the allusion to the goddess who renewed herself daily, a symbol of hope and of life's eternal wheel, was deliberate, too.

The babe was tiny and, apparently, feisty—having wriggled out of her swaddling to splay herself out across the mattress. Her skin was so delicate it was nearly transparent. Michael reached out a finger to follow the tiny trail of veins that stretched like lace across her open palm.

In her sleep, she grasped his finger, refusing to give it up.

"She's got a kung fu grip," Michael chuckled, wiggling his finger.

The lone female angel, Gabrielle, moved to Michael's side and tucked her arm into his.

"She's beautiful, Michael. Truly beautiful."

"I just wish Mona would change her mind and allow for a real christening," Raph, the last angel in the group, added gruffly.

"She'd see it as giving in to Don's old religious whims. She'll never do it. Besides, there's no need," Michael said, dismissing the concern as irrelevant. "We're here now. We'll be her witnesses."

"Real life fairy godmothers," Arthur chimed in, grinning.

Michael smiled despite himself. "Something like that."

He gently pulled his finger from Rorie's fist. "Everyone, it's time."

They took their places around the girl—each warrior angel taking the foot or side, Michael, their captain, retaining his place at the head.

Arthur shifted on his feet. "It doesn't seem right, doing this without Enoch. Or Hope." He looked pointedly at Michael.

"Enoch isn't a soldier," Michael responded, his eyes never moving from where they watched the slight rise and fall of Rorie's breathing, "and the time may come when we will have to fight for her. It wouldn't do to make pledges we cannot keep. And as for Hope," his voice broke with emotion as he spoke her name, "It's too soon. She cannot know of us. Not yet."

"I don't know why you don't tell her, Michael," Arthur argued softly. "As a reward for her service and sacrifice, you have been offered something almost unheard of—God has granted her the choice to be with you, either in Heaven, in angelic form, or here on Earth, with you cloaked in the flesh of full humanity. Yet you say nothing, letting her wonder if you have risen or not, letting her believe you have left her alone. Why?"

Michael's jaw stiffened. "We'll not speak of it."

"But why? You know she still spends all of her spare time looking for you. Her damned bedroom walls are covered with things she's printed off from her Internet searches, dribs and drabs she's hoping add up to proof that you are resurrected. She hides it well, but she hasn't gotten over you. She's suffering, and you let her."

"Do you think it's fair, Michael, to keep her choice from her?" Gabrielle, added, carefully appraising Michael's reaction. She did not wish to goad him; she honestly could not fathom what he was thinking.

The muscle in Michael's jaw tensed. He stood up, stretching his wings wide. Even in the half-light of dusk they glinted and sparkled, majestic.

"It's too soon to thrust such a choice upon her. I will tell her when the time is right. For now, it is just us. Just us four. Now."

He wrapped the crib rail in his massive hand, the scarred and bruised flesh a contrast against the carefully turned, bright pine. "Let us begin."

A sense of gravity came upon them as they considered what they were about to do.

"I'll start," Arthur began.

The angels closed their eyes as if by silent agreement as he took up his vow. He reached a gigantic hand over the baby's head in blessing.

"Daughter of God, we gather here as witnesses and to pledge you to Him. In His name, I offer you the gift of laughter to sustain you on your journey."

He withdrew his hand from the baby and Gabrielle's took its place.

"I offer you the gift of insight. May it guide you to wisdom in His path."

"I offer you the gift of strength, to sustain you in times of physical and emotional duress," Raph added quickly, his hand hesitating before reaching down to caress the crown of Rorie's head.

Michael stretched his muscular, scarred arm above the baby.

"I offer you bravery. May you have no need for it."

He raised his eyes and looked sternly at each of his comrades in turn. "Together, we pledge to come to your aid, to protect you in your need, to be your sword and your shield. In the name of Heaven, I swear it."

"I swear it," Gabrielle breathed.

"I swear it," Arthur added, his normally twinkling eyes suddenly grave.

There was a long pause. Michael looked at Raph, barely containing his impatience.

"I swear it," Raph muttered, knowing he had no choice. The tension in Michael's face finally dissipated.

"Now it is done. We are bound to her."

He turned to the other angels. "I know you do this for me and for no other reason. I thank you."

"Look, she's awake," Gabrielle whispered.

Everyone turned back to the crib. Rorie's eyes were wide open, a startling blue that was nearly violet. Her tiny arms flailed as she stretched, unable to control the movements of her body. Gabrielle leaned over to draw the baby up in her arms.

"Hello, baby girl. You're safe here, with us." She held Rorie against her chest, the baby's wee chin propped against her shoulder.

"She's such a good baby," she explained to nobody in particular. "She barely ever cries."

Michael gazed a little too intently at Gabrielle as she cradled Rorie in her arms. Gabrielle didn't need to see him to know what he was doing. She had seen that longing look on his face before as he'd hidden in the shadows, watching Hope holding her baby sister in much the same way.

"We should leave," Gabrielle said, gracefully interrupting the awkward moment.

"Yes, we should leave," Michael whispered, flushing, but unable to pull his eyes away.

Gabrielle buried her nose in Rorie's wispy fine hair, breathing in her sweet baby smell and avoiding Michael's gaze. "Your mama will be here for you soon, sweet girl." She kissed Rorie's head and laid her gently back in the crib before returning to the door.

"Goodbye," she said, giving the baby one last look.

Raph just scowled. "Don't think I'm going to like Hope, or any humans now, just because of a baby."

"Heaven forbid," Michael answered, trying to keep the corners of his mouth from betraying his amusement.

"Goodbye, Rorie," Michael whispered, backing away from the crib. "You'll keep us posted, won't you, Arthur?"

Arthur nodded. "Of course. Just like always. It will be easier now that Mona has decided to move into a more secure home. It will be strange for Hope, I'm sure, being behind a fence and gate, but with me living in their carriage house, I'll be sure they're kept safe. Whether it's from traffickers or the Fallen, I'll be there to watch over them." He clasped Michael's shoulder—warrior to warrior, brother to brother—and, with a shimmer, put away his wings, turning back into his human guise before slipping out of the room.

Wordlessly, the other angels began their own metamorphosis. From flesh and bone to shadow and air they shifted, swirling about the crib for a final look at the special little girl they had promised to watch over, the special little girl whose father had been sacrificed to the fulfillment of an angelic Prophecy not even a year ago. If any of them resented being pledged to her, they swallowed it down out of respect for Michael's role as commander of the heavenly army, and out of respect for Hope, for whom, they knew, Michael had done this. If he couldn't be with her, he had reasoned, he could at least be sure to protect her and those she loved.

Each angel had his own thoughts as they left the baby.

That it was unfair being pressed into service in this way. That it would never come to pass that they would need to defend her, anyway, making it an empty promise, a gesture but not more. That the babe seemed so sweet and helpless, yet strangely wise with her big, serious eyes.

And the wistful thought that Gabrielle kept brooding upon: that Hope looked so natural with a child in her arms, that she would be so beautiful with a child of her own. Something that might not ever happen if Michael continued down his foolish path, hiding himself from Hope while she clung to his memory. Gabrielle shrugged, thinking it best perhaps that Michael harden himself to his feelings for this girl. She was necessary to the fulfillment of the Prophecy; anything more than that, well . . . it was not suitable for an angel of Michael's stature.

They hoarded their feelings and thoughts to themselves as they floated away from the crib and out the window. They were too preoccupied to notice that there was another presence, hovering in the shadowy corner of the nursery a presence that shimmered and shifted like them, but with resentment and malevolence.

The presence waited for them to leave before moving from the dark corners of the room and weakly materializing itself beside the crib. It was an angel, too, but an angel of darkness. Evil radiated off him in waves as he sneered at the helpless child below him.

"They brought you gifts but didn't invite me to their party. You are claimed by God, now, and I suppose they think that will keep you safe. But I have brought you my own gift. For if I cannot take you for my own, I will bestow upon you the gift of endurance."

His lips twisted into a strange smile as he held his hand over the child, his image flickering as if he were too weak to remain substantial.

"May you have endurance to bear your suffering well. For suffer you shall. May you be able to bear the pain of doubt. Of rejection. Of loneliness. Of fear. Of pain so excruciating it makes you grind and crack your teeth and cry out for the release of death."

He paused, closing his eyes to imagine all the pain he could inflict upon this babe, so innocent.

He knew pain. After millennia of rejecting the One on High, he was crazed by it, hollowed out in his very soul from enduring the constancy of it.

Yes, he smiled to himself, he knew pain.

"May you endure all these things and yet not pass. May you be forced to carry on in the grip of loss so profound it would break the hearts of other mortals and send them early to their graves."

He let his eyes flutter open and rest upon the tiny girl, who stared up at him, wide-eyed, unmoved by his speech. He reached down and touched her cheek with his rough hand, which was so transparent it seemed to be absorbed into her very skin.

"You will be the instrument of my vengeance upon Michael and Hope," he whispered, eyes glittering in the dark. "Eventually, I will have my way."

The doorknob turned.

In a flash, the angel vanished.

Mona, the baby's mother, walked into the room. She paused just inside the doorway, tilting her head and sniffing the air. The curtain fluttered, the chill of the evening air seeping into the room. Mona pulled her fuzzy, worn bathrobe closer about her before striding over and firmly closing the window sash, shutting out the cold. She sniffed the air again, alert to any danger, real or imagined.

"I'll have to check the gas," she said to herself before walking to the crib and swooping her baby daughter up in her arms.

"For an instant, I thought it smelled like sulfur."

CPSIA information can be obtained at www.ICGtesting.com
Printed in the USA
LVOW11s0054050915

452957LV00002B/347/P

9 781632 99033